W9-CRQ-000

MARIE VIEUX-CHAUVET

Dance on the Volcano

Translated from the French
by Kaiama L. Glover

archipelago books

Archipelago Books
232 Third Street, #A111
Brooklyn, NY 11215
www.archipelagobooks.org

Library of Congress Cataloging-in-Publication Data
Title: Dance on the volcano / Marie Vieux-Chauvet ;
translated by Kaiama L Glover.
Other titles: Danse sur le volcan. (Paris : Plon, 1957).
LCCN 2016036853
ISBN 9780914671572 (paperback) | ISBN 9780914671589 (e-book)

Distributed to the trade by Penguin Random House
www.penguinrandomhouse.com

Cover art: Edouard Duval-Carrié

The publication of *Dance on the Volcano* was made possible
with support from Lannan Foundation,
the National Endowment for the Arts,
the New York State Council on the Arts, a state agency,
and the New York City Department of Cultural Affairs.

This work, published as part of a program providing publication assistance,
received financial support from the French Ministry of Foreign Affairs,
the Cultural Services of the French Embassy in the United States,
and FACE (French American Cultural Exchange).

PRINTED IN THE UNITED STATES OF AMERICA

Dance on the Volcano

I

ON THAT JUNE day, all of Port-au-Prince was at the harbor, joyously anticipating the arrival of the new Governor.

For the past two hours, armed soldiers had been keeping order among an immense crowd of men, women, and children of all sorts. The mulatto and Negro women were gathered a certain distance away, as was the custom; they had pulled out all the stops to rival the elegance of the white Creole and European ladies. Occasionally the freed-women's calico skirts, striped or flowered, brazenly brushed up against the white women's heavy taffeta skirts and diaphanous muslin *gaules*. Everywhere you looked, breasts barely covered by flimsy, see-through bodices attracted the delighted gaze of the men who, despite the horrendous heat of that summer morning, were dressed in velvet, with ruffled blouses, fitted coats, and vests. Beneath their curly wigs they were sweating more than the slaves. What bliss for them, then, whenever the ladies played flirtatiously with their fans! The jewels adorning the toes of the mulatto women – whom a new law had banned from wearing proper shoes – just made them all the more fascinating and desirable. Seeing their diamond-shod feet, the white women regretted having called for the new regulation directed at "those creatures" who had dared to imitate their clothing and hairstyles. Having complained to the Governor about the inexcusable offense, they had called for justice – without admitting, of course, that their real desire was to punish and humiliate these rivals who had become far too appealing to their own husbands and lovers. As always, society's laws were powerful. The white women had easily won their case against the freedwomen, products of the despised slave caste.

However, doubtless to get their revenge, at present "those creatures" were decorating their feet with the jewels their white lovers had given them. This was the height of insolence. No one could deny that they were utterly charming, coquettish, and captivating. They were without equal in the art of showing off their arched waistlines, the uniquely provocative curve of their breasts, their generous and supple hips. The combination of the two so vastly different blood strains had created the most prodigious beauty in these women. So in this regard, nature herself was responsible.

The officers in their sparkling uniforms – desired by all the women, be they white or mulatto – made no attempt to hide the lustful looks they were giving to the beautiful Negresses with their hair done up in madras scarves as sparkling with jewels as their feet. Their breasts half exposed, they smiled, and their perfect teeth traced a flash of light across their dark faces. From time to time, they broke out in great cascading bursts of laughter. But this noisy gaiety was by no means sincere, for their eyes were full of contempt, hatred, and provocation.

Among the women of Saint-Dominique, the rivalry had produced a fight to the death that was in fact at the heart of all relations in the colony: rivalry between white colonists and low-class Whites; between the officers and the government officials, between the *nouveaux riches,* with neither name nor titles, and the great nobles from France; rivalry also between the white planters and the freedmen planters, between the domestic slaves and the fieldworkers. This state of affairs, combined with the discontent of the freedmen and the silent protestation of the African Negroes who were treated little better than animals, had created a state of perpetual tension that produced a strange heaviness in the atmosphere.

Because of all of this, and despite the vibrancy, the laughter, and the elegant clothing and wigs, a sort of menace hung in the air. Yet, nothing was visible on the surface. As with all such days of great public celebration, rows of six-horse carriages, covered wagons, and closed carriages lined the road. The officers and colonists' opulent get-ups, the gold-trimmed cars, the women's elaborate hairstyles, make-up, gloves, and flowers – together with the trees, the insolent blue of the sky, and the radiant sun – created a marvelous tableau. People lingered, laughing, in front of the jewelers' and the perfumers' windows, and the women gave suggestive looks as they accepted gifts from the men. Groups of slaves in chains passed by, led by their master, and from time to time one could hear the snap of a whip lashing a naked torso.

All of a sudden, an immense clamor arose from the crowd; the long-awaited royal vessel had just appeared. Immediately, the bells rang out, the cannons resounded. The clergy, bearing banners and crosses, ornaments and incense burners, waited beneath a dais for the Governor, newly appointed by the King.

A hundred men went out in rowboats to greet him. Upon his arrival, the crowd applauded with cries of "Long live his majesty the King of France," and accompanied him to the church. Curious young children struggled with those trying to push them out of the way. A few of them protested loudly. The women seized the opportunity to shout insults at their rivals. A young mulatto woman met the gaze of an officer who had been looking her over. There was a blonde woman on his arm, totally absorbed by the spectacle of the Governor's welcome. The mulatto woman took a bouquet of flowers from her bodice and threw it to the man, who caught it smilingly. The blonde turned around immediately.

"Foul Negress," she screamed, "if you're looking for something to cool your fire, I'm sure there are some slaves who'd be more than happy to oblige you!"

Without responding, the mulatto woman turned her head toward the soldiers.

With all those uniformed men surrounding her, there was no way she could return the insult to that white wench! Ah, if only there hadn't been so many soldiers, she would have gouged out her eyes. After giving it some thought, she decided it was best to shrug her shoulders with an impertinent smile.

She wore a long white cotton skirt trimmed with red flowers and, gathered tight at the waist, a chambray bodice so transparent her breasts were all but exposed. A light wrap thrown carelessly over her shoulders came to a point on her back and revealed the low neckline of the bodice. Her madras scarf, adorned with costume jewels that sparkled in the sun, was set high atop her head, half covering her right eyebrow. With a slow, steady gait, in harmony with the swing of her hips, she went off in the direction of the crowd, sending flirtatious and seductive glances as she passed.

Someone shouted out to her, calling her "Kiss-Me-Lips." She smiled, turned around and, with a sweeping hand gesture, shouted in Creole: "But where are you? What, I can't see you any more?"

A man joined her – a white man in a jacket and cotton pants, wearing neither wig nor shoes with buckles.

"You're still being cuckolded, and yet you're not looking for a shoulder to cry on?" she asked, bursting into laughter.

"I'm resigned to being cuckolded," responded the man, taking her arm. "Come, 'Kiss-Me-Lips,' let's have a drink at the nearest cabaret. I know someone who makes a perfect rum punch…"

"Rum punch…if that's all you've got to offer!…"

"All right, come on – you can choose whatever you like."

"A sweet Bordeaux, that's what I want."

They went off in the direction of the central square as the crowd dispersed. In the streets, carriages manned by Negroes rolled along to the noisy clip-clop of hooves.

Two little girls, one twelve and the other ten, walked along holding hands. Shabbily dressed in faded calico skirts and bodices modestly held together with pins, they were barefoot and their hair was left loose. With their golden skin and long tresses, they looked at first like two little "poor white" girls. But upon closer inspection, one could see that they were in fact "mixed-bloods," for their black blood had added that extra spice – that slight note of originality – that any white person could detect at first glance. The elder one in particular, with her sensuous lips, her black eyes pulled slightly toward the temples, and her rebellious locks, was a perfect specimen of the *mestive*. They walked holding hands with a modest air that contradicted the gleam of curiosity in their eyes.

"Hey, Minette," a heavyset colored woman carrying a large basket of foodstuffs cried suddenly in Creole, "where are you and your little sister headed? Go back home or your mother will be cross with you…"

Barely had she finished her sentence before Minette took off at top speed, dragging her sister behind her. They passed right by the shops and the tents of the circus performers just arrived from France without so much as a look, and arrived breathless at the corner of Traversière Street. Then, hands pressed to their heart, they looked at each other, laughing. The market-women had set up their merchandise there and were calling out to the passersby to attract their attention. The two girls managed to carve a path through this chaos and made their way to a modest little house with spindly, whitewashed posts.

"Minette, Lise, where were you two?"

A mulatto woman, between about thirty-five and forty years old with thin, wearied features that nevertheless had retained some of their original beauty, rose from a small chair in front of the door and walked toward the little girls.

"Come on now, answer me. Where'd you run off to – so dirty, so badly dressed, and barefoot?"

She walked heavily, as if exhausted. Everything about her seemed dulled: her gaze, her voice, even her smile. Minette let go of her sister's hand, ran to her mother and circled her waist with both arms.

"We went to see the 'General,' who just arrived. Oh, Mama, it was beautiful – just beautiful. We saw all the most elegant gentlemen and ladies, we saw the sailors singing…"

"Like that, in that state?" interrupted her mother. "It's a miracle you weren't taken for a couple of maroons!"

"Us, Mama, oh no!" responded Minette with such conviction that her mother could not help but smile.

She brought the girls into the house and, chattering softly, served them a dish of red beans and rice that she had saved for their midday meal.

"Well, too bad for you, your food's cold," she said to them as she headed back outside.

They swallowed everything down with a hearty appetite and then, after rinsing their plate and cup, sat down with their mother amongst the colorful madras scarves, the trinkets, the soaps and cheap perfumes. They joined their voice to those of the other market-women: "Hey mister, hey lady – pretty handkerchiefs, 'smell-good' soaps – come have a look!…"

Their very first memories were of this place. Their first relationships were those they had formed here, on Traversière Street. Everyone they knew sold little odds and ends – *pacotilles* – just like their mother. There was nothing for them to worry about there. From their very first looks at the world, they had learned how to tell colored children from white children, rich colonists from the low-class Whites, slaves from the class of freedmen, to which they belonged. From their very first steps they had understood that there were places they would never be allowed to go; in the church, they had seen that there was a section for the Whites and another for the Blacks. They had seen, not without longing, the white children go to school, while they were obliged to learn to read in secret. Their mother had been their first teacher and, at night, by the light of a little lamp that barely illuminated their syllabary, she had taught them to write the letters of the alphabet. That was the extent of her own knowledge – and she deeply regretted it, as she had greater ambitions for her daughters. Without the means to pay a "poor white" to take the risk of teaching them, she patiently looked among the freedmen for a clandestine tutor, who would surely be less costly.

In the meantime, Minette and Lise grew up without any education, like all the other children of the neighborhood. These included a beautiful fourteen-year-old mulatto girl everyone called "Crazy Girl" because of her shameless behavior: she let the boys kiss her right in the middle of the street. But as Jasmine often reminded her daughters, Nicolette had neither mother nor father to watch over her. "Ah, po' motherless chile," exclaimed the neighborhood women in their languid Creole, "she surely gon' be lost." There was also a little *mestif* boy with curly locks and a delicate little mouth, who had been given the name Pitchoun by a white woman named Madame Guiole. In fact, no one knew of any other name for him, because although his father lived with his mother, the mulatto woman Ursule, he found him too dark-skinned to claim as his legitimate son. Pitchoun liked watching the soldiers march by and dreamed of becoming one eventually. He admired their uniforms: blue nankeen for the freedmen and white and red for the Whites. He made sabers for himself out of cardboard or wood, and sang battle hymns his tutor taught him. For, being one of the more privileged freedmen, he had a white tutor and was learning the goldsmith trade with Mme Guiole. Monsieur Sabès, although he did not much care for his son, had ceded to Ursule's entreaties. However, the latter was so sweet-natured and fearful that she did not dare protest whenever M Sabès hit the child for no reason, calling him a little nigger boy. The mother and son adored one another. It was their only consolation. Sometimes, when he saw his mother crying, Pitchoun ran out of his own home to the little house on Traversière Street, where Minette and Lise happily welcomed him like a brother. His greatest joy was to listen to them sing. If they needed coaxing, like a good little charmer he took out handfuls of candy from his pockets and found thousands of ways to flatter them.

"Oh come on, sing something for me and when I grow up I'll marry one of you."

"You're too young," replied Minette disdainfully. "We'll be young ladies and you'll still be nothing but a little fart."

At which point he stood up to show off his strong build, puffing up his chest and brandishing his sword while loudly singing battle hymns…

On that day, when the new Governor had been set up in his palace and the crowd had deserted the streets, several people had headed out to the cabarets and restaurants. The bells and cannons were silent. The only sounds were the crack of the whips and the horses' hooves hammering the ground. Fat clouds of dust rose up, hiding the pedestrians who prudently stood to the side to let the carriages pass. Because people of color were forbidden to walk through the King's Garden and along certain other streets, they turned instead onto the narrow side-streets where flimsy, whitewashed structures had been erected. Pitchoun, back from the popular demonstrations, arrived at Traversière Street accompanied by several friends. They made a showy entrance, pacing up and down the street, sabers drawn and singing a march. Once they had exhausted their repertoire, they surrounded Jasmine's stand, cheered on by the delighted market-women.

"Sing us something, my golden chickadees," Pitchoun said to Jasmine's daughters affectionately.

"We're tired. Go on, get out of here," protested Minette.

Pitchoun pulled a stalk of barley sugar out of his pocket and passed it under their noses. Minette grabbed it, laughing.

"A song, a song…"

A little crowd began to form. Some of the vendors gathered round, abandoning their stands.

"Jasmine's girls are going to sing…"

Minette raised her hand to keep the rhythm and give the signal to her sister. Immediately, their voices rose with surprising fullness and purity. They sang one of those many French ballads made popular in Saint Domingue by the sailors from the Metropolis who spilled out onto the island from the hundreds of boats that docked there over the course of any given year, along with the continuous flow of merchandise and adventurers.

"My Lord, do they sing beautifully!" exclaimed a poor, elderly white lady dressed in rags and powdered like a Harlequin. "True little prodigies…"

She opened her mouth in a circle, held out her hand and pointed with a deformed index finger: "I'm one to judge – I was a singer at the Royal Comédie." She leaned toward Jasmine: "I'm telling you, my dear, you should be proud…"

The girls' mother looked at her girls without smiling. Yes, they were gifted, but so what! Her staring eyes, opened wide, seemed to pierce right through them. Everything around her faded away. She was suddenly back in the past. This had been happening to her quite often lately. An unhealthy obsession kept her on a sort of leash, bringing her thoughts back to her very worst memories. She had visions of the large shack she had lived in as a child, of the market where she had been sold, the red-hot iron that had branded her right breast, the lashes of the whip that day she had been caught learning to read with an old slave, the eyes of her master on the night he had desired her, the hatred of her mistress and the numerous punishments it had earned her…She shivered without changing position and saw once again the birth of her daughters and, finally, the will that, upon the death of her master, made her a free woman.

Noticing her mother's fixed and unhappy stare, Minette abruptly stopped singing, let out a little cry, and went to bury her head in the folds of her mother's camisole. At twelve, she already understood many things. She accepted them as inevitable, yet questioned them all the same. Why? Why were things this way and not another? Why were some people rich and others poor? Why did people beat their slaves? Why were some masters kind and others cruel, some priests good and others evil? Why did catechism teach the things it did and why did the priests act the way they did? They said: we are all brothers, but then they bought slaves and beat or otherwise tortured them. Why should she have to hide herself in order to learn to read? Why had Rosélia, one of the neighborhood vendors, been imprisoned for hiding a runaway slave? And above all, why – knowing what could happen – had she hidden that slave, who she did not even know? Minette had the feeling her mother really did not want to answer whenever she posed these sorts of troubling questions. She had figured out on her own that money could buy everything: beautiful dresses, plantations, slaves, and carriages. Thinking like a true freedwoman, she thanked God she had not been born a slave; she made a point – following her mother's advice – always to speak French, so as to give the impression of refinement, and though she lamented the slaves' condition, she considered them an inferior and pitiable class. She was, however, unconsciously sensitive to the injustice of their situation, though she was still at the age where one easily confuses revolt with pity. And so it was not insignificant, she realized instinctively, that her mother's hand trembled in hers on market days when slaves were being sold. Still, she did not know everything about her mother's terrible past.

II

JUST A FEW days after the arrival of the new Governor, someone knocked on the door of the little house on Traversière Street. Minette ran to open it and found herself standing before an eighteen-year-old young man, dark-skinned with kinky hair. Of delicate appearance, he had extraordinarily honest eyes – eyes so full of candor that they gave his otherwise rather unlovely face a captivating expression of smiling goodness.

"Is your mother home?" he asked the girl, respectfully doffing his straw hat. "I am Joseph Ogé." And leaning toward her he added: "I've come as a tutor. I'm not here to ask for anything. Your mother will pay me as much as she can afford."

He expressed himself in perfect French yet with the slight lilt of a Creole accent. Minette slipped away to let her mother know. Jasmine came immediately. She looked at Joseph Ogé for a long time then spoke, leaning toward him: "I trust you, professor," she said aloud.

He burst out in frank and youthful laughter: "That's the fastest way to give ourselves away. Why don't you just call me Joseph. People like us don't have titles."

"Okay, then. Joseph."

The lessons began and the girls soon knew how to read perfectly. And so he brought them history books. With him, they entered into a whole new world. He spoke to them of the King of France, of the Queen, of their children, of their predecessors. He promised them that later he would introduce them to Racine, Corneille, Molière, and Jean-Jacques Rousseau. Lise yawned, while Minette – her eyes aglow – listened intently.

Soon Joseph was no longer their tutor but a friend none of them could imagine being without. Jasmine herself began to love him like a son.

For his part, as if long hungry for this kind of intimacy, Joseph became less and less reserved every day. He told them that he lived alone in a room he rented from a mulatto freedman, a real miserly sort – heartless…

One evening, he arrived drenched in sweat as if he had run a great distance. When he opened the door, he stood leaning against it without saying a word, trying to catch his breath. Jasmine and her daughters had him sit down and served him some leftover jam they had set aside for him.

But he was unable to eat and pushed away the plate.

Minette was the first to break his worrisome silence. "Joseph, why did you run over here?"

He rose from his seat and Jasmine was unsurprised to hear revolt rumbling in his voice when he answered: "I had to run from the police like a thief."

"Run? But why?"

"They caught me teaching some young slaves to read." He paced up and down the room, fists clenched and eyes brimming with tears. "They dress up our own brothers as policemen and have them chase us. They promise to pay them, to promote them – and they turn them into assassins…"

"Why?" asked Minette, standing up and blocking his path. "Why Joseph? I want to understand."

"Here's the truth," he responded with a deadened voice. "They're afraid of us becoming educated, because education encourages men to revolt. Ignorance creates resignation."

He sat down without looking at Minette and put his head in his hands before continuing: "Just like you and Lise, I learned to read in secret. When my mother died, I was left alone in the world. One day, I stole fruits from the market because I was hungry. Someone called the police and they chased me to a house where I was hidden. It was the home of a mulatto freedman named Labadie, plantation master and slaveholder. He put clothes on my back and protected me. I grew up with him. After giving me an education, he promised to send me to France to learn a trade. I was supposed to join my half-brother Vincent, who had already been studying overseas for several years, but a new law had been passed forbidding colored people from entering the mother country."

"Why doesn't your brother come back?"

"Come back for what?" he said with the same dull voice. "Everything is forbidden to us. Everything is closed to us. We can't even learn the trade we want."

He lowered his head as if overwhelmed:

"Me, I'd so like to…" He cut himself off, smiled sadly and made the unconscious gesture of placing his hand on his chest. "Let's just drop it."

Then, thinking better of it perhaps, he leaned toward Jasmine and looked her straight in the eyes: "Have you heard anything about the Black Code?"

She made a sign to indicate she had not.

"Well," he added, "this Code was drafted about a hundred years ago to lay out our political rights. Article 59 of this Code says that we, the freedmen, have the same rights and the same privileges as people born free."

"The Whites haven't kept their promises?"

"Labadie thinks they resent the fact that we've become educated, that we own land and, especially, that there are so many of us."

"Might they be afraid, Joseph? Might they be afraid?" asked Jasmine in a voice so passionate that for a second Minette wondered if it was really her mother who had spoken.

As for Joseph, he did not answer. But he looked at Jasmine with such intensity that she shivered. What did that look mean? Did he want to remind her of the runaway slaves hidden in the mountains and the disturbing messages they transmitted with their drums and *lambi* horns? But what could those poor souls possibly have in common with the class of freedmen, to which she now belonged? Had she not carefully hidden her old life from her entourage? For all of them, as for her, that past was dead, completely behind her. "Daughter of a slave" – people used those words as an insult. Was it not better to live peacefully, and to be more or less respected, by letting people believe that her daughters were born free? At the very core of her being, she kept hidden an immeasurable pity for her former brothers in misery. But what good was her pity? And what would be the use of confessing? Since she had

had the good fortune to be freed – since things had turned out that way, since in this world there would always be colonists, freedmen, and slaves – she might as well resign herself.

Resign herself! Joseph had just completely shaken that certitude. How he had looked at her when she dared – her, Jasmine – to talk about the white men's fear! The arrogant Whites who must tremble at night listening to the harsh and terrifying sounds of the *lambi* horns. How many times had she herself listened to them, alarmed, asking herself why they resounded so loudly and if everyone else was hearing them, too.

She hadn't forgotten about Makandal and his bloodthirsty rebels. Who could have possibly forgotten about them? He had been killed, it is true. But a leader who dies sets an example…Yes, those were all the things Joseph's look meant to express. Yes, the slaves were far less resigned than anyone thought and the Whites were truly ignorant if they took them for passive beasts of burden. So then, by the grace of the Lord, there was hope…that one day…No, it was not possible. That Joseph could think otherwise proved that he was nothing but a child.

"Has anyone ever seen the masters fear their dogs?" she blurted out, shaking her head sadly.

"Yes, when they become rabid," responded Joseph harshly. And as he spoke, he held Jasmine's gaze with the same searching intensity in his own eyes.

And immediately she understood that he was not speaking to her, Jasmine the freedwoman, but rather to the former slave, she who had been bought, beaten, humiliated – the former slave that she had never really stopped being, with her chronic fear and her woeful resignation.

"You've known, then?"…she asked softly. And she was surprised to feel herself overcome by a pleasant sense of peace. "It feels better not having anything more to hide from those we love," she added, and a sad smile crossed her lips, moving Joseph so deeply that he lowered his head.

Lise let out an awkward little cough, declaring the conversation mysterious and tiresome. Joseph looked at her: she had an annoyed and distant attitude, as if everything that had just been said had gone in one ear and out the other, without leaving the slightest trace. Minette, however, lowered a worried forehead and looked straight ahead, as if pondering something…

…Fortunately, not all of their evenings together took on this tragic tone. On the contrary, that instance where Joseph let himself go to the point of revealing his rebellious thoughts was the last time such a thing occurred. Generally, after their lessons or a group reading, Jasmine would take up some sewing and the girls would sing, while Joseph, happy and relaxed, listened to them smilingly. Sometimes friends from the neighborhood came by, requesting their favorite songs. And the girls, without needing to be begged, would delight their audience. Jasmine was proud. Within her, the beaten and debased former slave held her head high, forgot about the past, smiled at the future. But this brief feeling of joy lasted only as long as her daughters sang. As soon as the house was empty and her children asleep, she was once again overcome with worry, and trembled for her little ones. To the extent to which she could remember, she had learned this fear in her earliest childhood. She was afraid of her father the colonist, she was afraid when her mother died, she was afraid at the market where she was sold and also of her new master, the father of her children. She had been trembling with fear her entire life. In the end, it was possible – who knows – that she had been born to be married to one man, to be a protected woman with a legitimate name and a few kids hiding in her skirts. Life had been mistaken about her destiny and, in forcing her to accept this horrible condition, had destroyed all her strength. She had known others who were far more suited than she for battle and for vengeance. Her whole life, she had wanted to be protected, and faced with the horrors of reality, her damsel-in-distress nature had shrunken to the point of perishing. Only her daughters mattered to her in this world. And this child, this Joseph, who had educated them, molded them – how could she do anything but love him, too? He had come into their lives and been so generous that his salary amounted to little more than the affection she showed him. His eyes reminded her of those of a man she had once known, a long time ago, whose name and face she no longer remembered. It seemed to her to be a vague recollection that arrived in spurts but then faded just as quickly. But sometimes looking at him she said to herself, *This child's eyes remind me of someone else's I once knew – but whose?* And, confusingly, it seemed to her that if she loved him as much as she did it was likely because of this.

III

OFTENTIMES, WHEN Minette and Lise were singing, seated among the cheap wares of the market-women, the window of the neighboring house would open up suddenly and a blond head would lean out of it, astonished and delighted. Astonished, yes – for where had these two poor little colored girls gotten voices like that? Delighted, because this white woman was an artist to her core…Her name was Mme Acquaire. The rather modest house where she had rented a room bore a sign that read:

> SINGING, ELOCUTION, AND DANCING
> TAUGHT HERE.

An actress at the Comédie of Port-au-Prince, she lived with her husband, a white Creole like herself. Son of a wig-maker, the dancer and actor Acquaire was overwhelmed with debt. On his worst days – days where he had lost at the gambling table everything he had managed to earn the night before from a performance for which he had taken in the profits – he would knock on the door of François Mesplès, a filthy rich white usurer who had a reputation for heartlessness and scrupulousness…

"Hey, Scipion, there go those little nightingales from Traversière Street – singing away!"

An enormous black slave, with a smiling and open face, joined her at the window that morning. "Yes, mistress, those are the little nightingales."

Mme Acquaire listened a little longer to their pure, young voices, then, leaving the window wide open, sat down at the piano and once again said:

"Here's my favorite game, Scipion. I sing and the nightingales echo me."

She sang a tune from a popular opera. Then stopped and cocked her ears. The little girls had also gone quiet. Mme Acquaire began and then stopped again. All of a sudden, one of the voices responded so beautifully that she rose from her piano in a burst of enthusiasm and said to Scipion:

"One of these days, I'll bring them over here, do you hear me?"

"Yes, mistress," answered the slave, smiling.

He was one of those rare slaves who had been treated with humanity and, because of this, was entirely devoted to his masters. Because he, Scipion, was not beaten, because he was treated like a human being, and most of all because he could see the difference between his situation and that of the other slaves who were beaten, tortured, and tormented, he adored his masters. M Acquaire had bought him one day after a good turn at the gaming table; and, although he had been swearing ever since that he had wasted his money purchasing the jovial giant who served as a domestic for him and his wife, he did not really mean it at all, for he truly cared for him. Scipion put him to bed whenever he came home after his drinking binges, sullen and staggering. Scipion would put a bit of sliced lemon on his lips and pass a damp cloth over his forehead, and he never said a word about his master's escapades to Mme Acquaire. Scipion prepared their meals, did the housework and, on days when funds were scarce, waited for M Mesplès by the side of the road and asked for money. Scipion had become as indispensable as the piano. Just as the Acquaires could not imagine their life without that piano, they had arrived at a point where they simply could not do without Scipion. Mme Acquaire even went so far as to confide in him – sharing her worries, her hopes, and her plans.

Thus did he feel comfortable bringing up something with his mistress that was of great importance to him. Without fear of being beaten, he came back to the subject several times and spoke to her in flattering terms about the two little girls from Traversière Street.

"Bring them here to sing for you, mistress, I beg you."

"I've been giving it some thought, but quit harping on it…"

"At least let them see the piano, mistress. They're so poor and you're so kind," the slave insisted bravely.

Mme Acquaire did not answer, but now, whenever she passed by Jasmine's house, she would pretend to look over the merchandise so she could listen to the two sisters at her leisure.

One day, unable to hold out any longer, she left her house early in the morning. In the deserted street, the market-women had not yet laid out their wares. She knocked on Jasmine's door and, as the two sisters were still sleeping, she was able to speak freely with their mother.

"Jasmine," said Mme Acquaire, already thrilled by the effect she knew her words would have, "would you be willing to entrust your daughters to me so that I might offer them singing lessons?"

"Entrust my daughters to you!" The poor woman was trembling with happiness and would have gotten down on her knees to kiss the hem of Mme Acquaire's dress. But the Creole woman, satisfied by the joy she had just occasioned, kept her from doing so and said, somewhat dramatically:

"I will try, my dear girl, in some small measure, it is true, to right the wrong done by others of my kind."

Then she asked Jasmine to send the girls over to her every day from eight o'clock to ten o'clock in the morning.

With that settled, Mme Acquaire returned home to share the good news with Scipion. The slave, overjoyed, told Mme Acquaire that the good Lord would reward her a hundredfold for the good she was going to do and that she was now guaranteed a place in heaven. Mme Acquaire, skeptical regarding anything that concerned rewards in the afterlife, smiled and, opening her piano, began to play and sing. She was a woman of thirty or thirty-five years, not particularly beautiful, but slim and lively as a bird. Thanks to her training as a dancer, her figure was supple and flawless. As bohemian as her husband, she believed life consisted of moments of good luck and streaks of misfortune, both of which she accepted gaily. Before the death of her parents, important planters in Saint Domingue, she had left for France at the age of fifteen only to return at the age of twenty, having been trained in singing, elocution, and dance. She was a good catch – and thus did the Count of Chastel, an important property owner and slaveholder, ask for and win her hand in marriage. The wedding was to take place two months later, but then one night a great fire destroyed all the properties of the young Creole girl's parents. A slave who had been punished the night before was accused of the disaster – he was to be punished further but had disappeared. The Count of Chastel, upon hearing the news of his fiancée's ruin, claimed that he had to leave immediately for France to take care of some business matters. He only returned two years later, duly married to a white French woman from the mother country. The young Creole girl managed to hide her disappointment and agreed to marry M Acquaire, a Creole like herself, whose penniless father crafted wigs. From this sudden financial ruin and disillusionment, she understood that the Count – like all the men from the island's big families – had wanted to marry her for her fortune, and that the devastating fire, of which the slave had been accused, was in fact the consequence of all the ill-treatment to which the slaves had been subjected. As a girl, she had witnessed horrific tortures ordered by the colonists, both by friends of her father and her father himself – a man who never missed an opportunity to point out that it was necessary to treat "that species" as harshly as possible.

She had seen an entire family die from poisoning. No slave from that plantation had been willing to betray the guilty party. Three of them were tortured, to set an example, and they died screaming in pain without ever revealing their secret. From then on, the young girl had begun to think. Such instances of refusal and revolt, on the part of poor souls considered nothing more than animals, made her think that perhaps they were not really that unintelligent and that, hiding their rage, they only accepted their condition thanks to those sporadic opportunities for vengeance against their masters. She regretted nothing of the past, for she was not unhappy with M Acquaire. They had similar tastes.

Obsessed with dance and the arts, the same age as his wife and, like her, not particularly good-looking but well built, M Acquaire swore that he would never succeed at anything but the theater, having been born an artist and, as such, a natural enemy of commerce and politics. When the old garage that had been used as a performance hall since 1762 was destroyed by an earthquake eight years later, it was replaced by a beautiful space with seven hundred and fifty seats that merited the name the Comédie of Port-au-Prince. This was the moment when M Acquaire made the acquaintance of François Mesplès, agent for the new theater who, despite his greed, grudgingly agreed to advance them a few pounds, with interest, on days when money was especially tight. It soon became clear to François Saint-Martin, director of the theater, and to François Mesplès, the agent, that with their enthusiasm, their imagination, and their true love of the arts, the Acquaires had become indispensable to the functioning and, indeed, to the success of the Comédie. This earned them, on the one hand, the generous sympathy of the young director and, on the other, the admittedly self-serving tolerance of the agent.

While Mme Acquaire was still singing, the door opened and her husband appeared. As soon as he saw his master arrive, Scipion rushed to serve him some of his favorite rum punch with lemon and to help him remove his linen jacket.

"I'm just back from the Comédie," said M Acquaire, comfortably installed in an old, half-destroyed armchair. "I saw Mesplès. He advanced us a few pounds."

Mme Acquaire planted a few chords and sang: "Oh joy, life is good…"

Then she stopped herself and turned toward her husband:

"Do you know who I'll soon be giving lessons to? Guess… To Jasmine's little girls."

"The little neighborhood nightingales?" asked M Acquaire, abruptly closing his right eye.

He suffered from a tic.

"That's right."

"And are you being paid?"

"No. Not a single cent."

"And so, why do it?"

"It makes me happy."

"You play the benefactress and you live in a hovel. Ah! These Creole women, they wear their heart on their sleeve."

"Don't you go generalizing. I know plenty of Creoles who are more like that Mesplès of yours."

M Acquaire removed his shoes, tensed his feet in a perfect arch, and stretched. "I've been chasing after Mesplès for too long. My muscles hurt," he said, his tic twitching even more forcefully.

Mme Acquaire seemed to be pondering something. All of a sudden, she looked at her husband and said:

"Those little ones from next door, they have extraordinary voices. One of them in particular. I don't know yet if it's the elder or the younger, but that child sings the opera songs she hears from my window with amazing mastery."

"True," admitted M Acquaire, less enthusiastic than his wife, "she has a nice voice."

Mme Acquaire exploded:

"You call that a nice voice! Let me spell it out for you. If the child who sang back to me that complex melody from *Three Sultans* the other morning were to train her voice, she would become an extraordinary opera singer."

"You're getting carried away! What good will any of this do her? She can't even go to France with this new law they just enacted against colored people."

"It's unfair. It's disgusting."

"Let's not get political now, my darling. We're actors – don't forget that."

"I'm not forgetting anything, but I find all of this…disgusting. Don't stop me from saying it to you, otherwise I'll just suffocate."

M Acquaire yawned, played around again with the muscles of his feet, and reclined as comfortably as he could in the hole-ridden arm-chair.

The next day, Jasmine dressed her girls in the little cotton dresses she had starched the night before and placed in a drawer with nosegay flowers to perfume them. Then she gave them their sandals, rubbed with soot, and told them they glowed in the sunlight like mirrors.

"Be on your best behavior," she admonished them. "Speak French and be elegant – make your mother proud."

It was Scipion who opened the door to them. He smiled and, taking them by the hand, led them to the piano. They had never seen one before. They walked all around it, bent down to look at the pedals. It was open. Minette hesitantly put her finger on one of the keys, causing it to vibrate. They jumped back and Lise cried out gently.

"Don't be afraid," came the voice of Mme Acquaire. "I'm right here next to you, behind this screen. I'm just getting dressed. Go ahead, start again. Minette, put your finger on a note and then sing it."

Minette randomly placed her finger on a *mi*, more confidently this time. She opened her mouth and the note reverberated throughout the little room, resonant and pure.

"So you were the one who sang back to me so beautifully," said Mme Acquaire, emerging from behind the screen wearing a transparent chiffon tunic, her head wrapped in a handkerchief whose ends fell across one of her shoulders.

She drew Minette close enough to look her over. The girl's dark, slanted eyes looked into her own without the slightest shyness. Smiling, she caressed the girl's long braids and tanned cheeks, amused by the sensual and willful expression of the girl's full mouth, negroid and adorable. Minette had a special sort of charm that likely came from her dark, unwavering gaze – a gaze that did not falter, not even before a white person. A rare thing. The wings of her deliciously indented nose trembled with the slightest emotion, but never did the lashes lower to veil her eyes. Mme Acquaire, comparing the two sisters, found Lise to be the more beautiful of the two, with her less dark braids, her less slanted eyes, her less sensual mouth. But in Minette's type there was something that pleased the artist in her. Lise lowered her gaze when speaking to her and Minette surprised her by looking her straight in the eyes, not impertinently, but with calm assurance.

From the very first lesson, the Creole woman detected such a perfect understanding of music and so much character in her favorite of the two girls that she gathered her in her arms to embrace her.

"I'm going to make you a great, great opera singer," she promised her, laughing.

"And me?" asked Lise.

"You'll also sing very well, but I predict that Minette will be an extraordinary singer."

Over the course of the next few months, the two sisters came to their teacher's home nearly every morning. Oftentimes, M Acquaire and Scipion attended the lessons. The former, sunk deeply into his old armchair, his tic twitching each time Minette hit a beautiful note, and the latter seated on the floor, a blissful smile on his lips, his long legs stretched out before him and his eyes fixed on the singers' lips. During these months, the life of the two little girls from Traversière Street became exactly what their ambitious mother had always wanted for them. They had a schedule that kept them from idleness, that little sin to which so many women of the island succumbed – responsible, in Jasmine's opinion, for all of their other vices. In the morning, Minette and Lise practiced singing, and in the evening they continued their education with Joseph. He had recently brought them a book by Jean-Jacques Rousseau, in which Minette had discovered the phenomenon of a free white man obsessed with liberty and demanding it for all people, along with a play by Jean Racine, *Athalie*, through which she discovered the tragic form, classical art, resounding and forceful verse, and the harmonious rhythm of phrasing.

She was surprised to find herself reciting on her own the beautiful words the author had placed in the mouth of his heroine, taking care with her diction, in imitation of Joseph. Jasmine, overjoyed, listened to her rehearse and even went so far as to tell her – she who had always so carefully hidden her past from her daughters – that she had once known a young lady who, just like Minette, had recited beautiful verse before a crowd of listeners.

"Where?" asked the girl.

"Ah! A long time ago…it was a lady from…but that was so long ago…I've forgotten."

She stammered whenever it came to recalling her past. Ever since her daughters were old enough to understand, Jasmine had never gotten undressed in front of them, even though they slept in the same room. Certain marks she bore had to remain secret. She was free now, as were her children. She wanted to forget the past, banish it from her memory. The future remained dark, but she could hold out a little hope that her daughters, later on, would make their living teaching singing to rich colored people. For there were some very rich members of that class, plantation owners and slaveholders just like the white colonists. They were numerous, actually – too numerous, according to Joseph, not to attract the attention of the wealthy Whites. How could they possibly be content to find themselves now competing with a despised class that had been long kept in a state so inferior that even education was forbidden to them? Everything possible was now being done to prevent marriages between Whites and freedmen. They were barred from certain professions, even when they showed innate talent. It was a merciless struggle. One day, after a revolt of "maroons" where hundreds of Whites had perished, the colored freedmen had been brazenly disarmed, having been accused of supplying weapons to the rebellious slaves. Their soldiers' uniforms, different in every way from those of the Whites, of course, had become a ridiculous accoutrement, subject to insult from the "poor whites" who respected them even less since they had been disarmed. Just a few months earlier, however, Jasmine had seen the same men who were being humiliated today depart alongside the white soldiers for the battle of Savannah, from which they had returned victorious.

These same men, often searched in the middle of the street these days without the slightest apology, and from whom the tiniest little pocketknife could be seized, had surprised the Whites on the battlefield. Jasmine knew all of this through Joseph. Ever since he had been coming to the house, and especially since she began listening to him speak, long dormant impressions she believed to be well and properly buried were awakened in her. She no longer walked like an automaton, · head lowered and shoulders slumped. She looked around her like a curious child discovering the world. Thus did she notice the look in the eyes of a young black freedman being rudely searched by a white man. Something was brewing, though she would not have been able to say what it was. But after a long period of blindness, it seemed to her now that certain members of her entourage had changed. Still, more than ever before, the freedmen were being repressed; more than ever, the slaves were being mistreated, tortured; and with every revolt of the maroons, the reprisals of the Whites were that much more brutal. But to console herself, she noted that many of the freedmen were rich, and she praised their intelligence and success while thinking that one day they would make respectable matches for her daughters.

…That morning, Minette and Lise arrived at their lesson late and found Mme Acquaire lying down, sobbing and whimpering, with a compress on her forehead. They ran to kneel next to her bed and both began questioning her at the same time. But the Creole lady continued to weep without responding. A worried expression on his face, M Acquaire took long strides back and forth across the tiny room, turning in circles like a caged animal.

"Oh! Would you stop – would you stop pacing up and down!" begged Mme Acquaire, beside herself. "Your steps feel like a hammer drumming into my head."

M Acquaire sat down wearily on a stool that had been left at the foot of the bed, while his tic had his right eye twitching furiously.

Looking at him, Minette wondered whether he was kidding around, as his incessant winking gave him an unexpectedly playful appearance.

"Haven't you reached a decision yet?" he asked, looking at his wife.

"What do you want me to do? Sell the piano?" she responded.

At that moment there was a knock at the door and Mme Acquaire immediately stopped speaking. She made a nervous gesture toward her husband, who was bent over her.

"Those are the students," she whispered to him. "Send them away. They mustn't see Minette and Lise here."

"Yes, you're right."

M Acquaire opened the door slightly: three little white girls greeted him cheerily.

"Your teacher isn't feeling well," he explained to them. "She asks you to excuse her this morning."

"Couldn't we speak to her just for a moment?" one of them asked.

M Acquaire's eye twitched as he scratched his head nervously. "Ahem! I'm afraid she simply isn't able to see you…Ahem!…"

"I see," responded the girl, rather surprised. And not wanting to insist further:

"We'll come back tomorrow."

"Yes, please do. Tomorrow, then, tomorrow, young ladies…"

M Acquaire closed the door and let out a sigh of relief. "Phew!… That was a close one…"

Minette exchanged a glance with her little sister. She had just realized that Mme Acquaire was teaching them in secret! The only reason she had them come so early in the morning was so as not to risk the displeasure of her other students. They were being treated like they had the plague simply because of their color.

Minette's heart was heavy and her eyes filled with tears. They were nothing more than two poor colored girls that a white lady was teaching to sing out of pity! Minette stood up, took Lise's hand, and looked at Mme Acquaire, who continued whispering to her husband.

"May we leave, Madame?" she asked, in a plaintive little voice.

She sounded like a baby trying to hold back tears. Oh! She would not mention any of this to her mother. To what end? It was perfectly normal, and they had better accept it if they wanted to continue studying with Mme Acquaire. Likely that would be Jasmine's response.

"Yes, do. Go back home, children," answered the Creole woman insistently. "I'll have Scipion let you know just as soon as I'm feeling better. And don't forget that you mustn't come here after ten o'clock – not ever. Do you understand?"

"Yes, Madame."

"Good then, now off you go. Goodbye, my children."

"Thank you, Madame."

Once Minette and Lise had gone, Mme Acquaire was free to express her anxiety. She sat up in the bed, took the compress off her forehead, and dabbed at her reddened eyes.

"Yes, so now what would you have me do?"

"I don't know."

"Ah! Why, why did you gamble away that money we made with our last play?"

M Acquaire's tic was twitching so intensely that she felt sorry for him.

"So, Mesplès refuses to help us, you say?"

"Alas, yes! That scum claims he doesn't have a penny to spare – that he's half ruined himself. Exactly the kind of nonsense that a crook of his ilk shouldn't be spewing. To think that I tried to soften him up with thirty payments in a single week! Add to that all the rehearsals at the Comédie and I'm broke."

"My Lord, what are we going to do?" whimpered Mme Acquaire.

"There's one possible solution left."

"What's that?"

"Sell Scipion."

"You're not going to do that! You're not going to do that!" She was practically screaming.

"But we have no choice!"

Mme Acquaire let herself fall back on the bed, dissolving in sobs while holding the compress to her head with a trembling hand. Sell Scipion! No, it wasn't possible! Not for a second had she thought they could do with him what people did with other slaves. What did it matter to her if people sold wet nurses, suckling infants, half-dead elderly slaves whose value was measured by the ton like cattle, as long as Scipion remained hers! She had figured out that certain things in Saint Domingue would never change. Daughter of a planter, raised in the courtyard of a great house, she had been accustomed since girlhood to being served, adored; like all young Creoles, she had had a *cocotte* to whom she had confided her earliest secrets. She had let her be beaten – oh, never very much, but just enough so that her low-born confidante would understand that she was the mistress and that she alone held the power of life and death over her. Now, with age, she had learned to be indulgent toward that race, though the rebellion of one of its members had cost her her rank and her fortune.

While thinking about all this, an idea came to her in a flash. She quickly pulled herself together and cried out: "Now there's an idea!..."

"What is it?" asked M Acquaire, pulled out of the state of lethargy into which his misery had plunged him.

"Minette!" whispered Mme Acquaire to her husband, as if she did not dare to say the idea loud and clear…

"Well, what about Minette?"

She opened her arms dramatically and said, louder this time: "To attract a big audience to the theater, and to seduce our existing public, perhaps a bit tired of the same old act, we need something sensational, no?"

"Right!" responded M Acquaire, like someone still trying to understand.

"That something sensational will be Minette – in a duet with one of our young actors."

M Acquaire looked at his wife with what seemed like a combination of shock and pity, and said to her:

"You've gone mad."

"Mad? Not at all…"

"But they'd never let a girl of color perform on the stage of the Comédie! Are you trying to create a scandal, for heaven's sake? Have you forgotten who François Mesplès is?"

"No, I know who he is…Listen, our backs are against the wall. This scandal will either destroy all our hopes or save us.

M Acquaire's tic twitched as he stroked his chin – a sign that he was doing some serious thinking.

"It's true, that child has extraordinary talent."

Mme Acquaire took advantage of her husband's softening to press her point.

"Let me do it. What's the worst that can happen? We risk being expelled from the island. Big deal. If we fail, I promise you we can sell Scipion to pay for our trip overseas…"

The slave had heard everything. In a house that small, the walls have ears. And even though he was not making any particular effort, his masters' words reached him loud and clear. He understood that his fate no longer depended on the Acquaires, but on the little colored girl with the crystal clear voice. He already admired her; he began to adore her.

Mme Acquaire, whose excellent idea had immediately cured her of her malaise, put on a mauve silk *gaule*, beneath which she tied a modest underskirt, and ran to Jasmine's house.

When the door opened and she stood there before them, the girls let out a little cry of surprise, for they had just left her ailing in her bed.

Joseph rose and nodded to her. Mme Acquaire, overexcited, paid him no attention.

"My dears, where is your mother? Call her – I'd like to speak to her."

Jasmine hurried in, wiping her hands on her blue camisole. Sensing something unusual in the excitement of the Creole woman, the young people went out onto the patio so that she might speak freely.

"Jasmine, I have good news for you."

"Good news, Lady Acquaire?

How would Jasmine react? That question had not even occurred to the actress. She was certain that the poor freedwoman would be only too pleased to show off her daughter on a stage with white performers. Thus did she decide to forego any preamble and get straight to her proposal, saying: "I'm going to try and have Minette sing at the Comédie."

"The Comédie! You know very well that that's impossible, Lady Acquaire."

"I know the director of the theater – he's a white man, but not at all prejudiced. Entrust your daughter to me and you'll see."

Jasmine closed her eyes for a moment. Watching Minette grow up, she had been serene in the knowledge that with the education she had provided, her daughter would be all right – despite her beauty and the ambiance of vice and sensuality that reigned in the country. Although the atmosphere of the markets, the streets, and the public squares was a wide-open book where any young person could easily find ample opportunities for indecency and compromise, she had hoped to protect her children and to steer them toward a good marriage with a man of their race. She was not one of those former slaves who preferred to marry their daughters to some white adventurer rather than giving them to men of their own kind. She was ambitious, of course, but her ambition was legitimate and proper. What did she know about the Whites? There were the arrogant officers; the cruel seignorial planters, who made the men and women of her race bend under their yoke; and then there were the young, adventure-seeking libertines who spent their days chasing skirts. If benevolent, generous, honest white men actually existed, Jasmine had never encountered one. Yes, there was one – a Jesuit priest who had been run out of the country for teaching the slaves. Mme Acquaire, being Creole and poor, gave her the impression of not being so different from herself. But here she had wrested Minette from her influence, enticing her with a promise of access to the unforgiving white world.

"Why aren't you answering, Jasmine?"

"Lady Acquaire, it simply isn't possible."

"Not possible! But I'm telling you I can arrange everything. You have nothing to fear."

"It isn't what you think, Lady Acquaire."

Noting the tone of her response, Mme Acquaire understood that she was dealing with a particularly strong-willed woman who, unlike most women those days, was worried about her daughter's virtue.

"Listen, Jasmine. I promise you that I will watch over Minette as if she were my own daughter."

The colored woman smiled. What talent Minette must have for someone to plead her case like this!

"Think of her future, Jasmine. Think of the good she might do for others of her kind in revealing her talent to the Whites. For she has a splendid voice, Jasmine, a unique voice…"

Jasmine closed her eyes a second time. She envisioned Minette singing onstage, in a velvet gown and adorned with jewels, hundreds of hands clapping – white hands, the hands of important planters…She struggled with herself for an instant. Was she really going to refuse – did she have that right? No, it was not possible. And her emotions, which the mad leaping of her heart made obvious, did not escape the actress…Her daughter was going to appear onstage with white performers; she was going to be the first to break the impermeable color barrier – she, a fifteen-year-old girl. God was going to allow her, Jasmine, a former slave, to witness such a day!

She burst into tears, fell to her knees and, seizing Mme Acquaire's dress in both hands exclaimed: "Lady Acquaire, are you sure you can protect my child? I'm afraid, I just don't want to regret this…"

"You won't regret it, Jasmine," responded the actress, with the attitude of one who is sure of victory.

"That's all I ask, in the name of our Lord Jesus Christ," responded Jasmine, making the sign of the cross.

Once alone, she called in the girls from the patio, where Joseph had left them, and told them the good news. Minette, overjoyed, threw herself into her mother's arms. Lise wrested her away and, hanging on her neck, repeated:

"To the Comédie! To the Comédie!"

Her cries immediately brought Minette back to her senses. "The Comédie, you say, Mama? But they'll never allow…"

"Lady Acquaire says it's possible."

"Oh! Mama!…"

Jasmine let herself revel for a moment in her daughters' happiness. She asked Lise to take out the merchandise, then took Minette by the hand and pulled her into the bedroom, closing the door behind her.

"You're becoming a young lady, Minette, and your life is going to change. You'll encounter a new world – a world I've kept from you, for your own good and for your happiness. You may be praised and complimented. Whites will come to see you, to court you…don't let yourself be steered in the wrong direction."

As she spoke, she unbuttoned her blouse and Minette, who had been observing her, realized that she had never seen her mother undressed before.

"You must understand something, Minette. Life is much more than songs, laughter, and fancy clothing. There is something else. It will make you sad, my child, but there is something else. Look."

She took off her bodice and showed her daughter the brand on her right breast. She then turned around and showed her back, lined with scars.

Minette screamed and wanted to run away. Jasmine made a gesture to silence her – to take control and force her to stay put.

"You needed to know, do you understand? You needed to know."

Leaning down toward her daughter and with a voice broken by tiny hiccups of sorrow, she then whispered: "You will see white men, lots of white men. Never forget that your father was one of them, and that he was my master."

IV

THE DAYS PASSED. While Minette studied nonstop with Mme Acquaire, M Acquaire began preparing the public by announcing widely that there would be an extraordinary surprise that Christmas season.

What they were planning to do, without the permission of either the shareholders in the theater or its director, was extremely dangerous, for the atmosphere in that moment was especially tense. The colonists had lost a number of slaves to the ever-growing bands of maroons in the hills – and they had overtly accused the freedmen of helping them flee. For many weeks, not a day passed where one did not read at least one announcement in the local paper concerning one or several slaves who had fled their workhouse. Hanging from the trees, along the roads, the police had nailed signs that read:

FREEDMEN ARE STRICTLY PROHIBITED FROM
GIVING SHELTER TO MAROONS. ANY PERSON
FOUND GUILTY OF SUCH AN INFRACTION WILL
LOSE HIS LIBERTY, AS WILL ALL MEMBERS OF
HIS FAMILY RESIDING WITH HIM.

The town criers, who circulated the placards announcing the next Christmas spectacle at the theater, had no idea, as they stood beneath the trees bearing the official signs, that they themselves were drumming up publicity for a colored girl who would be performing the lead role in the comic opera *Isabelle and Gertrude*.

M Acquaire was not unconcerned about the welcome his protégée would receive. He shared his anxieties with Mme Acquaire who, either totally unaware of the politics of the moment or blindly optimistic, assured him that the evening would be a success. They would make a good profit and Mme Acquaire, who had managed to keep their creditors at bay until Christmas day, chased away any thoughts that could undermine her certainty.

"I have every confidence, you understand," she said to her husband whenever he seemed too nervous, "every confidence in both the talent and the charm of this girl."

"Talent and charm don't undo the fact that she's colored and that we're breaking the law."

"She has so little color to her that the law will be forgiving."

M Acquaire's tic started twitching nervously as he replied: "There's something about her that gives it away."

Mme Acquaire smiled mysteriously and responded: "That's precisely the thing I'm counting on to seduce the audience. And though the women may boo her, the men will cheer."

As the rehearsals were taking place secretly on Traversière Street, M Acquaire had been playing the role of the young actor, Claude Goulard, with whom Minette would sing the duet during the performance.

To familiarize her with the stage, they improvised one in the middle of the room. A large sheet served as curtain. As for the other actors, M Acquaire simply made use of the furniture.

"Look, this chair is Magdeleine Brousse. She sings the melody – you'll sing back to her. This portrait is the group of actors playing in the final scene. I'm Claude Goulard and Madame Acquaire is Madame Tessyre. Have you got that?"

Scipion played the role of stage manager and struck the partition with a stone three times, wherein the sheet was lowered and Minette walked onstage. She was perfectly natural, betraying not the slightest emotion, and was surprised at the idea that anyone could suffer from stage fright.

"How easy this is!" she exclaimed happily.

She sang back to the chair that was meant to be Magdeleine Brousse and to the painting that was standing in for the group of actors with the same self-assurance, and the Acquaires – well satisfied – pronounced her both astonishing and perfect.

"This is working beautifully," M Acquaire said finally, though still worried. He felt it would have been more honest to call a meeting of the shareholders in the theater to discuss Minette. But a refusal could ruin his high hopes and so he decided it would be best to confront the shareholders and the director with the done deal. The very intuitive Mme Acquaire knew in advance that she had nothing to fear from the liberal François Saint-Martin, director of the Comédie, and that he would be as taken by Minette as he was by all the beautiful mulatto girls in the country. As for François Mesplès, this was her way of getting revenge, she told herself. This vengeance, it was true, might end up hurting the two of them, but it would very certainly hurt him, Mesplès, and that made it well worth the risk.

Joseph Ogé, aware of what was being planned, hesitated to praise the plan and questioned Minette in a way that filled Jasmine with worry.

"Madame Acquaire wants to have you sing at the Whites-only Comédie. That's very courageous of her. But there's a mysteriousness to her preparations that doesn't sit right with me. Has she introduced you to the director?"

"No."

"Have you signed a contract?"

"No."

"Have you been to the Comédie?"

"The Acquaires…"

"The Acquaires, the Acquaires – but they're only actors! The Theater doesn't belong to them."

He was right to be concerned. Added to the colonists' rage at the escape of their best slaves was a wave of fear brought on by a number of poisoning deaths. Slaves committed suicide after having poisoned the masters and their cattle and, on Bonne-Foi Street, a certain Pradel had lost his freedom for having hidden two runaway slaves in his home. He had been hanged right on Main Street as an example, and for two days there was a line to go look at his contorted mouth, from which his thick purple tongue protruded. Desperate for new entertainment, the women went to the spectacle hoping to bring on a fainting spell, whereas the children thoughtlessly threw stones at the victim.

As a precautionary measure, the slaves were subsequently banned from their last remaining solace – they were forbidden to gather either at church or even outside, where they would listen to the "prairie preachers" who taught them that Jesus is the father of all men, independent of color, and that the slave must accept the yoke and serve his master with respect and devotion. These sermons were not always so innocent, and the colonists knew it well. They closed down the churches as soon as night fell. It was a grave mistake, for, deprived of this spiritual relief, those poor souls who believed naively everything religion taught them returned with renewed fervor to their old beliefs, and this time they held on intractably. Among them, a few enlightened ones, contemporaries of Makandal, strengthened their faith by establishing comparisons between the white man's God, who loved the Whites, and the African gods, who loved the Blacks. Vodou became powerful in the hands of the maroon leaders, who had found in that religion the necessary passion to awaken the most resigned slave.

Thus it was that in the hills and in the slave workhouses the drums and the *lambi* horns continued to communicate mysterious messages, especially during the night...

However, Jasmine, who was not unaware of any of this, interrupted when Joseph tried to question Minette again. She had made the decision to take her chances – and now that this decision had been made, she would not tolerate being discouraged by anyone.

Hope had made her heart soar. She said to herself, *One never knows* or *She sings so well!* and, to reassure herself, concluded that Mme Acquaire knew better than anyone what she was doing, and that she could be trusted.

Despite her ignorance, her maternal love had provided her with an uncommon psychological astuteness. This, coupled with her instinct, gave her antennae. The opportunity being offered to her daughter was unique; she knew that. The sad and miserable routine of her life was being rerouted by the Acquaire's project. Now when she thought about it, the future seemed to have been brightened by a luminous point that attracted her irresistibly.

"Let her have this chance, Joseph!" she said to the young man. "No matter what the risk, let her try…"

Joseph Ogé lowered his head, convinced that, in the end, it was better to close his eyes, put his head in the sand, and leave things in the Acquaires' hands. They were the darlings of the theater – maybe they would be able to fight for Minette. With no small effort, he chased away his bothersome fears and called the girls over for some reading aloud.

At around noon, as he was preparing to leave, the door opened suddenly and a woman from the neighborhood rushed toward Jasmine.

"They've just arrested a runaway slave," she burst out, trembling. "Apparently he had been hiding out on this street. Do you think they'll suspect us? My Lord! Here come the police!…"

Without answering, Jasmine went to the door, accompanied by Joseph and her daughters.

The slave was a very young man, about Joseph's age. Underneath the *tanga* barely covering his thighs, his supple and powerful muscles stood out like thick ropes. The guards had put a chain around his neck and while two of them held him on a leash, two others followed behind, muskets at the ready.

The people gathered in the street were trampling all over the vendors' wares to the great indignation of the latter, who yelled for them to clear off. Upper-class people dressed in hastily thrown-on transparent *gaules* geared up for the spectacle. Domestic slaves, crowded on doorsteps, craned their necks with curiosity, while the youngest among them cried out in Creole:

"They got him, they got him…"

Someone alerted the crowd:

"There's his master."

An older white man made a path through the frenzied crowd. He wore a three-piece linen suit, mud-covered gaiters, and a large straw hat. Standing before the slave, he unfurled a long leather strap and said:

"So you wanted to run away, too, huh?"

The slave said nothing. He simply raised his head, which had been lowered, and closed his eyes so as to avoid being blinded by his sweat.

"You're going to regret that little getaway!" continued the planter. "Now walk!"

Passing in front of Jasmine's door, the slave turned his head and looked at Joseph. He tensed his muscles as if to break his chains. The white man saw what he meant to do; his strap whistled through the air and landed with a single strike on the Negro's cheek. Minette let out a cry that was lost in the tumult of the crowd and the noise of the chains. The slave looked at her. She had grabbed on to Joseph and was weeping nervously: for she had just noticed fresh scars on his back and saw that his sweat carried with it bits of clotted blood as it ran down his torso. That must have been what her mother's back had been like just a few years earlier. Never had such a scene so overwhelmed her. Like all children in the country, from a very young age she had seen slaves beaten. That was their lot in life and not hers. But now that she knew that this had also been her mother's life, now that she understood that this very easily might have been her fate as well, Minette's conception of slavery had changed.

She had not cried out of pity, no. Something altogether different had suddenly gripped her, overwhelmed her, possessed her. Pity would not have tied her stomach in knots like that, it would not have tensed up her nerves to such a degree, it would not have made her nauseous or made her want to run up to that white man and strike him, bite him, curse him. All of this was provoked by the bloodied back she saw before her and that seemed as if it had come there expressly for her to see, if ever she had forgotten, what a slave's back could be when made to suffer the punishment of the whip. Her mama, her mama had suffered such things! Oh, the evil of the white man, oh! What swine! Galley slaves and white trash! Every Creole swearword she could think of passed her lips. On seeing her daughter cry, Jasmine lowered her head and sighed. Such spectacles were unbearable for her, too, for she hated anything that reminded her of her vile past. She brought Joseph and the girls inside and closed the door behind her. Minette sat down in a corner of the room and, with her hand covering her mouth, tried vainly to stop her sobs.

"It's her nerves," said Jasmine to Joseph. "She's at a difficult age. But it will pass."

Lise, taken aback, watched her sister crying. "But what's the matter with her today?" she seemed to be asking. Joseph went to get a glass of water and had her drink it, assuring her that it would calm her down.

"I hate him," said Minette with a painful hiccup.

"Who?"

"That white colonist. I could kill him…"

"Hush!" said Jasmine, terrified. She opened the door quietly and looked outside. A long scream of pain immediately rushed into the little room.

"Close the door, mama – I beg you," whimpered Minette.

"But what's the matter with you," asked Lise. "Is this the first time you've seen a slave get beaten?"

There was another scream, smothered this time. At that moment, Nicolette entered. Following the example of Kiss-Me-Lips, she was wearing silk madras scarves adorned with fake jewels and a transparent batiste blouse. She was often accompanied by white men, both young and old. She would emerge from their carriages arrogant and proud, disheveled and smug.

She gave Joseph a seductive sidelong glance and ran to preen before the little living room mirror.

"That slave is going to get what's coming to him," she stated in Creole, powdering the tip of her nose.

Not getting any response, she turned toward Minette. "Well, what's the matter with you? Why are you crying?"

"It's because of that slave they're beating," answered Lise.

"Because of a slave!…"

Minette stood up without a word, fists clenched. She passed in front of Nicolette, went into the bedroom, and closed the door behind her with such force that the little house shook.

V

DESPITE EVERYTHING, the next days were full of delight for Minette. The joyfulness of youth offered a soothing balm for her recent wounds. First of all, there was the bit of money Mme Acquaire gave Jasmine for her costumes. It was December 15, and the big day was approaching. These were days of unbridled joy during which the two girls ran from store to store. For the first time in her life, Minette experienced the pleasure of buying things. Heeding Mme Acquaire's advice, she bought herself a taffeta skirt at Miss Monnot's place on Bonne-Foi Street. Then she chose some transparent lace, earrings adorned with fake stones that she tried on laughingly in the mirror, and pink shoes that matched the color of her skirt. Lise got to keep a fan that she had been wanting for some time and that she held the whole way home with a ladylike attitude that delighted her sister.

"I'll be holding it on the day of the performance. Don't forget to look at me before you start to sing," she advised Minette.

They stopped, enchanted by the store windows of the jewelers and perfumers. But they had no more money and so were obliged to return home without having bought gloves or perfumes.

"Ah! Minette, how I would love to be rich enough to buy myself everything I want," sighed Lise, clutching her packages to her chest.

"Do you think there's anyone in the world who wouldn't want to be rich?" responded her sister…

…So as not to have to pay a dressmaker, they called on Nicolette, who immediately arrived armed with a pair of scissors that she claimed were "special," taking a mysterious tone that made clear to Jasmine that Nicolette held certain superstitions.

Whatever the case, she made herself so useful and was so spontaneously generous that Jasmine herself was grateful.

"Where are you off to with that get-up fit for a lady?" Nicolette asked Minette, "to the ball or to Vaux-Hall?"

"You'll know soon enough," she replied, with a secretive tone.

"Are you in love? Does he have a carriage? Is it a white man?"

"A white man!" exclaimed Minette with a peculiar tone of voice.

"Nicolette," scolded Jasmine, "Minette is still a child…"

"When I was fifteen," exclaimed the courtesan, "I already had two lovers."

"Enough, enough, Nicolette," interjected the mother, alarmed.

"All right, all right, I won't say anything more to your two little innocents. But believe me, they're as rare in this country as diamonds in the pockets of slaves. I was telling Minette recently about Kiss-Me-Lips – you know her, Jasmine – that young mulatto girl that the king's Bursar wanted to take for his mistress. She told me that in two years, Minette will be more beautiful than all the women in this country."

She left as soon as she had finished cutting out the dress, to the great relief of Jasmine, who worried about her influence on the girls. It was already enough for her to worry about the fact that Minette would soon be confronted with innumerable temptations…

Nevertheless, once they had put away their wares in the evening, they began sewing enthusiastically. The girls sang as they pulled the needle, and when Joseph Ogé knocked on the door, he stopped for a moment to look at the charming little group. Inspired, he recited a few phrases that Minette then integrated into the simple melodies she was inventing.

On Christmas Eve, Minette's robe was ready. Jasmine sprinkled it with jasmine-scented flower sachets. That evening, they gave what Lise called the general rehearsal with, for their audience, the Acquaires, Joseph, and a few neighbors that Jasmine had invited. When Lise opened the bedroom door to announce triumphantly: "She's ready," Minette was greeted with a buzz of admiration. She wore effortlessly the long taffeta skirt that had been perfectly tailored by Nicolette and upon which Jasmine had patiently embroidered large flowers with golden thread. Her lace bodice, though only slightly low cut, neverthe-less revealed the beginnings of the most perfect little breasts. Mme Acquaire rose, untied a package she had been holding in her hand, and took out a splendid tiara, which she placed on Minette's head saying:

"With this, you will be an irresistible Isabelle."

She kissed her, and everyone applauded.

M Acquaire, his tic twitching, gave her some last-minute advice on how to walk and curtsy. Then, taking her hand, he escorted her toward the makeshift crowd and bowed as he presented her to "her public." Minette smiled, completely undaunted. With her magnificent voice she let out two notes so perfect and so beautiful that the applause started up all over again. Mme Acquaire suggested to Jasmine that she put her to bed early that night, and then left with her husband and the other neighbors.

Joseph looked at Minette without speaking a word. He realized that Minette was no longer that studious little girl he had been teaching for the past two years, but had become a young woman of great beauty whose talent was going to allow her to cross the horrific barrier put in place by the Whites. If she managed it, success and – who knows? – great wealth were guaranteed! Her took her hands.

"You are very beautiful, Minette, and when I look at you I think that a girl like you is a true credit to her race."

"Because I'm beautiful?"

"No. Because despite your beauty, you are modest and discreet."

"Joseph!"

"You're afraid aren't you, Minette?"

"Yes."

"You've got to tell yourself you're playing for high stakes now. If you win, all the better. If you don't…"

"If I don't?"

"In that case you've got to say: 'too bad.' And then you'll keep singing – for yourself and for us. There will be 'other things' to help you get over it."

He spoke as if despite what he was telling her, he was not ready to share with her what those "other things" he had in mind might be. He placed his hand on his chest and looked her over from head to toe.

"You've grown up and you've become very brave, isn't that so, Minette?"

"I'm brave, but I'm afraid…of them."

He grabbed her abruptly by the shoulders. "If you fought them, would you be afraid?"

"Did you say fight them?"

"Yes. Your voice is your weapon and you're going to use it. And then…" Again, he hesitated, sighing and finally saying:

"Ah! Later, later, perhaps, you'll understand…"

The evening of the performance, Mme Acquaire came early to bring Minette to the theater. Nicolette was helping Jasmine to dress her, while Lise, absorbed in getting herself ready, stood in front of the room's little mirror and practiced fanning herself.

"Get out of here!" complained Nicolette. "Are you the one singing at the theater tonight? My Lord, at the white folks' theater! What luck! I'll be coming to hear you with my boyfriend, Minette. He's a young officer and he has a carriage. What a shame I'll have to be separated from him in the theater!…"

Mme Acquaire and Minette made quite a sensation in their beautiful clothing as they made their way from Traversière Street to the block where the theater was located. Cheers greeted them from all sides, and people pushed past one another in the doorways to get a better look at them. Mme Acquaire, wearing her ballerina costume and holding her slippers in her hand, walked with the lightness of a bird. She looked like a little girl with her gauzy calf-length skirt. Everything along the way seemed to astound Minette. It was as if she were seeing it all – the church she attended every Sunday, the fountains, the gardens, and the crowd gathered in front of the theater – for the very first time. At the entrance, the two women passed in front of the little refreshment stall where young white women dressed up as maids offered drinks to officers strapped into gleaming uniforms and to important planters in their velvet doublets and powdered wigs.

How often, returning from a stroll with her mother, had Minette been tempted to go in and see what was happening in that great room where she had heard that people sang, danced, and recited verse! But Jasmine had never had enough money to buy seats for them and, to console themselves, Minette and Lise would have Nicolette give them a full report of every detail of the performances. That night, she would be entering that space not as a mere spectator. She herself would play a role on the stage – the main role, that of Isabelle – in an opera that Mme Acquaire said had had a full two-month run in Cap-Français. Would she be equal to the task? She shivered and Mme Acquaire, who was holding Minette's hand in her own, felt it tremble. She threw a wide shawl over Minette's shoulders and brought her backstage.

Everything changed all at once for Minette. As before every performance, there was a very particular atmosphere: costumed actors arrived breathlessly, others showed up half dressed, costumes in their arms; still others, who were meant to play the role of Negroes in a Creole drama, swore as they slathered themselves in soot.

"Ah! This again," one of them said. "It's high time we got some Blacks in this company, confound it!"

"Hurry up," cried a voice. "It's almost time."

"Almost – what's that supposed to mean!" cried one of the soot-covered actors, exasperated. "Someone tell us exactly what time it is."

Minette was beginning to create a stir behind the curtains.

The first to notice her was the theater director himself, François Saint-Martin. He was young, dashing, and handsome. A true artist, he had no prejudices and chose his conquests from among the most beautiful mulatto girls of the country – conquests he flaunted as much out of inclination as bravado to humiliate the white girls who, he claimed, simply held no appeal for him. It was on this liberal mentality that the Acquaires were counting, knowing in advance that they would be excused their audacity.

Having set up house with a colored woman named Zabeth, who everyone said was crazy about him and who had given him two children, he was known to be a terrible husband. Mme Acquaire had left Minette to go hunting for Goulard, having half hidden her protégée in the folds of the curtain. It was there that Saint-Martin discovered her.

"What are you doing here, young lady?" he asked, looking at her in astonishment. "Is there someone you'd like to see?"

She did not know what to answer and her eyes darted around desperately looking for Mme Acquaire. It was the latter's husband, out of breath in his Venetian dancer's costume, who came to her rescue. His tic was twitching wildly as he informed Saint-Martin that Minette, under his supervision, would be making her stage debut in the role of Isabelle.

"In the role of Isabelle? That's quite a role for a debut. But why have you never told me anything about this young lady?"

His tic in full force, M Acquaire stammered as he turned his head to see whether his wife was coming, all of which the young director noticed.

"Anyway, I could care less," he said. "This night is all about you two. This is all your concern. I personally like seeing new talent encouraged, as long as the rules are respected…"

"Ahem!" muttered M Acquaire, uncomfortable.

"What is this young lady's name?"

M Acquaire turned sharply toward the director. "Listen, François," he said. "I'll tell you right after the performance – just trust me. I promise, I'll tell you everything."

"As you like. Who is she singing with tonight?"

"Goulard."

He looked at Minette for a moment, hesitating, as if trying to figure out exactly what type of beauty she was, so as to class her.

"For a white woman, she has something rather fiery about her," he whispered to himself as he left. "She must be from the South."

During this time, the theater was filling up. The nine boxes in the front, with seven seats each, were already full, as were the five screened-in boxes and the two balconies. As for the twenty-one others relegated to the back of the theater, those of the second tier known as "freedmen's heaven," they were full to the brim. As the time got closer to eight o'clock, the sound of chairs being moved and weapons clattering made it clear that the Governor and the town Bursar had taken their seats. Mme Acquaire had joined Minette in her little hideout and introduced her to Claude Goulard, who was as astonished and charmed as François Saint-Martin had been.

"Claude, this young lady will play opposite you. She'll be performing the role of Isabelle this evening."

He bowed politely, declaring himself most flattered to perform alongside such a beautiful person, and expressed his regret at not having had the opportunity to rehearse with her, which would have been far simpler and easier for both of them. But Mme Acquaire objected, saying that Minette had been ill and that, unable to leave the house, she had been obliged to rehearse at home.

"Don't worry, Claude," she reassured him. "She knows the role perfectly."

Ten minutes before the performance, she was presented to Magdeleine Brousse, the pretty twenty-year-old blonde playing the role of Gertrude.

"Hey there!" said Magdeleine Brousse. "What a mystery this show is. This has to be the first time we've ever rehearsed with one of the actors missing!"

But she smiled kindly at Minette and gently adjusted a lock of hair on her shoulders.

"She's beautiful, your little find, Mme Acquaire," she said gaily. "Between Gertrude and Isabelle, they'll have quite an embarrassment of riches."

She had made this last comment with an ironic air that made everyone burst out laughing.

As Saint-Martin was just passing by with great strides, seemingly absorbed in thought, the company began cheering him, and someone cried out: "Long live our director!"

Magdeleine threw him a kiss. Without stopping, he made a gesture with his hand and said: "Come on, come on – onstage!"

An actor Minette had only caught a glimpse of immediately stepped onstage. A chorus of applause welcomed him.

"Who's that?" Minette asked Mme Acquaire.

"The comedian Macarty. The audience loves him."

Minette barely heard what the actor was saying to the crowd. Her heart was beating wildly and she felt as if she would suffocate.

"You're pale," said Magdeleine Brousse, sympathetically. "It's always like that the first time – you always get stage fright and then you get used to it. Let me put a little blush on your cheeks and don't get upset if I'm a little familiar with you – that's how it is among actors. My God, you're tanned! You must spend a lot of time in the sun!"

She had hardly finished making up Minette before Mme Acquaire took the girl's hand and pushed her forward, telling her to take deep breaths so as to make her voice clearer.

"I'm afraid," murmured Minette.

"Don't say that," responded the actress. "It's bad luck."

The curtains had remained open after Macarty's exit. The three warning claps resounded like three strikes of a hammer in Minette's head. Saint-Martin passed through like a tornado shouting: "Isabelle – Isabelle and Gertrude! We're ready to introduce the opera. Strike up the orchestra."

Macarty had reappeared onstage to begin the play. "Ladies and Gentlemen," he announced with his singular accent. "Tonight, as you've all seen on our posters, a fifteen-year-old girl will make her debut on this stage, in the role of Isabelle. All preparations were made under the greatest secrecy by this evening's organizers, Monsieur and Madame Acquaire, who, in presenting their student to you, ask your indulgence, given her youth and inexperience."

The audience applauded.

"I'm told her voice is a revelation, and we are as impatient as all of you to hear her sing, as her rehearsals took place privately and in absolute secrecy."

Someone shouted: "How unconventional!"

He waved and then exited to thunderous applause. Minette was instantly unnerved, completely shaken. A voice murmured: "Onstage, onstage – get her onstage!"

Someone took her hand, the curtains parted, she was pushed forward, and then she was onstage. She looked out into the theater and was almost immediately dazzled. It was as if thousands of shooting stars were traversing the room – multicolored stars that twinkled with the clamorous sound of bells. Then they started to take on human form and Minette, half dead from fear, noticed one of the stars smiling at her – another was tilting its head, adorned with jewels, and still another, wearing officer's stripes, was pointing at her. Her legs were too limp to carry her any further forward, so she closed her eyes and stayed in place, arms rigid, hands clutching her skirt. When she opened her eyes, the stars had disappeared, and hundreds of men and women had taken their place – Whites, nothing but Whites, dressed in their most splendid attire.

The orchestra launched into the first few measures. She heard Mme Acquaire whisper from the wings: "Move around, walk, raise your hands to the sky."

Obeying mechanically, she heard the first note of the violin to which she was meant to respond. She opened her mouth to sing, but no sound came out. From the rustling of the curtain, the sound of hurried steps, and the whispering voices, Minette was all too aware of the anxiety of all the actors in the wings. As if hypnotized, she kept staring straight ahead, arms still raised above her head and mouth slightly opened. The violin went silent. The orchestra hit that first note with renewed vigor, as if trying to jog her memory. At that very moment, her eyes stopped seeing the extravagant, too-bright theater and focused further into the distance, higher up, toward the twenty-one boxes of the second tier where the people of color were seated. Jammed together and piled on top of one another, they seemed attached to each other in an immense solidarity that suddenly revealed itself to her. They were waiting, too. There was something so distressing in their eyes it made her want to scream. Immediately a series of images unfurled in her memory at a dizzying pace: images of backs riddled with lashes of the whip – one scarred over, the other still bleeding from fresh wounds. A long shudder traversed her body. She heard those lashes of the whip in that very moment, striking thousands of bloody backs with a loud, dull sound. Joseph's voice whispered in her ear: *You've got to tell yourself you're playing for high stakes now. Your voice is your weapon and you're going to use it.*

The violin went quiet for the second time. Then it hit the note a third time as the orchestra waited, craning its neck toward the stage like everyone else in the theater.

Minette opened her mouth, and this time her voice rang out, crystal clear, warm, and so full that a long murmur of admiration ran through the audience.

Now that she was singing, she did not see anything else; she did not hear anything else; she was entirely possessed by the incredible sounds pouring out of her. Everything else had disappeared: the theater, the orchestra, and even the twenty-one boxes where her friends were watching her. Something in her that came from far, far away was directing her gestures, her poses. When Goulard joined her onstage to sing with her, she saw the admiration and surprise in his eyes. He was young and handsome, and together they made such a perfect couple that the audience couldn't help but interrupt with its applause. Saint-Martin, in the wings with the rest of the actors, looked on astounded. Minette's voice came to him in sparkling bursts, intensified, then faded away with such sensuality and depth that he cried out:

"That child sings like a thirty-year-old woman. Where in France is she from?"

This was the moment the Acquaires chose to reveal their secret. Mme Acquaire, overjoyed, smiled and responded simply:

"She's a colored girl, François, a colored girl from my neighborhood."

"A colored girl!"

The declaration created such an uproar that the young director had to order the actors to quiet down.

"She has an extraordinary voice," said Macarty. "And what grace, what bearing!…"

Still overcome, Saint-Martin suddenly burst into laughter. "Ah! That's a good one – really, a good one. What a brilliant idea to play such a trick on all this high society with its ridiculous prejudices!…"

The Acquaires had counted on such a reaction and as M Acquaire's tic twitched with satisfaction, his wife started telling Saint-Martin about Minette. She recounted how she had met her, told him about their first lessons and about her decision to launch her stage career.

Saint-Martin became serious again. "That girl," he said, "has an exceptional talent that radiates not only in her voice but in every aspect of her bearing: she was born for the theater."

He parted the curtains again.

Minette was gliding across the stage without the slightest reserve – graceful, lithe, and supple. Goulard, as his role demanded, took her in his arms and together their voices sang words of love throughout the first part of the opera. Magdeleine Brousse entered the scene and then it was Macarty and the other actors' turn to play the comic roles.

"That's the very first time I've been fooled at first sight by a 'mixed-race' person," confided François Saint-Martin, dismayed, to M Acquaire.

"If it makes you feel any better," responded the latter, "you only saw her in the shadows, hidden by the curtains."

"Still," replied the young director, somewhat troubled, "her eyes don't mislead."

"Nothing about her is misleading, my friend, aside from that distinctive and distant air, slightly unusual for a colored girl," concluded M Acquaire.

"Shhhh!" said someone impatiently.

They were going to part the curtains once more. Impressed by the beauty and talent of the novice, the audience had become somewhat agitated. People were whispering, pointing at Minette. The Governor himself, after speaking in low tones with the King's Bursar, peeked his head out of his box and distinctly asked an officer seated in one of the first rows: "Just who is that 'young person'?"

As the question was repeated, without yielding any further information, it only heightened the audience's curiosity.

When, at the end of the opera, the actors waved before leaving the stage, the enthralled public gave them such an ovation that M Acquaire, beside himself, grabbed the young director by the shoulders and began shaking him, his eye twitching like a madman. So as to make their preference clear, a few spectators cried "Isabelle" as they clapped furiously. A young officer rose from his seat and cried: "Bravo, 'young person'!"

Minette was obliged to come back onstage. When she appeared, the delirious crowd stood and cheered.

Keeping her calm, she waved modestly and smiled, her eyes fixed on the seats in the back of the theater. There were the seats of those she loved: her mother, Lise, Joseph, Nicolette, and the others.

She was very emotional, however, and once she had made her way back to the wings she threw herself, sobbing, into the arms of Mme Acquaire. Even the young director, who was not easily moved, found himself touched by the sight.

An eight-year-old girl in a dancer's costume ran to bury herself in Goulard's open arms. "Why is the new actress crying?" the little girl asked him. "I heard Macarty say she has the most beautiful voice in the world."

Mme Acquaire, doing her best to calm Minette, introduced her to a few actors she had not yet met. After she had shaken hands with Mme Tesseyre and her young daughter, Rose – both of them dancers – to Favart and Depoix, to the set designer and painter Jean Peyret, and to the stagehand Julian, M Acquaire asked for five minutes of everyone's time so that the director might say a few words to them.

"My dear friends," began Saint-Martin, "today nearly all of us are here, aside from Nelanger, who's ailing, and Durand, who has gone to Saint-Marc for a few days. Tonight, I'm not addressing the men and women who make up this company, but only the artists you all are, with everything that word stands for – the self-sacrifice, free-spiritedness, love, and enthusiasm for true talent in whatever form. Tonight we have among us, for the first time in the history of theater in Saint Domingue, a young colored girl gifted with an extraordinary voice and an extraordinary talent. Although the law forbids her from coming into the theater, Monsieur and Madame Acquaire decided to roll the dice – and you've seen the incredible results. Before I meet with the theater's shareholders on Minette's behalf, can I count on you to welcome her and to treat her the way a true artist should be treated by other artists?"

Everyone applauded and Magdeleine Brousse came up to Minette and kissed her on behalf of the entire company. Saint-Martin then went up to her and said: "From this day on, you are part of our company, my dear."

"Thank you, Monsieur," Minette responded, her voice so overcome with emotion that he couldn't help but laugh, and added:

"Thank your talent. It alone is responsible for this miracle."

The Acquaires embraced her, laughing. It was indeed some miracle. That night, Minette had conquered both an audience and a man. That man was Goulard. He was young, unprejudiced, and honest, but poor. A close friend of François Saint-Martin, whom he admired for his passionate, bohemian, and liberal attitude, Goulard had made his stage debut in Saint Domingue as an adolescent. He had taken a small studio, for which he often was unable to pay the rent, near the young director. As faithful in friendship as in love, his head filled with the verses of Racine and Corneille, he yearned for a true passion that would hold him captive for the rest of his life. The passing flings he had enjoyed with various women had been nothing more than a way to prove himself as a man, as Saint-Martin would say. In Minette, he had found his ideal, and this revelation was a wonderful shock for him. He had long dreamt of falling in love with an artist, and she truly was one. She was young, beautiful, modest, and as poor as he. He was overjoyed.

That night, just like after every performance at the theater, there was an "evening ball" organized by the Acquaires. It would take place in an adjacent room, where several buffet tables had been set up. As soon as the votive candles had been lit, the orchestra launched into a country dance that brought merry groups of audience members to their feet. While Saint-Martin discussed the next night's performance with the actors, Minette, huddled in a corner of the curtains, watched the theater empty out. A few couples had begun to move about, and the dancers' wide silk skirts reflected flickerings of light here and there. A few people of color lingered in the upper boxes. They were not allowed to attend the after-party, so they contented themselves with admiring the finery and listening to the music from afar. Arms wrapped around one another, they danced in place, moving their upper bodies to the beat. Beautiful coiffed heads in madras scarves peeked out of the boxes, smiling and laughing.

When Minette joined her mother on the street, she was greeted with cheers. Goulard and Mme Acquaire accompanied her. The latter kissed her as she handed her over to her mother, saying: "I would give anything to bring you to the party, you understand that don't you, Minette?"

"I understand, Madame Acquaire."

Claude Goulard looked at her so lovingly that Joseph took note. Lise was holding Jasmine's hand. Wearing a flowered skirt and a calico bodice adorned with a little scarf, delicately held together with a pin, she was playing with her fan and acting the part of an elegant young lady. The little crowd of laughing, shouting colored folks went along arm in arm, singing rhyming couplets in Creole and sharing the latest gossip.

A few white women walked along amorously entwined in the arms of the officers, the bodices of their transparent *gaules* as plunging as those of the colored women. "Kiss-Me-Lips," devastatingly beautiful in a wide, bright-colored skirt, her breasts exposed underneath a transparent batiste bodice and her hair pinned up under her jewel-studded madras scarf, was accompanied by the King's Bursar. She wore a triumphant smile on her lips. Minette, watching amusedly as the crowd dissipated, noticed Nicolette get into a carriage driven by a black coachman in white livery with gold buttons. A heady, intoxicating scent permeated the air, tickling the nostrils and clouding the brain. The men shamelessly caressed the women's arms and kissed their seductively painted lips. Heavy six-horse carriages, decorated with velvet, tassels, and braiding, ran alongside more modest two-seater cabriolets and covered carriages, equipped with peek-through blinds and little taffeta cushions. Bejeweled masculine hands emerged through the curtains to help that night's conquest step up into the carriage. Gorgeous Negresses, mulatto girls, and white women fought over the most beautiful coaches and several altercations broke out among them. The horses' hooves raised the dust along the road in front of the inns, cabarets, clubs, and boutiques.

Minette raised her eyes to the sky. It was so beautiful, with its many stars and the immense suspended lantern of the moon. Gentle warmth suffused her heart. "Ah! To live happily under this very sky, to live like the others, to climb into a carriage and take the arm of a handsome white man, why not?"

Joseph, Jasmine, and Lise embraced Minette and then proceeded to let her know what the audience had been saying.

"A white man said you had the most beautiful voice he'd ever heard," said Lise.

"I'd say your risk paid off," said Joseph. "But they don't know your social class yet. Let's wait and see what tomorrow's paper says and then we'll know for certain."

Jasmine knew at last what happiness felt like. One of her daughters had just taken such an enormous step forward in life that she was over-whelmed just thinking about it. She had seen Minette onstage, singing alongside white folks. She had seen a crowd of white hands clapping for her. She had heard people call out her name, praise her beauty, talent, and grace. Her dream had become a reality. The Good Lord had per-formed this miracle. Did she dare rejoice already, or should she wait for tomorrow's paper, as Joseph had cautioned? Something told her that her little girl was not going to be stopped any time soon – that she would continue to rise very high. The emotions generated among the spectators from Minette's first notes could not possibly be diminished over a simple question of caste – it simply was not imaginable and she did not even want to consider it. For once in her life she would allow herself to be happy. She, who for so long had dragged behind her the weighty and tiresome burden of the past and who at the age of thirty-five already felt like an old woman, found herself suddenly reju-venated – as if the justice that her child had just been granted washed away all of her old wounds and restored her entirely.

It was with these thoughts in her head that Jasmine arrived that Christmas night at Vallières Square, cluttered with dozens of tents in front of which gesticulating street entertainers shouted out the price of admission and invited passersby to come see the acrobats and trained animals. A few young women ran over, followed by men offering to pay for their tickets. Two young Negresses stopped, out of breath, and lifted their skirts to wipe the sweat from their faces.

A delirious crowd hurried into the street. The coachmen snapped their whips to get their horses moving. Everything was lit up: the Governor and the Bursar's palaces, the barracks, the dance hall next to the Comédie, the Vaux-Halls, the cabarets, and the inns. Further ahead, the opulent residences of Bel-Air sparkled with an excess of light that made them look as if they were aflame. That evening, eighty torch lights illuminated the long path leading to the Marquis de Caradeux's mansion.

He was hosting a Christmas party and numerous carriages had entered the courtyard. The horses, blinded by all the torches, reared up and whinnied. The sound of their hooves somewhat muffled the shouts of the street entertainers and of the church bells calling the faithful to midnight mass. A few people entered the church, both white and colored. Jasmine and some other young people followed behind them. They turned around upon hearing the sound of the first fireworks being set off on the parade grounds. Illumined by the shafts of light, hands clapped, people embraced one another and shouted: "Hurrah for Christmas! Hurrah for Christmas!" as the bells rang even louder in the church, which had been suddenly lit up. A few congregants went in to kneel in prayer, as the priest and the choirboys intoned the hymns. Before the nativity scene where the statue of the Christ Child had been placed, people stopped to dip their fingers in holy water then crossed themselves. Kneeling next to Minette, Joseph prayed, head bent, forehead hidden in his hands. That evening, Jasmine saw him in a new light, and her affection for him grew. The former slave woman was suddenly overcome by memories that took her away for a moment. She saw herself seated next to an old man, a slave like her, who was teaching her.

Thanks to him, she had learned her letters and come to know Christ, the true lord, righteous God-in-Man who had suffered for all men and who called for the fusion of all classes, opening his arms to everyone, no matter what their station or color.

She had tried to show him to her daughters as he was and as she had been taught to love him, this man crucified by his fellow men for having cried out the truth, as he knew it. She remembered the old slave Mapiou. He knew how to read, write, and sing the hymns. Sold to Jesuit priests as a young boy, he had been taught to read. He became an apostle himself and, even after changing masters, continued to educate the Negroes from Africa, able to discern at first glance whether they came from his country or from another.

Jasmine sighed and looked over at her daughters. Minette's eyes were fixed on the Christ as if she was asking him something; Lise was yawning and trying to steal a glance at the people entering the church. Their mother saw no sign of true piety in either one of them. They did not pray with anything near Joseph's fervor. He was in true communion with a Being that he admired and venerated. When he raised his head, Jasmine was astonished to see in his magnificent eyes a reflection of the same flame she had once seen in those of the Jesuit priest who had taken her in with her daughters once they had been freed from their master's house...

When they left the church, the excitement had reached its peak. From one house, belonging to colored folks, the sounds of dance music and applause could be heard. The sound of the orchestras created a cacophony so deafening that there was no way to tell a minuet from a country dance.

Once home again, Jasmine and her daughters sat down on the beds for a moment, still chatting with each other about the evening and Minette's success. Before getting undressed, Jasmine asked her daughters to kneel down and thank God, and to ask him to keep them pure and without sin until their death.

"Ask Our Lord to help you keep the memory of the past in mind, and because you're the oldest, Minette," she added, looking at Minette meaningfully, "to keep you from becoming superficial and corrupted, like so many of the women in this country."

"Yes, Mama."

"Whenever you find yourself tempted, remember the past – yours…and mine."

"Yes, Mama."

Minette understood that her mother was speaking to her alone, as the eldest, to whom the former slave had revealed the humiliating marks left on her breast and back by her white master. Her mother was right. That memory had helped her onstage when it came time to sing. She would never forget it.

She lay down in the bed she shared with Lise and noticed that her mother was undressing behind the door, as she always did – her calico blouse was closed with a pin at the base of her neck so as to hide the scars imprinted on her skin. The emotions that had been running through her in the two long hours of Minette's performance had left her so exhausted that she fell asleep as soon as she went to bed. Minette, overexcited by that first evening in high society, was still unable to sleep an hour later. She decided to wake her sister.

"Hey, Lise – want to make some plans with me?"

"What?" asked the girl, waking with a start.

"Shhh! Don't wake Mama…I can't sleep."

"Why not?"

"This whole night, you know. All this success. The kindness of the actors. They're white, but they were so kind."

"You might not believe me," Lise whispered joyfully, "when I tell you what I was already dreaming about. I saw us riding in a green and gold carriage, with fine clothing and jewels."

Minette hugged her sister, a faraway look in her eyes.

"Do you think that could happen some day? Do you think we'll be rich?"

"Since you sing at the Comédie," Lise reasoned, "you'll be paid."

"True," said Minette, "but surely not enough for everything I'd like to do."

"And what would you like to do?"

"I want to buy all the slaves in the country so that I can free them."

"Free the slaves!"

"Yes."

"But then you'll never be a great lady, because you can't be one without having a slave in your service."

"Well, then I won't be a great lady."

"Your dream is impossible. It's completely crazy," responded Lise. "And believe me, you're even more of a little kid than your sister."

In the distance, the sound of a *lambi* horn suddenly pierced the silence. Minette shivered without knowing why.

"Listen," she said to her sister, holding up her index finger.

"What?" asked Lise, yawning.

"The sound of the *lambi*. Those are messages the maroons transmit to one another in the hills where they're hiding out."

"Why?"

"They want to be free, Joseph told me…All right, sleep now. It's late."

VI

THE NEXT DAY, early in the morning, even before Jasmine had laid out her wares, Mme Acquaire came knocking triumphantly at her door to tell her about all the accolades being lavished on Minette, praising her talent. She even mentioned the names of several planters and told her about a certain Mademoiselle de Caradeux who wanted to have her sing at a party in her home.

"Success, my dear, a resounding success!" she said to Minette. "At the next concert, you'll sing a grand aria and make a real splash."

She departed, leaving Jasmine so pleased that she had not for a minute considered asking Mme Acquaire what Minette's wages would be at the Comédie. It was already enough that she was being allowed to perform, she told herself, by way of excuse. "No demands just now, or everything could fall apart!"

She waited nervously to hear what the public had to say. The gazette, generally off-limits to Negroes and Mulattos, spoke flatteringly about the fifteen-year-old "young person" who had been such a success in the role of Isabelle. The article drew attention to the Saint-Martin players' liberal attitude in having a colored girl perform alongside them, and it applauded the welcome change to convention that showed the actors' independence and disdain for caste politics.

The article, while approving, was not without irony, and risked provoking the ire of the planters, already up to their necks – largely for economic reasons – in the politics of race. They easily could have protested and demanded justice from the government. Fortunately, as they were always in the midst of some dispute or another with the latter, they made no complaint, proving by their indifference how little thought they gave to actors in general, be they white or black. It did not harm them personally in any way and really only concerned the Governor. They looked the other way, declaring that such talent in the colony was so rare that they would continue to applaud the "young person" at her next performance.

The Governor sent for François Saint-Martin and made him promise, in an effort to keep order, not to let the theater be invaded by "those creatures" and only to promote true talents.

"Certainly you will agree, Your Governorship, that this young girl has exceptional talent," said the director of the Comédie.

"My dear Monsieur Saint-Martin, we Governors have eyes and ears like every other man, believe me. That 'young person' is devastatingly beautiful and sings like an angel. Promote her, yes, but for heaven's sake, make sure she remains the only one…"

There was a devilish twinkle in his eye that did not fool Saint-Martin.

"These women are beautiful," he added, "and from what I've heard, the Bursar and the King himself pay tribute to them in ways that are a bit too…public for my taste."

He excused Saint-Martin, rapping him on the shoulder and calling him lucky, which made the director smile. With his white wig and laughing eyes, the Governor seemed to him like an old letch, only too happy to admire pretty young girls like Minette on the stage.

Charles Mozard, owner of the gazette, may have been a bad poet, but at least he had enough good taste to appreciate talent in other people. Agent, slave-trader, printer, playwright, and poet, he was as active with his various projects as was Saint-Martin with his theater. Married to a modest, not particularly beautiful Frenchwoman, he had just put on his first play – *African Vengeance, or, the Effects of Hatred and Jealously* – that very year in Cap-Français. The authorities were displeased by certain somewhat suggestive scenes containing kidnapping and revenge. Disappointed by the cold and reproachful reception, and annoyed that people had gone so far as to suggest that he lacked talent, he came back to Port-au-Prince, where he took up his old activities. He was taking perverse pleasure in praising Minette's charm and talent, thus avenging his recent frustrations.

Mme Acquaire, holding the paper triumphantly in her hand, had run over to Jasmine's house for the second time, only to find Joseph Ogé and Minette there reading Jean-Jacques Rousseau's *The Village Soothsayer*. It was Joseph who was first to read nervously through Charles Mozard's article. When he had finished, he folded up the newspaper, took Minette by the shoulders and, looking her in the eyes, said:

"I think you've won," he said to her. "I'm as proud of you and as happy as if I were your…brother."

"But, you are my brother, Joseph."

"Thank you, Minette."

Beside herself with joy, Lise called Jasmine, jumping up and down and clapping her hands – for once forgetting to behave like the young lady she so wanted to be. Jasmine, who was in the middle of setting up her stand, was so overcome with emotion that she let her wares fall to the ground, which was cause for screams of protest and a general outburst of laughter. While everyone was helping to clean up the mess, Mme Acquaire went to tell Minette that they would soon begin rehearsals again, given that on February 13 Saint-Martin planned to put up a new opera, *The Fifteen-Year-Old Lovers*, in which she would once again play the lead role.

"Monsieur Saint-Martin expects to play you in a fairy-like decor this time. He'll take in the proceeds from the evening and will pay for your costumes himself."

Joseph looked at Jasmine. Minette was not going to be paid, it seemed. She would perform for the benefit of others and be at once exploited and protected. Not qualified to broach the subject, he did not dare give his opinion in front of Mme Acquaire. But he was waiting for her departure to open Jasmine's eyes and advise Minette. He was more than surprised to see the latter approach the Creole woman, look her straight in the eyes, and say to her unabashedly:

"And what will I get out of this arrangement, Mme Acquaire?"

Joseph again looked over at Jasmine, seeing her just as astonished as he was, and then turned away to hide his smile.

"I'd like a night where I take home the proceeds, Mme Acquaire," she added with the same tone.

"You take home proceeds one night…well yes, naturally. I'll have to speak to the Director…"

She looked at Minette as if she were seeing her for the very first time.

"It's true you've really grown up, indeed. We'll have to keep that in mind from now on…"

She quickly met Joseph and Jasmine's eyes then, again observing Minette, gave her a light tap on the cheek and said:

"Don't you worry, we'll sort it all out."

"Thank you, Madame."

Once the actress had left, Joseph burst into laughter:

"Well, well!" he said to Minette, "you're quite the businesswoman!"

"I'm not going to let myself be…" she thought for a moment, as if looking for the right word, "…exploited," she concluded. "You've explained that word to me and I absolutely loathe the idea."

Jasmine smiled hearing her speak.

Though she may not have been made for fighting that battle, her elder daughter would be able to defend herself. At fifteen she already saw things for what they were and would never let anyone lead her anywhere by the nose.

"The thing is, Minette needs lots of money," declared Lise with the attitude of someone who knows they are about to make someone angry by revealing a secret.

"A lot of money," replied Joseph, turning toward the young girl with a worried look. "And what for?"

"Be quiet!" cried Minette, rushing toward her sister.

"Speak," interrupted Jasmine, as worried as Joseph. "Is it to buy yourself jewelry, dresses, and…"

She stopped herself and hesitated, as if it were too difficult to say the word.

Lise ventured a sorrowful glance toward her sister. She saw how tense she was, her eyes flashing and fists clenched.

"Go ahead, speak then, you little idiot," Minette hissed angrily. "Finish what you've started to tell."

And then turning toward her mother and Joseph, Lise continued:

"She wants to buy all the slaves so that she can free them and then…"

"You little fool!" Minette screamed at her and, leaving them all standing right there, she went to hide in her room, her sobs audible.

Joseph asked Jasmine's permission to go after her, which she granted with a slight nod of the head. The young man went to kneel beside the bed where Minette was crying, curled up in a ball. He lifted her chin, took a handkerchief from his pocket, and wiped her eyes.

"It's wonderful, just wonderful to have such lovely and generous thoughts," he said to her. "Stop crying. Come, I brought a book with me today. A priest wrote it. His name is Father Raynal. Come listen to what he says about the right to freedom and the condition of slaves… After that, we can all go see my old professor, Labadie. I'm sure you'll like him…"

…They found the old man seated at his worktable, on which piles of scholarly books were stacked.

"Would you ever want to know that much?" he asked Lise.

"Me? Oh! No, I'd go mad."

"And you?" he again asked, looking at Minette.

"Yes, I think so..." she hesitated and then added, "Sir."

"Don't bother calling me Sir, my child; the law is the same for all people of color."

Taking them by the hand, he led them out to the garden, which gave onto an immense sugarcane field. Hundreds of voices gave rhythm to the Negro songs out there, in the workhouse. "Some slaves are treated with humanity," he had said to Joseph. Likely affected by those words, it seemed to them that the voices they heard were neither muffled nor monotone and that, on the contrary, they were declaring an act of faith and gratitude. In the garden, birds chirped, locked inside bamboo cages, and goldfish chased each other in a shallow basin surrounded by flowers.

"He's rich," Minette thought to herself. "Rich like all those white planters." And she could not help feeling proud of that fact.

Labadie looked at the girls as they gushed over his treasures. Standing up in the middle of the garden he appeared small. His white, silky hair framed a prominent forehead, under which his gray eyes shone with a gaze so meditative that it seemed cold. He spoke simply, but with elegance, and to hear him speak one would think he had studied in France.

"Their voice is marvelous," he said, once the songs had died down. "I understand why the Whites see in their talent a divine attribute."

Then, he kissed the girls and offered them some flowers and candies.

As they left, Lise begged Joseph to take them to the town square where there would certainly be something going on that evening.

Acrobats and jugglers would be putting on a show. The prices were displayed on various posters:

ENTRY: ONE GOURDE-PIASTRE FOR WHITES,
TWO GOURDINS FOR MULATTOS, AND TWO
ESCALINS FOR NEGROES.

They were disappointed, not having enough money to pay for tickets.

"How much money do you have, Joseph?" asked Lise.

"Six escalins."

"I have an idea. Let's coat our faces with tar and pass for Negroes."

"Lise!" exclaimed Minette.

Joseph let go of the young girls' hands and looked at Lise, his face strained.

"What's the matter? Why are you looking at me like that. You're scaring me."

He didn't answer, and took her hand again.

That night it became clear: Minette was his favorite.

VII

In less than two weeks, Minette had learned her entire part and done the fitting for the costumes, which had been made for her this time by a French vendor recommended by Magdeleine Brousse and Mme Acquaire. She had been overjoyed to find herself back among the theater folk: Goulard, as attentive as he was charming; Mme Tesseyre and little Rose, who worked tirelessly on their dance routine; Depoix and Favart, top-notch actors with whom she was meant to perform in the February 13 show; and Macarty, the comedian who always delighted her, making her laugh with his terrifying grimaces. In the meantime, Durand had returned from Saint-Marc and had said, in her presence, after hearing her sing, that he found her extraordinary. Nelanger, still convalescing, plucked his guitar to keep his fingers nimble.

A Creole set piece, a ball, and an opera were all part of the new program, *The Fifteen-Year-Old Lovers*. Minette listened uncomfortably to the rehearsals for *Mirebalaisian Love Stories*, a Negro parody of Jean-Jacques Rousseau's *The Village Soothsayer*. The gestures and lines in Creole rubbed her the wrong way. In her mind, the theater was Racine, Corneille, Molière, etc., and she could not understand how one could waste time singing vulgar ditties in the local patois. She found it degrading to one's talent to perform such facile and superficial plays. "If they could even be said to serve some greater purpose," she thought to herself. "If they could speak the truth, cry out in the slaves' own language their sufferings and their desire for freedom!" But on the contrary, theater being subject to censorship by the authorities, what deserved to be spoken was instead ridiculed, and the planters always came out smelling like roses.

That evening, Saint-Martin invited the group of actors to his home to raise a glass, as he put it, to Minette's prodigious talent. For all that he admired her as a man, the artist in him was too thoroughly and sincerely in awe of her talent to allow him to in any way jeopardize Minette's future. Of course, he would have loved to take her in his arms, to show her off to the public as a delicious conquest, and then to drop her – as he had done with so many other women. But he feared that such disappointment might somehow affect that exceptional voice that he had promised himself to exploit to everyone's advantage. There was no bad faith in his dealings with Minette. Mme Acquaire had told him she was calling for a salary, and he wanted to grant her request but found that he usually lost the money he owed her at the gambling table. He was always sorry afterward, but that hardly made things right. Goulard had also advocated for her and, most recently, his argument had been so fierce that Saint-Martin had looked at him mockingly and said:

"So, my poor friend, you're smitten to that extent?"

To which Goulard had responded with a revealing silence.

After leaving the theater, Minette had gone to let her mother know that she had been invited to Saint-Martin's home.

"To drink alcohol with the other actors, my dear!" Jasmine exclaimed.

Joseph interrupted:

"Let her go, Jasmine, and trust her."

But Jasmine had nonetheless put on her best dress and accompanied her daughter to Mme Acquaire's house, entrusting her to the latter.

"Take her yourself, Madame, I beg you. Mothers have great responsibilities," she said to her, lowering her head.

As they spoke, the group of actors roamed the streets, to the delight of the passersby, who cheered them laughingly. Durand, a pale, thin blond with impeccable diction, recited a few lines. Macarty answered him with a tirade that Nelanger punctuated with plucks of his guitar. They were charming, and received ovations as they passed, which inspired Macarty to exclaim with a comic grimace:

"Hey, what's this – do they take us for street performers?"

That simple comment set off a fit of giggles. Claude Goulard was walking next to Minette. He had offered her his arm, which she had refused to take and – with her shining eyes, easy stride, and breasts modestly covered by a thick scarf – calmly observed the passersby, carrying herself with put-on indifference alongside the elegantly dressed white women with their noisy skirts and the men in officer's stripes who turned to admire them.

Two young white girls, recognizing her, pointed in her direction, one of them saying distinctly:

"It's the 'young person,' there she is – the 'young person'!" which aroused the curiosity of the passersby.

"Look at that – you're famous, Minette," said Saint-Martin.

"Not yet," she replied with such a confident tone that he laughed heartily, calling her a "young upstart."

A few minutes later, they arrived at Saint-Martin's home. He opened the door and a young Mulatto woman, two children hanging on her skirts, ran toward him.

"Monsieur François," she exclaimed with such a passionate tone that Minette looked at her, shocked, "how late you are!"

"Good evening, Zabeth," he answered, pinching her cheek distractedly. "I've brought you the whole group, along with this lovely young lady, a free colored like yourself who sings at the Comédie."

"Hello, Zabeth," said all the actors in turn.

Her eyes were somewhat similar to Minette's in their form, but their frightened expression was completely different.

The two children, two and three years old, lifted their sweet little faces – the faces of a baby Saint-Martin, because to see them was to know without a doubt that he was their father. As she prepared the glasses, Zabeth stared at Minette, who was caressing the children. As they approached him, their father pushed them away with an impatient gesture that was not lost on anyone. Saint-Martin had filled the glasses and, raising his own glass high in the air, said:

"My friends, let us drink tonight to Minette, the young girl with the divine voice. May her talent sow glory and success on her path."

"To Minette!" they all cried.

As he drank, Claude Goulard kept his eyes fixed on her. The little ones forced their way over to him and climbed onto his lap with familiarity.

At the other end of the table, Zabeth also watched Saint-Martin, and Minette – who was watching her – noticed an expression of such pride and such love on her face that she was deeply moved. For that expression was the same one she saw on Claude Goulard's face when he looked at her, and she understood that he must truly love her, Minette, as much as Zabeth loved Saint-Martin. "Love – what is love, really?" she wondered in that moment. She was not in love with anyone and felt strangely independent and carefree. She would not be bogged down with such a troublesome, such a demanding sentiment that filled one's eyes with sadness, as she had noticed with Goulard and Zabeth. It was important for her to remain herself, so as to succeed in her career, and receive – without any remorse – compliments and declarations of love from Whites. She would soon be sixteen. She was going to earn money. She would dress like a lady and break hearts without mercy. She was loath to cut her teeth on Goulard. He was white, that was true, but like the Acquaires he seemed different from the others and was part of the company. And the company was sacred for Minette. Had not Saint-Martin himself said that artists are not people like everyone else when he first presented her to the group? That was where she was in her thoughts when Mme Acquaire, standing up, pointed out the lateness of the hour and suggested they leave. The children had fallen asleep in Goulard's arms. He gave them over to their mother, saying:

"If the clergy didn't prohibit us from holding these children over the baptismal fount, at least one of them would be my godchild."

He smiled ruefully and turned to Saint-Martin:

"Do you remember, François, that night when you barged through the doors of the church to ring the bells for little Morange's funeral?"

"She was so sweet," commented Macarty, draining the glass he had raised again from the table.

"And me, too young not to protest the injustice of the clergy," added Saint-Martin with an expression he had never had before then.

In effect, his face had changed suddenly. His slightly cynical mask had softened, and the revival of some memory had brought a twinge of sadness to his eyes.

"Of what crime, exactly, do these men accuse us?" asked Durand.

"And of what crime was little Morange guilty?" answered Saint-Martin, with a slightly bitter voice. "I saw her grow up; she was a sweet and pure little girl."

In that instant, Zabeth's face took on such a worried expression that, seeing it, Minette felt her own heart tighten. Saint-Martin had loved the little French actress, he must love her still – and so desperately that his heart was forever closed to others. And Zabeth knew it. Her face revealed each of her thoughts like an open book.

"It's like we have the plague," concluded Macarty, with a frightening grimace.

Saint-Martin laughed, a bit nervously, in fact. And noticing that, Goulard almost regretted having initiated the conversation.

"We're denied the cemetery or proper burial ceremonies, and, for lack of a godfather and godmother, my children couldn't be baptized since the only friends I have are actors…It's true I could care less about all those things. But sometimes I just want to grab a priest by the throat and tell him to go to hell…"

He turned to Minette and apologized.

"It's fine. Don't apologize," said M Acquaire, his tic appearing as he smiled. "She'll have to get used to it. But if her dear mother were to ever find out…"

"I know how to use swear words, too, Monsieur Acquaire," responded Minette so amusingly that everyone burst into laughter.

Everyone left on that rather happy note, planning to meet at the theater the next morning at ten o'clock.

On returning home, Minette was careful not to wake Lise and her mother. She needed to be alone to think about everything she had just seen and heard at Saint-Martin's house. First, the secret sorrow the latter hid behind his rather tough mask and that was due, she was sure of it, to the death of the young actress he had loved; and then to know about the injustice they all suffered and that was not only, as she had believed, her people's lot. In Saint-Martin's voice she had sensed the stirrings of a different version of the same revolt Joseph had revealed to her that one night. The Whites could also suffer the injustice of the Law! She remembered Joseph explaining to her that the planters' greatest enemies were the poor whites. Discontent, hatred, and revolt thus existed on a human scale and not only within the black race, despised and enslaved?

She fell asleep with these thoughts and did not wake until Lise called her in the morning. It was eight o'clock and the vendors were already setting up their stalls on the public thoroughfare with a cheerful clamor.

VIII

FOR THIS NEW performance, the sets had been transformed from top to bottom, just as Saint-Martin had promised. Jean Peyret, the set designer, along with the stagehand, Julian, had worked on it for twenty days without a break.

On the evening of February 13, an enormous crowd began filing into the theater as early as six o'clock. Some of the theatergoers, hoping to get the best seats, preferred to spend two hours waiting inside the theater to avoid getting stuck in the last rows, near the Negresses.

That evening, once the curtains had opened and the orchestra launched into the first bars of music, a shiver of pleasure ran through the crowd upon Minette's appearance onstage. The audience was there for her just as much as for either Macarty or Durand. The evening was a triumph, and ended in so much applause that the actors were obliged to return to the stage three times. A chorus of voices called out for Minette, shouting:

"Long live the 'young person'!"

When she reappeared onstage, the crowd's enthusiasm became absolute delirium. Love letters were thrown at her feet, flowers torn hastily from boutonnieres rained down on her. When she returned backstage, she once again wept on Mme Acquaire's shoulder, overcome with emotion. Her mentor was equally moved. M Acquaire was so thrilled that his right eye had all but disappeared from the mad blinking of his tic, and little Tesseyre, completely fascinated, standing on her toes in preparation for a curtsy, forgot to resume first position.

Despite this incredible success, Minette was not allowed to join the crowd in the ballroom. Obliged to assist his friend Saint-Martin, Goulard reluctantly left Minette after lovingly kissing her hand. Clutching the curtains, Minette watched the dancing couples for a moment – she caught sight of Magdeleine Brousse, Goulard, and Saint-Martin, who had entered the brightly lit room through a side door – and then left to join her mother and sister in front of the theater. She felt humiliated. The very public that had just cheered for her, that had cried out for more of her as if the sole reason they had left their homes that evening was to hear her sing, was the same public that now refused to allow her into the ball. This was how it had always been, and it had to be respected and accepted as divine law. But she, Minette, had broken that law by appearing onstage and, worse still, she had forced white hands to applaud her, disdainful mouths to cry out for her, and this by the sole distinction of her talent. That talent had opened a door for her, and it would open others, if she wanted it to, if she truly wanted it the way one had to want something in order to make it happen, she told herself. One day, she would enter that great room – that room from which she now had been twice turned away – triumphantly and on the arm of a white man. Saint-Martin and the Acquaires had done enough for her, and she understood that. They did not dare push things any further, for fear of being punished. The laws of prejudice had been established on high and had to be respected. It was one thing to serve as entertainment, to be the kind of jester that Joseph told her kings possessed. That was where the possibility of transgressing the law ended for her protectors, and they had done a lot for her…

Jasmine was with Lise, Joseph, and a few other people of color from the neighborhood. Mme Acquaire arrived in a magnificent, rustling taffeta dress she had had sent from France. In her hand she held little folded notes, which she proffered to Minette, saying:

"Your first love letters, my dear. I picked them up from the stage. They're from your white admirers. You can read them tonight."

She slipped them into Minette's bodice. The young girl blushed, but made no attempt to stop her.

"It's just wonderful to get love letters," sighed Lise, looking enviously at her sister's bodice. "Oh, my dear, you'll buy me a little parasol, won't you? I so long for a parasol."

Lise had tired of playing the lady with her fan and let it drop as she dreamed of a parasol. Joseph smiled, thinking that she was already as flirtatious as an eighteen-year-old. Jasmine must have thought the same thing, for she dragged Lise off into a corner to scold her. A few young women of color approached Minette and invited her to join them at the freedmen's ball being hosted that night by Célimene. Lise begged her mother with her eyes and, since Joseph had no objection, Jasmine consented, heady with her elder daughter's success.

The colored woman's ballroom was as rich and splendorous as that of the theater. Scores of people were crowded into the space and one could make out a few young white men who, having left their own salons, were dancing with the colored girls in their madras headscarves.

Upon Minette's arrival, those who had attended her performance at the theater began cheering her, and she was immediately surrounded by admirers inviting her to dance. Not knowing how to choose, she regarded each of them in turn, as if to select the one she liked best. At that very instant, her gaze fell on a young man of about twenty, dark-skinned, leaning against one of the columns and looking at her unsmilingly.

He was dressed in a striped cotton shirt and white pants. His hair was cut short, exposing a perfect forehead. His thin nose, its nostrils flared, seemed to sniff at the people around him with a disdain that amplified the harsh expression of his mouth. His eyes, so wide and elongated that they somehow contradicted everything else about his face, seemed naively surprised and trusting. He was slim but well built, and his hands, which were splayed nonchalantly on his hips, appeared slender and refined. He had one of those faces without real beauty but that could not go unremarked. A face that held your attention and whose every expression seemed to reveal each thought. For the moment, his expression was mocking, wary, and yet so tender and so passionate that it overwhelmed Minette.

"Close your eyes," suggested one of her potential dance partners, "and just pick one of us at random."

She pushed them all away, shaking her head, and headed toward him. For a moment, their eyes met and Minette felt an unexpected shock run through her. Her heart pounded, her hands trembled, and she felt as if she was gently shivering.

"And you, would you have any interest in dancing with me?"

What was this new voice of hers – breathy, toneless, and almost pleading?

The young man smiled and immediately his face transformed, becoming joyful and luminous. "Is it the brightness of his teeth?" Minette wondered.

Bowing, he raised his hands in a gesture of regret.

"My apologies," he said, "but I am disabled."

Though it was said without bitterness, his statement shook Minette even further. For a moment, her embarrassed, searching gaze held the young man's eyes.

"Pardon me," she murmured by way of apology.

"That's all right," he answered.

And bowing his head, he walked away, limping and dragging his right leg behind him.

Hundreds of women dressed in long flowered skirts spun all around Minette as they danced, wrapped in the arms of partners wearing striped or solid-colored short pants and colorful shirts; they all sang along with the band. A man in a yellow silk shirt emerged from her circle of admirers and pushed Jasmine, Lise, and Joseph into the middle of the room, gathered some chairs, sat them down and shouted:

"Minette's going to sing!"

"What's going on?" asked the dancing couples, who hadn't yet noticed.

"Minette's going to sing!" the man in the yellow shirt shouted again. "Someone quiet the band!"

The man approached Minette and took her by the hand.

"Since you won't dance, lovely lady, sing for us," he said.

She smiled.

Obediently, the band had stopped immediately, and the dancers gathered in an enormous circle, surrounding her and cheering.

"What shall we play, young goddess?" asked the eccentric character. "Your wish is our command."

Chin raised, Minette followed the young disabled man, who was still walking away. Without responding, she opened her mouth and let out a note so wondrously pure that he stopped in his tracks, turning around to look at her. She was alone in the middle of the ballroom, hands clutching her skirts, eyes fixed on him. He smiled at her again. Then she began a melody she had often heard coming through Mme Acquaire's window and that as a little girl she had hummed, seated on the bench in front of her mother's stand. It was the aria from *The Beautiful Arsène*, which began with these words: "Can there be a more glorious fate…"

When her voice died out on the final note, she saw the young man turn and walk away, with his limping gait. For a moment, she remained silent, not hearing the cheers and cries of enthusiasm. Once he had disappeared, she turned her head and looked around for her mother, Joseph, and Lise. She ran up to them, saying she was ready to leave. Her admirers protested, so Joseph told them Minette was tired and not feeling well. She waved goodbye, then took Joseph's arm and headed toward the exit.

Once outside, she took deep breaths – the way one breathes when one is fifteen years old and feeling happy. Lise, now jealous of her sister, since no one had asked her to dance although she had so wanted to, was now calling the young men of the ball a bunch of "ugly cretins."

"They were all so ugly and so stupid looking, those men who asked you to dance," she said to her sister.

"It's true," Minette responded. "I thought they were really quite ugly and stupid."

And turning toward Joseph:

"Did you see the man I asked to dance the first dance with me?"

"The one who turned you down," added Lise with a mocking tone.

"He was...disabled, and I hadn't realized."

Joseph barely held back a burst of laughter.

"That guy, disabled? That's a good one. One of Jean-Baptiste Lapointe's better jokes."

"So that's his name?" questioned Minette nervously.

"A name that shouldn't interest you much, believe me," answered Joseph.

"Why not?"

"He's a man with a very bad reputation. He lives in Arcahaie, owns slaves, and has a vast fortune. He is said to live a debauched and flamboyant life."

"Doesn't that describe all men?" objected Lise, intrigued, while a worried-looking Minette seemed to think this over.

"No, not all men, Lise," answered Joseph. "There are a few at least who manage to avoid such temptations..."

"Yes, I know, you're one of them. But you...you...you're not a man like all the rest."

"How's that, I'm not a man like all the rest?"

"Lise just means that you have so many excellent qualities that it's like you're a different kind of being."

"Yes, that's what I meant, I guess," added the young girl. "You aren't the kind of man one would want to…dance with, and I don't really see you kissing a girl."

"Lise!" exclaimed Jasmine.

Minette was thinking. And so the young man she had sung for had been making fun of her? He had preferred pretending to limp and had no trouble saying he was disabled just to avoid dancing with her! A dull feeling of anger was making her heart pound. She, who had thought herself irresistible! She recalled the white-toothed smile that had brightened his young face and the eyes widened in false surprise. Now she understood what they were really expressing: mockery. Oh! She would get her revenge, she swore it. Someday, she would meet him again and make him regret that insult. Refusing to dance with her, Minette, who had just sung at the Comédie and been admired by the Whites. She would make him regret his behavior – even if it took ten years. What a shame he lived so far away! But once she had earned enough money, she would head to Arcahaie for a little vacation. She would see him that day and he would be sorry.

"I hate him," she sighed, tightening Joseph's arm around her waist.

"Who?" he asked, for he had already forgotten their conversation.

"Him, Jean-Baptiste Lapointe!"

"You're still thinking about him?" questioned Lise teasingly.

"Refusing to dance with me! Oh! I'll have my revenge!"

That night, Minette had trouble falling asleep. The love letters she had taken out of her bodice as she undressed were now strewn about on the table near the bed. She picked them up, careful not to wake Lise and her mother, and went out of the room to read them. She realized with surprise that one of them was signed by the Marquis de Chastenoye and was an invitation to come to his home to have champagne with him. He praised her beauty in the most flattering terms and called her a "young goddess." She smiled, flattered, and found Lapointe's behavior even more baffling, given these compliments from such an important person. Lapointe was young and very attractive but, after all, he was no more than a person of color like herself. He had refused her that dance but a Marquis had invited her to his home. She found him stupid, self-important, and completely impolite. She compared him to Claude Goulard, so attentive and sweet, and thought happily about his love-struck gaze. She went back to her bed and fell asleep at once flattered by the letters, delighted by Goulard's affection, and furious about the trick Lapointe had pulled on her.

IX

LISE WENT TO Mme Acquaire's house every day for her lesson. She had made such great progress that her teacher expected soon to launch her into an arena entirely different from Minette's, though also very much in vogue at the time. The popular theater shows had reached new heights of success that year. In Cap-Français, in Saint-Marc, in Léogane, in Les Cayes, and even in Port-au-Prince, they were being applauded by a public more interested in a little distraction than in any particular genre – one that frequented the theater as much for the classics as for the latest local comedies. Thanks to the most recent performance they hosted, the Acquaires had managed to settle a few old debts, though they had incurred a few new ones, too. M Acquaire had been playing dice and his wife had refreshed her wardrobe a bit. The vicious circle had closed yet again and they had to come up with a new performance to satisfy their lenders. Lise was her latest find. They would soon have her singing and attracting people to the Comédie using some clever announcement where they would make clear that this new singer was the sister of the "young person." They had not yet spoken of their plans to anyone. Saint-Martin had reminded them that the Governor, though he had accorded his protection to Minette, had asked that they not attempt to present any other people of color at the Comédie.

It was eight o'clock in the morning when Minette, wearing a flowered skirt and silk madras scarf, left her house to meet up with Mme Acquaire to go to rehearsal. Scipion was there alone doing housework. He welcomed her with an admiring gaze, a gaze Minette already knew well and that tickled her every time to see in the eyes of the large black man. He related to her that his mistress had left very early for the Comédie, having been summoned there by M Saint-Martin. Thus did Minette arrive alone and stumble upon a meeting of the theater's stockholders. Not wanting to interrupt their discussion, which she immediately understood to be particularly heated, she sat down behind a curtain and, opening her music book, went over the opera. The tone of the conversation distracted her from her study. She pulled back the curtain and observed the scene. There was a table around which sat M Saint-Martin, the Acquaires, Durand, Depoix, Favard, and some white men Minette did not recognize. One of them, about forty-five or fifty years old with a large belly and heavy, well-defined features, spoke in an imperious and harsh voice. Interrupting Saint-Martin, he struck the table and said:

"But she should be grateful to us. We allowed her to perform onstage, which isn't without risk."

Minette saw M Acquaire's tic going wild, while Saint-Martin smiled and gave little reassuring taps on the man's shoulder, as if to calm him down.

"Come, come, Mesplès!" he said. "Her talent has brought us huge crowds lately, and with this new opera I'm preparing, she'll guarantee its success."

"She's made you go soft, my dear Saint-Martin," answered Mesplès, "but I'm not one to be indignant about your taste for Mulattresses. I have the same weakness and…"

He cut himself short to indulge a coarse, unpleasant laugh as Saint-Martin protested.

"That young person has a certain talent, I'm not disagreeing, but what does that even matter for a person of color? Nothing, absolutely nothing. Without the Acquaires, she'd still be singing in front of her mother's stand like any other street performer. Believe me, if you have her sign a contract, she'll take herself for a white woman. Next thing you know she'll be arrogant, unbearable. I'm used to her kind."

Mme Acquaire looked at her husband, who winked at her without saying anything. It was Durand who, having spoken in low tones to Depoix and Favart, argued:

"But really, she's part of the company…"

"She isn't part of any company," insisted Mesplès.

"Ah, no! Excuse me," interrupted Saint-Martin. "But we welcomed her and celebrated her just as we do all our new actors."

"That was imprudent," said Mesplès.

"Look," answered M Acquaire, conciliatory, "let's admit that she isn't part of the company. But given that she's asking for wages…"

"Let's offer her every now and again a performance where she takes home the profits – twenty percent – which we will promise to her without any contract, which will keep her from thinking she's indispensable…"

This was all expressed in a cynical, derisive tone that chilled Minette. She could not listen to any more. Rising without making a sound, she went down the little wooden staircase leading backstage and ran away.

She walked very quickly, as if spurred on by some nervous energy that, in her inexperience, she took for anger. However, it was much more than that. Everything she knew about the prejudices held against those of her station had not been painful when they were not direct attacks on her person. She had felt the disadvantage when it was a question of her performing at the Comédie. If she had been worried, she had not suffered from it, finding perfectly normal the order of things as they had been accepted by everyone around her. Today, listening to François Mesplès, stockholder in the theater, she had experienced for the first time in her life the absolute and unsettling ill will of the white man toward free people of color. She was still too young to immediately become aware of this and to judge the milieu she lived in from the outside. Everything was still limited to her own experience. However, certain of Joseph Ogé's words came back to her memory. She remembered the Black Code and its articles, as well as other confusing things she could not manage to disentangle from her impression of personal revolt. Ah! That man had said those things! Ah! That man had spoken about her in that despicable tone and had refused to accept the very principle of a contract linking her to the Comédie. Certain words came back to her: "What does talent matter for a person of color? Without the Acquaires, she'd still be singing in front of her mother's stand like any other street performer." She was overwhelmed by a desire to curse the blood and the race that was the source of all her misfortunes. Because she had a few drops of black blood in her veins she had to resign herself to being humiliated and insulted her whole life! Because she descended from a race that the colonists' brutality relegated to enslavement, she would have to spend her life with her shoulders hunched in resignation!

Oh! Why am I a colored girl – why, Lord? she was surprised to hear herself wonder.

Ashamed, she hurried on. Without meaning to, she arrived at the seafront, where the daily crowd bustled about, joyfully oblivious. A few sailors, arrivals on the most recent ship, began fanning out into the streets, singing. Some of them, half drunk, shouted out couplets as they waved their berets about and leered at women. A slave-trader prodded forward a group of Blacks chained together, making them advance under the whip, like so many animals. The sun beat down on the ground and the trees with rays so hot that they seemed red like fire.

Minette, who was walking straight ahead with her head down and her heart heavy, ran right into a sailor, who immediately took her in his arms and held her to him.

"Hey there, my little chickadee, you walk like a blind woman!" She tried in vain to free herself.

"Let me go, just let me go..."

"Not before you tell me where you live."

He staggered a bit as he clutched her to him. Minette's madras scarf fell off, and her hair spilled over her shoulders. He began to grope her shamelessly, as she kicked at him and tried to bite him, insulting him all the while.

"Let me go, let me go, you drunk, you white trash, you beast!"

Just as he was trying to kiss her and a crowd of curious revelers began gathering around them, a man on horseback galloped by, then stopped so suddenly that his horse reared up before approaching. Minette continued to cry as she struggled, while the sailor laughed and held her even more firmly. No one knew where the blow came from, but the man, his back pierced by a knife, suddenly fell backward. Some women began screaming immediately, and others started running as the circle tightened around Minette and the wounded sailor. Completely distraught, Minette raised her head and looked around. Stopped at a distance away from the drama, the horse pranced about, as if trying to get her attention. She recognized its rider and a shiver traversed her body. Jean-Baptiste Lapointe, his face framed by a wide straw hat, was looking at her with an expression so odd that for a moment she forgot all about the sailor, the crowd, and the drama. He had turned his horse around and taken off in a furious gallop. As the police arrived, someone cried:

"Every man for himself!"

All the people of color, the poor whites, and the children scattered frantically. A carriage came to a stop, and a very well-dressed older gentleman emerged, walking forward while demanding an explanation. Several were offered noisily. He noticed Minette, standing next to the injured sailor and said, surprised:

"Well, if it isn't the 'young person.' What's she doing here?"

Minette immediately saw that this imposing character could be her savior. She ran to him with her hands clasped:

"Monsieur, I don't know what happened. The sailor was drunk and was trying to make me kiss him. I was struggling, and then someone struck him…"

"It's true," someone else insisted while moving toward the man from the carriage. "I'm a white Creole and a jeweler on Bonne-Foi Street. My name is Bascave. This young lady was in the sailor's arms when someone struck him from behind."

The police, who had been bent over the sailor, stood up and announced:

"He's dead!"

Horrified, Minette hid her face in her hands.

"What were you doing here, in…in the arms of…of…the sailor," asked a policeman, with a stutter.

Everybody laughed; then someone responded:

"What's a woman usually doing in the arms of a man?"

The jeweler from Bonne-Foi Street again attested to Minette's innocence, recounting how she had been brutalized by the sailor, who refused to let her go despite her protestations.

"This 'young person' simply cannot be responsible for what happened. The knife was thrown from a great distance and with extraordinary force," said the man from the carriage.

It was noted that the blade had penetrated all the way through the body. The policemen spoke in low tones with the man from the carriage who, taking Minette's arm, said to her:

"You're clearly upset, my child. Step into my coach. I'll take you home."

As the police had begun arbitrarily arresting people of color, a massive effort to flee had begun, during which several people were knocked over, trampled, and hurt. Minette, abruptly separated by the crowd from her savior with the carriage, looked around for him for a moment before starting to run herself, overcome by panic. When she stopped to rest, completely out of breath, she noticed that she was leaning against the door of a little house right on the edge of the road. To her great surprise, the door opened slowly and a hand pulled her inside. When she turned around, half unconscious with fear and fatigue, she found herself facing four black people: an elderly couple, a young woman in her thirties, and a thirty-five-year-old man with a burning look in his eye, and who seemed – when he stood – to be taller than any man she had ever seen before. *Even Scipion can't be as tall as he is,* she thought to herself as he looked at her.

"Tell me what happened," he said to Minette, in a voice as harsh and trenchant as an axe.

"Let her rest, Jean-Pierre," said one of the old people in Creole, a hunched-over woman whose dull and frightened expression reminded her of her mother. "Indeed, the poor thing truly seems worn out!"

And then, pointing to a chair: "Sit down, my child," she added.

During the brief moment that the old woman's intervention had lasted, Minette had been able to look more closely at the four people gathered in the room. Aside from the elderly couple and the tall young man named Jean-Pierre, there was also a young woman at the end of the table. Truly beautiful, her gaze and her face had something tragic to them that made one almost ill at ease.

"You've lost your madras," she said in a quiet, almost muffled voice.

Minette brought her hand to her hair.

"Yes, it fell off as I was struggling."

"Struggling, young lady – against whom?" asked the old man, who had not yet spoken.

She turned toward him to respond and was struck by the resemblance between his eyes and those of the two young people. Their three sets of eyes were identical in both their shape and their expression, and completely different from those of the old woman. For as timid and fearful as were the latter's, those of the others flashed proudly with a terrible expression of defiance. Minette sustained the gaze of the old man without flinching, though she saw what seemed like burning sparks glowing in his eyes.

"Yes, I struggled with a white sailor who wanted to kiss me."

"And it's because he wanted to kiss you that you were running like you were afraid?"

"The sailor was killed," said Minette.

"Killed! And by whom?" asked the young man, so anxiously that he seemed out of breath.

"No one knows."

The young woman looked at Jean-Pierre and the same wild flame burned in both of their gazes. The latter leaned forward suddenly.

"Hide her, Zoé," he said to the young woman. "They're coming this way."

"No one has accused me," began Minette. "A white man…"

"Be quiet," whispered Jean-Pierre, waving his hand.

There was such authority in his voice that Minette obeyed instantly. She followed Zoé into the next room and left the two old people and the young man. Zoé had not yet closed the door to the bedroom when someone entered the front room without knocking. They heard the click of a sword and someone swearing. It was a former slave, broken by his training with the constabulary, for whom capturing maroons or law-breaking freedmen was a lucrative and entertaining business.

"Who are you looking for?" asked Jean-Pierre.

"A man of color. He's suspected of killing a sailor. Are there others here with you?"

"Yes, two women in the bedroom. Feel free to go check for yourself."

He walked over without a word and immediately a cry of surprise escaped him when he recognized Minette.

"What? It's you! What the hell are you doing here? I thought you'd left with the Marquis de Chastenoye."

"I lost him in the crowd."

"Is this where you live?"

"No, this is...my friends' house," responded Minette, terribly worried.

"I should have arrested you," continued the policeman, looking strangely at Minette and Zoé, "but that old fool paid me a hefty sum to leave you alone. And then, the white bystanders agreed that you had no part in the incident. Was it perhaps a lover of yours who did the deed?" he questioned, suddenly suspicious.

Minette immediately altered her expression, becoming a little girl, innocent and awkward.

"Oh, dear!" she protested, "at my age!..."

"At your age, what? There are girls younger than you in the life, don't you know?"

"No, I don't know anything about that..."

"Fine. I'd love to believe you. Maybe those blasted 'malcontents' have struck again."

He left the room, passed through the front room and left without saying another word to anyone.

Zoé took Minette's hand and dragged her along after her.

"Jean-Pierre," she began, "he mentioned 'malcontents,' and this young lady isn't a suspect."

"It's just shameful!" he exclaimed, rage boiling in his voice. "To hear such words in the mouth of one of our brothers!"

He turned to Minette. For a brief moment his burning gaze fell on her.

"Listen," he said to her, "you can trust us. Who do you suspect did this?"

"Suspect! Well, no one…" stammered Minette, as she saw in her mind a bronze horseman wearing a straw hat. Jean-Baptiste Lapointe's gaze had overwhelmed her. She remembered it and now realized that it had burned with hatred and disgust at the sight of the sailor who was mistreating her. Yes, that gaze could well be that of a criminal or a vigilante. But why, why would he have killed a white man? For her? That wasn't possible. He did not seem at all like a great admirer of hers or like a jealous lover and, clear evidence of his total indifference toward her, he had refused her a dance at the ball.

All four of them were looking at her with such apprehension that she felt compelled to speak. But at the same time, she was suspicious. Who were these four? They seemed like good people, especially the old man and woman, but the other two – such passion in their gaze, such fever in their voice and gestures! Why were they interrogating her with such curiosity, such impatience? Why were they so interested in this whole affair?

"Don't give us a name, if that bothers you, young lady," said Jean-Pierre, "but speak – it will help us, believe me."

For a moment he remained rooted right in front of her and his immense eyes opened so exorbitantly in his dark face that Minette was afraid.

"Do you suspect a white man of having killed that sailor?…"

"A white man?" replied Minette quickly. "Oh, no!…"

"So you do suspect someone."

"I don't dare…I don't want to…"

"Don't say his name, if that's a problem," said Zoé encouragingly.

"It was a *griffe*," admitted Minette, "a *griffe* on horseback – tall, handsome, and young."

Suddenly the atmosphere changed. Jean-Pierre and Zoé threw themselves into one another's arms and embraced as if delirious with joy.

"It's him!" cried Zoé, "It's him – I'm sure of it!…"

"Calm yourselves, children, calm yourselves," said the old woman gently as she looked outside nervously. "For heaven's sake, calm down!"

Jean-Pierre had become serious again, not in obedience to the old woman's admonitions, but because he seemed to be following a thought that made him throw himself against the chair in which the old man was seated. Their eyes met, and Minette was once again struck by their resemblance.

"Ah! Their reprisals will become more violent every day. We can expect a movement of solidarity very soon, isn't that right, father?…"

"Very soon," the old man answered, "no one can say if it will be soon. I'll die perhaps before seeing it come to pass, but it will happen…yes."

Minette got the impression they had forgotten about her, but then they remembered her presence and abruptly turned in her direction. In an instant, they seemed to come together and a sort of secret, tacit understanding established itself among them. Zoé turned to Minette.

"How old are you?" she asked her.

"Fifteen."

"At fifteen I already understood quite a lot of things…"

She stood up, came toward Minette and placed her hands on her shoulders.

"You are the daughter of a mulatto woman and a white man, and I am the daughter of two Negroes. Your skin is different than mine but we are both free women of color and the laws are the same for both of us, no?"

Breathless, Minette nodded yes. *Where was she going with this, for heaven's sake? What tragic eyes and what terrible passion!* she said to herself.

"Your story is as follows," continued Zoé, "your mother was a slave, she suffered the advances of her master and you were the result, right?"

"Yes, but how do you know?"

"It's the eternal story of all pretty little mixed-race girls like you. And before you, your mother was born in the same circumstances, and your freedom is nothing but the result of chance."

She began walking, and kept her eyes on Minette as she paced up and down the room. And Minette got the impression that what Zoé was saying right then she had already repeated to hundreds of people with a goal that she, Minette, did not yet understand.

"My parents were slaves, slaves in Martinique, which is a country that absolutely resembles Saint-Domingue, as far as suffering and injustice are concerned."

The word "injustice" was spoken with such bitterness that Minette felt like she was hearing it for the very first time.

Injustice! Who had said that before Zoé? she thought. Who? Injustice had kept slaves in irons, allowed them to be beaten, tortured, killed. Injustice toward the freedmen, the same injustice that prohibited them from performing at the Comédie, from going to the Whites' ball, from getting an education…all those unjust laws, this entire order of things, unjust, this social prejudice, unjust…But who had said all these things before Zoé? Joseph? Father Raynal? No, it was a painful sensation she felt manifesting itself all around her and that had been revealed to her, not because anyone had pointed it out to her but because in herself she had felt a muted revolt against so much absurdity. This revolt had been brewing for some time. It had taken shape the very day when she understood that she and Lise, because they had a few drops of black blood in them, were put in quarantine even by little white girls their own age. In effect, she had continued to live with her revolt without even realizing it was there, eating her up, sleeping, as she envied the life of the Whites just like all the others in her social class. But in listening to Zoé, a veil had been torn off, exposing everything that had been so well hidden inside her and that undoubtedly had inspired this need to insult the Whites, to spit in their faces, and to hate them. Joseph had helped her to see things clearly within herself. The work Zoé was doing on Minette's narrow little freedwoman's consciousness had been initiated by Joseph, but more gently, more patiently and, above all, more prudently.

Zoé pulled back a curtain and revealed a few shelves filled with books.

"That's where I learned to read and how I continue to teach myself. An old freedman lent me his books. He's rich and his courtyard is a veritable paradise, with birds and fish everywhere."

"Labadie!" cried Minette.

"You know him?"

"Yes. I learned from his books, too."

"Ah!…"

She put her arms around Minette's shoulders with an affectionate gesture so unexpected that Minette could not help but look at her in surprise. But Zoé was no longer thinking about Minette. She had run to her brother and was speaking to him in low tones, in a persuasive, passionate voice. He listened to her, a faraway look in his eye.

At that very moment, the door that gave onto the street opened up and a mulatto woman entered. She had long braids pinned back in a thick bun at the nape of her neck and was dressed in a severely cut black dress and a long-sleeved blouse that covered half her hands. On her arrival, Zoé let out a cry of surprise:

"Louise," she called out, and ran to embrace her.

The mulatto woman let her worried gaze linger on the elderly couple, kissed them and held out her hand to Jean-Pierre.

"Have you seen Beauvais, Lambert?" she asked.

"No, not in three days," he answered, "but he promised me he'd come, so he'll come."

She let her gaze travel over the narrow room and seemed to notice Minette for the first time.

"And who is this – a friend of yours, Zoé?" she said, looking over Minette suspiciously.

"A friend?" responded Zoé, looking Minette in the eyes. "Yes, I think so…I think we can count on her, too."

"Good," said the mulatto woman, taking Jean-Pierre Lambert by the hand.

"Excuse us," she said, leading him into the bedroom. "Something confidential."

Minette felt weary. Too many things had happened in the course of that one morning. She had only one desire: to leave, to go home, to go to bed, to not see anything else, to not hear anything else. She got up and, without saying a word, hugged Zoé and gave her a kiss.

"Tell me your name?"

"Minette."

"Where do you live?"

"Traversière Street."

"We'll meet again, Minette."

"I hope so, Zoé. Goodbye Papa. Goodbye Mama."

"Goodbye, my daughter," responded the old people.

It was almost one o'clock when Minette arrived at her home. Her mother had already brought in the stand to serve lunch. For the first time in her life, the young girl was keeping secrets from her mother. She did not tell her about the murdered sailor, or about Jean-Baptiste Lapointe or the Lamberts. Her worried air, while she ate the traditional meal of peas and rice, did not escape Lise, who began questioning her about her morning. Had she been with Mme Acquaire at the Comédie? How had the rehearsal gone? Had Goulard paid her any compliments?

"I wasn't at the Comédie," admitted Minette, so as to put an end to her sister's rather annoying investigation. "I felt like going for a walk, so I went for a walk."

"Speak French!" begged Jasmine.

And suddenly realizing what Minette had just said:

"What? What are you saying, my daughter? You went for a walk? With whom?"

"Oh! By myself, Mama," responded Minette, exasperated.

She was holding back with some difficulty the tears that had begun streaming down her cheeks.

"I'm tired," she said with a voice so shaky and plaintive that Lise, whose eyes had been lowered on her plate, looked up at her and cried:

"You're crying? What's the matter with you?"

Minette pushed away her plate and stood up. What she wouldn't have given to be alone for a moment, just a moment. *Oh, to have a room of my own, to be able to close myself up somewhere to think and to cry as much as I want!* she thought to herself. Everything she had lived through that morning was knocking around inside her in feverish disorder: the stakeholder in the theater, the sailor, the horseman, Zoé and Jean-Pierre! Oh! She simply could not handle it. She was going to start screaming, screaming like a madwoman. Jasmine looked at her like a mother hen fearing her chick would run away; Lise wore the expression of a surprised and stupid little goose. Did she not have the right to keep to herself things she had no desire to talk about? How would she talk about them? She herself could barely manage to understand what had been going on inside her and around her from the moment she had left the Comédie. How could she possibly tell Jasmine that she had been out walking alone, that a sailor who had kissed her had been killed, and that she suspected a certain Lapointe had done it? Oh! All of that was too complicated and Jasmine would have a reason to whimper, to weep, to look her in the eye to remind her of her scarred back, to force her to repent, to retreat back into herself. She left the dining room without a word and entered into the only bedroom, closing the door after her. For a minute she listened to the sound of Lise and her mother's voices, pricked up her ears to be sure they had not followed her. Then she lay down in her bed, buried her head in her pillow and wept despairingly.

X

FOLLOWING THE sailor's murder, the planters hung two men of color as an example. Though they swore they had been mere innocent bystanders, they were brought to the public square and hung from lampposts after a mockery of a trial. Coincidentally, as if they had been tipped off, a group of free colored women, abandoning their sandals, their Indian-style skirts, and their madras scarves, but decked out in velvet and lace, chose that same day to display themselves ostentatiously on the arms of the most handsome officers of the colony.

Moreover, their feet were shod, which infuriated the white Creoles and European women. Wearing the jewels that their white lovers had offered them the night before, adorned like so many human shrines, the free women of color went to witness the freedmen's ordeal.

The accused were two young men, perhaps twenty or twenty-five years old. The younger of the two screamed and attempted to escape the clutches of the soldiers. Their mothers and other relatives followed behind them, wailing, screaming, and praying aloud. "Mercy, mercy," they cried, "Lord God, have mercy." One of their mothers rolled on the ground in despair and, when they placed the rope around her son's neck, leapt on a police officer and bit his arm. She was arrested immediately. Curious onlookers pressed forward, jostling one another so as to get a better look at the swinging bodies with tongues that had begun to stick out, purple and swollen, from the mouths of the hanged men.

Among the free people of color there was Nicolette, in velvet skirt and lace bodice, as well as Kiss-Me-Lips, her face half hidden beneath a fringed parasol. The way they were dressed could not exactly be considered a form of vengeance, yet, gathered together at the scene of the hanging in that way, they were so striking in their luxury that, despite the childishness of the gesture, they nonetheless seemed to issue some manner of protest. Some of the white women, recognizing their husbands or lovers among the companions of the beautiful colored women, shouted at the latter – calling them dirty niggers, bastards, and *gens de la côte*. These were serious insults: the colored women took them without flinching – as if they had planned it – and behaved as if impervious.

Having attended the hanging with unreadable expressions on their faces, they dispersed along with the rest of the crowd and, from that moment on, only ever appeared dressed as ladies. The murder of the soldier, the provocative attitude of the free colored women, and multiple cases of marooning created a horrible state of tension that turned the tide against Minette. And, as she was visible and had been the first to begin wearing such expensive garments, she became a prime target. She was attacked immediately in the local gazette, criticized for her extravagant tastes and compared unfavorably to Mme Marsan, a white actress from Cap-Français, so as to destroy her in public opinion. The paper contrasted the two women's talent, their beauty, and their social standing. It lamented Port-au-Prince's apparent appreciation for a little half-breed that local whites – too indulgent and in complete disregard for the law – had supported in a career that allowed her to show herself in public, and so risked weakening the power of prejudice and pushing "those creatures" to take on inappropriate airs. The paper openly reproached the Governor for having encouraged such attacks on the edicts of the King in fortifying, by his weakness, unacceptable aspirations and desires. The day after the hanging, Minette's name was dragged into the drama that had taken place at the seaside and the "young person" who sang at the Comédie was revealed as the woman who had been in the arms of the sailor at the moment of his murder.

Horrified by the two freedmen's ordeal, Minette spent the day in her room, weeping and cursing the dead sailor, the judges, and the planters. Now that she had heard the word "injustice" used by Zoé Lambert, she had begun using it as something of a mantra, repeating it to herself constantly. When Joseph arrived, she spat it out at him with the same fervor she had heard in Zoé's tone.

"Such injustice, such cruel injustice – killing those poor men! I know for a fact they didn't do anything."

Without responding, Joseph unfolded the newspaper he had brought with him and showed the article to Minette.

"How mixed up are you in this sad affair, Minette?" he asked.

As he had spoken loudly, she made a gesture to silence him.

"There's no point in Mama and Lise knowing about this. Come over here, I'll tell you everything."

When she had finished speaking, Joseph nodded his head.

"You really owe that Marquis de Chastenoye. Without him, you'd have been arrested and put on trial."

"He seemed like a kind old man."

"Don't be too sure of that. He likely has a…personal interest in protecting you."

"A personal interest!…"

"Look, let's drop it and talk about that terrible article that's working to undermine your incredible theater debut. Have you seen Saint-Martin or the Acquaires?"

"No. I haven't left the house since yesterday."

"They might have come here."

While Minette and Joseph were discussing the infamous article, the Acquaires – furious – had run to Charles Mozard's office.

"Why would you write an article like that about our protégée?" Mme Acquaire had asked him, trying to contain her outrage.

"It's for her own good, believe me," the journalist had responded, unmoved. "She wants to climb too high. The higher we let her rise, the more terrible her fall will be."

M Acquaire, blinking his eye disconcertingly, alleged that the Governor had given his word to Saint-Martin that he would offer his total protection to the "young person," in whom he recognized a true talent, and that if he, Mozard, continued to attack Minette, he would bring his complaint to the Governor. Mme Acquaire tugged at her husband's arm to calm him down, for she feared angering the journalist. But the latter burst out laughing and suggested they go have some drinks together at a nearby café. Mme Acquaire accepted, hoping to have the chance to convince him. But after laying out all her arguments, she had to admit defeat.

"But you were so complimentary and encouraging when all of this began, my dear Monsieur Mozard," Mme Acquaire murmured to him with a tone that implied he had allowed his opinion to be bought.

"That was then," responded the journalist, unperturbed as he sipped his drink. "Since then, your protégée has had her little moment, and now that's enough."

"So you reproach her…"

"Her affinity for the garish and for tacky and expensive clothes that the Negro in her shows off with such distasteful vulgarity."

"But those are costumes…"

"More showy than realistic, you yourself will admit."

Mme Acquaire placed her hand on the journalist's arm and adopted a decidedly seductive and coaxing tone:

"Just try not to be so harsh next time, I beg you…"

"Send her to me and have her ask me herself."

"Oh!" exclaimed Mme Acquaire, shocked. "Are we making a deal here?"

"My dear lady, you appreciate straight talk, even if it's tough to hear; you yourself use a veil, even if it's fairly transparent…"

Mme Acquaire made a disgusted little grimace, stood up, took her husband's arm and dragged him away.

"He must have pocketed a nice little sum, our dear Monsieur Mozard!"

"Which he'd be happy to spend on Minette."

"That – never!" protested Mme Acquaire. "That girl is only fifteen years old and I promised her mother…"

"Nonsense," interrupted M Acquaire. "The day she decides to sleep…to fall, she'll be damned certain not to ask her mother for permission."

As they walked along, they arrived at Jasmine's house, where they found Minette, calmer, seated in the front room sewing a bodice.

Mme Acquaire, overexcited, did not understand the young girl's signal for her to be discreet and began talking about everything in front of Jasmine and Lise. Jasmine raised her hands to her head in a gesture of despair and nearly knocked over her tea.

"My Lord God," she screamed. "Minette, why didn't you tell me anything about all of this?"

Minette immediately spoke up in her own defense. She put down her work on the table and slowly said:

"From what I've understood in all of this, Madame Acquaire, I'm being reproached for rising too high too fast…"

"Monsieur Mozard nonetheless has a certain…admiration…for you."

"Well, he has a strange way of showing it. Madame Acquaire, I won't forget the gratitude I owe you – and since I'm becoming a source of trouble for you, I'll stop singing at the Comédie."

"Come now, Minette, everything will work out," said the Creole woman, her tone slightly changed. "The public will call for you, you'll see."

"I won't be able to be a part of the company without the respect and the freedom of action accorded to my fellow cast members. It's enough that I'm being exploited. I've resigned myself to the fact that I work without a contract and get paid whatever you all want to pay me, but now I'm angry and I just want peace."

"Minette," protested Jasmine, "show Madame some respect."

"I do respect her, Mama…"

"Listen, Minette," said M Acquaire, inserting himself into the conversation, "we've been defending you, and we'll keep doing it, and as far as your contract is concerned, if everything calms down we hope to be able to convince François Mesplès."

"François Mesplès!" exclaimed Minette, as if she wanted to retain the name. "I would love to meet that man."

Mme Acquaire quickly exchanged a glance with her husband.

"That's a wonderful idea, my dear," she said obligingly. "You can go to his home. You know where he lives, no?"

"Who in Port-au-Prince doesn't know where to find the home of the wealthy Monsieur Mesplès?"

"Be sweet, beseeching, and above all don't wear any jewels," continued the Creole woman.

Minette's eyes had a worried expression that her mother didn't fail to notice. As the Acquaires took their leave, she observed her daughter, who, with her gaze fixed on something invisible, seemed hypnotized.

She had just come up with a plan that she would keep to herself and that she swore to execute. This M Mesplès, was he not the white man who had so chagrined her that morning at the Comédie? Because of him, she had truly suffered, for she had not forgotten the hateful disdain in his voice when he had spoken of her presumed rights and her future at the Comédie.

At around ten in the morning, she brought Lise to her lesson with Mme Acquaire, despite Jasmine's tearful insistence that none of this mattered now that M Mozard's article had ruined everything. Knowing that some Whites disapproved of her daughter's performance on the Comédie stage made her tremble, and she had already lowered her head, defeated, like a person used to obeying and to bowing and scraping.

But for Minette, this was not the end. She was going to fight – with her beauty, her youth, and her talent. She already had a little list: the Marquis de Chastenoye, the Governor, and all those officers who had written her love letters. If she gave the signal, they would all be at her feet. When she returned home, she was surprised to find Joseph there waiting for her. This was not his usual time, which worried her even more, given that he was looking at her like he wanted to probe the depths of her soul.

"Minette," he began, "do you know who killed the sailor?"

She turned her head and answered:

"All I have are suspicions, nothing but suspicions. I couldn't accuse anyone."

"I've seen the Lamberts, Minette."

"The Lamberts! You know them?"

"Yes."

"What did they tell you?"

"That they'd brought you into their group despite your youth. I've been tasked with talking to you."

"Into their group!"

"Be discreet and take care. God has just placed you on a path rife with troubles and roadblocks. In order to navigate it, you'll have to let go of certain dreams, disregard certain things. I, too, have been pleading your case because I believe you're ready."

"Speak, Joseph…"

"Lambert is one of the heads of the insurgency. He hides runaways and helps them escape."

Minette shivered and clasped her hands.

"But why?"

Joseph brought his mouth close to her ear and said a few words to her in a low voice.

Immediately, her expression changed. A sort of brutal contentment colored her features and gave her an almost ferocious air.

"So you, too, then?…"

"Yes, me, too, Minette. Although, as Lise has said so well, I seem… different from the others. I'm part of their group. I fight with them because they're the weakest. God knows that this is my calling. I feel like I can tell you everything now…"

A burning flame shone for a moment in his eyes.

"I would have so loved to be a priest!"

In a burst of emotion, the young girl took his hands.

"So that was it!"

"Fighting with them to obtain their rights, I'm convinced I'm fighting to get closer to God."

The burning flame had disappeared from his eyes, and was replaced by a glow so tender, sweet, and compassionate that Minette's eyes filled with tears.

"Ah, Joseph!" she exclaimed, "You have to hope. Haven't I managed to take a step forward? And I'll keep going, despite the obstacles. I swear it."

She had spoken too bitterly.

Joseph immediately lowered his gaze to rest on her. She saw such worry in his eyes that she tried to reassure him.

"Don't worry. I've got my head on straight. Nothing can derail me."

He made a gesture of contented acquiescence and, taking her hand, brought her out to the street, where Jasmine was crouched behind her stand, selling her wares. The two of them sat down next to her and smiled as they listened to Lise's voice, whose well-practiced and careful trills they could hear clearly.

"Clearly, she's been working hard!" noted Joseph with satisfaction.

Jasmine heard him. She looked up at him, her eyes once again dulled with sadness.

"What's the use, now," she sighed. "The gazette has ruined everything…"

Joseph left, then came back in the afternoon and sat down near the stand where Jasmine and Minette were still seated. He had been there for a few minutes when suddenly something strange created a commotion among the vendors. The sounds of women screaming rang out, terrified and strident. And then, knocking everything over, as if in a state of madness, a tall, strapping man, branded on both arms and half naked, hurled himself into the crowd of market-women. He ran blindly, his eyes protruding and mouth hanging open. Minette seized Joseph's hand. *Oh! What can I do, for the love of God, I want to do something*, she said to herself.

Standing now a mere ten paces from Jasmine's stand, the slave was looking wildly around in desperation. Abruptly, he fell to the ground and crawled toward Joseph. At the very same moment, police swarmed the street. The slave, curled up at Joseph's feet, remained motionless, his head lowered to the ground.

The silence had become distressing, and so unbearable that, apparently coming to some sudden resolution, Joseph furiously began throwing Jasmine's madras scarves and fabrics from nearby stands on the poor man's body, grabbing anything he could get his hands on. He then cried out, following through on the subterfuge:

"Hello, Sir, Madame, c'mon over and have a look at our beautiful handkerchiefs, fabrics, soaps, and perfumes…"

Of all the witnesses to the scene, only one person might have betrayed him. An old, poorly dressed white man who had stopped to haggle over fabric with Jasmine. One of the slave's feet was badly covered. The old man threw the handkerchief he was holding over it. Ten constabularies passed by, peering into faces and screaming about the punishment awaiting anyone who hid runaway slaves. But what could they possibly see, what could they hope to make out in this tumult of voices calling for customers – out of these hundreds of dark-colored arms brandishing soaps, madras scarves, and fabrics?

Even once the soldiers had left, the excitement continued apace, keeping up the same energy so as to throw off the scent. The panting slave began moving the fabrics.

"Be still, my friend," said Joseph to him in Creole. "They're gone and soon it will be nighttime."

For more than two hours he remained there, hunched over, paralyzed, and trembling with fear. Once night had fallen and they were sure the district was no longer under suspicion, Joseph had the slave crawl into the courtyard where, without losing any time, they dressed him in one of Jasmine's camisoles. Lise, who had gone to see Pitchoun, came home at this very moment, and passed by the stand without noticing anything unusual. With his head wrapped in a scarf and unrecognizably dressed as a woman, the slave was then about to leave the house, accompanied by Joseph, when Lise came out to the courtyard.

"Good evening…neighbor," she said, looking at the slave in surprise.

And she whispered into her mother's ear:

"Who's that? I don't recognize her."

"A friend of Joseph's," responded Jasmine.

Minette looked at her mother and was astonished by the expression on her face. Everything that had been dulled in her features had been reanimated, as if she had come into contact with a powerful breath of galvanizing air. Of course, her trembling hands revealed her worry and she was breathing as if she were suffocating. But at the same time, for a brief moment, her expression reminded Minette of Zoé. She was standing before a slave and looking him straight in the eyes. She undoubtedly saw something familiar there, for she shook her head quiescently, as if to say that she understood.

"Goodbye," said Joseph then.

And pushing the slave in front of him, escorted him out.

"Is Joseph's friend mute?" Lise then asked her mother.

"You talk too much," interrupted Minette, exasperated.

"What's the matter with you?" replied the young girl.

"Speak French," interjected Jasmine, in her habitual droning monotone.

"How did your lesson go?" asked Minette, to change the subject.

"Fine. And Madame Acquaire promised me that she would sort out everything with that Monsieur Mozard."

As if overcome with remorse, Minette kissed her little sister and went into the bedroom. Once there, she sat down on the bed and clasped her hands. There were things she had kept from her mother, believing her incapable of withstanding certain dangers. And now the two of them were accomplices in something that could cost them their freedom. Did they have the right to risk Lise's future in that way? She was so young, so carefree, so unfit for serious things! Minette thought of Joseph and trembled. He was in grave danger. So as not to have to speak to Lise when she came in, Minette preferred to undress and go to bed right away. That whole night she suffered horrific dreams in which women and children were tortured as she looked on.

XI

THE FOLLOWING DAY the director of the theater paid Minette a visit, accompanied by the other actors. This goodwill visit proved the performers' overwhelming solidarity and confirmed Minette's conviction that they represented a distinct class vis-à-vis all the other Whites in the country. Goulard, more smitten than ever, was looking for an encouraging sign from her which she still could not quite muster. Saint-Martin, who had approached the Governor a second time seeking protection for Minette, guaranteed her that she had nothing to fear from that quarter and promised her that at the next performance both the public and even Mozard would be so charmed by her voice that they would come around unreservedly. They all shook her hand affectionately and Goulard offered to take her for a walk around Vallières Square, where acrobats from France were giving a free show. She thought of Joseph and turned him down, too worried to have fun.

"Won't you come with me, Minette?" pleaded Goulard.

"Not this evening, but another time, I promise."

She waited in vain for Joseph, stealing a glance in the direction of her mother from time to time to see if she, too, was worrying. In the distance, the rolling of a drum resounded and was answered, as always, by the harsh sound of the *lambi*. Startled, Jasmine, who had stooped down to pick up some laundry she had left to dry in the sun, remained frozen in that position for a moment, listening to the doleful plaints. Inside, Lise was doing her singing exercises, a music notebook in her hand, and Minette, silent, her hands crossed on her lap, awaited Joseph's return. At nine o'clock she had to go to sleep, as Jasmine had called her to bed. After Lise had fallen asleep, she saw her mother rise and get dressed.

"Stay put. I'm going to see what I can find out," she said to Minette dryly.

"Mama!"

"Shhh! Be quiet and wait for me to come back."

She returned two hours later and Minette, who had not been able to sleep at all, rushed into the front room as soon as she heard the door open.

"And so, Mama?" she whispered.

"Nothing. I couldn't find out anything. The doors of the house where he rents his room were all closed. I couldn't find out anything."

Joseph arrived very early the next morning, as if he knew his friends would have been too worried to sleep. He waited to speak to them until Lise had left, and then recounted how he had been able to help the slave escape without raising the slightest suspicion – and how the slave had thanked him, kneeling down to kiss his hands.

"And now he's somewhere safe," he concluded.

"Quiet," warned Minette. "Someone's coming."

Almost immediately, the door was pushed open and M and Mme Acquaire entered. Talking over one another, they tried to explain to Minette that she was needed, that she had to sing, that a prominent personage was expected, that the Governor himself had asked her to accept the next role because of the arrival of this esteemed personage, etc. Completely stunned, Minette covered her ears with her hands.

"I'm not sure I understand, Madame Acquaire."

"She's right," responded the latter, looking at her husband with what was meant to be a fierce expression. "You're interrupting me, you're speaking over me, you're stuttering…"

"And your tic is going full force," finished M Acquaire, imitating his wife.

"And your tic is going full force," retorted Mme Acquaire. "Which makes a mess of everything. Let me speak to the poor child…Listen here, Minette, we've come to you as a delegation. The government is anticipating a visit from the Duke of Lancaster, third son of the King of England, in exactly two weeks. We've been asked to organize an evening in his honor. Do you realize what that means?"

"Yes, Madame Acquaire."

"You'll play the part of Myris in *The Beautiful Arsène*. This'll be an incredible opportunity for you to confront the public, as they won't dare to show any ill will in front of such an important personage."

Joseph nodded his approval while Jasmine clasped her hands. Her daughter was going to sing before the son of the King of England! Minette ran to get dressed and followed the Acquaires to the theater where they met up with Saint-Martin and the actors.

"There's our beautiful Myris!" shouted the young director on seeing her.

Joyful and enthusiastic, he explained to her that they would showcase her this time in a fairytale decor.

"It's a very popular opera that's taken Paris by storm. I'm sure you'll be up to the task."

"You can count on me, Monsieur."

"And I have some good news for you. If you're as successful as I predict you'll be, I'll personally make it my business to hire you for the next three years."

"Under contract?"

"Patience, Minette – take things as they come. Monsieur Mesplès doesn't want you to have a contract."

"Well, then I won't sing in this opera, Monsieur."

"What are you saying?"

"I'm saying that I demand an evening where I keep the profits and I insist on being hired with a contract. If you refuse, I'll quit the Comédie."

"You can't be serious. Miss this opportunity to win over the public for a question of pride! What do you think – that we haven't lifted a finger to convince Mesplès? Ask Goulard – who fought maybe even a little too hard for your rights – how he was almost fired from the theater!"

"Well, then I'll go see Monsieur Mesplès."

"What? You…"

"I'll go see Monsieur Mesplès. I'd already been considering it."

Saint-Martin seemed to think this over for a moment and had a strange smile on his face. This little wisp of a woman, rebellious and proud, appealed to him. He extended his hand to her.

"You never know what can happen. I wish you luck, Minette."

"Thank you, Monsieur."

As she went on her way, she saw Goulard running after her. He took her hand.

"So when are we going for that walk, Minette?" he asked.

"Where can this possibly lead, Claude?"

He leaned over her and said breathily:

"To love. You know perfectly well that I love you."

"Yes, I know you're sincere."

"I'd like to see you alone. I need to speak to you. I'm begging you, Minette!"

She took her hand out of his and smiled, slightly embarrassed.

"Don't tempt me."

"I'm begging you!"

She hesitated, then said abruptly:

"Tonight, Vallières Square. I'll be there."

With that she escaped, leaving the young actor dizzy with hope and joy.

She returned home and took out the trunk containing her most beautiful dress – the one she had worn to play the role of Isabelle and that Nicolette had tailored using enchanted scissors. For what she was going to do that evening, she would have to lie to Jasmine. She did not hesitate for a second: she would lie. She believed, confusedly, that in order to truly have the "freedom to act," as she put it, she would first have to escape her mother's supervision, even at the risk of disappointing her. Naturally, she would spare her as much as possible, but now that she understood that nothing in life could be attained by sitting around, arms crossed and complaining, she had bravely opened her eyes to the world and would defy it.

That afternoon, Jasmine was complaining of back pains and asked Minette to go to the market for the day's provisions. She went off while Lise studied with Mme Acquaire. She crossed through the diverse crowd of people, where planters' wives in European dress, rag-clad vendors, languorous Creoles in transparent *gaules* and billowy madras scarves, flanked by their ladies-in-waiting, arrogant planters armed with whips, bewigged civil servants in frilly lace shirts, and slaves waiting to be sold like animals all mingled together.

Minette carved out a path for herself among this excitable crowd of people laughing, debating, and calling out to one another. In the corner where the slaves had been thrown together, the crowd was so dense that she had to stop. A planter was haggling over two young black boys, inspecting them as invasively as possible; another one, poking a young Mulatto girl with the end of his whip, made her stand up and walk for him, after which he pulled down the straps of her dress, lifted her skirts and demanded that she smile.

"How much?" he said, addressing the merchant.

"Two thousand pounds, Monsieur. Look at her – she's a real beauty. Get undressed," ordered the merchant, shoving the young slave.

She was crying as she removed her dress. Soon she was naked.

"She's too expensive," said the planter, grimacing. "She's skinny."

"Skinny – this beauty?"

And to force the potential buyer to appreciate the merchandise, he turned her every which way, praising her long hair, the curve of her hips, the firmness of her breasts.

"One thousand five hundred pounds," said the planter coldly.

The deal done, the slave got dressed, crying as she followed her new master.

"She's a virgin," shouted the merchant to the planter as the latter walked away. "You got a good deal."

Minette, overwhelmed, followed the young slave with her eyes.

Her heart was beating as if it would burst, for as she watched the scene she saw her mother's past, that past that Zoé had evoked so vehemently that she had been marked by it from that moment on. In that instant, a horrific revolt welled up inside her and she was overcome by such energy that she felt capable of killing someone. Oh! It would be so easy, truly, to thrust a knife in a few necks, to poison people, to start fires. She shivered and realized that her gaze must have been suffused with as much fever and passion as that of the Lamberts, and she understood that there was a metamorphosis happening inside her. At an age when she should have been thinking about clothes and love, jewels and seductions, a threatening lesson was spelling itself out incoherently inside her young girl's heart. What was in this lesson? She did not know yet. But she knew that it had begun to destroy in her the young girl she had once been, and to transform her from that moment on into the woman she would be soon, reducing her to a mere machine in the service of destiny. She had planned a rendezvous with Goulard that evening. How nice it would be to love him, to let him kiss her, and to experience the unfettered joys she dreamed about sometimes.

She bought the provisions without even bargaining, risking a scolding from Jasmine, and went home to get dressed. Disregarding Mme Acquaire's advice, she put on some jewels and let Jasmine know she was going out.

"Going out! And where to?"

She lied and answered:

"To the Comédie, Mama."

"Are you performing tonight?"

She did not have the heart to continue lying.

"Yes, an important role."

"Minette," shouted Jasmine, "be careful!"

She went over to her mother, and took her head in her hands.

"My poor, sweet mama," she murmured.

Jasmine squirmed abruptly out of her grasp.

"Oh, let me be," she said. "You're hiding something from me. As you've gotten older you've become a stranger to me. I no longer recognize you."

"Come now, Mama."

"No, I don't recognize you anymore. You think secretively, you act secretively, and you've learned to lie."

Her eyes brimming with tears, she looked at Minette and repeated:

"I have no more children, I have no more children," dabbing at her cheeks with an old cloth she was darning.

Minette looked at her mother reproachfully and, with a loud sigh, walked out. It was early. She walked slowly, trying to think about what this interview would be like, preparing lines she then immediately replaced with different ones in the very next instant. In front of the painter Perrosier's house, she heard someone calling her. Perrosier was on his doorstep, his palette and brushes in hand. His hair was a mess and his shirt stained with ink. He was smiling at her admiringly.

For the last few weeks, he had set himself up on Traversière Street, in a minuscule two-room house whose appearance was even more wretched than that of Jasmine's. On some nights, he got drunk and painted busts of black women with their breasts exposed, which he called his masterpieces. He was known to stagger by the market-women, who called him the "old white drunkard," and Minette thought he was perhaps the dirtiest white man in the whole country.

"You're beautiful," he said to her. "I want to paint your portrait."

He took a few halting steps toward her.

"I have no money to pay you, Monsieur," answered Minette, laughing.

"But I've heard you work at the white people's theater."

"Yes, but I earn very little."

"Always the same problem – class exploitation," he spat out, mealy-mouthed, and with the attitude of someone unaware of the importance of his words. "Get what's due to you, my dear, otherwise they'll have you working for free. Myself, I…"

He was about to launch into what was likely a familiar speech when Minette, eager to put an end to these confidences, interrupted him saying:

"Monsieur Perrosier, I'm in a bit of a hurry. I promise I'll come by and knock on your door one of these days."

"Promise?" he insisted.

She laughed again and made a friendly gesture with her hand. She thought he was a nice guy, that scruffy young bohemian tramp. He was of the poor white class, devoid of hatred and envy, with art his unique passion.

For him, the social classes all melted together; they represented, without distinction of blood or wealth, no more than the group of individuals that might pique his interest according to his inspiration of the moment. Thus had he never been able to make his fortune in those five years since a boat from Nantes had off-loaded him in Saint-Domingue. In the beginning, luck had smiled on him. Having learned of his arrival, a M Renodeau came calling to ask that he commit the mawkish blond beauty of his drab and ethereal sixteen-year-old daughter to canvas.

This was an incredible chance for the young painter to establish his reputation. But in the middle of the first sitting, a young slave – dark-skinned and half-naked – came into the room. On noticing her, Perrosier let out a shriek of admiration, put down his brushes and cried:

"My God, she's beautiful – how I'd love to paint her portrait!"

Lady Renodeau, annoyed that someone would admire a slave in her presence, turned her back on the astounded painter, who was immediately escorted out by a black servant. As for the slave girl, she was made to pay for the white painter's ill-placed tribute with twenty-five lashes of the whip.

From then on, Perrosier lived in utter misery. He took to getting drunk, and turned into a wandering painter, sketching the lascivious and sensual silhouettes of the free colored women on the public square for a few coins here and there.

Nicolette, who had in her room several of Perrosier's sketches of her own fiery little being, recounted this story to Minette, telling her that the young painter was a fervent admirer of hers and that he had asked her, Nicolette, to bring Minette to him.

"He swears that you'll be the masterpiece that helps him reestablish his reputation in the country," said the young courtesan.

"He'll be even more reviled – I'm nothing but a poor colored woman."

Minette was still thinking about the painter's story as she arrived at Vallières Square. She raised her eyes to the sky: big, dark clouds were gathering, thinning the air and stirring up great waves of heat. Despite the threat of rain, a small crowd was jostling to cheer on a new group of acrobats who had situated themselves under large tents set up right in the middle of the square. Soldiers on horseback puffed out their chests and waved around their riding crops to attract the attention of the women. Two little white children, shod in worn slippers, held a monkey dressed as a free colored person on a leash, prodding it forward and crying:

"Who wants to see a monkey dance on a tightrope? Fifty shillings, for fifty shillings you can watch this monkey dance on a tightrope."

A horse ridden by a soldier in high boots galloped past the monkey and his trainers and nearly knocked them over.

"Make way, make way, for the King's Bursar," someone shouted.

Minette arrived at the edge of the sea, where the daily flow of sailors, travelling merchants, and prostitutes bustled about. She headed toward the Bel-Air district. Wooden houses, erected between tall posts, stood side by side with their clay roofs and immense galleries. Imported elm trees lined the paved streets and cast little corners of shadow where men looking for a little adventure positioned themselves to watch the women pass by.

A streak of lightning traversed the sky, lighting up the edges of the black clouds like flashes of fire. A terrible crash of thunder resounded and, immediately, fat drops streamed from the sky and chased away the crowd of pedestrians, who raced toward the inns and cabarets for shelter. Minette sped up. It was only seven o'clock and already the streetlamps and the houses were illuminated. In the street, the crowd bustled about in a strange concert of laughter, screams, wheels turning, and the cracking of whips. Spacious homes lined the street on both sides and, right on the corner, she distinctly saw the Marquis de Caradeux's house, fully illuminated by the multiple torches placed along the immense lane. She approached a stone house with a shingled roof, lined with galleries, and knocked on the door. A young slave came to let her in. Minette was astonished by the modest and uncomfortable furnishings that reminded her of the furnishings in her own little house on Traversière Street, revealing her humble, if not to say miserable situation. How could a man as wealthy as M Mesplès live in such a badly furnished home? She had dressed up like an elegant lady to make this visit, planning to fan herself flirtatiously in the middle of an elegant salon as she observed herself in large mirrors, seated in one of the over-stuffed velvet armchairs Nicolette had told her about. The slave bowed low and gestured toward a chair.

"Would it please Madame to sit and repose," he said in impeccable French, only his *r*s somewhat distorted. "Whom shall I announce to my master?"

She smiled. The slave took her for a lady. This was a good sign and she felt flattered. But what name should she give? She thought for a moment and said in flawless French:

"Tell your master that 'Mademoiselle' Minette would like to speak to him."

The slave slipped away and returned almost immediately, bowing this time with more reserve:

"My master will not be able to see you."

"But I must speak to him."

Up until that first obstacle, she had not felt at all nervous. She had thought about her clothes – about the impression her great beauty would make on the white man, about his surprise at her speaking to him without lowering her chin, at her holding his gaze as she had so enjoyed doing for some time when facing her superiors. Yes, she had thought of everything except of Mesplès' refusal to receive her. What could she do to change his mind? She bit her finger in her confusion. The slave leaned toward her.

"There's only one way," he said with a sly smile. "But I warn you, it doesn't always yield good results."

Minette's lip trembled. To use such subterfuge to gain access to the white man and then to play cat-and-mouse with him – a game the Whites found so exciting, apparently, that it led them to grant all sorts of favors. The many stories Nicolette had told her may have seemed shocking before but, now that she would be using them to her own advantage, had become perfectly clear. She looked at the slave. He was still leaning over her and waiting for her response.

"Yes," she at last said softly.

The slave disappeared a second time. This time, Minette's heart was beating so quickly that she could barely catch her breath. The door opened at the other side of the room and the slave called to her: "Come." And when she got there, he pushed her into the bedroom and closed the door behind him.

François Mesplès was in his bathrobe, stretched out on his bed and smoking a pipe. He let her in without saying a word and Minette could look him over at her leisure: a strikingly aquiline nose gave his chubby face an air of incredible brutality. *The face of a parrot*, thought Minette, disgusted. The thin mouth and receding hairline of a thinking man were belied by his prominent belly – the belly of a bon vivant, a big eater and drinker – making clear she was dealing with a devout disciple of Epicurus. As soon as he noticed her, he exclaimed:

"The 'young person'!…So then, you're here to seduce me? I warn you, I've grown tired of all the games you wenches try to play…"

Pronounced in a harsh and indifferent tone, his declaration made Minette's blood run cold. *There's no point with this one*, she said to herself. And she wondered what Nicolette would have done in such a situation, with such a person. For a moment, she regretted not having sought advice before coming and, closing her fan, abandoned her expression of borrowed coquettishness. *I hate him*, she thought to herself. *He's old and ugly and doesn't even seem to find me pretty*. She understood her mistake when, taking a long drag on his pipe, he said to her:

"Come over here. I like your voice, at least. I just can't figure out how a little hussy like you can possibly have a voice like that!"

He knocked out the ashes from the bowl of his pipe into an ashtray on the table near the bed. And as Minette had not moved:

"Come on, get over here. My word, you're quite the little lady. Who bought all those jewels for you, huh, who? I don't know what you all are thinking lately, always trying to imitate white ladies. You copy their gestures like monkeys and you gain nothing from all this frippery. What's the matter – you scared?"

Although she was shaking in his presence and felt humiliated by the scene, she made an effort to speak.

"No, Monsieur," she said. "I'm not scared, but if I've come here, it's merely for the honor of speaking with you."

"Are you playing some kind of game with me, by chance?"

"No, Monsieur. I'd planned to but I couldn't do it. I'm poor and I could never afford a toy as costly as you."

He looked at her, surprised, and spit out – as if he could barely contain himself:

"Is this some sort of joke?"

"No, sir, only those with means have the luxury of joking."

"Well then, shut up and come over here. Oho! You're looking me straight in the eyes – you're a proud one, almost shameless."

He rose, put his hands in his pockets and walked toward her.

"Why have you come here?"

Minette took a deep breath. Whatever happened, she had come to talk and she would speak. He was certainly used to colored courtesans, flattering and hypocritical, speaking to him on their knees. But she would shock him by speaking to him as his equal, without shame, but with all the respect she knew she owed him.

"Monsieur Mesplès…" she began.

He interrupted her.

"If you've come to beg for money from me, you've wasted your time!" he shouted at her.

It was her turn to interrupt:

"Monsieur Mesplès, I've decided to leave the Comédie."

He started in surprise, a gesture which did not escape Minette. She immediately thought to herself: *Ah! You're trembling. You need me for the next opera because the King of England's son is coming. You need me to double your sales but you want me to sing for free.*

"What's this you're telling me?"

"I'm leaving the Comédie, Monsieur, if I'm not given a contract."

"So that's what this is. You've pulled that right out of your bag of tricks. I warned Saint-Martin you'd get uppity."

Anger suffused his face.

"So you want a contract?"

"Yes, sir, what I'm given is barely enough to pay for my costumes."

"Well," he answered, looking at her with disgust. "It's clear you like luxury."

"I'm beginning to appreciate beautiful things, Monsieur, and also to place myself on the same level as the other members of the company I belong to."

"You don't belong to any company!" he shouted at her again. "We allow you to sing – that's all!"

She lost her composure and raised her voice like a willful and spoiled child. *I don't owe this man any respect*, she said to herself. *He wants...* she hesitated *...to exploit me.*

"It's unfair, unfair, unfair!"

She screamed these last words with violence and at the same moment saw a hand reach out and slap her face. He hit her once, twice, three times – so brutally that she began to scream.

"There's your contract. Now get out of here. I've wasted enough time with you. Allowing myself to be tricked by a little slut – me! Me!"

Furious, he was about to strike her again, and she began to run out.

"That's right – get out of here if you don't want me to throttle you, you dirty little Negress!"

The door opened as if to help her escape. When she left the room, she saw that the young slave was holding the doorknob.

"Go," he whispered to her. "Get out of here. He's a monster and might come after you."

As it was pouring rain, she ran to shelter herself under an awning where several others were already huddled. A thin line of blood trickled from her mouth. She wiped it away with her handkerchief and stared at the stain as if trying to understand where it had come from. Blood! Her blood! She had been struck so hard that her mouth had been torn. Why? As she watched the rain come down, she tried to recall the scene. What had she said that had enraged M Mesplès to that point? She could not remember. An immense weariness forced her to lean against the wall. Eight chimes rang out from a nearby church. *Eight o'clock!* she said to herself. Heavy tears welled in her throat, but her pride pushed them back to the point of almost choking her. No, she would not cry, no, no! When the rain stopped, she walked until she reached Vallières Square. Someone ran to catch up with her. It was Goulard.

"Minette!" he called.

She raised her stricken face to him.

"What's happened to you?"

"Oh! Leave me be, just leave me alone. I hate you, I hate you all – you and all your kind!"

A few passersby stopped.

"Shhh!" said Goulard. "Calm yourself. My poor child, how you must be suffering to be saying such things!"

The young man's voice seemed so sincere and compassionate that Minette suddenly threw herself against his comforting shoulder and began to sob. They came from a very deep place, her sobs. They had been stifled for so long that they came out as hiccups, spasmodic and despairing. Goulard led her into a darkened corner, to shield her from the curious passersby.

"My child!"

"Claude, if you only knew…"

"Tell me, if it will make you feel better."

"Monsieur Mesplès!…"

"Him! What did he do?"

He peered anxiously into her face.

"He hit me again, and again, and again – look, my mouth is bloodied. And all because I asked for a contract," she explained feverishly.

"That brute!" he said, relieved that it had not been much worse.

He took her in his arms and lovingly pressed his cheek against hers.

"Promise me one thing, Minette. Let me speak about all of this to Saint-Martin. And above all, with or without a contract, perform the role of Myris. It's the best way to get your revenge."

XII

THE FOLLOWING DAY, Minette, accompanied by Lise, left the house early to go to the Comédie.

"Do you know what Mama said to me this morning?" Lise asked her.

"What did she say?"

"That the white people's theater has stolen her little girls from her and that she doesn't recognize you anymore."

"I'm growing up, that's all."

"No, Minette, you've really changed."

"But you've changed, too. I'm telling you, we're just getting older…"

"Do you remember all our plans, our marvelous plans?"

"Ah, yes! To ride in a carriage on the arm of a handsome white man, wearing expensive dresses and jewels!"

"You've already got the jewelry and the dresses…"

"My jewels are fake, you know that perfectly well; and as for my dresses, I buy them for the stage."

"How I'd love to do the same," Lise sighed longingly.

As they spoke, they arrived at the theater. The whole company was there, aside from Mme Tesseyre and her daughter Rose. Goulard had probably let Saint-Martin know about the incident that had transpired the evening prior between Minette and Mesplès, for he ran over to greet her. Taking her face in his hands, he looked her over carefully, like a true artist fearing some alteration to a beloved work of art.

"Thank God," he began, "he seems not to have left a mark…"

With a quick movement of her head, Minette gestured toward Lise.

"I'd rather speak to you privately, if you don't mind, Monsieur."

She left Lise with Mme Acquaire, who sat down immediately at the piano to begin a lesson with the young girl. Once they were alone, Saint-Martin said to Minette:

"We were wrong to encourage you to go to that man's house. Goulard told me everything, and he's right that things could have been much worse. In any case, Monsieur Mesplès behaved like an absolute brute. And so, with the support of the entire company, I've decided to make things right for you. You'll sign a private contract allotting you eight thousand pounds as an annual fee and acknowledging that the Comédie owes you for the past two years, during which you've performed non-stop. How does that sound?"

"Oh, Monsieur Saint-Martin!"

"Whatever the gazette says about you, you are a part of this company. I'm sure certain obstacles will arise down the line, but we're here to help you surmount them when they do."

"Thank you, thank you, Monsieur."

The offer was too generous. Not one of the actors there believed it to be sincere. But Minette was overcome with joy.

What a consolation after the previous day's horrific disappointment! Life was good and fair after all. After her suffering, this was just the balm she needed to heal her wounds. She was going to sign a contract – to be on equal footing with the other artists, and even be compensated for her two years of work! Oh, how wonderful it would be to look M Mesplès in the eyes and see him defeated! The director and all the performers in the company were protecting her. What did it matter that it was their own self-interest that had pushed them to support her, as long as they agreed to her terms and respected her. They had been wonderful to her, and Goulard had shown himself to be a charming and selfless suitor. All these thoughts moved her so greatly that she grabbed Saint-Martin's hand and pressed her lips to it.

"I'll never forget this, Monsieur."

He caressed her face.

"You're sweet. Come, let's sign that contract."

Giddy with joy, Goulard placed it before her.

A rush of blood flooded her cheeks! She was ashamed of her name: Minette – "Kitten"! What had her mother been thinking to choose such a name! It screamed her social status. It was banal, stupid, without personality. It did not suit her at all, she realized. As a little girl, she had suffered when the children in the neighborhood, crouched in shadowy corners, would meow at her as she passed by. And now, this was the name she was going to use to sign that contract. How he would laugh, that M Mesplès, when he saw it! Ah! A curse on that white man, her father, who had brought her into this world and abandoned her with nothing.

"Go ahead and sign it, my dear!"

She raised her eyes to Goulard. Emboldened by the affection in his gaze, she signed.

"A final bit of good news," announced Saint-Martin, clapping his hands together. "I've decided that profits from the next performance will go to Minette....And now, let's not lose any more time. Madame Acquaire, will you begin rehearsals? Depoix and Fayart, to your instruments. Macarty, your flute – look, it's over there in the dust. You're going to end up with a rash!"

Macarty, ever the comedian, picked up his flute with a grimace so horrifying that Magdeleine Brousse swore she was about to faint, which of course made him do it all over again – this time right under the nose of the beautiful actress who, instead of passing out, gave him a kiss and ran off.

"Hey, Magdeleine – you aren't going to rehearse your part?" shouted Saint-Martin.

"I'd love to, my dear handsome director, but an actress also has the right to her little romantic trysts, no?"

"No, I'm not denying that, certainly. But you'll go to your rendezvous after the performance!"

Disobedient, she immediately slipped away, while Saint-Martin shook his head indulgently, as if to say she was completely crazy.

Leaning on the piano, Goulard ran lines with Minette, and when it was her turn to sing, Mme Acquaire turned the piano over to the orchestra's pianist, who had just arrived, late and completely out of breath. She was meant to sing a duo with her husband and, observing her, Minette could see clearly how much she loved her profession.

After the rehearsal, as Macarty expressed his concern about the absence of Mme Tessyre and her daughter, Saint-Martin told them that Rose had fallen ill and that they would all go together to check in on her.

"Before we leave to see the little one," he added, "I'd like to speak to you all about a project I've sworn to see through."

"Boom, boom," interrupted Nelanger, plucking his guitar.

"Silence!" shouted M Acquaire, his eye twitching…

"You," interrupted Mme Acquaire, addressing her husband, "you're taking this twitching business a little far. I was watching you as you were singing and you'd completely forgotten about your tic."

"Yes, I know. I had it hidden in my pocket."

Everyone began laughing.

"Well, turn the key on that pocket of yours."

"Sure thing, my little turtledove. And I'll only open it when we're alone."

"Silence!" shouted Saint-Martin this time.

They all stifled their laughter with some difficulty.

"And so," said Durand, "what about this project?"

"Here it is. You all know that I've been in preliminary talks with the former director of the Saint-Marc Theater, for which I hope soon to become the agent. My dream is to run the theaters in every city in Saint-Domingue…"

"Bravo, bravo!" screamed Macarty, doing a little pirouette.

"After Saint-Marc, Les Cayes. In fact, we'll soonstage a performance in Les Cayes, for which I plan to bring Lise."

"But, Monsieur!"

"Yes, you. You have a lovely voice. Didn't you know that?"

"No, Monsieur."

"Well then – now you do, little chickadee," he said, pinching her cheek.

Overcome with joy, Lise ran to Minette.

"Did you hear that? Did you hear?"

"Well, aren't you happy," Minette replied, hugging her sister. "Have you thought to thank our director?"

"No, not yet."

"Well go ahead, then."

She ran to Saint-Martin and, in her excitement, flung her arms around his neck.

Saint-Martin smiled and looked at Magdeleine Brousse, who was just coming back. Jealous, she thumbed her nose at him.

"Oh, come on now. She's just a child!"

He caught up to Goulard and, as he headed toward the exit, said to him:

"I love that kind of woman. Full of spontaneity and precocious charm. Honestly, I don't see how a man can have any taste for white women once he's held one of those girls in his arms…"

Goulard interrupted him, placing his hand gently on his shoulder:

"You were too generous with Minette. You won't keep your promises."

Saint-Martin protested:

"Who do you take me for? This very evening I'm going to try to win the money I owe her. I adore those girls…"

"You appreciate them with your 'senses.'"

"And that's the best way, trust me. Besides, what's love if not a game of the senses?"

"What about the heart?"

"But the heart itself is a sense. The proof is the way it behaves when it's in love."

Goulard burst into laughter, but became serious again just as quickly.

"Listen, François. I've wanted to talk to you about this for some time now. In all of your big projects, what do you plan to do with Zabeth and your kids?"

Saint-Martin looked at Goulard as if seeking to read his thoughts.

"You don't think I'd ever leave them to starve, do you?"

"I do."

"Surely not! That's rather harsh. You could be a little gentler, you know."

"You're capable of incredible acts of generosity and of the cruelest selfishness. I'm younger than you, dear friend, but I've watched you over the past six years, don't forget. For you, Zabeth is the slave you managed to buy yourself and who you ended up sleeping with. But now there are those kids."

They had been speaking while walking at a certain distance from the actors, who followed behind. When they stopped to wait for the others, Saint-Martin nodded his chin toward Minette and said to Goulard:

"You love that girl, don't you?"

"Yes. And if there weren't some stupid law forbidding marriage between Whites and people of color, I'd marry her."

"Write to the King of France."

"You're making fun of me."

"I don't mean any harm, you know that."

They arrived at Mme Tessyre's home on the Islet of the Comédie – a modest, shabbily furnished room that she shared with her daughter. They could not all enter at the same time, so only Macarty and Magdeleine Brousse went inside. They knocked on the door as the others went back down to the courtyard. Mme Tessyre came to open the door and gestured silently toward little Rose, who – burning with fever – whimpered in her sleep. Magdeleine bent over the bed, took the little girl's hand and called her name.

"How deeply she sleeps!" said the actress, worried.

"No, she isn't sleeping," responded her mother. "She's been in that state for the past four hours."

"And you haven't called a doctor?"

"Yes. But he wasn't able to come. He's too busy. Look."

She opened the window and Macarty and Magdeleine leaned out.

"There he is, the doctor, fighting since this morning to keep three little children alive. Apparently there's an epidemic."

"But surely he's not the only doctor," suggested Macarty.

"He's the only one I know of."

At that very moment, a very thin Negro woman entered, dressed in a work shirt. She had a full cup of yellowish herbal tea in her hand, and handed it to Mme Tessyre.

"Here, Lady Tessyre," she said in Creole. "Have her drink this. It's good for fever."

"Thank you, Mélinise."

She took the cup from the Negro woman's hands and placed it on the table.

"You called me very late," said the woman reproachfully, leaning over Rose.

She raised the little girl's eyelids and, leaning farther forward, smelled her breath.

"Give her the 'tea,'" she suggested, "and then call the doctor."

She was about to leave when a series of heartrending cries filled the room.

"My Lord God," she said, making the sign of the cross. "Death has come to our neighborhood."

She left quickly, followed by Magdeleine Brousse, who raced down the stairs. She passed by the other actors and nearly knocked them down in her hurry.

"Hey!" shouted Durand. "What's going on? What are those screams?"

She made a vague gesture with her hand and ran to find the doctor, who had just come out of a neighboring house. When she came back with him, the little Tessyre girl had just opened her eyes. A blackish foam dribbled from either side of her mouth. Her tongue was protruded, dry and swollen.

"She's thirsty," said the doctor. "Give her something to drink."

Mme Tessyre took the cup of tea from the table.

"What is that?" he asked.

"An herbal infusion prepared by one of the Negro women in the neighborhood."

He looked at it suspiciously then brought the cup to his nostrils.

"Sometimes these remedies are just what's needed. Those people often know better than we doctors how to treat certain diseases in this country…Give her the tea."

Mme Tessyre placed her arm around the child's neck and, raising her head, poured a few drops into her mouth.

The doctor kneeled down at the girl's bedside and took her pulse while examining her nails. He nodded his head.

As soon as she'd drunk the tea, the child threw it back up with a painful retching. A fetid odor immediately suffused the little room. The doctor leaned over her. He raised her eyelids just as the Negro woman had done. The skin on the girl's face, so pale just minutes before, had taken on a yellowish color. Her mouth tensed and became difficult to open.

"This is the end," whispered the doctor, leaning toward Macarty. "I've come too late."

Suddenly, he let go of the little hand he had been holding in his own and looked at Mme Tessyre.

"Doctor," whispered Magdeleine Brousse, suddenly overcome, "she isn't breathing anymore."

As if he'd been waiting to hear that in order to act, the doctor began to pull the sheet, slowly, very slowly, over the little girl. She had died.

Immediately, Mme Tessyre threw herself on the bed and began to scream. And Magdeleine Brousse, weeping, could not keep her from taking the dead child in her arms and rocking her as she cried out her name. Macarty was crying too. He had seen little Rose's progress at the

Comédie; he had watched her grow up. Like all the actors, she was part of the company – and for four years she had charmed them with her grace and talent.

On hearing Mme Tessyre's cries, the actors – François Saint-Martin at the head – ran to knock on the door.

"Are you all crazy?" screamed Macarty, sticking his head out the half-open door. "One person, only one, can enter at a time. You, François, come."

And then, looking at the others:

"The little one is dead."

As Saint-Martin entered, the doctor, picking up his hat, prepared himself to leave. Macarty leaned toward him and pointed at the body.

"Doctor," he asked, "what did the poor child die of?"

"Fever. Always the fever. I've logged more than a hundred cases this month alone. Only Whites. Comfort her mother. Farewell, good people."

Mme Tessyre, on her knees by the bed, wept and called out her daughter's name. Saint-Martin had his arm around her shoulder. She raised her head.

"François, François, my poor little girl. You remember how she loved to dance? You remember how graceful she was? How will I go on without her? What will I do?"

Saint-Martin wiped his tears, then called Magdeleine Brousse to Mme Tessyre's side.

"Stay with her. We'll take up a collection to buy the coffin and have a vault made for the child."

The burial took place the day after, but without Magdeleine Brousse. She was still keeping the girl's distraught mother company. Macarty and Saint-Martin carried the coffin, followed by the other actors, the musicians from the orchestra who had known Rose, the stagehands, the set designer Jean Peyret, and the mason. They passed by the Whites-only cemetery with seeming indifference, and after a great distance arrived at an out-of-the-way corner where they had all buried their dead. Goulard was walking next to Minette, when suddenly a horseman arrived at a furious pace and pulled so sharply on the reins that his horse bucked into the air and spun around on its back hooves before coming to a stop. It was Jean Lapointe, in a straw hat with his shirt open at the neck. Bold, handsome, with fire in his eyes and nervously holding his crop, he watched the funeral procession file by. He waved, abruptly removing his wide straw hat. He had the same harsh little sneer that tightened the corners of his lips. But when he noticed Minette, he shuddered, the arch of his eyebrows lifted, betraying his surprise, and his lips formed a brief smile. He spurred his horse on, then directed it toward a house built at the very back of an immense property and disappeared. Minette recognized him. She had noticed his surprise and his smile. It was the third time he had smiled at her, though he seemed rather sparing with them, with his usual serious and cynical expression. Minette's heart had beaten faster upon noticing the handsome horseman and, seeing her reaction, Goulard said:

"What's going on? You seem scared."

There was no need for her to respond: the rider had disappeared and they had all arrived at the grave site. A few hundred modest gravestones stood facing the place where Lapointe had just disappeared. The mason set up his equipment on the ground and, picking up his pickaxe, dug the hole into which they lowered the little coffin. The bell of a neighboring church, as if to avenge the injustice done to the innocent artist, began to peal. It was eight in the morning and mass had just ended. In that moment, everyone remembered the night when a defiant Saint-Martin had forced open the door of the church and climbed up to the bell tower to sound the knell for the young Morange girl on her death, something the clergy had denied her. He was also the one who asked Minette to sing for Rose Tessyre.

"That will be her burial mass," he said, with a heartbreaking smile.

Minette took Lise's hand and took a step forward toward the gravestone the mason had just placed. They sang a Creole lullaby, infinitely sad and nostalgic – a lullaby that their mother had taught them and that ended with the words: "Sleep, sleep, little one, close your eyes." The whole group wept and Saint-Martin etched the name of little Rose, eight years old, into the stone.

The makeshift cemetery was located outside the town, just behind the Governor's palace and next to the house Lapointe had entered. As the actors headed for the exit, a woman dressed in a horse-riding dress passed by on a chestnut-colored horse before entering into that same house.

"There goes Louise Rasteau," said Durand. "How I love seeing her on a horse!"

Minette had also recognized her. She remembered the day she had met her at Lambert's house and the distrustful way the woman had looked her over. Lapointe at Louise Rasteau's house! Louise Rasteau a friend of the Lamberts! The Lamberts, what had they said when she had spoken of the person she suspected of killing the sailor? Had they not cried: "It's him! It's him!" And had they not danced with joy afterward? So it was Lapointe, then? All these ideas came crashing together in her head and she was so concentrated on trying to understand them that she almost let herself be knocked down by a carriage rushing by at top speed. Goulard grabbed her by the arm, calling her imprudent.

Driven by a Negro, the carriage sped past the actors toward Louise Rasteau's house. Three men got out and headed quickly inside the house. Of the three men, two were black and the other a young *griffe* who Minette and Lise recognized as Joseph Ogé.

"Joseph!" cried Lise, surprised.

Her sister covered her mouth imperiously.

"Shh! You didn't recognize him."

"But why? I recognized him perfectly well. It was Joseph."

"Be quiet, you little fool, and stop shouting out his name."

The carriage left the courtyard, again passed by the group of actors, and disappeared in a cloud of dust in the direction leading away from the town. At that same moment, a gold-fringed coach, trimmed with crimson, came out onto the opposite street and drove slowly in front of Louise Rasteau's home. A broad-shouldered Negro, about twenty years old, was driving.

"Hey there, stop!" shouted a voice from inside the coach.

The door opened slightly and a white man's head appeared. He was young-looking, with a thin nose and aristocratic mouth. Noticing the actors, the white man gestured with his hand.

"Hey, you over there! Did you see a carriage pass this way?"

Minette had the impression she had seen that face before.

"Who's he talking to?" asked Macarty, looking suspiciously toward the coach.

"Let's just play deaf," suggested Mme Acquaire.

"And blind," added M Acquaire, twitching in the direction of the planter.

"Did you hear me, you all? Did you see any runaway slaves around here?"

Everyone looked around stupidly, shrugging their shoulders as if to say: "What's that planter going on about?"

For her part, Minette was observing the coachman. His eyes were fixed on her and his hands trembled horribly as they held the reins.

"Hold on, you there, young lady – looking at my driver. Come over here and tell me what you know. I'll make it worth your while."

Minette was still looking at the driver. Where had she seen that face before? She was turning it over in her memory, trying to recall, when she felt as if the man was making a subtle sign with his hand. The index finger of his right hand, which was holding the reins, was bent like a hook, and moved rhythmically as if to call her over, as he held her gaze with his own. Minette suddenly remembered a young slave, held on a leash, his back bloodied. A planter, the very same one seated in the coach, had been striking him in the face with a long strap: it was M de Caradeux and his slave – that rebel slave that he had not gone so far as to kill because he was so handsome and strong. That purebred Senega-lese slave, his pride and joy, sitting high up in the seat of his magnificent coach, whom he had beaten relentlessly the day he tried to escape and whom he had imprudently kept in his service as a domestic – ah! how blinded he was by his disdain! For his master, the slave was merely a handsome animal without the capacity for imagination or reflection – a handsome creature that could be subdued just as one tamed a wild horse.

Had Saint-Martin gotten wind of the coachman's ruse or did he fear Minette might respond thoughtlessly to the planter? He rushed toward Minette and took her arm.

"We don't get involved in politics, Minette. We're artists, nothing but artists – don't forget that," he whispered to her.

"I haven't forgotten, Monsieur."

"Well then, come along."

She wrested her arm out of Saint-Martin's grasp and tried to meet the coachman's eyes. He had lowered his head and looked down stupidly.

The planter became impatient. He swung the door open wide. "This house may be under suspicion," thought Minette to herself. "We've got to get this coach away from here." As if to prove her point, Goulard whispered to Depoix:

"The slaves he's looking for were surely brought to this house just a few minutes ago. But this isn't our concern."

Yes, but it was Minette's concern. She remembered Zoé, Jean-Pierre, and Joseph! To hell with the actors' indifference! She was the daughter of a former slave and what they would never understand was up to her, Minette, to understand. M de Caradeux, in looking at her more closely, had in fact just realized who she was and exclaimed:

"Well, well – you're the 'young person'! In the flesh! Why are you refusing to speak?"

He was becoming agitated and his expression changed.

"Come, come, young lady. Leave your friends here and come with me. You won't regret it."

All of them looked at her. Oh! Such apprehension in Goulard's eyes! With an attitude of silent disgust, Saint-Martin looked at her as if to say: "Well, go ahead, then. You're just like the rest of them. You all end up doing the same thing."

The coachman's finger again began to stir deceitfully to call her over, but he kept his head lowered and his eyes bore no expression.

She turned toward Goulard with sudden resolve.

"I'm leaving my sister in your care, Claude. Be a dear and bring her back home."

Then, looking at the others:

"Please excuse me…I've waited for this moment for so long – to ride in a coach on the arm of a handsome white man. Don't you remember, Lise?"

And with that, she left the group, went up to the coach, put her hand in that of the planter and climbed into the carriage. The planter issued a brief command to his coachman.

"Minette!" screamed Lise.

The carriage advanced slowly for several minutes. Minette, emotional, looked around at the silk cushions, the gold handles, and the dusty embroidered rugs. Suddenly, the planter seized her arm and began to massage it.

"I've heard you sing. Who doesn't go to the Comédie to hear you sing? My niece herself!…Ah! How lovely you are! And young! How old are you?"

"Sixteen, Monsieur."

"I'd have bet on it! I love little green fruits – still slightly bitter. In my book, a twenty-five-year-old woman is already an old lady. It's what I've been trying to explain to that sanctimonious niece of mine, who keeps her little maids off-limits like a bunch of saints…Ah!"

He took Minette in his arms and nibbled at her cheek.

"Ah! My little dumpling! We're going to have some fun together!"

He was getting excited and his hands wandered toward the décolleté of her blouse, squeezed her curved and narrow waist, and began trying to raise her skirts.

"Are you scared? That must mean you're a virgin. If you are, I'll pay you handsomely. My Lord, she's beautiful! I've had an army of little wenches in my lifetime, believe me, but not one of them was as beautiful as you are. You see, I play fair and I never undervalue the merchandise."

Minette's face flushed. She tried to push away his too-aggressive hands, squeezing herself as far as possible into the corner.

"Monsieur, Monsieur!…"

When will this coach ever stop? she thought to herself. *When can I get away from this man?* For what seemed like an eternity, she was forced to tolerate the impertinent caresses of the planter, as if outside her own body. Finally, the coach came to a stop.

"We're here. Come with me."

His tone left no room for discussion. He turned his head to shout a new order to the driver. Minette, taking advantage of his momentary inattention, opened the door and jumped onto the street.

"Wait, wait…Ah! You little bitch," he shouted after her, "you'll pay for this!"

Afraid of being seen in public running after the colored girl, he let her go. Minette looked at the driver. He was still seated, back straight, on his bench.

"Drive into the courtyard," shouted the planter.

At that very moment, the slave raised his hands as if to let go of the reins and a ball of rolled-up paper hit Minette in the shoulder and fell at her feet. For a brief second, her eyes met those of the driver, who whipped the horses and made them turn into the long driveway. Minette bent down and picked up the paper. Unfolding it, she read the following words, written in an unpracticed hand:

Warn Lambert. They suspect his house.

He wanted to get a message to Lambert. But why had he chosen her – her! – for such a delicate mission? As she walked toward Zoé's house, she thought back to the scene during which the young slave – bleeding, dragged like an animal – had tried to break through his chains when he saw Joseph. Joseph – that was it! He knew him and had seen him at Minette's house. She understood everything now. But my God, my Lord, why did she have to be mixed up in all of this? Why could everyone not just let her be? She was only sixteen. And then, as Saint-Martin had said to her, artists should live for their art alone. But while she was having all of these thoughts, she nevertheless had tucked away the note safely in her bodice and hurried her step. In her haste, she bumped into a young mulatto girl who nearly lost her shawl. A vulgar swear word followed by an exclamation of surprise escaped the girl's lips. It was Nicolette, in a pick taffeta dress and shawl.

"What are you doing here, by yourself?"

She burst out laughing.

"I bet you were meeting someone."

A six-horse carriage passed by, stirring up a cloud of dust. Nicolette pointed at a cabaret where a smiling and bloated Negro carrying a tray loaded with glasses was painted on the shop front.

"Let's go to Big Poppa's, and I'll treat you to one of those coconut liqueurs…"

"No, no," answered Minette.

"Come on, we can catch up. I've got tons of stories for you."

She spoke loudly and in Creole. Minette felt a bit embarrassed.

"Nicolette, I'll see you tonight, I promise, but not now, not now, I can't."

"So that's it, you're meeting someone? What a story, my friends! All right, I'll see you later, my dear."

Once again, she burst into laughter and then left with a gentle sway of the head and hips.

Minette nearly ran to the street where the Lambert's house stood. Somewhere in the neighborhood by the seaside, she remembered it well. After much hesitation, she finally recognized the dirty little house – the house where people like her lived, without money, without slaves. She ran over and pushed the door open. This time, it seemed to be blocked from the inside, but the sound of chairs being moved let her know that someone was coming to let her in. It was Zoé herself.

"Minette," she exclaimed, "I'm so happy to see you!"

"Where's your brother, Zoé?"

Zoé suddenly looked at her attentively.

"Why?"

Minette hastily pulled the note out of her bodice and handed it to Zoé who, after reading it, seized her hand and brought her inside. The old man and woman rocked silently in their rocking chairs. Respectfully, Minette went to greet them.

"Hello, Mama, hello Papa," she said.

"Hello, daughter," they answered.

Jean-Pierre Lambert was in his carpenter's workshop. He had a hammer in his hand and was getting ready to nail some planks together when Minette and Zoé arrived. The workshop was a narrow room, a sort of shed with a broken-down roof where planks, furniture in need of repair, and all sorts of woodworking tools had been piled together.

"Jean-Pierre!" called Zoé.

She handed him the note Minette had brought.

He read it over, frowned and said:

"Who gave you this message?"

"A young coachman."

"Do you know his name?"

Minette shook her head.

"What did he look like?" continued Lambert.

"Very tall, very strong."

"It's Samuel," he said simply. "That man is gifted with an unparalleled intellect and Monsieur de Caradeux should watch out."

He looked at Zoé.

"You see," he added. "I'm speaking freely in front of your friend. I trust my gut with her."

Zoé put a hand on Minette's shoulder as a response.

"Have I ever been wrong, Jean-Pierre?"

"You haven't, I'll admit it."

"I'm blessed with a sixth sense, you've said it yourself. But according to our father, it's this 'lucky charm' that makes me 'gifted.'"

And she pulled from underneath her skirt a minuscule black bag sewn together at the four corners.

She regained her tragic air and fixed Lambert with her strangely gleaming eyes. Lambert read over the note again.

"I'm not worried," he said. "I'm strong, too, and I've taken precautions. Let them come, the police, I dare them..."

The door to the workshop opened abruptly and a man entered. It was Beauvais, Lambert's friend. He was the legitimate son of a white man and a Mulatress and had skin as fair as Minette's, silky curls, and a round mouth, stubborn and tight. He was wearing white linen breeches and a straw hat.

"Look what this young girl has brought me," Lambert said to him, holding out the note. "For the moment, I'm not worried at all. The last ones I hid are already at Louise's place and they'll soon head for the mountains. What do you think Louis?"

Beauvais put his chin in his hand with a familiar gesture.

"What do I think? Well! You're not taking enough precautions. I've always said that. More than ever before, our young colored brothers in the constabulary, prodded by the compensation the Whites are offering them, are being particularly zealous. I'd recommend prudence, extreme prudence."

He spoke the perfect French of students trained in schools in

France. He had spent his youth there. Lambert shook his head as if to say to his friend that sometimes boldness was called for and that he did not like to hesitate before acting.

Beauvais turned toward Lambert and, indicating Minette:

"Who's she?" he asked.

Zoé was the one to respond.

"A young colored girl who's been breaking the law."

"How's that?"

"She sings at the Comédie."

"Ah! She's the one!..."

Beauvais looked at Minette for a long time. From head to toe, she thought, without admiration and without particular interest – simply with indifference mixed with a kind of psychological curiosity. When he looked at you it was as if he took no note of the physical but saw instead what was hidden inside – that which, according to him, the eyes or the mouth could dissimulate. So his prolonged visual interrogation was generally somewhat unnerving for whoever was being made to sustain his probing gaze, so dark, impenetrable, and cold. *What a difference,* said Minette to herself, *between Lambert and Beauvais! The one is disconcerting, and seems to turn over ideas in his head a hundred times before expressing them; the other is all fire, spontaneity, and rashness.*

As she sustained Beauvais' gaze with a boldness he found greatly amusing, she took note of the fact that he, too, had heard of her – that no matter what, she was something of a celebrity. These ideas went to her head like clouds of incense. Her pride and her youthful vanity had found a perfect pretext for their expression. Among these thousands of people of color – bullied, humiliated – she had carved out a path for herself. She had been chosen by destiny to represent them in the world of the Whites, and to prove through her talent that their so-despised race had produced exceptional beings. A white public had put her on a pedestal, and from that pedestal she looked down and saw everything unmasked. And what she saw was horrific. It was a shame. How lovely it would be to be rich, celebrated, adored, without regret. She sighed without lowering her eyes from Beauvais' gaze. He smiled. Decidedly, she had a gift for pulling smiles from the most strained lips.

"What a strange little woman!" said Beauvais.

And then, planting himself right in front of her:

"Have you ever lowered your eyes before anyone?" he asked her.

"Never, Monsieur, not even before a white man."

"Not even, huh!"

He laughed. Lambert made a sign to Zoé, who immediately left with Minette. The two men stayed there alone.

XIII

THE BIG DAY had arrived. The preparations had been completed since the previous night. Enormous sums had been spent on the sets and the costumes. Saint-Martin, lacking funds, had been obliged to appeal to the Governor's generosity. The seats and benches of the theater had been completely restored; the whole place had been repainted. Everything was sparkling clean, from the orchestra to the upper tiers. Minette's dress, in white velvet embroidered with gold, was laid out on her bed. The ship carrying Prince William was expected since that morning. The Governor, dressed in velvet, and shod in gold-buckled shoes, inspected the soldiers-in-arms who were lined up to welcome his illustrious personage with great fanfare.

A colorful crowd invaded the square, flowered, bewigged, gloved, and bustling. Also since that morning, people had been passing by Jasmine's home to admire Minette's costume. "Lord, she'll be beautiful!" people exclaimed. "Lord! She's so lucky – to sing for a prince at the Whites' theater!"

A few ladies in the neighborhood enthusiastically called Jasmine into the corner to give her a few *makandals* or *simples* to bring her luck, enjoining her to have Minette wear them. Torn between her superstitions and her desire to follow the advice of the old Jesuit priest who had taken her in, dying of starvation, with her daughters, on the day she had left the plantation of her dead master, Jasmine hid them in a drawer, not daring to get rid of them. She had never been so happy before. As people came by to congratulate her, they spoke of her daughter as a separate being, thus making clear to her that she now had to resign herself to Minette's ascent – that all future happiness would come from Minette and that she should show her daughter great respect, venerate her like a goddess. Immediately, she would change tactics. Everything Minette said, everything she did was to be accepted without contradiction. If she had been able to rise so high, it was because she had been born with a blessing that put her above her peers. She would be the source of money, of joy, and of respect from the Whites. She was the fortunate one and, in the same way one respected a plant or a good luck charm, Jasmine and the people of the neighborhood now saw her as something of a sacred being. Scipion brought her flowers and kneeled to kiss her hand and the hem of her dress. She received fruits from the neighbors, jams and jellies from little girls, and small plates of food from grandmothers. Strangely, no one was jealous of her talent and her success. She was the one the gods had chosen to bring honor to them all and they would cheer for her at the theater with as much pride as Jasmine herself.

Little Pitchoun came over early that day. He was wearing shoes and his curls were well tamed. He took Minette to the side and brought her to the outer courtyard under a male orange tree, strong and heavy with scent. He pulled a little metal object out of his pocket and handed it to the young girl.

"Here," he said. "It's a ring. I made it for you."

It was a little pewter circle decorated with flowerets along the exterior. Minette put it on her finger and kissed the boy to thank him. He was three years younger than she but it did not seem so, given how tall and well built he was.

He ran quickly away after promising her that he would be at the theater that evening with his mother and that he would applaud her till his fingers broke.

"See you tonight, Minette," he cried from the street. "Don't forget to look up toward our seats. I'll be there with my mother."

Minette turned the ring around her finger.

"Thank you for the ring, Pitchoun," she answered.

When the cannon announced the arrival of the boat in the harbor, she could not run down to the square with Lise, for Mme and M Acquaire had just arrived in a state of nervous agitation.

"Don't go into the sun this morning, my dear. You'll tire yourself out," advised the Creole woman. "Stay in bed for a bit, stay in bed."

"Remember," added M Acquaire, "you're performing for His Royal Highness tonight, Prince William, Duke of Lancaster!"

Jasmine clasped her hands together and ran to arrange the pillow under her daughter's head. Minette let out a little sigh of annoyance.

For the past two days, she had heard no news from Joseph. At noon, she had not been able to eat anything, despite the parade of appetizing little dishes that had been offered to her by the neighborhood women.

"Look at the marinades that 'Gratine' Rosa sent you!" said her mother.

"And this grenadine jelly," offered Lise, tasting all the dishes greedily.

Nicolette also came by to admire Minette's costume. She had brought along Kiss-Me-Lips, who tapped her pink slippers with the tip of her fringed parasol, just like a European lady.

"Lord, aren't you chic!" exclaimed Lise, clapping her hands. "Look, Minette, I want a parasol just like the one Kiss-Me-Lips has. Please, Minette..."

And as her sister had no response:

"Well, anyway, since I'm going to be working soon, I'll buy that parasol myself."

"Is that true?" asked Nicolette, curious.

"Soon I'll be going with Monsieur Saint-Martin to Les Cayes, where I'll make my stage debut."

"Les Cayes?" repeated Kiss-Me-Lips. "My children, your navels were surely cut with golden scissors. I've never seen such good fortune!"

They went on to admire Minette's Myris costume, which they found dazzling, and then ran off when the cannon exploded a second time. Prince William had just arrived. The whole wealthy white population of the island had risen to its feet. The planters surrounded the Governor and the other representatives of the government. The Marquis de Caradeux, having returned from his property, had spent the whole night traveling in the hopes of meeting the Prince. He had practically forced his daughter Céliane, who secretly harbored an inclination for a religious life, to join him. For the moment, she stayed close to him in her white dress and looked like a schoolgirl with her high collar and long sleeves.

The Marquis of Caradeux was popular among the planters. Very wealthy, he had more than three hundred slaves in his workhouses and, on his magnificent Bel-Air dwelling, more than fifty domestic slaves cluttered the immense dining room during receptions. A brash politician, he was the leader of an ostensibly high society club where the richest and the most subversive planters gathered. The club overtly flaunted its antipathy for the government and its desire to undermine its authority. The idea of separatism had even taken shape in some of the more daring minds – those who, to fortify their audacious plans for revolt, invoked the Boston Massacre, still fresh in everyone's minds.

The Marquis de Caradeux smiled at the Governor, however, as he shook his hand, each man well aware of where he stood with respect to the other, despite this outward show of goodwill. The new Governor knew that, on several occasions already, the planters in the club had written to the Metropolis to complain about him. Both of them men of the world, the Marquis de Caradeux and the Governor smiled despite their mutual hatred. Governors had been revoked and replaced too often. Sometimes, too, tired of the depressing atmosphere of petty plotting, they decommissioned and left for the Metropolis, loudly denouncing the planters as outcasts and anarchists. The King's Bursar made a point to cry far and wide such evidence of ineptitude and, in long letters addressed to the powers-that-be, proclaimed the incompetency of these governors faced with the hostility of the planters.

However, for the moment, each one made an effort to put his personal grievances aside. The point was to greet the King of England in the most pompous and entertaining possible manner. An entire program had been laid out: dinners, theater, fireworks, musical fanfare, music-hall revue. As the cannon and the bells mingled their bass and light soprano voices, the clergy – in their holiday cassocks – and the wealthiest of the island's population advanced toward the illustrious visitor. The Marquis de Caradeux offered his daughter his arm and, as she curtsied, bowed and said:

"Monseigneur, I hope you will honor my home with your presence. May I count on you for tomorrow evening…"

The King's Bursar interrupted him, shouting:

"Long live His Majesty the King of England and long live the King of France!"

The crowd repeated after him and they all headed toward the government palace where cool drinks were being served. Young and handsome, Prince William seemed to be enjoying himself. He looked around, bewitched by the skies the color of faded indigo, the trees with their persistent perfumes, leaves rustled by the warm winds, the flowery and heavily made-up Mulatresses, the white women in their crinoline skirts, the shirtless slaves, and the Negresses with their sparkling smiles and provocative hips.

Lise and Pitchoun had run into Kiss-Me-Lips and Nicolette on the square. Pressed up against the young courtesans, they watched – awestruck – as the procession went by. Hearing all the fanfare, Pitchoun was unable to control himself and began marching in step, his wooden sword on his shoulder.

"Look at Mademoiselle de Caradeux," said Kiss-Me-Lips to Nicolette. "She looks like a martyr."

"She's lovely," said Pitchoun, "but sad."

"But why? After all, she's rich," noted Lise.

During this time, Minette, lying on a mat that Jasmine had spread out for her in the tiny courtyard, under the orange tree, was thinking about Joseph. A half hour after Lise had gone, she stood up, dressed herself and said to Jasmine:

"Mama, I won't be able to sing tonight unless I know what's happened to Joseph."

"Where are you going, my child?" her mother asked.

"To Labadie's."

"Go on," was all Jasmine said, every day less able to control her eldest daughter.

Minette found the old man in his garden, reading a book of ancient history.

"Hello, Professor," she said.

"Hello, my child. But why do you so insist on giving me a title?" he added, looking at Minette curiously. "Surely it must be a bit troubling for a young girl like you to call an old man like me by his first name. But why don't you call me 'Papa' or 'Uncle,' as is the custom among our people."

Minette shook her head stubbornly.

"You're a great scholar."

"I've studied a lot, but have no title."

"If it weren't for the injustice of our condition, you'd be a doctor, a physicist, an astronomer – Joseph told me."

"But I'm all of that because I studied. What does it matter if I'm called 'Papa' or 'Uncle.'"

He took Minette by the shoulders, adjusted his glasses, and looked at her affectionately.

"You've said some astonishing things," he concluded. "And since

I'm a bit of a soothsayer, I'll guess why you've come here this morning. You want to know about Joseph, don't you?"

"Yes, Professor."

"Don't worry about him. He's safe."

"Is that true?"

"I give you my word."

Joyfully, she threw her arms around Labadie's neck and hugged him. Then she ran to the birdcage, put her lips against the bars and let out two trills so beautiful that the birds listened as they fluttered about nervously.

When she arrived back home, Lise had already returned. Excitedly, her sister recounted everything she had seen at the seaside. She imitated the Prince's gait, gushed over his smile and eyes, and declared that she thought him a very handsome fellow.

Jasmine had to interrupt her, saying she was tiring Minette and suggested that the latter lie down again on the mat, in the shade of the orange tree.

At about three in the afternoon, Joseph arrived, as affectionate, as enthusiastic, and as charming as ever. Jasmine took him in her arms like a son and then turned him over to the two girls, who exhibited a thousand signs of their affection.

"Where were you, you terrible man?"

"Why did you stay away for three days?"

He took a wrinkled little book out of his pocket, and held it up triumphantly.

"I was at school, young ladies."

"At school!"

"Yes, at the school of Bossuet."

"Bossuet?"

"Okay, listen to this."

Then he recited a few passages from *The Sermons* out loud: "Of whatever superb distinction certain men may claim, they all come from the same place and this origin is small."

"Listen to this, too: 'But perhaps in the absence of good fortune, our qualities of the intellect, grand plans, and vast ideas can distinguish us from the other men! Greatness and glory! Can we still hear those names in the triumph of death? No, Sirs, I can no longer support these great words that humanity in its arrogance uses to numb itself faced with the void.'"

"How strange. You just read with the voice of a priest," remarked Lise.

Minette, however, said nothing. She had understood not only the meaning of the passages, but also that Joseph, carried away by his unrealizable ideals, was consoling himself reading revolutionary books.

"Tell me about Bossuet," she said sweetly.

"He was a priest."

Then she made a great gesture of surprise.

"A priest!"…

They looked at one another in silence. Then Joseph began laughing. He seemed rejuvenated, happy, relaxed. He had closed himself up for three days at Louise Rasteau's house with *The Sermons*! And for three days he had been addressing an imaginary crowd, with sweeping gestures of the arms and a tone of voice full of moving persuasion. Once he found himself alone with Minette, he told her that he had met a Jesuit at Labadie's house who, on learning what vocation was calling him, had taken an old book out of his cassock and said:

"Because the laws of this country designate the servitors of God by the color of their blood, read this my son and, without cassock and without the priesthood, plead your people's cause."

"I shut myself up in Louise's house for three days. I know the book more or less by heart. There are spots where the prose is sublime…"

He sighed and bent down toward Minette.

"Ah! If only I could speak to my brothers. If I could gather them all together, my words would reach every last one of them."

Joseph's exaltation dazzled Minette. Never had she seen him as impatient, as boldly carried away by his ideals.

"How wonderful it must be to feel a miracle emerge from a crowd one has galvanized oneself. To watch it become conscious of itself and to be able then to say, 'This is the work of God having chosen me to enlighten them.'"

It was seven o'clock. Jasmine immediately called for Minette.

When Minette left the back courtyard, she found the front room bustling with people. Men, women, and children from the neighborhood were there, all waiting to escort her to the Comédie.

An hour later, perfectly elegant in her white and gold velvet dress, she arrived at the Comédie. She noticed that Goulard was avoiding her. Ever since that day she had agreed to get into the planter's coach, Goulard had not been the same. He avoided looking at her, or being alone with her – even speaking to her. Saint-Martin had lost his exaggeratedly polite attitude and impertinently undressed her with his eyes. In that, too, she noted another sort of injustice – the injustice of gossip that condemns based on appearances without seeking the truth of things.

She was hurt. That Claude Goulard and Saint-Martin, up to that point so affectionate and respectful, would so abruptly change their attitude toward her without even according her the benefit of the doubt proved to her that they had only ever held her in the lowest esteem. *The natural opinion of a white person with respect to any person of color,* she told herself, and the thought made her bitter. *Well, too bad for them. I'm not their slave.* The Acquaires and Magdeleine Brousse welcomed her graciously. Mme Tessyre, obliged to perform that evening despite her sorrow, wiped away furtive tears that everyone did his or her best not to see, so as not to be too moved. Only Saint-Martin, as he passed near her, pinched her cheek in a gesture that tried to be brusque, but that was full of compassion.

Macarty stopped near Minette. His hands on his hips, he examined her costume and, staring at her jewels with a disapproving gaze said:

"Be prepared to read very nasty things in tomorrow's paper. You're too beautiful and you're wearing too many jewels."

Minette's lips tightened in annoyance:

"My jewels are fake…"

"Your beauty enhances their value and makes them look real."

He took her hand and made her turn around as he whistled knowingly.

Saint-Martin shouted:

"It's time to go onstage. Gather round, gather round. The Prince is in the Governor's box. Macarty – onstage for the opening of the curtains. Get ready!…"

Three warning claps and the curtains parted. For a moment, the spectators were truly transported to Paris, and a great pride came over them all, producing a wave of enthusiasm that exploded in a long round of applause.

Macarty waved, opened his arms wide to call for silence, and thanked Prince William for having honored them with his presence. The orchestra then played a British fanfare, for which everyone rose and cheered with cries of "Long live His Majesty, King of England! Long live His Majesty, King of France!"

When Minette entered the stage, she was obliged to stay silent for a long moment, so prolonged was the applause that welcomed her. She took the opportunity to scan the hall. In the Governor's box, she saw the Prince and a very beautiful and very blonde young girl, dressed in a dark dress with a high and severe collar. She was leaning forward and looked at Minette openmouthed, her eyes wide and thoughtful.

In the upper loges, she spotted her mother, Lise, Joseph, Nicolette, Kiss-Me-Lips, Beauvais, the two Lamberts, Labadie, Louise Rasteau, and everyone from her neighborhood, along with the rest of the colored population.

Once she began to sing, the public hung on her every word, utterly transported. The fantastical set, her costume, her beauty, and her talent all together created an extraordinary atmosphere. The young Prince leaned toward the Governor and said a few words. The latter agreed with a respectful nod of the head.

At that moment, their hands enlaced, Goulard and Minette were mixing their voices in a duet. Minette, her face close to his, looked into his eyes smilingly. "How stupid you are," she seemed to say, "to blame me for something I didn't do!"

At the end of the opera, her triumph was absolute, and as she left the stage to the sound of thunderous applause and in a hail of flowers and notes, a white constabulary officer came to tell her that Prince William was awaiting her in his box to present his compliments. Mme Acquaire, who had rushed onto the stage to gather up the flowers and letters, gave them to Minette, drawing attention to one in particular.

"Here," she said. "Someone just brought this for you."

"Who?"

"A young man. He said his name's Pitchoun."

"Ah!"

She then took a little bouquet of roses from Mme Acquaire's hands along with a folded note she put in her bodice, asking that the rest be given to her mother. Then she followed the officer to the Prince's box. Trembling with emotion, she made a deep and graceful curtsy.

"Rise, 'Mademoiselle,'" said the King of England's son to her. "I appreciate your talent and am grateful for your beautiful singing. May the Lord grant you a long life."

As she lowered for another curtsy, the Prince took her hand and raised it, joining his fingers to her own:

"I invite you," he added with a charming smile, "to accompany me to the ball this evening."

"Monseigneur, I would never dare," stammered Minette.

"I am inviting you," the Prince insisted.

The Governor turned bright red and let out an uncomfortable

cough, then, rising, offered his hand to the young blonde girl with him. Minette's heart stopped beating for a moment. No, it was not possible that she had heard the Prince correctly. That she would go to the Whites' ball on the arm of the son of the King of England! She shut her eyes, just as she always did when overcome with emotion. When she was able to look at Prince William again, she had the impression that his blue eyes were sparkling with gaiety and amusement.

In the theater, where the spectators were waiting for the Prince to depart before they could leave, people began whispering as they looked toward the Governor's box.

The ballroom was entirely illuminated. A tight little crowd had gathered in two rows, waiting for the Prince's arrival. The people of color applauded Minette from their section. Jasmine, seated between Lise and Joseph, took her handkerchief from her pocket to wipe away her tears of emotion and joy.

When Minette entered the ballroom on the arm of the Prince, they were met with a low murmur of disapproval. It did not last long, for the Governor, fearing protest, was the first to applaud them. Everyone immediately followed suit. Minette's talent put her above the others of her race. Having gone out of their way to hear her sing, the Whites could just as well tolerate her presence among them that evening, said the guests, as if to justify their indulgence. Nevertheless, several of the ladies, closing their fans with a snap, headed discreetly for the exit. Everyone pretended not to notice.

Alongside the Prince, passing by all those white people she could barely look at, so much was she trembling, Minette noticed a man who was applauding ostentatiously and bowing even lower than the others:

it was François Mesplès, in a velvet suit. Oh! How triumphant she felt looking in his eyes, her waist supple and curved, her head tilted back, and smiling with a smile at once moved and proud. Despite everything, she had to thank him, because the sight of him enabled her to pull herself together.

The Prince, imperturbable, opened the ball with her. His eyes sparkled with an amusement he was trying mightily to make inoffensive. But everything in his demeanor seemed to be saying: "I won't stop you from going to my colonies and doing the very same thing, if you want, but for the moment I'm having fun, my dear Frenchmen, I'm having fun…"

The young blonde girl with the Governor exchanged conspiratorial glances with the Prince from time to time. She, too, despite her incongruously austere outfit and her serenely sweet brown eyes, seemed to be enormously amused whenever she looked at the Governor's uncomfortable rubicund face and at her father's outright disapproving air as he chatted with the King's Bursar. When Minette went back to the table and the Prince went to dance with other ladies, she leaned toward Minette and said:

"I'm Céliane de Caradeux. You have the most beautiful voice I've ever heard. I'd like to ask you something: would you come sing at my home for my next Christmas party?"

"Of course, Mademoiselle," said Minette, unable to hide her astonishment.

So that was Céliane de Caradeux! The wealthiest white heiress in the country and daughter of the cruelest, most evil of all the planters! How could that girl – sweet, simple, so humbly and severely dressed –

be the daughter of the Marquis de Caradeux? For Minette, so young and inexperienced, all the planters' daughters had to be as evil and perverse as their fathers.

The actors had just arrived in the ballroom and were received with cheers. Goulard, struggling with himself in vain, came to ask Minette for a dance.

"Go ahead," said Mlle de Caradeux, "don't break his heart."

Decidedly, that young lady was delightful, and Minette sang her praises to Goulard, saying:

"My word, she's gentle and lovely, that planter's daughter!"

The young actor's lips trembled as he responded:

"Was it her uncle's case she was making so passionately?"

"Don't be stupid, Claude."

"Minette, why? Why did you get into that man's coach?"

"Oh, you're so annoying!"

"I thought you were an honest girl."

"I believe that I am."

"Swear to me that's true."

She felt sorry for him, thinking to herself, *How can he possibly love me so much?* And so to be done with the whole thing said:

"I swear it."

But she realized he still had doubts when he declared:

"I curse that filthy man and wish I had the right to challenge him to a duel."

That evening, seeing him so carried away with jealousy made her want to kiss him. He asked her to leave with him and she agreed, lowering her eyes. She then returned to the table and, after curtsying to the Prince, clasped her hands to her heart, as any good artist knows how to do, and said:

"Monseigneur, I shall never in my life forget the honor you have done me."

"Farewell," said Prince William, "and give thanks to your own talent. It will open the doors of heaven to you."

She kissed Goulard under a lone almond tree standing along Bursar's Square and, pressed against him, her arms around his neck, her mouth raised to his, swore to him that he was the first man to ever hold her in his arms.

When she left him, they had made up. But despite the burning traces of his kisses and the delightful sensations he had revealed to her, she looked deep into her own heart and was surprised not to discover that marvelous flame she expected love would have illuminated.

XIV

WHEN MINETTE came back home that night, she found the house still full of people. Decidedly, celebrity made solitude impossible. There was such excitement in the air that neighboring dogs worriedly came over to join in the festivities, and then began barking nervously. Everyone wanted to embrace her. Lise insisted that she demonstrate the curtsy she had done for the Prince and declared that she, too, hoped someday to be presented to such important people.

Joseph was as proud of Minette's success as Jasmine and Lise, but deep down he feared that all of this would change something in his little sister, as he called her. Jasmine's authority had further diminished, for at present she blindly accepted her elder daughter's slightest whim. Used to being dominated by her masters, it seemed natural to her to bend to the will of the privileged young girl she had carried in her own womb, and to adore her like a goddess. As strict, chattering, and mother hen-like as Jasmine had been before, Joseph felt that this had been a true lifesaver for her children. In her sorrowful eyes, which nervously observed the slightest of their faults, there was a sort of guiding light that allowed her to see their errors and to find the best way to influence them. This guiding light had been transformed into an expression of pride, of which Minette had become all too aware and which risked leading her to become indifferent to her mother's authority. This was what the young man was thinking.

That night, once the friends and neighbors had left, he looked for an opportunity to speak to Jasmine alone. The girls were undressing in the bedroom and, as their mother was about to wash the dirty dishes in the courtyard, Joseph called to her with a silent gesture. She put down the basin full of dishes on the little table and came over to him.

"Jasmine," he said, "even though you're proud of your elder daughter, don't show it too much and keep hold of your authority as her mother."

Though she made no answer, her eyes shone strangely.

"It's for the good of both of you that I'm speaking this way. Minette is very young."

Jasmine briefly looked toward the door to the bedroom.

"Oh, Joseph, my son, that child has a great destiny," she whispered, as if fearing to be overheard by someone other than the young man. "She has a great destiny. She has her father's blood in her and it seems to me that nothing courses through her veins but that white blood, that terrible paternal blood, full of fearlessness and arrogance. I'm weak, and she is strong; I'm fearful, and she is brave. Believe me, there is nothing of the slave in that child. Her father's white blood has marked her. He was a nobleman, a great lord, full of cunning and harshness."

She spoke fearfully, quickly, as if compelled to reveal herself.

"I realized all of this recently, seeing her on the stage, proud and completely unperturbed, sustaining the gaze of a thousand Whites."

"Jasmine!"

"Before realizing all of this, in order to protect her, to teach her to hate them, I showed her my back and my breast. Oh, Joseph! Sometimes I have the impression she wants to avenge me, and that she hates the entire world."

"I'm sure you're wrong about that."

Hearing the door creak, Jasmine lowered her head to wipe away her tears furtively.

Lise came into the room, followed by Minette, who was completely beside her self with rage.

"Lise, give me back that paper!" she screamed.

Lise dodged between the furniture, all the while trying to read what was written on the paper.

"Lise, give that back to me…"

"Not before I've read it…"

Minette bent down, took off one of her shoes and threw it at her sister's face. It hit her in the forehead and a bright spot of blood appeared.

"Minette!" shouted Jasmine.

In her emotion, Lise had let the paper fall to the ground. Without a word, Minette picked it up and stuffed it in her bodice. Then, looking at Lise she said:

"I never would've done it if I didn't have every right, you know – and all three of you know it. My letters belong to me and I won't have my little sister…"

"Minette, please," begged Jasmine, looking at Joseph as if to say: "Now do you see what I'm saying?"

Minette left the room, went into the bedroom, and quietly closed the door. She sat down on the bed and took out a little bouquet of roses, smelling them with her eyes shut. Then she read the letter. It was short. Signed Jean-Baptiste Lapointe, it read:

Come to Arcahaie. We will welcome you like a queen. I am your admirer.

Her heart was beating furiously. It was beating now the way it should have beaten when Claude Goulard had kissed her. She lay down on her back and smiled. *So it would seem I've snared them all in my web,* she said to herself, *white men and men of color, too.* She sat up, opened a bag and took out several letters, which she let rain down on her skirt as she smiled. This was all only the beginning. She had entered the ballroom on the arm of a Prince. And she would do even better. What? She had no idea, but she was sure of one thing: that nothing would stop her and that she would continue to rise – to rise to the most dizzying heights. She went to bed and pretended to sleep when Lise and her mother entered. The letter signed Jean-Baptiste Lapointe that Pitchoun had passed to Mme Acquaire was hidden along with the red roses between her breasts. The next morning, she stowed them away in her trunk with all of her most precious affairs and among which there was the little pewter ring Pitchoun had made for her.

At around eight o'clock, she rose, took a bath and got dressed. Lise had a bandage on her forehead. Minette looked away and ate her breakfast without saying a word. But when Jasmine went to set up her stand, Minette helped her bring it into the street before leaving for the theater. She had not forgotten that she was to receive the profits from the performance, and so she was going to claim what was owed to her.

In passing by the Acquaire's house, she noticed Scipion, who ran toward her to offer her a pinkish amber hibiscus that he had picked just for her. He still called her "the little nightingale" and looked at her like a savior; he was sure that it was thanks to her success at the Comédie that his masters would never have to sell him.

Saint-Martin was waiting for her. When she arrived, he raised his arms enthusiastically, took a little newspaper from his pocket and held it out to her.

"The critics are raving about you. You owe Prince William a huge debt. Here, read it yourself."

The evening's performance had been written up eloquently. The review praised her costume, her beauty, and her talent. But nothing was said about her entrance into the ballroom with the Prince and that silence was like a slap in the face in its ostentatious insult. It was as if it had not even happened, but it was clear that this attitude was due solely to the respect held for the Duke of Lancaster, and that no reaction would come until after his departure.

Saint-Martin then handed over the profits from the performance and, in front of her, took out the expenses for the organization of the ball and the making of the costumes. That morning, she made a small fortune of nine hundred pounds and felt no emotion on receiving the envelope, which she stuffed into her pocket, thanking him in a perfectly clear and natural tone. But to herself she resolved to handle everything personally the next time it was her turn to receive the profits and, like the other actors at the Comédie, to take charge of organizing the sets and the direction of the performance. That would be easy enough for her to demand, she thought, since the director was heading for Les Cayes.

"Soon you'll get those two years of salary the Comédie owes you," he promised her.

A few days later, Saint-Martin, after long negotiations, had become the contract-holder for the Saint-Marc Theater. The current number of actors at the Comédie was insufficient to perform certain plays. He was thrilled to note that there were some top-level actors there, like Mme de Vanancé, Mlle Duchelot, and three actors – Desroches, Sainville, and Duchainet – who had had brilliant debuts in Paris. Saint-Martin expected them the following day and planned to have them perform in a new play alongside Magdeleine Brousse, Minette, and Mme Tessyre.

The trip to Les Cayes having been planned for the next week, Saint-Martin was preparing to go to Jasmine's house to discuss Lise, when two talented actresses arrived from France.

It was about ten o'clock in the morning.

Minette, her hand on the heavy envelope stuffed in her pocket, was chatting with Goulard, leaning against a big empty trunk that was used to store rags. A little ways away, Saint-Martin was discussing the next play with Durand, Depoix, and Favart. Macarty was polishing his flute and Mme Tessyre, her face drawn and sorrowful, was embroidering a handkerchief while listening to Magdeleine Brousse's silly stories. All of a sudden, from the back of the theater, two feminine voices launched into a duet – a song no one had heard before. The voices were lovely and their trills were technically brilliant. Everyone turned around, astonished, to see two elegant young women, dressed in the latest Parisian fashion. They had a relaxed attitude and introduced themselves with studied, coquettish mannerisms.

"Madame Valville," said the elder of the two, a redhead with a wide smile and a turned-up nose sprinkled with freckles.

"Mademoiselle Dubuisson," said the other, a brown-haired girl, short and chubby, like a little doll. "We've just arrived from France. What's the theater like around here?"

Saint-Martin, always excited when it came to new artists, welcomed them with open arms and told all of them about an idea he had been considering for several months.

"We now have enough artists here to put on the biggest operas from Paris. No more limited-distribution plays. For our next performance, we'll put on one of the greatest French operas."

The introductions took place right then and there, and when Minette and Goulard left the Comédie, the question of contracts was already being discussed.

Before going back home, Minette wandered a bit through the streets and went to a few stores with Goulard. At Mme Guien's, on Bursar's Square, she bought the parasol Lise wanted and at Mlle Monnot's she bought a chambray scarf for Jasmine. Her shopping finished, she made her way home with Claude, who refused to leave her. She sat down in the front room and called to her sister and Jasmine, who were preparing lunch. When Lise unwrapped the package and saw the magnificent parasol, trimmed with pink fringe, she forgot all about her wound and her resentment, and jumped up and down, hugging Minette.

"But I warn you," Minette admonished her, "no more of your nosiness – you've got to respect other people's privacy."

Jasmine offered Goulard a glass of grenadine and some cookies. Once he had left, Minette took the money out of her pocket, gave it to her mother and said:

"Mama, if I earn this much money every month, do you think we might rent a house where I'd have my own little room? I'm growing up, Mama…"

Jasmine took the envelope, counted the money and, trembling, responded:

"Very well, my dear. I'll see what I can find in the neighborhood and we'll change houses."

Lise, in an effort to seem more elegant, had already taken off her bandage and, standing in front of the little mirror, was twirling her parasol on her shoulder like a real courtesan.

Jasmine interrupted this little game and asked her to take out the merchandise, which Lise did begrudgingly after closing her parasol with a big sigh.

It was May and great gusts of hot air already announced the arrival of summer. With the heat came several cases of fever, as happened every year. The hospitals pushed poor Whites out onto the street, where they ended up dying after three or four days of illness.

That was where things were when, one morning, a terrific beating of drums and the harsh, gloomy, and sinister sound of the conch shell could be heard in the nearby mountains. It was not the usual faraway sound interspersed with rhythmic moans, but rather a deafening concert that was coming closer every minute. In the streets, as if suddenly very anxious, people began to run. Mothers on doorsteps, ears cocked, called to their children and made them come indoors. Stagecoaches and horse-drawn carriages went by more quickly than usual. Riders from the constabulary, armed to the teeth, spurred on their horses and passed by at a gallop.

"Five hundred pound reward for every maroon captured," they let it be known.

A white man dressed in a torn shirt and wearing a straw hat full of holes raised his hands to the sky:

"Maroons – the maroons are coming!"

A few gunshots rang out, followed quickly by the sound of screams and a wild dash by a group of people coming from the market. A few children out running errands, surprised by the scramble, ran away whimpering.

The townspeople never knew what was happening. The fight had taken place some ways away from Port-au-Prince and a hundred or so wounded had been brought to the already overflowing hospital. In the sudden excitement brought on by the maroons' attack, several slaves had escaped the plantation houses and neighboring workhouses. The planters, furious, were forced to sign a peace treaty with the insurgent Blacks, whose only condition was the right to be baptized at Neybe and acknowledgment of the freedom they had paid for with their blood. That day, ten freedmen accused of having aided the flight of domestic and field slaves were arrested and put before a firing squad in the middle of the parade grounds without even a semblance of a trial. That night, two white families were poisoned during their meal: two families, including eight children between the ages of three and fifteen years old. Not even the most brutal torture could get any of the slaves to talk. The alarm bells at the church rang all night long in mourning, and the following day the priest blessed twelve coffins placed in the nave, before which the Whites tearfully left flowers. M de Caradeux's vengeance was swift and terrible. He had lost two families who were his friends and, as much for them as to preemptively remove any thought of similar plans for revolt among his own slaves, he tortured three of them by pouring hot lead into their ears and burying them alive up to the neck. All of Bel-Air, in complete turmoil, heard the screams of the poor wretches that night, and no one could sleep, so loud and piercing were their cries – loud enough to reach neighboring areas.

Joseph stayed late at Jasmine's. Silently, he watched Lise, who was covering her ears so not to hear the slaves' screams, while Minette nervously chewed her handkerchief with a drawn and tense expression on her face. She refused to eat, claiming her stomach was too tied up in knots and, with that same closed expression, began singing an opera solo at the top of her lungs. Joseph alone understood how greatly she was suffering when, completely spent, she let herself fall into a chair, panting, her eyes dry. When he left and Jasmine turned out the light, she stayed awake, listening to the faraway voices that gradually got fainter and fainter. At dawn, it was silent. The slaves were dead. It was only then, hiding her head under her pillow, that she fell into a deep and dreamless sleep, not waking until late that morning, her eyes red and throat dry.

The Duke of Lancaster had also slept poorly. He woke up that morning in a very bad mood. He was meant to have dinner that evening at M de Caradeux's home. He went there yawning after declaring frankly to the Governor, at whose residence he was staying, that there was nothing safe nor pleasant about the country other than the actors at the theater. In less than five days, he had witnessed a maroon revolt, mass poisonings, and torture. He declared he had had quite enough and decided to leave the very next day.

"Monseigneur," the saddened Governor began to explain, "it's just an unfortunate incident, believe me. You'll have to come back."

"Your country is beautiful and the women are ravishing, I'll admit," answered the young Prince, "but things just aren't right here. Discontent and hatred reign here far more absolutely than the King of France himself."

The Governor lowered his eyes and changed the subject. He would have liked to blame the planters for the state of things, but he did not dare accuse anyone. Certain of the King's edicts had recently favored the planters and, like an experienced diplomat, he preferred to keep quiet on the matter. Eighty torches illuminated the driveway leading to M de Caradeux's home. When the Governor's carriage entered, fifty or so other vehicles were already crowded into the courtyard. Céliane de Caradeux, very pale in an ivory silk dress, greeted the guests at the door. The Prince, noticing her, saw that she had not slept that night either and that she was making a superhuman effort to attend the dinner. He was seated next to her at the table. More than fifty slaves, dressed as lackeys, were posted behind the guests' chairs, anticipating their slightest gestures and, despite the wide-open doors, the heat in the dining room was suffocating. Flowers and expensive dishes decorated the table; Bordeaux was served in crystal glasses with chiseled silver stems. M de Caradeux's nervousness did not escape the Prince. He sniffed at the food suspiciously and jumped up, startled, when the sound of a conch suddenly pierced the air. Some of the women, shivering, cocked their ears and M de Chastenoye held his fork suspended in the air as he listened intently. The slaves, stoic, acted as if they heard nothing. Only their eyes seemed livened in their otherwise enigmatic faces and for a brief moment they exchanged conspiratorial glances. Céliane de Caradeux seemed as calm as all the slaves. A sad little smile danced periodically across her pale lips and, when the Prince observed the slave serving her, he understood that because of this young girl, sweet and pure, the Blacks would enact no vengeance that might put her life in danger. She must have done her best to repair the damage done by her uncle and father, and the slaves probably loved her for it. The Prince leaned toward her.

"I will leave this place with two wonderful memories," he said to her, "you and that evening at the theater."

He left the following day.

The paper had the decency to wait for his departure before attacking Minette. A scathing article appeared immediately afterward. It argued that someone needed to put a stop to the relaxing of customs that had allowed for the admission of a young person of color, perfectly thrilled to show off her triumph, into high society events. It criticized the extravagant luxury of Minette's Myris costume and the Duke of Lancaster's presumptuous eccentricity.

François Mesplès had been waiting for things to backfire before reacting. He went to the Comédie and there, in the presence of the actors who had come from Saint-Marc as well as Mesdames Valville and Dubuisson, began insulting Minette. François Saint-Martin and

Goulard intervened; Macarty and Depoix even had to hold back Goulard, who was ready to fight and screamed at Mesplès that he was a brute.

"She slept with you, huh? She suckered you and you let yourself be taken, you imbecile."

"Shut up, Mesplès!" Saint-Martin screamed at him.

"And you, too, you're going to let yourself be played for a fool – if it hasn't happened already," continued the ultra-rich loan shark, beside himself. "But it sickens me to see this little colored wench wrapping all of you around her little finger. Giving her all the profits from that exceptional evening? What, have you all gone mad? Twenty percent would have been more than sufficient. All the profits? All the profits? And then when you're broke, it'll be: 'Mesplès, give me a little advance for this…Mesplès, just a little advance for that…' As long as you're giving performances for her benefit, I won't lend you another dime, got it?"

He left and Saint-Martin lowered his head. They had been friends for many years and they had never had any trouble. Saint-Martin was perhaps the only one toward whom Mesplès had ever shown himself completely selfless and he had to admit that the loan shark had gotten him out of tough spots more than once without ever asking for anything in return. Their friendship dated back to the time when Saint-Martin still went by his real name, La Claverie. After the scandal that had followed the death of young Morange, the scandal that had obliged him to change his name, news of his prowess reached Mesplès, who went to shake his hand and nicknamed him "The Bell-Ringer." That particular character trait revealed a certain bravery in the actor that Mesplès quite admired. Quick-tempered and violent, he was more than happy to find these same tendencies in other people – as long as those people were white, it goes without saying. Filled with color and racial prejudice, he passionately detested all those who had the slightest drop of African blood in their veins. Slaves and freedmen were to him one and the same and, in his bad faith, he made no distinction between them.

Minette, rage in her heart, had wiped away Mesplès' insults in silence. When he left, a certain tension began to be felt between the actors newly arrived from France and from Saint-Marc and those from the Port-au-Prince theater. The newcomers seemed to think that the stockholder Mesplès was in the right.

There were plenty of white actors now, and to continue to favor this colored girl was to declare that they lacked talent. When Minette decided to escape the uncomfortable atmosphere at the theater, leaving without a word to anyone, only Goulard went after her. During the entire duration of the walk from the Comédie to Traversière Street, they did not exchange a word. But when she arrived in front of her house, Minette turned to Goulard and held out her hand.

"Thank you, Claude," was all she said to him.

"I beg you," he advised her, "not to make any hasty decisions. Wait till things settle down. Other Prince Williams will travel through the country and they'll need you."

She shook her head.

"I won't quit the Comédie, my dear Claude. I have a contract. I earn eight thousand francs a year and I'm part of the company."

"Bravo!" responded Goulard. "There's a girl who knows what she wants."

He seized her hand and brought it to his lips. Then he asked when he might kiss her again.

"When I return from Arcahaie," she answered him, so serenely that he understood that she was not at all in love with him.

His heart tightened in his chest and his face immediately darkened.

"What are you going to do in Arcahaie?" he then asked her, with a tone he hoped would sound indifferent.

"I have a meeting there."

She laughed and then added:

"And I'm going to make them miss me by refusing to collaborate with Saint-Martin this time. They'll perform without me and we'll see."

When Joseph came that night, she told him everything that had happened at the Comédie and repeated to him word for word all the insults Mesplès had thrown in her face. Then, she spoke to him of her plan to leave for Arcahaie for a little trip.

"Why choose Arcahaie, Minette?" he asked her with his vibrant, direct voice.

She offered no answer.

"Why, Minette?"

"Joseph, I care for you very much, you know that. You're my brother. But I'll be seventeen soon and I can't let anyone push me around, not even my brother. I promised you that nothing and no one would distract me. And I'll keep my word. That's all I can tell you."

"Life can be cruel and men disappointing."

"I've known that for a long time."

He put his hand on her shoulder and tried to look in her eyes.

"All things considered, you're right. You've reached the age where you can determine your own fate. Take your chances, but never forget that whatever you do will reflect on the whole of your race – this race you represent in the eyes of all the Whites who know you."

She lowered her head without answering. Did she not have the right to live her life in peace? She had already done enough for her people. Was she obliged to think of others every moment of her existence before lifting her little finger?

When Joseph left, she told her mother that she was going to leave to Arcahaie soon.

"With the company?"

"No, alone, Mama."

"Very well, my dear."

"And Mama, wait a bit before renting that new house. We just can't know, you understand, we can never know what'll happen."

She handed her mother half of the money she had earned and asked her to dispose of it as she pleased. Then she left to purchase a little trousseau, which she brought to Nicolette.

"How much would it cost me for you to make me three skirts, two bodices, and two underskirts?" she asked the dressmaker.

"Give me a red necklace from Miss Monnot's," she said.

That was a worthless bauble. Minette embraced her in gratitude.

"Yes, a red necklace, and not another word about it."

She had taken out her famous scissors, which she kept in a tin chest adorned with dry leaves and bird feathers.

"Look at my little chest. 'Arranged' as it is, it forces my scissors to do only the best work."

She cut through the fabrics with confidence.

The skirts, the blouses, the underskirts were trimmed and sewn in no time. Minette, watching her work, thought to herself that never in her life had she seen fingers work a needle so well.

"This time, don't tell me that you're not going to meet someone. It wouldn't be normal for a girl your age not to have a lover," said Nicolette, looking at her with laughing eyes.

Minette, taking a conspiratorial tone, told her that, in fact, she was going to Arcahaie to meet a handsome young man she fancied.

"My mother doesn't know anything. Don't betray me."

Which caused Nicolette to respond reproachfully:

"Do we women ever betray one another?"

Then, she gave her some advice that she assured her was practical and based on years of experience.

"This is your first lover, right?" asked the young courtesan. "Well, put your pockets before your heart and remember that your good sense must come before your feelings. Otherwise you're done for."

She promised Minette that she would bring the new dresses herself, first thing the next morning.

"I'll iron them for you, too. You'll just have to put them in your trunk."

Once back home, Minette saw Jasmine setting three plates on the table alongside a fragrant bowl of spicy-smelling broth.

"Where's Lise?" she asked.

"At her lesson with the Acquaires," answered Jasmine.

She had hardly finished her sentence when Lise walked in, followed by Mme Acquaire. Out of prudence, Mme Acquaire made no mention of the scene with Mesplès and, taking an air of great enthusiasm, tried to explain to Minette her new passion for local plays, how she'd gotten the taste for them and why she and Saint-Martin were interested.

"In fact, why don't you try to perform local plays, Minette?" she asked the young girl once she thought she had made her best pitch.

"Me, Madame?"

"Well yes, why not?"

"Perhaps you've just discovered that I'd be more easily forgiven that sort of easy triumph, Madame?"

"My, how you take things the wrong way!"

"No, Madame. I see things clearly, that's all."

It was futile to insist. Never, and Mme Acquaire understood it well, would Minette agree to perform in one of those degrading plays. *I could never depict the atrocities my people have suffered with the buffoonery of a badly written comedy*, said Minette to herself. She added, so to better hide her thoughts:

"You've crafted my taste. I've been marked, definitively, by that which is beautiful and grand. The local plays, Madame Acquaire? How could you have thought for even a moment that I'd agree?…"

Lise, who did not understand all of this fuss over the exact thing that was going to launch her on the stage, smoothed her hair coquettishly before the mirror.

"But they're plays like any other. Monsieur Saint-Martin told me himself that *Love in Mirebalais* is a masterpiece. It's a parody of Rousseau's *The Village Soothsayer*, you know."

Minette looked at her without the slightest disdain. That she could declare that a local play written by a bad local poet was a masterpiece – there was nothing surprising there. But she was certain of one thing: Saint-Martin had lied in telling her that.

Mme Acquaire sighed. Her future in the theater had to be terribly uncertain for the good woman to have proposed such a thing to her, Minette said to herself. They didn't want to lose her at the Comédie. She was earning them a lot of money, after all. They were trying to keep her without upsetting M Mesplès too greatly.

"This is all so tiresome – so tiresome!" exclaimed the Creole woman with another sigh.

Once Mme Acquaire had left, it was Magdeleine Brousse who came by with words of encouragement, the same promises of success for Minette if she accepted the lead role in the next local comedy.

"Come on, what does it matter to you, dear? What do you want, to earn a little money, right? And at least that way no one will bother you."

Minette, who had had just about enough, was making a real effort to control herself. She had a crazy desire to scream insults at the Acquaires, at Magdeleine Brousse, and at François Saint-Martin himself. As for Mesplès, she swore to get back at him when the time came. He would get what he deserved. Twice he had put himself in her way and she was starting to lose patience. For the moment, it was easy for Mesplès to pay her back for the smug and victorious little attitude she had shown him on the night of the ball. But she was going to become powerful and he would come to fear her, she swore it to herself. Even if she had to offer herself to all the great heads of state in the country. This worthless chastity was starting to wear on her. Nicolette had done well. Letting it be known that she was with the King's Bursar gave her respect and consideration. Yes, she too would need a powerful protector: the Marquis de Chastenoye, for example. He was old, rich, and well established. She would be known as the protégeé of a great personage and people would admire her. Joseph, with his pure and intransigent priestly ideas, could he possibly understand her horrific situation? Certain aspects of life were just beyond his comprehension. It was evident in the clarity and serenity of his gaze. But it was impossible that he had not seen all around him the planter priests, businessmen and slave-owners; he could not have grown up and not seen, just as she had, that the struggle was merciless and that at some point it was necessary to ignore one's heart and one's honor, to seize life with two hands and squeeze one's fingers around it, like around the neck of an enemy one has vanquished. Oh, she would fight! All the François Meslèses put together would not keep her from moving forward and finally making it.

"So you refuse, then?" insisted the blonde actress, having been tasked with trying to convince her.

"I can't, I just can't," Minette repeated with a stubborn little air. "Beautiful music and beautiful verse – that alone is theater in my eyes. It's not my fault."

When she pronounced those words, Magdeleine Brousse leaned toward her and embraced her.

"And you're absolutely right, my dear," she said to her. "If you had given in, the director himself might very well have been angry with you. Hold tight, and we'll see what happens."

XV

WITH THE ARRIVAL of the new actresses from France, both Saint-Martin's trip to Les Cayes and Minette's trip to Arcahaie were postponed for several weeks. There was too much to do for the new play, in which Minette, for reasons she would not reveal, refused to perform. Believing it to be some whim of hers, Saint-Martin had not insisted. For this one time, he had very honorably replaced her with Mlle Dubuisson. Once the play had been performed, he redoubled his efforts to get Jasmine to entrust him with Lise. It had not been an easy task. Her younger daughter was still very young, indeed, and Saint-Martin had a bad reputation, thought Jasmine. But just like Minette, Lise was becoming more distant: an ambitious girl, she had long dreamt of making her debut on the stage and being cheered and praised just like her sister. Her pride had registered, without the slightest jealousy, all of Minette's successes; nevertheless, that had strengthened her deepest resolve to be known, to make money, and to become famous – because she, too, had a lovely, well-honed voice. She recognized, for that matter, that Minette was more hot-blooded than she and that her sister's voice was fuller and had more range than hers. She said proudly, imitating Mme Acquaire's coquettish tone: "My sister is a contralto and

I'm a light soprano," which meant: "Between the two of us, there's something for everyone." Less complicated than Minette, she knew exactly where she wanted to go and why. The theater would allow her to earn money and with that money she would buy all those beautiful things she was so tired of desiring without being able to afford. She had no interest in pursuing a libertine path like Nicolette's. She was flirtatious without sensuality and had no desire to sleep with old men for money or jewels. She found it more practical and certainly less disgusting to earn that money performing local or other plays at the Comédie.

As certain complications did not torment her as of yet, she accepted indifferently the way things were, seeing everything with the same serene regard and dreaming at night about clothes, carriages, and fame.

There was none of that fervent desire to defy, to shock, and to conquer in her. When she spoke to Mme Acquaire or to the actors at the theater, she maintained the modest demeanor of a well-bred little girl who, very young, had learned not to look Whites in the eyes, to always be docile and conciliatory, and above all to always show exaggerated gratitude. The Whites were her superiors. The French she spoke was the language of the masters and symbolized the good taste and refinement of a proper education.

Their mother, who had learned to speak French in the masters' house, repeated ten or twenty times a day: "Speak French, speak French." Lise and Minette had heard that little phrase throughout their entire childhood. In the local plays, the only degrading aspect, as far as Lise was concerned, was that Creole was spoken – and Minette's refusal to perform in them had a bit to do with the same aversion. She who spoke only of Grétry's music and who, imitating Mme Acquaire, recited the most beautiful classical verses – to ask her to babble away in Creole while playing the buffoon! Lise vaguely understood that feeling of revolt. But the other side of the question, the more serious side, escaped her: she never would have believed that it disgusted Minette to exhibit the physical and moral suffering of the unfortunate slaves via the buffoonery of a comedy. If she had been able, Lise would have bought herself a slave or two the very next day. The wealthy freedmen, Blacks, and Mulattos owned slaves, why should she not do the same? She would have bought some even if she had known of her mother's past. Jasmine was so certain of this that she preferred not to bother reliving that past in vain. Lise loved her dearly; she knew that. Seeing the scars on her back, she would cry – but she would forget about it two days later.

When it came to Minette, however, it seemed that her gesture had not been for nothing. Nevertheless, she sometimes believed, as she had intimated to Joseph, that the master's blood had stirred up all its inheritances in her daughter's veins, pushing her toward formidable, unchecked aspirations. The terrible pride of the father – that wealthy, nouveau riche white man who had bought himself a title – had been resuscitated in his female offspring, to whom he had left as sole legacy his white blood, infused with neuroses and pride. She resembled him unmistakably. Each passing day made that even clearer to Jasmine. There were times when she suspected Minette of living, even within the confines of that tiny little room the three of them shared, a dangerous life in which frivolity already had very little place. Minette had shocked her on that day when Joseph had hidden the slave at their house. Her behavior had not been that of a scared little girl, but that of a woman playing a high-stakes game. She had kept the secret without betraying him and had never spoken about it again.

She was also the one who had known how to weaken her resistance the day Saint-Martin had come to talk to her about Lise.

"Mama," she had said with a calm and measured tone, "let Lise go, don't stand in her way. She'll resent you for it later."

She had acquiesced immediately, weeping the way all mothers weep when faced with situations beyond their control.

Minette had taken that same measured tone to speak to Joseph about her plan to leave for Arcahaie. Although she had looked him straight in the eyes as always, he had realized that she would never admit to him the real reason for her trip. She had not come up with any alibi to mislead him and had spoken to him of her decision with a tone that allowed for no interrogation. Yet, there had been such affection and respect in her attitude toward him. He could trust a girl like that. He only feared that her own nature would get the better of her, and that her pride would lead her to confuse wrong for right. This faith he had in her, he had been happy to find that Zoé and Lambert felt the same. And they had only met her twice. Even Beauvais, distrustful Beauvais, had spoke of her in flattering terms, saying that she possessed the most honest and impertinent regard he had ever seen in a woman. However, despite everything Joseph said to reassure himself, he could not help thinking of Jean-Baptiste Lapointe and the impression he had made on Minette on the night of the ball. Was she going to reignite things? He was having a hard time letting go of a nagging feeling that was painful for him to confront. Deep inside, he knew what it was – what the answer to the question was. But since there was nothing he could do about it, he kept quiet, and merely hoped that Minette would return soon enough – praying for his little sister's salvation in the manner of all pious souls.

Lise's journey was necessary, as he himself had said to Jasmine. Despite his religious ideals, he was not one of those close-minded men who saw evil everywhere. Thanks to Labadie, he had made contact with a whole host of things that, opening his mind, had guided him naturally along the path for which it seemed he had been born. He would stand among those good priests who defend the right to justice, who demand the light of instruction and Christian charity for the oppressed, all the while remaining a man and, above all, understanding the human in every man.

Lise wanted to leave to try her luck. He weighed in on her behalf and reasoned with Jasmine, saying to her:

"You'll have to resign yourself sooner or later. Let her go, Jasmine…"

The day of the two sisters' departure, Minette brought Joseph into an isolated corner of the back courtyard.

"Tell the Lamberts I haven't forgotten anything," she said to him. "No matter when and no matter where I am, I'll be with them. This trip, this trip…"

Joseph put his hand to her mouth.

"Keep your secret, my sister," he said to her. "That, too, is what freedom means."

…The little house was full of people: people from the neighborhood and a few actors from the Comédie crowded the front room.

Saint-Martin, relieved to learn that Minette only planned to go away for a short while, eagerly supported the idea. He figured it might be a good thing for the public either to forget her or to suffer from her absence to the point of calling her back to the stage. He gave her a letter of introduction for Mme Saint-Ar, a European woman who had married a Creole planter from Arcahaie. Saint-Martin told Minette that they were reputed to be free-spirited people, neither prejudiced nor snobs, and he insisted that she pay them a visit.

"You'll be there for the third Thursday in Lent. Don't miss the chance to attend one of Madame Saint-Ar's balls. That'll be one of your best memories."

He had added, doubtless just to make small talk:

"And so, is it true? Are you deserting the theater – are you abandoning us?"

Without giving him an answer, she left her house with him and went to say her goodbyes at the Comédie. There they came upon a cheery and enthusiastic scene, which made clear to Minette that she had been perfectly well replaced. M Mesplès, present that day, cynically and ostentatiously praised the talents of the new actresses in her presence, using the most flattering terms in talking about Mlle Dubuisson's singing voice. The latter missed no occasion to flutter her eyelashes at him, all the while smiling her seductive, pursed-lip smile for the benefit of all the other men there.

"She's already Saint-Martin's mistress," Magdeleine Brousse had confided jealously.

"So you're off on holiday, my dear," said Mlle Dubuisson to Minette with a patronizing and disdainful little tone.

"I'm going to take a moment to recover from my success," Minette responded, trembling with rage and looking her straight in the eye.

That unexpected response from a young person she had meant to insult astonished the actress.

"You'll be back soon enough," was her impertinent response. "Yes, you'll always be back soon enough for the public to realize it's had enough of you."

Goulard did not defend her this time. A lover's spitefulness and jealousy had made him bitter.

Nevertheless, he accompanied her to the stagecoach alongside Joseph and Jasmine, though without speaking a word and full of resentment toward her. They shook hands in silence and he did not even ask for a farewell kiss. His lover's instinct told him that this trip was bringing his beloved to someone new, which he took exception to. His manly pride was deeply hurt by such a show of casual indifference.

"Our love was only just born, but I think it would be best to bury it now," he said to her bitterly.

"Who knows?" she answered. "Perhaps I'll come back more in love with you."

"Do you have to cut your teeth on someone else before you can love me? Farewell, Minette. I expect to be completely over you by the time you return."

"Well that's too bad for you, you cruel man!"

She smiled at him and, after kissing her mother and Joseph, gave Lise a thousand little bits of advice and wished her luck. The stagecoach, into which several people of color traveling to Arcahaie had been sandwiched, awaited just a few steps away. She ran over to it without looking back, and then disappeared from sight.

Everyone was quiet as they headed back down the road that led toward the south.

Saint-Martin had already arrived, accompanied by Scipion, who carried his bags. Lise, dressed up like a proper lady, wore one of Minette's dresses, which Jasmine had fitted for her. She looked ravishing. Looking her over, Saint-Martin thought it would be amusing to have her pass for a white lady by bringing her with him into the select coach. It was one more opportunity to make a mockery of the country's ridiculous prejudices. A few minutes before the departure of the car headed for Les Cayes, the actors showed up in a mad bunch.

"Goodbye, Lise," said Mme Acquaire. "Be sure to write and tell us about all your successes."

"Farewell, little sister," called Joseph. "And remember: whenever you put your heart into what you do, success is guaranteed."

Lise wept as she kissed her mother and Joseph. Interrupting the sad farewells, Saint-Martin pointed toward Zabeth and his sons as they hurried toward him.

"Look at them, Lise," he said. "I'm leaving them without shedding a tear. There, there, we'll be back soon."

Zabeth was trying to drag the children along as quickly as possible. They were barely able to keep up with her and stumbled, crying, as they clutched at her skirts.

By the time she had managed to reach the actors, the travelers had already taken their seats in the stagecoach. She bent down, took her sons in her arms, and began crying out:

"Monsieur François, Monsieur François!…"

Saint-Martin stuck his smiling head through the open window.

"Farewell, Zabeth," he said. "Don't think too much about me, it'll make you look sickly. Take care of yourself and wait for me."

"François!…"

She sobbed desperately. Goulard took one of the children and put his arm around the young Mulatress' shoulders.

"There, there, Zabeth, calm yourself. Remember, François hates tears."

"Monsieur Goulard, he's leaving!"

"This isn't the first time."

"I don't know what's the matter with me, I just don't know," she repeated so despairingly that Claude Goulard shivered.

The scene had dampened the mood of a farewell that everyone had hoped would be cheerful, and the actors – without understanding why – felt nervous as they watched the car head off into the distance.

Macarty was the first to snap out of it and chase away the gloomy atmosphere. Taking the tiny hand of the child Goulard was carrying, he waved it back and forth shouting:

"Bye-bye, see you soon!"

Everyone immediately followed suit and Jasmine had to turn away to hide her tears. She was alone now, more alone than Zabeth, even, who had her little ones to console her. That's what it meant to be a mother: to kill yourself working to raise little beings, to watch them anxiously as they grow up and then, one day, to let them go, saying only: "Go live your life; you don't need me anymore."

Joseph put his hand on her shoulder and walked back toward home with her.

A year had passed since the signing of the famous contract, but Joseph and Jasmine were surely unaware that, although she had signed that contract in a private agreement, Minette still worked at the Comédie without even daring to demand her wages.

XVI

THE COACH ROLLED along on the rocky, potholed road. Sandwiched between a dull-looking elderly black man and a young, heavily made-up *câpresse* with her hair covered by a jeweled madras scarf, Minette dozed intermittently and watched the landscape pass by through the old cart's poorly sealed flaps. It was pouring rain. Fat drops of water splashed the passengers from time to time and the black driver, warmly wrapped up in a waterproof cloak, swore in a booming voice:

"Hey, this way! Damn it – to the right, you crazy 'orses – to the right, damn it!"

He was barely avoiding the potholes and the mud-caked wheels rattled as if they would soon fly right off.

"What awful luck having to travel in such weather," sighed a fat, ruddy woman as she made the sign of the cross.

"It's rather surprising for March," responded a young black man seated just across from Minette. "But there's nothing to do but get used to it."

Knocked about and shaken up, the travelers who had been sleeping were abruptly awakened by terrible claps of thunder that seemed to explode right next to the coach.

For three hours, the flooded cart rolled along the road lined with trees whose waterlogged leaves lay flattened into the mud. When it finally came to a stop and the driver shouted: "Arcahaie, Arcahaie – anyone for Arcahaie," the rain had only just stopped.

Minette was first to disembark. She went to collect her things from the driver and stood for a moment on the street. A few minutes later, the young black man – the man who had been sitting across from her – got out as well. All he had by way of baggage was a bundle of clothes he tossed nimbly over his shoulder. He stopped next to her and raised his head to the sky. Above them, the trees were shaking off the rain in the refreshing breeze. Minette lifted her skirt slightly and held it clutched in her hand to keep from dirtying it; her slippers were already covered in mud. All along the street large puddles had formed and people could not help but splash each other as they walked through them. Two Negro soldiers from the constabulary passed by on mud-splattered horses; a covered carriage driven by an elderly black coachman rolled straight through the puddles. A few beggars, missing limbs and covered in rags, looked pleadingly at the passersby.

Houses with shingled and slate roofs rose up at the end of driveways lined with orange and flame trees.

Minette looked up and down the street. Which way was she meant to go? At that very moment, the young black man with the bundle of clothing turned to her.

"May I be of some service?" he asked her in an only slightly accented French.

"Thank you, yes. Which road do I take to reach Jean-Baptiste Lapointe's estate?"

"Jean-Baptiste Lapointe, the *griffe* of Arcahaie! Why, he lives quite a ways from here, in Boucassin. You'll have to go there by horse and head back a bit the way you came."

"Ah!"

"It's a half an hour from here; in the countryside."

"Where can I find a horse?"

"Well, that you can get anywhere. Look, walk over to that gate over there. Ask for Nicolas and tell him Simon sent you. He'll help you."

He adjusted his bundle on his shoulder and raised his straw hat.

"Normally, I'd take you over there myself, but I'm a slave. I'm running errands and I'm already late."

Minette looked at him attentively.

He wore short cotton pants from Vitré and a long-sleeved shirt buttoned up to the neck. On his feet he wore sandals whose straps exposed his toes. Minette had seen domestic slaves with Vitré or Morlaix cotton shirts before, in the streets of Port-au-Prince. But what seemed absolutely new to her was the expression of contentment and serenity on the slave's face. Of course she had already seen Negroes dressed in livery serving as valets and lackeys, drivers dressed in gold-buttoned shirts like M de Caradeux's coachman, but they all wore a sort of closed, darkly unhappy expression on their face, which immediately revealed their social station. This young Negro was different; he seemed happy. Could there possibly exist, other than Scipion, a single slave who wasn't beaten, spied on, distrusted, and ill-treated – who enjoyed his master's confidence? She had always known that the slaves were so unhappy that they only awaited the right moment to flee into the hills; and that the masters, because they were masters – be they white, black, or mixed-race – treated them like beasts of burden.

She left the young slave with a smile and watched him walk off as she kept thinking about what she had seen. She finally began walking. After a few steps, her skirts were soaked and so dirty that she stopped paying attention. Once at Nicolas' gate, she noticed a little wood house lined with galleries and a large courtyard where a few horses were tied up, eating cut grass. An elderly one-armed man came over to her and asked what she needed in a lisping Creole.

"Simon sent me," she answered. "I'd like a horse to take me to Boucassin."

"Right away, right away," answered the one-armed man. "And you'll have a guide as well; you're not from around here – you'll need a guide. Fifty escalins for the horse and twenty escalins for the guide. Will that be all right?"

"Yes," she answered.

And she immediately took a little purse from her bodice and emptied its contents into her hand.

Once she had paid, she looked at her feet and at the hem of her skirt. They were caked in mud. Softened by the humidity, her madras headscarf was wrinkled and leaned too much to one side. She straightened it. Alas! Was this the state she would be in for this rendezvous? Her chambray bodice, her silk shawl, and the little clutch bag Nicolette had so carefully embroidered were all crumpled. She looked like one of those young freedwomen who sold meat, pork, and fish at the market.

A saddled horse was brought to her and a young black boy of about twelve, wearing only a waistcloth, helped her to mount.

A six-horse carriage passed by the gate. A smiling Mulatto was driving and made a friendly gesture to Nicolas with his whip.

"Who's that?" Minette asked the young boy holding the reins of her horse.

"That's Michel, Mistress – Madame Saint-Ar's driver."

Mme Saint-Ar, she thought immediately. Why, I have that letter for her from Saint-Martin. She quickly turned to look at the young guide.

"Does Madame Saint-Ar live near here?"

"Yes, Mistress. Look, over there – that big estate. It's called 'Les Vases.' It belongs to Madame Saint-Ar! She's a nice white lady."

The horse turned off the road and followed the young boy along a deserted path, lined with cotton plants. After about a half an hour, the guide, who was carrying Minette's bag on his head, pointed toward a little hill where there was a flat house with a red slate roof and a single gallery on its right wing.

"We're here," he said.

Uncomfortable on her horse, Minette shook out her long, flowered skirt to clean it as best she could. Holding on to the saddle with one hand, she tried to arrange her madras headscarf. But as the horse was making its way up the rough incline, she fell to the side and fell squarely in a puddle of red mud, which splattered her bodice and face. She swore violently and pushed away the guide as he tried to help her up. She rose to stand, furious.

"I'm supposed to look perfect," she spat out in Creole, as she did whenever she was angry with herself.

The guide, doing his best not to laugh, helped her back up into the saddle.

"Hold on tight, Mistress," he advised. "The slope is very steep."

Five minutes later, the horse stopped in front of the gallery abutting the right wing of the house, where three slaves, dressed just like the guide in a rough cotton waistcloth, ran up beside her. They helped her down from the horse by holding out their hands for her to place her feet. Two enormous dogs came toward her, barking and with their teeth bared. Terrified, Minette began to scream.

"Hey, what's going on?" someone immediately questioned. "Settle down, Lucifer and Satan, settle down."

The door to one of the rooms of the house opened and Jean-Baptiste Lapointe appeared.

He wore a pair of white linen pants and a sheer chambray shirt unbuttoned halfway, exposing his strong neck and the glistening skin of his young, muscular chest. For a moment, he looked at her curiously, before coming down the stone stairs situated beneath the gallery. Recognizing Minette, he made a brief gesture of surprise and then burst into laughter as he looked her over. He laughed so long and hard that tears ran down his cheeks. Each time he tried to get a hold of himself, he ended up sputtering and doubling over even more violently.

Minette observed him, her eyebrows raised. She was standing before a madman. Jean-Baptiste Lapointe was completely mad. What kind of mess had she gotten herself into?

When he was finally able to calm down, she realized that he was only having a good laugh. He apologized for having greeted her in such a manner and held out his hand to help her up the stairs.

The dogs, now as gentle as lambs, rubbed against the young man with plaintive little yaps, subdued by the sound of his voice alone. He pushed open the outer door and Minette found herself in a great hall, decorated with meticulously clean wood furniture, hanging Indian-style curtains, and an abundance of plants growing in earthenware vases.

"Your home is beautiful," she said with a coquettish smile.

She turned and looked into a large mirror, about to remove her madras headscarf, and was suddenly paralyzed with shock.

She was completely soiled from head to toe. Her face was flecked with little bits of coagulated mud; her dress was stained from the hem of her skirt up to the waist, and her damp madras headscarf was folded over like a clown's hat. She burst out laughing, just as Lapointe had done.

"An explanation for my slightly mirthful welcome won't be necessary, then," affirmed Lapointe, still laughing. "But you'll still need to have a bath and a chance to change clothes."

"But, your parents – might I greet them first?

"Well it's just that…there must be some misunderstanding. I've always lived here alone."

"What?"

Once again she saw that cynical and unsettling look on his face, with his dark eyes stretching toward his temples.

"I live alone."

"Then I must go immediately," said Minette, mortified. "You were disabled, and now you're not. You invited me to your family home, but you live alone. I detest complicated situations."

"Well, then you must detest life itself. Nothing is uncomplicated in this world."

Minette looked at him out of the corner of her eye.

Standing, fist on his hip, he awaited her decision with a false show of indifference. A great weariness came over her. She longed to lie down, right there at his feet and sleep – to sleep to the point of oblivion. There was no way she could agree to remain there alone with him.

She would have to take that long ride again on horseback, holding on to the saddle; and the muscles of her arms hurt so much, she felt them hanging like dead weights at her side.

"Farewell," she said nevertheless.

And at the same time, she passed her hand across her face to wipe away the flecks of dried mud.

"I won't eat you up if you want to have a bath and change your clothes. I'm not a werewolf after all."

He had smiled sweetly as he said that. She looked at him and saw that his hands were trembling slightly.

"All right for the bath," she said, making an abrupt decision, the way she often did.

In moments like those, she trusted her instinct over any sense of reason – an instinct to which her natural temerity was all too happy to cede.

It was this same force, she thought to herself, that gave her those accents and attitudes onstage and that had compelled her to come to Arcahaie. She believed in that force like some mysterious thing that lived inside her and served her well. Her reaction was normal: ever since her childhood, the superstitions common to people of her race did battle with the doctrines of Christianity so often read and commented on by Joseph. Where was the truth? Some feared the gods of Guinée worshipped by the Negroes, others recognized the superiority of a single God, father of the Christ made man. She had often heard the old neighborhood healer tell Jasmine that the Whites' god was a "resident" of the skies, just as white as the Whites themselves, and that he did not understand a word of the Creole spoken by the suffering Blacks. As she became more educated, Minette had managed to shed such naive beliefs. But, despite that, like a proper child of Guinée, she had faith in multiple little things – predictions, dreams, cursed days, and blessed days – she took them all into account.

She would have rather died than be caught telling stories in the middle of the day, or eating the top of a honeydew melon. One day, her mother had taken a stern and frightened tone to scold Lise for pointing at a rainbow. Jasmine had a talisman that an old Negro named Mapiou had given her when she was still on the plantation. All the while teaching the slaves in secret, he had spoken to them of the power of the *lwa*, the gods of Vodou. Minette had seen that talisman tucked away in her mother's large trunk one day when she had gone looking for clean clothes. She had understood that this was a *makandal* like the one Nicolette wore pinned to her shirt to protect her from the evil eye. It was a sort of little bag filled with tiny objects as mysterious as the power of the thing itself. Lise and Minette touched it with a combination of revulsion and respect. "You never know," they said to themselves. There were plenty of nice stories in catechism, but the ladies of the neighborhood had seen incredible things with their own eyes. That was enough to sow doubt and fear in the two young girls.

The night she sang at the Comédie for the first time, she had always thought deep inside that it was perhaps thanks to the *makandal* her mother had pinned to her skirt that she had recovered her voice.

In that moment, the force was speaking to her and said: stay. And she obeyed. She knew that she could have tried to resist, but the force would always be stronger. It was the same state of mind that Nicolette referred to whenever she declared, "My gut tells me to," or "My gut tells me not to," and that would suffice to convince her to do things one way or another.

Yes, she would stay. She had to. After all, she had not gone to all this trouble just to attend Mme Saint-Ar's ball, as M Saint-Martin had recommended, nor had she come there to admire the landscape. She was being honest with herself: it was for Lapointe alone that she had decided to take this trip. The problems at the Comédie had pushed her to escape, to forget, to be happy. It was for a chance to be happy or to forget that she had come there now. For heaven's sake, she was not going to leave because Lapointe had lied by telling her he lived with his family. How Nicolette would have laughed at her behaving like a scared little chicken. But how Joseph and Jasmine would have suffered to know about the situation she was in!

Lapointe had clapped his hand. Instantly, the door to the second room had opened and two young *câpresses* appeared, barefoot and wearing gingham dresses. They had long, wiry hair that fanned out over their shoulders in waves, and skin the color of sapodilla. Their faces bore no expression, as they kept their eyes lowered.

"Here are your bodyguards," said Lapointe to Minette. "For your safety, they'll lie at your feet. You, Fleurette, take care of Mistress's bath," he said to the slave with a little beauty mark over her upper lip, "and you, Roseline, take that bag and accompany Mistress to the blue room. You are not to leave her unless she requests it."

"Yes, Master," they responded.

Minette followed them. It was actually quite amusing to be served like an important lady. *So this is how wealthy free women live*, mused the young girl. *Slaves who call them Mistress, little companions as attentive as lapdogs — who follow them around and anticipate their every desire, men and women they purchase and over whom they have the power of life and death. What luxury!* "We'll receive you like a queen." Lapointe had certainly kept his promise about that: he was introducing her to the high life.

The two slaves brought Minette to a room decorated with blue curtains, a bed made of white wood, and a table topped by a beveled mirror. A few books were placed on the shelves. A plant with pink flowers bloomed in a crystal vase, set on a small table.

"Lie down, Mistress," said Fleurette, taking off Minette's madras headscarf.

"I'll go heat the bath water," said Roseline, removing Minette's shoes.

She took away the mud-encrusted shoes for cleaning.

Minette felt uncomfortable. Being served like this without wanting to protest, without trying to do for oneself the things being done by a slave kneeling at your feet, without offering a word or a look of thanks must take a great deal of getting used to. Abandoning herself to Fleurette's eager hands, she had let herself be undressed somewhat despite herself. She found it daunting to be nude. She tried to tell herself that Fleurette was merely a slave, bought by Lapointe and placed in her service for a couple of days, but she could not help but feel uncomfortable in front of this stranger who was going through her suitcase and removing her blouse. When Roseline came to get her for the bath, she was unpleasantly surprised to see her enter carrying a bathrobe, in which she wrapped Minette and then removed skillfully before guiding her into the bath. Minette let herself relax into the wide, tin-plate bath filled with warm water, into which fresh leaves, smelling of marjoram, had been crumbled. Then, the two slave girls rubbed her back, her arms, and her legs while softly humming a Creole song to themselves. Not the slightest indiscreet glance. Nothing but great assiduousness in their gestures and an expression that made plain their desire to please and to do a good job.

Minette stepped out of the bath, refreshed and perfumed.

When she went back into the bedroom, Fleurette had already laid out one of her outfits, with matching madras scarf and shawl on the bed. As Roseline hurried to dress her in a clean shirt, Minette stopped her and took her hands.

"That's enough now, my dears," she said to them in her abrupt manner. "You may leave me now."

Fleurette chewed on her upper lip, with its beauty mark just above it, and Roseline lowered her head guiltily.

"Mistress was not satisfied?"

Seeing their chagrined faces, Minette felt a twinge of remorse, which she quickly stifled, for she found the presence of the two girls discomfiting. Would she be obliged during the length of her stay there (for she would certainly stay, she knew that now) – would she be obliged to have these two over-eager attendants hanging around her constantly, encroaching on her solitude? They were very young – they seemed to be between fourteen and sixteen years old. They were cheerful, healthy, and dull. Never would she agree to such company.

"Would you like us to scratch your head, Mistress?"

"To tickle the soles of your feet?

"To massage your hands?"

"Your back?"

Minette smiled. That was the way of the Creole slave: hypocritical, flattering, perverse. *Poor little things!* she then said to herself. *It isn't their fault.* Jasmine must have had to do the same things. They were the product of their circumstances, and from their earliest childhood they had learned to honor their master's slightest whim. *How could they possibly resign themselves to that? I would die – or I'd maroon*, thought Minette. They had begun to roll on the floor, weeping.

"The master will punish us," whimpered Roseline, kissing her feet. "Please let us stay, Mistress, let us stay."

This could not be true. Lapointe allowed his slaves to be beaten? She could not believe it. *The girls must be exaggerating to get a reaction from me*, she said to herself again.

"Why are you lying?" she shouted at them. "You've never been beaten."

They looked at one another slyly for a moment and took on a closed and hypocritical expression.

Without looking at them again, Minette put on a green skirt and white blouse. She then tied a flowered shawl around her chest and added the brooch she had bought with Magdeleine Brousse at Miss Monnot's shop. She did not put on her madras headscarf but gathered her hair into two thick braids, which she tied with a green ribbon. Then she took the slaves by the hand and went out onto the gallery with them.

Jean-Baptiste Lapointe was waiting for her at the bottom of the stairs between two saddled and bridled horses. Seeing her so beautiful, he trembled as he walked to meet her.

"We meet again," he said in a low voice.

"That's a man for you – can't stand even a minute of dissatisfaction."

"I love you," he said to her, again without hesitation.

"Oh, no! Not in front of witnesses."

"What witnesses?"

"Those two, over there."

She gestured toward the two girls.

"Them! But they're slaves."

He said this with a horribly disdainful tone.

Minette was petrified with surprise. And so it was true. He was a slave-driver like any other. He was one of those vicious planters who considered the poor souls he bought as little more than animals! Without suspecting what was going on inside Minette, Lapointe signaled for the slave girls to leave them. He then clasped Minette's hand and brought it to his lips.

"Oh, leave me be!" she shouted at him.

"I love you," he repeated.

"Yes, but I cannot love a man of my race who calls his slaves 'slaves' with the same voice as a white planter."

His expression changed suddenly. Any trace of tenderness disappeared from his face. He crossed his arms over his chest.

"I was speaking to you of love," he spat out harshly.

"What's love, if one doesn't admire the person one wants to love."

He pretended not to understand her.

"But I adore you."

"I don't feel the same."

"Do you have reason not to?"

"I hate planters."

"And I hate them just as much as I hate slaves."

"Yet, the latter have made you rich."

He began to walk. An expression of dreadful rancor hardened his face; a wrinkle appeared between his brows, just in the middle of his forehead.

"They remind me of my own circumstances in this society. Oh! You'll never understand me…"

Despite that observation, he went on, as if pushed by some terrible force:

"My whole life I've suffered being who I am. My whole life, I've been insulted, ridiculed, and humiliated. I studied – is there any book I haven't read? Those that preach resignation as well as those calling for revolt. And when you read them, what do you find – hot air, nothing but hot air. You cross your arms and say to yourself, 'Well now, I know a lot of things, but what does it all get me?'"

He broke a branch off a bush while walking, and sharply whipped the side of his pants.

"This – this is life…"

He opened his arms wide as if to embrace a great expanse.

"Yes, this – taking, earning as much as possible, accumulating, imposing yourself through money, countering all the insults as much as possible, killing, beating, taking revenge, and viciously biting into all the little joys life offers."

She looked at him. Despite his violent attitude, there was something charming – both infantile and cruel – emanating from him. In pronouncing those last words, he had bitten his lip and his beautiful teeth were like a white stain on his dark mouth.

"I hate the Whites as much as the Blacks. The former despise me

and the latter debase me. I hate the female slave that was my mother –
her race is cursed."

"Your mother isn't responsible for anything. You know that perfectly well," protested Minette.

"Oh! All that's nothing but words. Female slaves sleep with any
master and we suffer the consequences. I didn't ask to be born. What
do I have running through my veins? The bastard blood of a Mulatto
– and that of an ignorant and superstitious African. I hate them both."

He burst out into hollow and desperate laughter.

"How could you have imagined for even one second that I lived in
some stupid sort of cozy little freedman's family?"

"You wrote to me…"

"You misunderstood the tone of my letter. The 'we,' though perhaps ambivalent, meant the slaves and me. I have nothing to be sorry
for. In any case, be clear on one thing: I have never violated a woman
in my life – my pride would never allow it."

She felt she needed to say something to him.

"I trust you," she murmured.

Yes, she knew he would never be content with doing such things.
He would do worse perhaps: his eyes, his gestures, his words – they all
suggested as much. He would do worse, there was no question – for
nothing in him sought to deceive. His gaze had the force of steel; his
body was built for battle. He gave the impression of an immovable rock,
and his strength seemed prodigious.

"Those are just words," he spat. "Usually, people detest me, and
that's normal."

That admission revealed such great suffering to Minette that she turned toward him. He had stopped walking, out of breath, his eyes aflame, and his shaking hands breaking the branch into the tiniest pieces.

"Can I ask you a question?" she said, overwhelmed.

"I always answer questions."

"Why did you kill that white sailor?"

"Which one? I've killed many. I'd kill a thousand Whites every day for pure sport. I hate them."

"Do you realize that you've just called yourself a murderer?"

"But there are nothing but assassins all around me. What do you call the Whites who maim their slaves and torture them to death?"

"Oh!" exclaimed Minette.

Finding nothing to respond, she threw herself onto the wet grass of the garden and began to weep. He knelt down beside her and said: "No, no, don't cry," and then stayed quiet for a long moment, until she finally raised her head.

And then, as if inspired by painful memories he could not wait to share with her, he went on.

"I didn't want to hate, believe me. No, I don't think I was born for that…There was once a time, oh! I was very young, and interested in science. I hoped someday to become a great doctor…I was made to understand that such a profession was forbidden to us…"

He was quiet for a moment then continued:

"A few months ago, I boarded a ship heading for Cap-Français. I met a young white lady on board who had come from France, and she found me charming. That evening, she joined me on the bridge reserved for people of color. When we disembarked, I found myself mixed up among the white passengers. The young lady had taken my arm. On seeing us, several people couldn't hide their shock. Knowing what was going to happen, I was looking for a way to get away from the young lady and escape when two planters came up to me and threatened to strike me if I didn't leave immediately.

"'But why?' asked the lady.

"'He's colored,' answered one of the Whites.

"'Colored?' exclaimed the lady uncomprehending.

"'Yes, the son of a slave. He has to respect the law, which forbids him to mingle with us.'"

He lowered his head and closed his eyes as if to hold back tears.

"And it's always been like that, for all of us…"

"Hush," protested Minette. "You're getting upset."

"Upset," he responded. "I'm used to it by now."

Then, cutting himself off, he ran his hand over his eyes, shivered as if just waking from a bad dream, and became distant again.

"Excuse me for bothering you with all of this."

He turned his head toward the house.

"The horses are ready. Do you want me to accompany you back to town?"

"I came to stay."

"You will, then?"

Immediately, his face became youthful again and so tender that Minette's heart melted with sweetness. *Oh! To love him – to love him despite it all. To close my eyes and just say, "Oh, well." To accept him as he is, or to transform him through love.*

"You will, then? Oh! I've been so thrilled to welcome you here.

With each passing day I said to myself, 'She's going to come, she's going to come,' and now you're here."

"And now I'm here," responded Minette.

He was suddenly a completely different man.

"I refused to dance with you," he said, chewing on a blade of grass. "Ask me why."

"I refuse."

"Go ahead, you prideful one, you – ask me why. Fine, you refuse. Well then, I'm still going to tell you, so there'll be no misunderstandings between us. You were dressed like a white woman. I detested you."

"And when did you begin to love me?"

"I loved you from the first moment I saw you."

His voice had become serious again. He turned toward her.

"Minette, people close to me call me Jean."

"Jean," she said.

He took her in his arms and crushed her into him.

She had tipped her head back and her lips were parted in a smile. He took her mouth so greedily that she moaned. He growled with desire and, without pulling away from her, stood up and carried her to the door of the salon, which two slaves had opened for him.

When Minette was standing again, he held her with such violence that she resisted.

"Ow! You're hurting me!"

He stepped back for a moment and went to lean against the windowsill. Minette went to join him. From the distance, the sound of an old Creole song reached their ears. Hundreds of voices chanted a sweet, sad melody to the rhythm of drums.

"Listen," said Lapointe to her. "The slaves are singing!"

"Yours?"

"Yes. The workhouse is just a few yards from here. I'll take you there tomorrow if you'd like."

The sound of the conch suddenly pierced the silence. The two dogs barked at full throttle and the slaves stopped singing as if cocking their ears.

"The conch!" cried Minette.

"The maroons' conch," added Lapointe. "My Negroes have stopped singing – they're interpreting the message. They'll be nervous tomorrow. It's a pity, but I'll send orders to the overseer to watch them closely. The work mustn't suffer because of this. I've got more than fifty sacks of sugar to send out next month."

The spell was broken. Minette, a faraway look in her eyes, saw in her mind the immense workhouse, the sordid huts, the backs hunched over under the arid sun, the overseer's whip, the punishments, the tortures…

She turned toward him. He was looking out the window again at the neighboring hills, upright like gigantic dark masses under the suddenly bright sky. He pointed a finger in the direction of one corner of the sky.

"Hauts Pitons Mountain!" he said. "They're all running toward that hill but they'll leave it someday."

"Please, don't talk about all of that," begged Minette. "It's one thing I just can't understand about you."

He took her roughly by the shoulders and pulled her to him.

"Do you at least understand the rest of me?"

He searched her face and it was as if his black eyes were shooting flames into her.

"Oh!" sighed Minette, "What a misfortune it is to love you!"

He silenced her with a kiss.

"To love without bounds would be true happiness."

She resisted briefly and extracted herself from his grasp.

"But why, why? Oh! There are so many questions I want to ask you...To know, to understand who you are. It's no easy task. You're impenetrable."

Despite it all, she remembered his attitude, his expressions, the other side of his personality that had made his hands tremble and had contorted his young face while he told her about himself. What did he mean when he said, "I hate the Whites as much as I hate the Negroes." He had suffered – she had the proof in those revelations he had made, and now he was taking his revenge as an anarchist who took neither one nor the other side and was content with selfish satisfactions. But he could be forgiven, thought Minette.

"But still, you work with Lambert," she said suddenly, without realizing that she was betraying a secret.

He jumped as if he had just been struck by a whip on the nape of his neck.

"Lambert!" he exclaimed. "How do you know about that?"

He burst into laughter and continued:

"Oh, I see – you're one of Zoé's recruits!"

"And you?"

"Me, I'm an individualist who fanatics like de Beauvais and Lambert take for a destroyer of Whites. And besides, their cause interests me in one way: I swore that before my death I'd enjoy the privileges laid out in the Black Code. I will claim our civil and political rights, along with all the others."

She threw herself against him, delirious with happiness.

"Jean, Jean," she murmured. "I was so afraid. Finally, I've understood. I feared loving you, while hating you at the same time…"

He cut her off and, moving away, looked her straight in the eyes.

"Hold on there, I'm not one to help slaves run away."

What does that matter? Minette said to herself, *as long as he understands the situation – as long as he's close to Joseph and the Lamberts. What does it matter – that touch of cynicism in his voice – as long as he's brave, rebellious, and a fighter. No, he isn't an assassin and he was right to kill!* She herself had felt that temptation one day at the market when she had watched young slaves being sold as they wept.

"Oh, it's all just so wrong, it's just so wrong," she sighed.

She walked away from him and looked up at the sky. An immense glow was visible through the branches of a mango tree, like a moving lantern. The young man came over to embrace her. They went back down the stone staircase and walked toward the alley lined with heavy-smelling orange trees in bloom.

He picked some flowers, which she put in her hair. Then he told her she resembled Myris, and how much he had liked one of the melodies from *The Beautiful Arsène.*

"I made the trip just to see you perform," he admitted to her.

So she immediately began singing for him:

I seem young,
But I'm more than a hundred years old.

I remember that in my youth
A particular fairy, to whom I was too precious,
Gave me a gift – it was the gift of pleasing
Grace, talent, beauty, the art of seducing,
That was my fate…
You see me in my original form
I see myself again at fifteen years old.

"What a voice you have!" said Lapointe, looking at her admiringly.

Roseline and Fleurette came to offer them dinner. Two place settings had been laid in the front room. They sat down and four young male slaves immediately began to flutter around them, anticipating their slightest gestures.

It was a veritable pageant of delicious courses and Minette, remembering Jasmine's meager meals, enthusiastically consumed the chicken and many desserts. Lapointe poured her a drink and raised his glass to her health. At the end of the meal, the two of them had managed to empty a good bottle of Bordeaux. When Minette wanted to rise from her seat, she stumbled a bit and, laughing, leaned against the table. He put his arm around her and led her outdoors beneath the trees, where the slaves had set up hammocks. She refused to lie down, claiming she had eaten too much.

"You're not a true Creole, then," he said to her.

"Yes," she responded, "but no one's ever gotten me accustomed to such luxury."

The young man's face darkened. He got into a hammock and was immediately joined by Roseline and Fleurette. Kneeling next to him, one began scratching his head, while the other, squatting, hummed and played a mandolin. She sang a lascivious and melancholy song while staring at her master with eyes filled with devotion.

"Minette," said Jean-Baptiste Lapointe all of a sudden, "allow me not to make any changes to my lifestyle during your time here."

He rose from the hammock and whistled for his enormous dogs, who immediately ran over.

He turned to his servants:

"Watch over your mistress."

Before they could even respond, Minette protested.

"Oh, no – you aren't going to impose these two girls on me. I, for one, do not need slaves."

"Will you feel safe without your 'bodyguards'?"

"What do I have to fear?" responded Minette. "Only your dogs scare me."

"You don't recognize your fiercest protectors, then."

"Perhaps, but I prefer to be alone."

"You should feel perfectly at home here."

He clapped his hands twice and the two girls left them.

He had changed yet again. *Why?* said Minette to herself. *Now what's going on inside him?* Might as well try to resolve an enigma. He looked at her in silence, in the half-light of the moon. A delightful feeling of trust spread over her, however, and relieved her of all worry. She had not thought for a moment about the Comédie or about Mesplès and her disappointment. A sweet lassitude spread through her limbs. *Oh, to spend my life here*, she thought. *To lounge in a hammock myself – to hear myself called Mistress and deliver myself into the hands of adoring servants I would reign over with kindness!* She raised her eyes to Lapointe. He was looking at her silently:

"You are very beautiful," he simply said.

She lowered her head. She was not going to let herself get carried away. No. She desired him too much for that. Why wasn't he speaking? Why wasn't he trying to do anything about the awkwardness between them?

"Farewell," he said quietly.

"Jean!"

She cried out to him – throwing herself into his arms.

In the little wood house, the candles burned out one by one. Slaves lying on mats slept in the gallery. Fleurette and Roseline had disappeared. Only the night stood between the lovers, a night rendered golden by the moon, whose rays penetrated into the bedroom, sprinkling Minette's loosened hair with shimmering scales that Lapointe collected with his lips.

XVII

For three days, they holed up together, speaking softly in their somewhat cramped quarters, which afforded them little privacy. An elderly slave, hunchbacked and toothless, who everyone called Ninninne, was the only person Minette was willing to receive in the bedroom. Ninninne brought them food, grumbled as she tidied the room, and observed their embraces unflinchingly. Unused to having slaves, Minette did not realize that all of them would have shown the same indifference, out of respect for the master. Lapointe refused to speak to an overseer who had come with important news to give him, and he left his bookkeeper at the door as well.

When, on the morning of the fourth day, he left the room, he learned that two of his best slaves had escaped. The spell was broken immediately. He insulted the bookkeeper and struck one of his overseers in the face with a leather strap. Minette screamed at him for this overreaction. She reproached him his brutality and he asked her not to meddle in things that were his affairs. Despite his refusal, she followed him to the workhouse and mounted a horse whose reins were held by a young slave. Lapointe threatened her. Despite her cries and protestations, he punished three Negroes and the wives of the slaves accused of having helped in the escape. Weeping, Minette got back on her horse and took off. She had hardly noticed the immense field of sugarcane, the naked little black children panting as they carried bundles of grass, the disabled old slaves weeding, the hundreds of black and brown backs bent over and the arms who raised machetes to cut the stalks, as she was already convulsed in tears. All of these laboring faces, streaming with sweat, nervously anticipating the overseers' whip, were screaming out a truth she refused to acknowledge. Everything, from the leaf-covered huts to the factory with its mill, its ovens, and its chimney – the entire existence of the exploitative and pitiless planter, rendered indifferent and vicious by the love of profit, was all spread out right before her.

The entire time it took to go back, Minette had not stopped weeping. She had been too happy and the wake-up was horrific. Once at the house, she immediately packed her things and hugged Ninninne.

"He ain't so bad," said the old slave, caressing her hair. "He fightin' and he fightin' – and he wanna fight the whole world. Don' leave now, don' leave – else he gon' get real mad."

Roseline and Fleurette, hidden in the doorway, looked at her hypocritically. If Mistress was leaving, if Mistress was crying, it must be that Master was finished with her. They rejoiced in the news without daring to smile.

Just before leaving, Minette was tempted to leave a note for Lapointe, but she decided against it and, calling for one of the slaves, asked to be driven to town.

Another storm was gathering. Ominous dark clouds hung in the sky like so many dirty rags. Intermittent bolts of lightning flashed in the sky, brewing silently.

Minette had hidden Saint-Martin's letter in her bodice and headed to see Mme Saint-Ar at the "Les Vases" estate. Though it was eleven in the morning, the somber weather cast an air of melancholy in the atmosphere, making it feel more like the late afternoon.

She got off her horse at Mme Saint-Ar's gate and saw that the many puddles of water had dried out. The streets seemed cleaner and more navigable. She adjusted her skirts and shawl and, carrying her bag, entered the property, at the end of which was a very beautiful house, adorned with long vines of red hibiscus. The house was dazzling: wide galleries enclosed by intricately decorated railings that attached to a staircase supported by white columns. The garden was filled with imported plants and, at its center, there stood a little Cupid-shaped fountain, water spraying from its smile. Magnificent lemon trees let fall golden fruits whose heavy scent lingered in the air.

Minette climbed the stairs and knocked on the front door. A little dog with long white hair like that of a sheep began to yap sharply. The door opened, and she was greeted by a smiling young black girl in a white apron and bonnet.

"Madame Saint-Ar?" asked Minette, looking around in surprise.

Immediately, she began to make the comparison: in her mind, she once again saw Lapointe's little wooden house with its one tiny gallery. To think she had found that beautiful and luxurious! Next to Mme Saint-Ar's heavy, carved wood furniture, mirrors, paintings, vases, carpets, and velvet wall-coverings, Lapointe's life was, despite his fortune, very simple, she realized – different in every way from that of the white planters. This immense living room, with its crystal chandeliers and silver candelabras, its overstuffed silk armchairs and gold ashtrays, revealed a luxury she had never seen before.

The black maid looked attentively at Minette. "Now who is this girl?" she seemed to be asking herself. "A white woman or a person of color?"

"Who shall I say is here?" she asked in a lilting French.

"I've come with a letter," answered Minette, taking the folded note from her bodice.

The maid took the letter and, with a slight hesitation, gestured toward a chair.

"Would Miss like to sit?"

She looked her up and down and, apparently, was satisfied with what she saw, as she offered a broad smile of welcome before exiting the room.

A violin played a Grétry melody in one of the adjacent rooms and, from time to time, the sound of a happy young woman's laugh reached her ears.

The black maid returned:

"Mistress is waiting for you."

Minette followed her through a string of rooms, each one more luxuriously appointed than the next, and found Mme Saint-Ar seated outdoors, in a large mahogany rocker. At her feet knelt a young girl of about fifteen or sixteen, with milky white skin and even features framed by silky black curls. Both wore silk *gaules* trimmed with lace, and atop Mme Saint-Ar's white hair sat a chambray bonnet with pleated flounces. Her cheeks were painted pink and her double chin gave her a friendly and vivacious air. She fixed her youthful blue eyes on Minette, as her heavily bejeweled fingers gestured in welcome.

"Come in, my child, come in," she said to Minette. "My dear friend Monsieur Saint-Martin told me marvelous things about you and your talent. I loved the theater when I was young and I'm happy to have you here with us."

"Thank you, Madame," answered Minette.

"Give this young lady a chair, Marie-Rose, take her bag, and then have someone bring her a nice, cool glass of fruit juice."

Marie-Rose stood up in a rustle of silks, smiled at Minette and took her bundle.

"Which room, godmother?"

"The pink one, dear."

"So, I'm told you sing at the Comédie?" said Mme Saint-Ar to Minette once they were alone.

"Yes, Madame."

"You've had the honor of dancing with the Duke of Lancaster?"

"Yes, Madame."

"My word! What charming modesty…Have you come here just to see me?"

The slightly malicious tone, with its innuendo, made Minette flush to the tips of her ears.

"Oh, my, my – by the Virgin Mother, isn't she just so lovely! I'm not asking you to tell me your secrets, my dear. I've had plenty of my own…Have you thought about having dresses made for my ball? In two days it will be the third Thursday in Lent and that very evening we'll have a grand ball, followed by a masked ball."

"Madame, it's just that…" Minette stammered, embarrassed, "Monsieur Saint-Martin must have forgotten to mention…"

She stopped and looked Mme Saint-Ar straight in the eyes.

"What, my child, that you're a colored girl? Do you think that isn't obvious at first glance?"

Minette lowered her head.

"And why would I care about the color of your blood? I'm not one of those racist French people. The only prejudices my husband and I have are against vulgarity and ugliness."

Laughing, she added:

"It's not very forgiving, but what can I do?"

Without answering, Minette threw herself at the older woman's feet and kissed her hand.

"My word, my word!" exclaimed Mme Saint-Ar with a smile, "So much gratitude for such a small thing. Come now, get up and come sit here by me. By the Virgin Mother, isn't she just lovely, with her golden skin and her dark eyes!" she repeated. "And to think, they say you've also got a marvelous voice…why, yes, you'll sing something for me on the night of the party…"

She got up heavily from her rocker and began inspecting Minette.

"Let's see, what sort of costume shall I have you wear? A Harlequin, a Pierrot – that would be too obvious…"

She pondered for a moment as she turned round and round the young girl.

"A narrow waist and perfectly curved, and what posture!…You'd make a wonderful Iseult, that's it. But I'll need a Tristan. Who is your paramour, my dear, go ahead, tell me – do you have a paramour? Tell me his name and I'll see what kind of taste you've got."

Minette, unsettled by this flood of kindness and courtesy, suddenly burst into sobs. Since her departure from Jean-Baptiste Lapointe's home, she had bravely held back her tears. But her heart, full with bitterness, suddenly burst like an abscess from the prodding of a lancet. A white woman had welcomed her without the slightest haughtiness or pity. And what a white woman! A great lady, wife of a planter, and impossibly rich, whose home even had a suite for the Governor!

Mme Saint-Ar watched her cry for a moment then, shaking her white curls and the folds of her bodice, asked:

"How old are you?"

"Seventeen, Madame," Minette sputtered.

"Now, now, I know all about that. You've got a case of heartbreak. I know just what you need: some solitude. Go to your room and don't you come out until I say so. I'm going to take care of you, all right?"

"Thank you, Madame," said Minette as she dabbed at her eyes with a handkerchief.

Mme Saint-Ar clapped her hands. Immediately, the door opened and a slave appeared. Minette jumped in surprise. It was the young traveler, Simon, who had helped her to find Lapointe's house. He bowed to Mme Saint-Ar and awaited her orders.

"My dear Simon," she said to the slave, "accompany Mistress to the pink bedroom and ask my goddaughter to have her meals brought to her there until you hear differently from me."

"Very well, my lady."

"Put yourself at her disposition and make sure she wants for nothing."

"Very well, my lady."

"Where are the gentlemen?"

"In the library, my lady. They're playing a game of craps."

"My word, what an obsession! They might have waited a bit!"

Minette followed the slave as they traversed a long corridor lined by a series of rooms on either side. On the back gallery, twenty or so slaves – cleanly dressed men, women, and children – washed dishes, shelled peas, and prepared the fire, all the while speaking in low tones. A delicious harmony seemed to reign over everything. On the countenance of the slave who accompanied her, just as with all the others, Minette was surprised to note a sort of blissful, trusting air of satisfaction.

The slave opened the door to a bedroom and said:

"Please make yourself at home, Mistress."

"Thank you, Simon. Funny we should meet again."

"I'm very glad of it, Mistress."

He bowed and closed the door after him. Minette went over to the window and looked out. As far as she could see rose up white huts, and gray smoke poured from a red brick chimney. The odor of sugarcane juice and freshly milled cane emanated in gusts. A Negro melody, taken up by hundreds of voices in a jumbled and deafening chorus, rose into the air to the rhythm of the drums. The workhouse! thought Minette. She closed her eyes and again saw Lapointe and his terrible expression of pitiless hatred; she saw again the hands of the overseers tearing off the slaves' clothes; she saw the whips they raised. Oh! The cries of the poor wretches – would she ever be able to forget them? How could he have done this? He was heartless – soulless! My God, it was all so irreparable! She threw herself on the bed and buried her head in the pillow. Once she had calmed down a bit, she looked around her and admired the pink silk curtains, the four-poster bed, the white mosquito netting, and the large mirror toward which she rushed over. Her eyes were a pair of red embers, with dark circles around them. She was suffering – her, Minette – because of an unworthy man. She clenched her fists and beat them against the mirror. Forget him, forget him. She went to her suitcase, opened it, and took out a clean dress, which she laid out on the armchair. The sound of a violin made her perk up her ears. Someone was playing, quite expertly, a melody from *The Beautiful Arsène*, which she had sung only recently for Lapointe. She ran to the window and looked into the courtyard. The violinist was the young slave, Simon. "Oh," cried Minette, so startled that she dropped the scarf she had been holding in her hand. The violin stopped and the slave turned his head toward her window. He bowed to her with a wide smile and, picking up the scarf, climbed the stairs and knocked on her door. As he handed her the scarf, Minette was struck by the refinement of his manners.

"Tell me, Simon, who taught you to play the violin?"

"Why, Monsieur Saint-Ar himself, Mistress. He's a great violinist and people come from quite far to hear him play."

He bowed, awaiting her orders.

"That's all. You may go."

He brought his violin back to his shoulder and played as he walked away. A wave of memories flooded over Minette. Once again she saw the little house perched on the hillside. The Indian-style curtains in the bedroom. A shiver passed through her. Her blood still burned from the man's embrace. She remembered his youthful laugh, the sadness of his expression, his careful lovemaking, his tender attentions. She blocked her ears so as not to hear the violin.

At that moment, someone rapped gently on the door and, before she could even answer, Marie-Rose's lovely head appeared.

"May I come in?"

"By all means, Miss."

"Oh, no – call me Marie-Rose. No formalities between people of color," she said as she gently closed the shutter of the door.

"You, Miss!" Minette let out, so astonished that she promptly forgot what the girl had asked.

"Yes, me. I'm the daughter of a white man and one of Madame Saint-Ar's slaves. My mother died giving birth to me, and so people think I'm Madame's relative."

"I never would have thought…" said Minette, looking at her closely.

"Why – because my skin is so fair? My mother was a Mulatress."

She was spirited, slight, and spoke with childishly charming inflections. As they chatted, she admired Minette's dress spread out on the armchair.

"Do you have a gown for the ball? Let me see your trousseau. There will be quite a lot of people – we sent invitations as far away as Les Cayes."

Minette felt the sadness wash away. She knelt down on the floor with Marie-Rose and took out the dresses Nicolette had made for her.

"They're pretty well made and the fabrics are lovely. But at a great ball, the women only wear low-cut gowns. I'll speak to my godmother… Don't you worry about a thing."

Ten minutes later, they had become such good friends that Marie-Rose confessed, laughing gaily, that she was in love.

"I have a lover, you know. His name is Fernand de Rolac. He's a young White who's just arrived in the country…He's young, he's handsome…you'll see him soon enough, at the ball…"

She hugged Minette and kissed her on the cheek.

"I'll have someone send you some food. You must be starved.

Goodbye for now. I'll come back to help you choose your costume and your gown."

"Thank you, Marie-Rose."

She made a funny little face, showing her affection for Minette, and then rushed out of the room.

XVIII

FINAL PREPARATIONS for the ball were made against the backdrop of the most gorgeous weather. An incandescent sun gleamed in the sky. The leaves sparkled on the trees, and the little "Love" fountain spouted a stream of water, heated by the warm weather.

Since that morning, carriages had been arriving non-stop, depositing a steady flow of *gaule*-wearing women and bewigged gentlemen.

Fifty or so slaves had been mobilized and put in the charge of a "master chef," a sturdy Congolese Negro with a prominent belly and deep voice who barked sharp orders that could be heard echoing through the residence. Twenty or so cooks and kitchen hands bustled about the food warmers underneath an arbor. Little Negro girls and boys on their knees noisily fanned the wood fires using straw hats.

Minette arose at ten o'clock in the morning. Mme Saint-Ar was right: a bit of solitude had helped her. She felt less sad and a great deal calmer. Since arriving in that house, all her convictions had been completely destabilized. She had learned not to put all the white planters in the same category and, in allowing her hatred to dissipate somewhat, her heart had been greatly unburdened. *So it's true, then, that slaves can be happy with their masters*, she kept repeating to herself, naively indifferent to the superficiality of her question. Having discovered goodness in some masters, she absolved them quickly, all too happy not to have to condemn the lot of them or to hate them all. Hatred is a heavy load to bear; to unload it is a relief. Minette's youthful nature was far better suited to joyfulness and untroubled gaiety than to a somber ideal of sorrow and bitterness. She was saddened to have discovered in Mme Saint-Ar the indulgence and the decency that she so desperately had hoped to find in Lapointe. Here, the Blacks were happy, whereas her beloved treated them like animals. She was not aware at the time that certain, more even-tempered planters found that they could get better results from their slaves with kind words and little treats than with blows. She was not aware that exploitation, camouflaged or not, had but one objective, which, in the cold light of day, bore the same face of suffering and horror. She would later learn that M Saint-Ar, as kindly and smiling as he appeared, resold his old, infirm slaves by the ton so as to replace them with new "recruits" whose strength and fitness assured the smooth functioning of the machines in his workhouse. For the moment, it sufficed for her to learn that some Whites actually bought violins for their slaves for her to feel just like the slaves themselves – infinitely grateful.

Besides, the welcome she had received was flattering, and further enhanced her gratitude. The slaves called her "Miss," and for the first time in her life she was an "invited guest" in a white salon. She was not being forced on anyone – she was being welcomed just like everyone else. Her golden skin and her beauty were admired by all, and M Saint-Ar had kissed her hand with a smile. All the mocking courtesy and Machiavellian diplomacy hidden in those gestures had escaped Minette. Their objective was too well concealed and she allowed herself to be caught up, despite her intelligence, in the gears of a clever ruse.

She first began to come to her senses when one of the slaves caught his hand in the mill. When the bell went off, the guests left their rooms and, curious, ran to gather on the back gallery where the sweating Negroes were preparing the banquet. A portly old slave woman who had been kneeling and blowing on a bundle of sticks stood up and nervously looked toward the workhouse along with all the others. A magnificent, unusually tall slave came in, held up by two other slaves who murmured words of comfort in his ear. One of the poor wretch's hands had been torn off to the elbow, and bright red blood poured from his frightful, shredded stump. Heavy beads of sweat dripped from his forehead, blinding him, and he moaned without even opening his mouth.

M Saint-Ar made his way through the crowd of guests and was soon in the front row of spectators with Minette and Marie-Rose.

"Bring him to the medic!" cried M Saint-Ar to those holding up the wounded slave.

The two of them ran up the staircase.

"He wants to speak to you, Master."

"My dear friend," said a bewigged man wearing shoes with gold buckles, just like those of M Saint-Ar, "how can you possibly think to allow your slaves to come disturb you in your home? Your kindness to these creatures truly has no limits."

The wounded slave wrested his arm away from his companions and he ran to throw himself at M Saint-Ar's feet.

"Do you see Master, do you see?"

And seeing that his Master was looking at him severely:

"It wasn't my fault, Master, I swear it. Oh, Master, you were so proud of my strength and my endurance. You called me your good Congo and you spoiled me. But now, Master, I'm disabled. You won't sell me like the others, Master, you aren't going to sell me?"

He got down on his knees to kiss M Saint-Ar's feet. The latter remained impassive.

"Master, say you won't sell me."

"We'll have to see, Michel, we'll see," said the planter in an annoyed tone.

"Oh, Master, Master, I'd rather die."

"Do you think any work would ever get done if I kept on a bunch of cripples and old men?…Let's go, take him to the clinic and get him fixed up."

The slave rose to his feet, weeping. With his good hand, he pressed forcefully on his horrific wound.

"What kindness," exclaimed a young woman whose transparent chiffon *gaule* exposed half her bosom. "My dear Monsieur Saint-Ar, how can you waste your time listening to a slave go on like that? He deserves a good beating, I'd say."

"Aren't you a pretty little monster," responded M Saint-Ar, taking her in his arms.

The guests headed back to their rooms, still chatting about the incident.

"That big ape interrupted my nap," said a young girl in a mauve *gaule*. "I'll have terrible color this evening. Are you coming, Louise?"

She wrapped her arm around a blonde girl who was laughing loudly at the comments made by a young man wearing a blue vest and white pants.

"What kind of story is that devil Fernand telling you now?"

"It's about colored girls. He says that…"

She leaned in to whisper some hilarious story in her friend's ear, making the latter burst out laughing.

"Let's go, my dear. It smells like billy goat in here," she said, looking around at the slaves and scrunching up her nose.

Minette saw Marie-Rose turn pale and took her hand. *Was the smug-looking young blond man telling obscene stories about colored girls her lover?* Minette wondered.

"Come, Marie-Rose, let's go to my room."

"Dear Miss Briand," interrupted Fernand de Rolac suddenly, "are you leaving?"

The blond man stopped in front of Minette and Marie-Rose and bowed.

"Oh, Fernand," murmured Marie-Rose plaintively.

"What's the matter, my sweet?"

"Me, nothing really…"

As he spoke, he stared at Minette. "Where have I seen that face before," he seemed to be asking himself. He bowed graciously.

"Will I see you later on, dear Marie-Rose?"

"Of course, Fernand."

He went off and the two young girls remained alone.

"Let's go," said Minette.

Two carriages came furiously up the driveway. Two couples emerged and Mme Saint-Ar went to greet them.

Marie-Rose sighed:

"I must go help Godmother. I'll come back and see you a bit later."

"All right."

Minette returned to her room and sat down on the bed. Her heart was beating so fast she could hardly breathe. Fleeing for a moment from the truth that had just been revealed, she vainly sought to figure out the cause of her distress. What was happening? Why had she felt something suspect and hypocritically inhuman in M Saint-Ar's attitude? Didn't he love his slaves? He didn't beat them, he fed them, he spoiled them, he cared for them. Wasn't that the truth? Still refusing to understand, she put her head in her hands. *What is it about me, dear Lord, that my thinking about things only makes me suffer?* she said to herself. *Why can't I resign myself to my fate and just accept that of others?*

She thought about Jasmine, about Joseph and, walking over to a little desk, took out a piece of paper and a long quill pen, which she dipped in a nearly overflowing inkwell.

Dear Mother, she wrote.

> *Do not worry about me. I am at the home of Mme Saint-Ar, to whom M Saint-Martin had the kindness to introduce me. She is a very rich white lady, married to a Creole from Arcahaie. I am surrounded by slaves who seem happy, and who cry at the very idea that they might ever be sold elsewhere. Marie-Rose, Mme Saint-Ar's goddaughter, lives as an equal with her godmother, although she's a quadroon. They call me "Miss," and M Saint-Ar kissed my hand when I presented it, as if I were a lady. Tell Joseph that certain white masters are less evil and less cruel than some black and mulatto masters...*

It was one o'clock by the time she had finished her letter. The lunch bell called the guests into the dining room. Minette rose and ran to the mirror to fix her hair. She was about to leave to head to the dining room when there was a knock on her door. She opened, and Simon entered with a large platter filled with food.

"Your lunch, Miss."

"But, I was planning to go to the dining room."

"Madame thinks you may still be tired and that it would be best were you to eat in your room."

"Oh!"

The truth suddenly hit her, though she pushed it away. She picked up the sealed letter and handed it to the slave.

"Would you please have this letter sent to my mother in Port-au-Prince?" she asked him.

Simon turned over the envelope to read the address.

The one they call Jasmine
Traversière Street
Next to Mme Acquaire's house

He raised his eyes to Minette and answered her in a strange voice: "Very well, 'Miss.'"

His tone bore a slight, though not unkind, trace of mockery.

He bowed politely, nonetheless, before leaving her.

Since her arrival, Minette had not left her room other than one time, to see the wounded slave. She would have been very happy, though, to join the others in the dining room.

She opened her door and poked her head out in curiosity. The muted voices of the servants mixed with the sound of clanking silverware and dishes. Twenty or so Negresses in white aprons and bonnets came and went between the dining room and the back gallery.

The "head chef" sweated profusely as he chopped the veal quarters and grimaced from the hot oil.

A violin played an unfamiliar melody. Minette left her room and slunk among the plants of the gallery on the right. The door to one of the bedrooms opened and she flattened herself against the wall like a thief. The sound of voices reached her ears. She craned her neck. A few steps away from her, on the immense table made even longer by added leaves, fifty or so Whites ate and chatted together. A multitude of slaves cluttered the room, posted behind their chairs. They were decked out in their most luxurious livery, white linen and gold buttons. All around the table, the black housemaids moved discreetly about, offering food, while the valets served the drinks. In a corner of the room, Simon played violin for the entertainment of the guests.

"In fact," said a voice Minette thought belonged perhaps to Céliane de Caradeux's uncle, "which masters are in the right?"

"What do you mean, dear Monsieur de Caradeux?" questioned M Saint-Ar.

"Which of the two of you – between my brother and yourself, Monsieur Saint-Ar – is correct? My brother claims that we must treat even the most docile slaves like animals, and you believe the contrary."

"My technique has always yielded full and complete satisfaction."

"But certainly you'll agree with me when I say that my brother produces the best sugar on the island. Perhaps he owes his success to his harshness."

"Others who make lesser sugar are just as wealthy," answered the master of the house with a polite and derisive little smile. "I'm no stickler, as long as my sugar sells."

Mme Saint-Ar interrupted by asking Simon to play her favorite melody.

"Walk around the table as you play, my dear," she told him.

Minette returned to her room and sat down before the rich platter of food. She barely touched anything. Something seemed stuck in her throat and after several unsuccessful attempts to swallow she pushed away the platter. The violin continued to play. Minette spread herself out on the bed but then rose to open the door to a black maid, who had brought her dresses sent to her by Marie-Rose.

"But isn't she in the dining room with the guests?"

"No, Miss is in her room with the seamstress."

Like all the slaves, she distorted her *r*s, pronounced *is* like *us* and drawled in something of a singsong. *In this house*, thought Minette, *everyone speaks French, more or less.*

She took the large cardboard box with the two dresses from the slave: they were taffeta, trimmed with lace, necklaces, and chiffon. The ball gown was pink and the Iseult costume was green, trimmed with ivory lace.

"My Lord, they're beautiful!" exclaimed Minette.

She dismissed the slave and threw the dresses on the armchair. Marie-Rose was also eating in her room. What could this mean? Perhaps she was tired and Mme Saint-Ar had probably asked her to rest.

The violin was still playing. It went on without interruption for the entire three hours of the lunch. Minette heard footsteps near her door, then the dull sound of a body falling to the floor. She quickly went out: two slaves were lifting Simon into a chair, while another poured rum into his mouth. He was sweating profusely and his mouth was so pale it seemed like a wide white streak against his dark face.

"What's wrong with him?" asked the young girl.

"He fainted. Oh, that happens every time he plays for too long."

The slave regained consciousness. He spread his trembling hands in front of his face and massaged his wrists with a painful grimace.

"These damn cramps," he sighed.

In the dining room, the guests rose from their seats. The house-maids and valets caring for Simon hurried to head back inside the house.

M Saint-Ar, no sooner having risen from the table, had unbuttoned his vest and removed his wig, following the example of his guests. He came out to the gallery, mopping at his forehead. Noticing Minette, he cried out:

"Well then, young beauty, still tired?"

"I haven't been tired for a while now, Monsieur."

"Pish tosh, that's just little girl's nonsense. You're all the same, you'd wear yourselves out without even noticing it."

Simon was still seated. He smiled at M. Saint-Ar, making a concerted effort not to show his discomfort.

"What's the matter, my boy?"

"Nothing, Master, I'm just resting to make sure I'm ready to make you proud later this evening."

"You played very well this afternoon."

He rapped him happily on the shoulder.

"Be in the salon early this evening. You'll play a solo for us. Oh! Monsieur de Caradeux will be green with envy," he added, punching his fist into his open palm.

"Thank you, Master."

M Saint-Ar then turned to the other domestics.

"Everyone will celebrate tonight. Make merry, I'll grant you quarter-liters of rum. Let them know in the workhouse."

A purr of satisfaction arose from the group of slaves.

"Thank you, Master!" they cried, happily. "Thank you, our dear Master."

M Saint-Ar called the head chef over and, placing his hand familiarly on the slave's shoulder, said:

"You, César, be sure to stay on top of things. Don't let the rum go to your head. An unsuccessful dinner is a dishonor for a great planter. Don't you forget that – and watch that you don't overdo it. Remember your title – you're the 'head chef.'"

The portly slave rubbed his chubby cheek with his thick hand.

"As far as the rum goes, Master, there's a risk. I've been on my feet since dawn and I've still got to work tonight. If I drink even a drop I'll fall asleep."

"Well then don't have any."

"Very well, Master. Thank you, Master."

The brass band from Port-au-Prince had just arrived in a carriage driven by a white coachman. Their instruments in hand, the musicians removed their hats to greet the master of the house and, following one or another of the slaves, went to the rooms that had been set aside for them. The guests began installing themselves under the trees for their afternoon nap. Young Creole girls stretched out on mats, heads leaning on a folded arm, smiled at the compliments offered by lightly clad gentlemen with flushed cheeks. Kneeling near the mats, young slaves with large earrings and their heads wrapped in brightly colored scarves used straw fans to swat away the mosquitoes.

Marie-Rose came and went among the guests, offering them refreshments and little hors-d'œuvres on silver trays.

"I've never met a Creole less lazy than Marie-Rose," someone pointed out admiringly.

Fernand de Rolac, seated next to the young blonde with whom he had been speaking that morning, had moved the conversation into slightly thorny territory. He was telling the story of how he had won a duel in France over a woman who had left him two days later and run off with his adversary.

"European women are both heartless and heartbreakers."

The little joke had been thrown out by a balding young man, lazily stretched out in a hammock and attended to by two slaves holding fans at the ready.

His comment had inspired cries of protest and reproach.

"European women are no worse than any others. There are good and bad women everywhere."

"Of course, even among the colored girls," said the man, bursting into laughter.

"They have one quality, at least," declared Fernand de Rolac. "They don't fade easily."

"That's what they say," said the young woman in the chiffon *gaule* to whom M Saint-Ar had offered his arm a few hours earlier.

"Is it true that they smell bad?" asked the young blonde seated next to Fernand de Rolac, with a burst of laughter.

"Louise," he interrupted, "you just can't keep anything to yourself..."

Marie-Rose's hands trembled so much that she let the platter drop.

"What's the matter, my beauty?"

Fernand ran to her and placed his arm around her, but she shrugged him off and ran away.

She knocked on Minette's door.

"My God, what's the matter, Marie-Rose?"

Without responding, the young girl let herself fall onto the bed. The charming, youthful features of her lovely face were all distorted and tears streamed down her cheeks.

"They're insulting colored girls."

Minette shrugged her shoulders.

"They're just showing off. They don't really believe it. Believe me."

"Even Fernard..."

"Let me ask you something, though it might seem indiscreet...Are you sure that Monsieur de Rolac loves you?"

"That's what he's told me."

"Have you spoken about all of this with your godmother?"

"She's encouraging it."

"Do you plan to let Monsieur de Rolac know the truth about your status?"

"Oh, no – never! Godmother has forbidden it."

"I see...is he the first man to court you?"

She lowered her head and sighed deeply.

"No. But the other was a quadroon and Godmother didn't approve. He knew everything and…he loved me."

Thus, out of this delicate and lovely girl they had also created a torn, tortured creature that they tossed around at will, even deciding her fate. Why had they revealed her social condition if only to have her pass for a White? Why, if they truly loved her, were they encouraging her to accept this smug little nobleman who would never make her happy?

Marie-Rose wept softly. She rose from the bed and hugged Minette.

"They're good to me, so good to me – both of them. And yet… sometimes…oh! Minette, don't betray me, please don't ever betray me…"

She kissed her friend and went to the mirror.

"Oh my, they mustn't see that I've been crying."

"Lie down here and rest."

"I can't – I don't have time. I've got to check on the table, put flowers in the vases, and count the silver. Then I've got to help Godmother get dressed."

She laughed.

"I'm the only one she'll let near her, really…She finds the slaves clumsy and calls me 'her little white maid.'"

She too had been given a flattering little title. A pretty title that kept her from realizing that she was being taken advantage of and that made her believe she was loved.

"Marie-Rose! May I talk to you like an adult? May I give you some advice? You've shared your secrets with me, and I won't betray you. Will you do the same for me?"

"I swear it, Minette."

"Where is the quadroon you once loved?"

"He lives near here."

"Find him and marry him."

"What?"

She became so pale and trembled so much that she had to hold on to one of the bedposts.

"You're advising me to leave Godmother, to go find this man without telling her? How ungrateful I would be! Have you not understood all that she's done for me? My mother was a slave, have you forgotten?"

She began to sob, hiding her face from Minette.

"I've been harsh. It was my way of telling you plainly how things really are. Marie-Rose, if what I'm saying makes you hate me, I understand that you would be well within your rights."

"Minette!"

She looked at her friend, terrified, opened the door and fled from the room, her handkerchief covering her eyes.

XIX

As THE GUESTS who had been present throughout the day began to file into the salon in all their finery, additional carriages continuously brought less intimate acquaintances from all corners of the country. A crowd of curiosity-seekers backed away from the rearing horses: poor Whites, people of color, and local domestics gathered at the carriage entrance and tried to catch a glimpse of whatever bit of the gala they could.

The marching band launched into a minuet. M Saint-Ar opened the ball with the laughing blonde Louise, and immediately other couples followed them.

Minette, relegated with Marie-Rose to the room reserved for the young people, observed the splendorous decorations all around her: the flickering lights of the crystal chandeliers, the sumptuousness of the clothing, the grace and elegance of the dancers, the immense tables laid for the dinner – she found it all ravishing. In this room, where she found herself with Marie-Rose, a few planters' daughters – all younger than they – were making their society debut that evening. Young Creole girls, buttoned-up and shy, having lived like so many rare birds under the iron rule of their parents; and adolescent boys who, with their smooth-faced smiles and awkward gestures, slyly caressed exposed young necks with their eyes...

Marie-Rose, in her white brocade ensemble, tapped Minette on the shoulder with her fan and made a face in the direction of the youths.

"We have our pick. Who should we dance with?" she whispered.

Minette smiled.

"And so now I've got to go greet this bunch and be nice to them? How stupid they seem!" she added.

The band struck up a contredanse following the minuet.

"When can we go into the ballroom?" asked Minette.

"When one of the dancers gives us a sign."

"Well, then, let's go get these gentlemen."

"How awful!"

"Make a decision…"

"Okay, let's go…"

Opening their fans, they headed boldly for the group of young people.

"Well, now, gentlemen – are you afraid of a little heat?" asked Marie-Rose mockingly.

"We've been waiting around like wallflowers all this time," added Minette.

There was an immediate scramble in the face of this unexpected gift. The ten youths who found themselves there immediately began to bow before the two beautiful young ladies.

"Come, come, now, there are plenty of us to go around," said Marie-Rose, prodding some of them toward the young girls who, thrilled, rose hastily to their feet.

They left the room on the arm of their partners and entered the ballroom.

"Wait," advised Marie-Rose, "this dance is ending."

And turning to her partner:

"Do you even know how to dance?"

"Well…um…yes…of course," stammered the young man, turning beet red.

The orchestra had gone quiet. Hidden in the doorway, the young people waited. M Saint-Ar, passing by on the arm of a very young man, stopped near the door without noticing them.

"Yes, my dear Monsieur de Laujon, they've been subjected to a harsh disciplinary regime, no matter what Monsieur de Caradeux thinks. Without them even realizing it, I get them to work their hardest. They're decent creatures, and in exchange for my running this show without whips or torture, I never have to worry about fires or poison," said M Saint-Ar.

"Are they even capable of things like that?" asked the young man, inquisitively.

"You're new to this country, and it shows. Yes, Monsieur de Laujon, they're capable of great destruction – and even of destroying themselves. Their vengeance can be horrendous. Whatever happens, anyway, those of us here in the Vases region – we'll be just fine. There isn't a single one of my slaves who wouldn't die for me."

The young man smiled sardonically.

"And how do you feel about mixed-bloods, dear Monsieur Saint-Ar?"

"I keep them happy, all the while steering as clear as possible. Sometimes I go so far as to invite them into my home. Frankly, some of them are pretty stand-up people. But since you never know with their kind, I handle them just like I handle my slaves and…"

The rest of his sentence was muffled by the first bars of a quadrille. Minette and Marie-Rose had not missed a word of their discussion.

"Now do you see what I told you was true?" Minette whispered to Marie-Rose pitilessly.

Marie-Rose followed her partner into the ballroom. But now, she had no desire to dance – none whatsoever. A feeling of confusion mixed with an incomprehensible need for solitude gripped her heart. M Saint-Ar's voice still rang in her ears. "I handle them just like I handle my slaves…" So that was what it was – his affection! And it was surely the same thing for Mme Saint-Ar…Both of them must have been "handling" her the way they "handled" all the rest…How could she have believed for even a minute that they thought of her as "the young lady of the house" – her, the daughter of a slave?

These last words drummed against her temples to the point of making her dizzy. She let go of her partner's hand, let out a slight cry, and lost consciousness.

Minette, abandoning her own partner, rushed over to her. Raising her head, she called her name. Someone passed her a vial of smelling salts and suggested:

"Tell Madame Saint-Ar."

Someone else jostled past the dancers impatiently.

"Excuse me, excuse me…"

It was Fernand de Rolac. He bent over, picked up Marie-Rose in his arms and, followed by Minette and Mme Saint-Ar, headed for the nearest bedroom in the house.

"What happened?" asked Mme Saint-Ar, in a tone that suggested slight annoyance.

"She was dancing, Madame," answered Minette, holding the vial of salts near the young girl's nose.

"With you, Fernand?"

"Alas, no, dear Madame."

"And I had specifically asked her not to leave the 'young person's room' until I called for her."

"Ah, temptation…" Fernand dared to comment.

"This child has never disobeyed me…Oh! She's opening her eyes… Are you feeling any better?"

Marie-Rose passed a trembling hand across her face.

"What happened? How silly of me."

With great effort, she sat up and smiled.

"Not to worry, it's nothing."

She looked at Mme Saint-Ar and her lips trembled.

"I'm sorry, Madame."

"You've made yourself a bit of a spoilsport, but it's nothing, as you say. Come now, are you feeling well enough to go back to the ballroom or would you prefer to be in your room?"

Mechanically, she caressed her goddaughter's hair.

"My goodness, she's beautiful, my little goddaughter!"

She said it without enthusiasm, in a monotone voice Minette found chilling.

"If you permit, Madame, I will bring your goddaughter to her bedroom myself."

She helped the young girl to stand.

Fernand de Rolac took Marie-Rose's trembling hand and pressed his lips to it with a bow.

"I'm so sorry about this troublesome little incident…"

"As am I."

"Speaking of, my child," said Mme Saint-Ar to Minette in a friendly voice, "you promised to sing a little something for me. I believe you'll be sensational as Iseult. Do you like the outfits I had made for you?"

"I'd have liked to come thank you, Madame, but didn't want to disturb you."

"That's very well, not another word…We've got to end the first part of the ball in just a few moments. Dinner is at midnight. What time do you have, Fernand?"

The young man consulted his watch:

"Nine-thirty."

"Good. And now that you know the secret, keep it to yourself. It's got to be a surprise. It would appear that this young lady has a voice…"

She took M de Rolac's arm and headed back to her guests. Minette accompanied Marie-Rose to her bedroom.

They closed and locked the door and then sat on the bed without speaking. Marie-Rose had a faraway look as she nervously crumpled her handkerchief in her palm. Bursts of women's laughter could be heard among the rustling of silks and the tapping of high heels on the wood floor of the corridor.

"The masked ball will soon begin," noted Marie-Rose tonelessly. "The guests are coming to put on their costumes."

"Yes."

Her attitude suddenly changed and her eyes began to shine.

"Tell me more about yourself, would you?"

"What do you want to know?"

"Everything. Till now, I've only lived with my own little story. This house, the workhouse filled with slaves, and the domestics in my service have been my whole world…I imagined the entire world to be just like this world I see here every day. A simple caress, a banal compliment sufficed to flatter me – like a dog. Since no one had ever told me about my mother's past, I was satisfied with just about anything – the slightest thing made me perfectly content. Look at my dress – it's brocade. Never before have I asked myself where all this money comes from…"

The costumed guests left their rooms and called out to one another from one end of the corridor to the other. The orchestra welcomed them with a sarabande.

"When I was very little," continued Marie-Rose, not realizing that she was speaking instead of Minette, "when I was very little, I understood so many things. But they settled there, deep inside me, as if in reserve. Take those barrels where we store the wine. They all burst after a while. I feel just like them – I'm too full and now I've burst…Even though I had nothing to compare my life to, some little voice told me: careful, things aren't supposed to be this way. I don't even know if they're worse elsewhere."

"In a way, they're worse, yes," answered Minette. "Because it's always better to tell yourself you're happy, even if you're in denial."

"Oh, no – that's exactly what's criminal about this. It would have been better if they'd humiliated me, beaten me, tortured me!" she spat out loudly.

Minette started and placed her hand over Marie-Rose's mouth.

"Are you mad?"

"I had to tell myself over and over, 'They love you – can't you see that they love you!'" she finished softly and with such a humble air that Minette's heart tightened, so young did Marie-Rose appear in that moment. "When I went to the workhouse, the slaves' sweating faces made me weep. I'd become very attached to an old one-armed man who told me stories from his country in Creole. Monsieur Saint-Ar sold him in spite of my tears and the slave's tears. Since then, I've seen so many sold that it doesn't even affect me anymore."

She went over to the window and leaned out.

Shadows lit up by the torches emerged from the workhouse.

"The slaves," she murmured, "they're going to celebrate. In a few hours, someone will toss them the leftovers – as if they're dogs. They'll get drunk and believe they're happy. They've been tossing me leftovers, too, but I didn't realize it."

Minette put her hand on Marie-Rose's shoulder and also looked outside.

A few slave couples were dancing the "chica," bumping hips, while others played with sticks – swearing and tapping their feet in the dust.

Under the arbor, the head chef watched over the food preparation, surrounded by several kitchen hands. When the sound of the *lambi* rang out, they turned instinctively toward the mountains, their gestures suspended in mid-air.

Marie-Rose shivered and looked with Minette in the direction of the hills.

"My old 'storyteller' used to say to me, 'They won't forget Makandal any time soon…The *lwas* spirits speak with the voice of the *lambi* and when the Negroes hear it, they hear messages from the gods of Africa. A day will come when they'll all rally around that voice.'"

She stopped for a moment, as if thinking, then added:

"I never knew who Makandal was."

"He was a maroon leader. On his orders, the slaves launched a campaign of poison and fire and they fled to the hills, where they remain to this day."

"Are there other leaders?"

"That's what they say."

Marie-Rose closed the window and remained leaning against the shutters for a moment, trembling.

"I'm afraid," she murmured.

"You mustn't be, my darling."

"My old one-armed friend used to say the same thing – but the sound of the *lambi* always frightened me…"

With that, she sat down abruptly on the bed.

The masked guests passed by the room, laughing gaily.

"The masked ball," exclaimed Minette. "I promised Madame Saint-Ar I'd sing."

Marie-Rose rose quickly to her feet.

"I'm coming, too."

She began rifling around feverishly in a drawer and tossed two black eye masks into Minette's hands.

"We'll be incognito. Godmother has barely seen my costume – she won't recognize me. Besides, there'll likely be dozens of Columbinas."

"But if you're going to faint again…"

"That's nonsense. I'll hold up till morning."

When they entered the salon, a hundred Harlequins, Columbinas, shepherds, and Tritons were holding hands as they ran about in a furious farandole. The two girls were immediately snatched up by glee-fully insistent hands, while someone shouted: "Follow along, follow along, keep moving…" The group rushed passed Mme Saint-Ar, imposing in her chatelaine's costume. Dressed as a Triton, M Saint-Ar chatted with a Spanish dancer, who was none other than M de Cara-deux, and a charming shepherd – Alfred de Laujon. The farandole passed near them and grabbed the latter, despite himself.

"They're choosing the young ones," noted M Saint-Ar, as if to pro-voke M de Caradeux.

"Oh! Well I prefer to dance. Excuse me, my dear friend."

He went to bow before a somewhat out-of-place-looking mid-dle-aged woman, who smilingly offered him a seat.

In the meantime, the farandole had made its way out into the gar-den. When it reached the hedges, someone cried out: "Break the chain," and immediately a hundred voices repeated: "Break the chain!" Minette had her right hand in that of Alfred de Laujon. Once the farandole had scattered, he kept her hand in his.

"And who are you, lovely Iseult?" he whispered to her.

"Iseult, herself."

"And I'm Tristan in a shepherd's costume. Show me your eyes."

"No."

She tore her hand from the young man and began to run.

"Wait, Iseult, wait."

Couples embraced under the groves, avoiding the lights.

Looking for Marie-Rose, Minette returned to the salon and went to curtsy before Mme Saint-Ar.

"Is it time, Madame?"

"Ah, yes! Is that you, my child? Your costume suits you well. And the idea of the mask is perfect. Monsieur de Laujon," she called out, "where has that young man gotten to?"

"Here I am, Madame. I was chasing after a charming Iseult but, if I'm not mistaken, this is her right here."

"You don't have to chase her anymore, my young friend," answered Mme Saint-Ar, rapping him lightly on the arm with her fan. "Now come help me prepare a surprise that, I'm sure, will be very much appreciated…"

She walked away with the young man who, after listening to her, headed straight over to the orchestra. The pianist played several chords to call for silence.

"Ladies and Gentlemen…" began Alfred de Laujon. But his voice was lost among the laughter and noisy shouting.

"Ladies and Gentlemen," he said more forcefully. "May I have your attention for a moment?"

"Hoorah!" someone shouted.

Everyone gathered round, suppressing their laughter, and the couples that had been lingering in the garden hurried back, their hair in disarray.

"Ladies and Gentlemen, our delightful hostess, Madame Saint-Ar, has asked me to inform you that there will be three great surprises this evening: the first will be a song recital, performed by a young lady who prefers to remain incognito."

Cheers burst out.

"The two other surprises have to do with all those in costume here tonight. Two prizes will be distributed: the first will go to to the funniest costume and the second to the most beautiful…"

"Hoorah!"

"And now, I ask for your absolute silence. The performance is about to begin."

In the same moment, a man in a yellow domino costume, face hidden by an eye mask and hands gloved, entered the room and stood in the doorway, facing the piano. Alfred de Laujon, spurred on by the little raps of a fan and some sidelong glances, smiled his charming smile and discreetly gave out compliments and pecks on the hand. He made his way out of the crowd of ladies and joined Mme Saint-Ar, who was directing Minette toward the piano.

"What will you sing, lovely Iseult?" he asked.

"The melody from *The Beautiful Arsène*."

And, leaning toward Mme Saint-Ar:

"Who will accompany her, Madame?"

"Monsieur Saint-Ar himself."

At that moment, the man in the yellow domino costume took a few steps forward and placed himself just in front of Minette.

Simon handed a violin on a silver platter to M Saint-Ar, who struck up the first measures.

Dressed in her Iseult costume, Minette began to intrigue the crowd.

Once she began to sing, everyone looked at her in astonishment.

Some of those who had heard her at the Comédie in Port-au-Prince whispered as they looked on. M de Caradeux, standing next to the man in the yellow domino costume, immediately exclaimed:

"My word! It's the 'young person'!"

And then, turning to a powdered and paunchy marquis:

"Oh! My good Lugé, what are these times we're living in? Our dear Monsieur Saint-Ar – height of eccentricity – has opened his doors to some colored wench and brought her among our wives and daughters!"

The man in the domino costume made an abrupt gesture, as if he were about to lean toward M de Caradeux to say something. Then he seemed to think better of it.

"Madame," said Alfred de Laujon to Mme Saint-Ar, "this young girl has the most beautiful voice I have ever heard…Now who is she?"

She leaned in to whisper a few words into his ear. Then, so that everyone might hear:

"Bring the young girl to me, Alfred. She deserves a kiss from you," she added.

The final note of the little aria had just been sung and was met by enthusiastic applause. As she waved and bowed, Minette observed the man in the yellow domino costume. He smiled at her and her heart leapt. Still she did not want to believe it. At that moment, M de Caradeux, an impertinent expression on his face, walked up to the piano, where he stopped and addressed M Saint-Ar:

"My dear man," he said, "to amuse your guests you've gone so far as to break the law; do you really think we can abide such eccentricity and such derring-do?…"

And turning to Minette:

"We would very much like to see the eyes of this Iseult," he finished.

With an abrupt gesture that nothing in his attitude would have prepared them for, he tore off her eye mask and threw it at her feet.

Stony-faced, she looked him directly in the eyes.

"So I was right – it's that young colored actress that's got everyone talking," he declared.

The dubious comment was interrupted by stifled exclamations and whispers.

"I don't appreciate Monsieur de Caradeux's actions one bit," said Alfred de Laujon indignantly.

"But she's a colored girl, after all," reasoned Fernand de Rolac.

"Leave the salon, my dear," advised M Saint-Ar, with an embarrassed air. "That would be for the best."

At that moment, the hand of the man in the yellow domino costume landed on M de Caradeux's shoulder.

"If you are not a coward, Monsieur…"

The voice made Minette shiver. It was Lapointe. She had to do whatever it took to prevent this duel or it would be the death penalty for him.

"My Lord!" she murmured.

She scanned the room for Marie-Rose and saw the young girl waiting for her, hidden from Mme Saint-Ar. She was first to raise her hand in a subtle gesture, and Minette ran to join her.

"Who is that?" she whispered.

"He's my lover."

"Is he white?"

"No…"

"Oh! This is incredible!"

And she crushed Minette's hand in her own.

"What weapon, Monsieur?" said M de Caradeux.

"I'll leave that up to you."

"Swords."

The man in the domino costume smiled.

His lips were painted and the bottom half of his face was hidden by the mask.

"So be it."

M Saint-Ar made a sign to Simon, who rushed into another room and then returned with two swords, lain on a silver platter.

"Here are your weapons, gentlemen," said the master of the house with an incomprehensible smile. "Now let's take this into the garden."

"Holy Mother Mary," whimpered Mme Saint-Ar, "my poor supper!…"

They went down the long stone staircase.

"Remove your mask," said Caradeux, brandishing his sword.

"You put one on."

The clanking of the weapons mixed with the cries of the women and the exclamations of the men. Lapointe, taller and stronger than his adversary, immediately had the upper hand.

"Well then, Monsieur," he cried, "it seems you're about to be skewered."

M de Caradeux, beside himself, grew livid, dropping his head.

"Who are you?"

"Your pride will suffer less if you don't know…"

Minette, once again separated from Marie-Rose, who was pressed up against a tree, seemed not to know what to do with herself. Someone touched her arm. It was Alfred de Laujon. He bowed, took her hand, and kissed it.

The sincerity of his gesture comforted her.

"Leave, Mademoiselle. That would be for the best, believe me," he told her.

She bowed her head and went to her bedroom. She took her things, piled them into her little suitcase, and then quietly went back out to the garden. At that very moment, a cry rang out: Lapointe had just disarmed Caradeux and was holding the tip of his sword against the old man's chest.

She forgot to be prudent and threw herself between them.

"Minette," shouted Marie-Rose…

"You owe her your life," screamed Lapointe. He then slashed Caradeux's white shirt twice, grazing him slightly. He removed the man's hat and held it on the tip of his sword like a trophy. "I'll keep this as a memento…"

And then he burst into a horrifying laugh.

"Who is that man? Someone take off his mask…"

Minette fled. She heard Marie-Rose calling after her but did not turn around.

Jostling the curious onlookers who had gathered around the gate, she managed to force her way through to the street. A horrible chill spread through her body. *Now, I'm not going to faint like Marie-Rose*, she said to herself. *I'm perfectly used to such insults, such humiliations.* She breathed deeply and heard a horse galloping behind her. Two large dogs surrounded her and licked her hands.

The horseman came up to her at a gallop, bent down, and swept her into his arms. He sat her just in front of him.

"Oh," she sighed. "Why did you come?"

He took off his mask, galloping all the while.

"And you? What were you looking for with those nice Frenchies there?"

"Humiliation, as you saw."

He laughed his sonorous laugh.

"The Saint-Ars! The nice, sweet Whites who love their slaves!" he cried. "So what did you think? Lapointe beats his wretches and Monsieur Saint-Ar spoils them…That's it, isn't it?"

"Leave me alone."

"You run away from my house, you abandon me because I have a few slaves whipped. Foolish, foolish girl…"

The horse climbed the path and stopped at the stone staircase leading to the lone little gallery. Lapointe set Minette down and passed the reins to a slave.

"How pitiful my home must seem to you after so much luxury!"

"Oh, just be quiet!"

He turned her around suddenly and took her in his arms.

"I thought you'd left forever. I beat more than ten slaves that day."

"You're nothing but a monster."

"What does that matter, since I'm in love with you?"

He took her mouth and plunged his hand in her hair in a gesture of loving tenderness.

She freed herself and wiped her lips with the back of her hand:

"You won't beat anyone as long as I'm here?"

"You're imposing conditions?"

"Just the one."

"And if I refuse?"

She brought her face close to his.

"That will mean you don't love me."

He pressed her against him, kissed her face wildly and, opening the door to the bedroom, had her enter first.

He kept his promise. During the eight days Minette spent under his roof, he refrained from getting angry. She only allowed herself to be served by Ninninne. He did not object and sent away the two Mulatresses of the house. He behaved perfectly and spoiled her immensely. The two dogs became friends whose caresses she accepted and who she rolled around with, laughing, in the garden. For eight days, they led a carefree life troubled only, for Minette, by the sorrowful songs coming from the workhouse.

One morning, Lapointe went to Arcahaie and came back with a hidden note, which he passed to her.

"The coachman was going to bring this to Madame Saint-Ar, but I said I'd take care of it. I've got some mail of my own."

His face darkened suddenly.

"Kiss me," said Minette.

He ignored her and caressed her hair.

"Read your letter."

She unfolded it and read aloud.

My dear Minette,

The public is calling for you. The first performances given by Mmes Dubuisson and Valville were real successes but the public now seems weary of them. Mlle Dubuisson missed a note and was booed.

You've had your revenge – as you can see. Our director wrote us that your younger sister has had great success in Les Cayes. He is counting on you to take up your work – especially given that your contract is reaching its term and he will soon have to pay you the agreed upon three thousand pounds. We await your return and send you our love.

Mme Acquaire

Minette could not help but be overjoyed.

"The death-blow," muttered Lapointe darkly.

She put her arms around his neck.

"We'll be together again. Life must go on."

"For me, it will stop after you leave. Oh, if only you loved me enough to give it all up. I'd marry you…"

She murmured:

"Jean, my career is also a part of my life."

He lost his temper at that.

"Well then go back to your career!" he shouted at her.

She saw that he was in pain and tried to reason with him.

"We both have things that are important to us. We're both bitter. You said to me one day that having the workhouse and those slaves would help you to do what you want. Well, my voice is the only thing I possess…"

"You're the only possession that truly matters to me."

She felt such distress in his voice that she moved away from him, for fear of crying herself.

She went into the bedroom and folded her dresses to put in her suitcase. He remained alone on the gallery for a moment; then Minette heard the sound of a galloping horse. He did not return until that evening, muddied and half drunk. She welcomed him without reproach and helped him to undress.

"When are you leaving?" he asked her.

"Tomorrow."

He stretched out on the bed, groaning, and pretended to sleep.

He did not touch her and she did not dare fuel his desire. During the night she heard him wake quietly. He went into the next room and returned with a bottle of rum, which he put down at the foot of the bed. Three times he got up ever so quietly and took long swigs from the bottle. The third time, he fell back on the bed, completely drunk. So she tucked him in like a child and cried. When she left the house the next morning, he was still sleeping. She kissed Ninninne and gave her a note to pass on to Marie-Rose.

"Go to Madame Saint-Ar's. Ask for Miss Marie-Rose. Do you understand?"

"Miss Marie-Rose at Madame Saint-Ar's," she repeated. Then, taking Minette's hands:

"Like this, you're leaving us, Mistress?"

"Alas, yes, Ninninne."

"You're abandoning him. What will he do without you?"

"Watch over him, do you hear me? And when you want to send me news, go find Miss Marie-Rose. She'll help you."

"Very well, Mistress."

"Farewell, my dear woman."

"God be with you."

A slave helped her onto the horse and she left the little Boucassin house where she had lived moments she would never forget.

XX

IT WAS ELEVEN o'clock in the morning when she arrived in Port-au-Prince. Jasmine burst into tears upon seeing her, then wrested her away from all the market-women and pulled her into the house.

"Christ have mercy, how you've grown, how you've changed!"

"My sweet Mama, in just two weeks?"

"It's true – you've changed. There's something different – it's the look in your eyes."

As she spoke, she brought Minette's bags into their narrow little bedroom.

"Have you had lunch? Do you want to eat something?"

"I can hold off for a bit. Tell me what Joseph and Lise have been up to."

"They're both doing well. Lise is having a lot of success in Les Cayes and she's been writing me the craziest letters…"

"She must be just perfectly thrilled, my dear little sister."

Jasmine kept talking as she unpacked Minette's things. Stretched out on her bed, Minette observed her mother out of the corner of her eye. She noticed the gray hairs mixed throughout her messily piled up chignon. She saw the deep wrinkles etched in the sagging cheek of her mother's prematurely aged face.

"Mama, you're the one who's changed," she could not help pointing out.

Jasmine turned away quickly as if terrified by Minette's gaze.

"I'm an old woman, you know that – an old abandoned woman."

She left the room and returned a few moments later with a cup filled with a yellowish liquid.

"Here," she said to Minette, "I made you a lemongrass tea – strong, just the way you like it."

Minette took the cup in her hands and swallowed a few sips of tea.

"Mama, don't you have anything to tell me?"

She placed the cup on the little table near the bed.

"Mama!"

At that moment someone pushed violently on the front door. Relieved, Jasmine left the bedroom to see who had come in. Minette heard Nicolette's strident voice. She had the impression Jasmine was whispering, for there was a brief silence during which she heard nothing.

She rose from the bed and left the bedroom.

"Ah! There you are," cried Nicolette in her lilting Creole. "How good you look! Let me give you a hug…And the dresses, were they a success?"

She let out a crude little giggle.

"The air in Arcahaie did you some good…"

She then took a note from her bodice and handed it to Minette.

"Read this to me, will you," she begged. "My sweetheart thought it was a good idea to send me a love note. I never dared to tell him I don't know how to read."

"It's high time you educate yourself," said Minette, looking over the note.

"Why? None of that matters. You can't learn to make love from a book."

Jasmine looked at her with an offended air and walked away.

"So what does it say," she asked, taking the note out of Minette's hands.

"It isn't a love note," answered Minette. "He's ending things."

"What?"

"This gentleman is letting you know that he's soon to be married and warning you not to try to see him ever again."

"Oh! The pig! It's clear he's no aristocrat. Oh! And anyway, I don't care. There's plenty more fish in the sea…"

She tore up the note and, bending over Minette, said:

"And so, your rendez-vous? Is he a faithful white man at least?"

"He isn't a white man at all."

"Lord have mercy! So we're all the same. We sleep with Whites to get money and show off a bit, but for true love we turn to the freedmen. Even Kiss-Me-Lips…"

She launched into the story of her friend's strange love affair, torn between the love of a "poor White" and a young Mulatto with "silken hair," thank you very much. The "poor White" intentionally insulted the young Mulatto, who responded in kind. So the former had the latter arrested, claiming that he had raised a hand to him. The tribunal had the young Mulatto whipped, and he died soon afterward of indignation. According to Nicolette, this was the cause of the debauched life Kiss-Me-Lips now led.

"Back then, she went by her given name: Marie-Rose…"

"Marie-Rose," murmured Minette.

She was suddenly overwhelmed by a flood of memories so great that she became dizzy: the image of her lover filled her heart and she felt the salty taste in her mouth that comes right before tears. She ushered Nicolette out, pretending a sudden fatigue, and went back into the bedroom, where she found Jasmine.

"That Nicolette is shameless," said Jasmine.

"She's not a bad person, Mama."

"It's true she lost her mother very young, but what a rough way of speaking she has!"

"She didn't grow up in the 'big house' like us."

"What do you mean by that?"

"She was born free, and so was her mother."

At that moment, Minette noticed her mother shiver and had the feeling she was hiding something.

She stood up abruptly and clutched her mother, crying:

"Speak, Mama, speak – I'm begging you."

"Oh! I wanted to have at least one day with you," she complained. "I wanted to spare you the bad news for at least one day. My hair has gotten whiter, my face has a new wrinkle – it's because of this situation, this horrible situation…"

"Come on now, speak, Mama!" cried Minette.

And in her terrible impatience, she was almost hurting the poor woman, completely distraught.

"It's Joseph," began Jasmine.

"What's happened to him?"

"They found a runaway at his place and the police have brought him to Monsieur de Caradeux."

"Joseph, my God!"

"We haven't managed to find out anything yet. The day after his arrest, Labadie came over here with a very beautiful young black girl."

"Zoé!" Minette immediately exclaimed.

She smoothed her hair, holding back her tears. Joseph taken to M de Caradeux – Joseph enslaved – no, it wasn't possible!

"What are you going to do, Minette? There's nothing we can do. It's no use. Stay with me, stay with me."

She grabbed her bag and, embracing Jasmine:

"My poor, sweet Mama! How hard this life is!" she said simply.

She squeezed her in her arms and then ran outside, where the merchants and neighbors welcomed her once again with joyful greetings. She responded to their show of affection with a forced smile and crossed the street, cluttered with little stands and stalls. Avoiding the block where the Comédie stood, as well as the Acquaires' house, she headed down Bretagne Street and passed by the King's Garden to arrive at the Lamberts'.

The street was abuzz with the tumult of the big city and the colorful crowds of inhabitants. A carriage passed close to her. The driver tugged at the reins and slowed down. A head leaned out through the curtains: it was the Marquis de Chastenoye.

"Where have you been hiding, lovely child?" said the old man to Minette.

"Excuse me, Sir – thank you, Sir. You do me a real honor, Sir."

She was so distracted that she almost failed to recognize him. As she stammered out the niceties required for addressing all white men of his standing, she remembered the day he had saved her from certain arrest. He was powerful; he could help her. She looked at him more closely: he was old, so old he seemed decrepit. She smiled at him as she recalled the wave of memories that the slightest word brought to mind – to the point of making her dizzy. Everything was coming to her in a sort of free association of thoughts, bringing her, breathless, back to the little house in Boucassin.

"Would you like to join me?" pleaded the old man with his quavering voice.

Minette's lips trembled. Was she going to be able to stand the half-impotent old man's bold and libertine gropings? My God, they were brave, those girls who sold themselves to such wrecks for a few bucks!

When she was seated next to him, she was surprised to see him keep his distance. He spoke to her protectively and respectfully, and told her how much the public missed her presence at the theater.

She turned and looked at him squarely.

"I'm nothing more than a buffoon for them, Monsieur."

He took her hand gently and with such fatherly concern that she looked at him with curiosity.

He had fine features that once must have been filled with life, and his blue eyes, with their faded lids, looked into hers with something more akin to sympathy than disdain. His old powdered face was framed by a wig, whose curls cascaded down his frilled shirt. A gold chain, from which there hung a heavy charm attached with a diamond-encrusted pin, knocked against his vest.

"Don't be bitter, my child. A clown exerts himself flattering people and making them smile, whereas you…"

He stopped himself and let Minette's hand fall on her skirt, as if to prove to her that there was nothing untoward in his actions.

"You," he continued, "you charm and you seduce. It's a big difference…"

"Thank you, Monsieur."

"You look people in the eye. It's important to be able to look people in the eye. I have a soft spot for you: your voice reminds me strangely of the voice of a woman I once knew, way back when…oh! it's been a long time. I'm old and I live on memories."

The carriage crossed the King's Garden in the reverse direction and reached the block where the Comédie was situated.

"Here you are in front of your theater, my child."

"In front of the theater! But I wasn't going to the theater…"

"The driver will stop wherever you wish to go."

She was suddenly afraid of him. An irrational fear that he knew she was headed to the Lamberts' and that he had figured everything out. She felt the same chill that came over her every time one of those bewigged white men spoke to her. It was the fear of the oppressed before the master who, with a gesture, could save or crush them. She began to tremble.

"What's wrong, my child?"

"Me, Monsieur? Nothing at all."

"I have no desire to harm you, believe me."

"Yes, Monsieur."

"Didn't I save you once before?"

"Yes, Monsieur."

"So why are you trembling?"

"I don't know, Monsieur."

"You look people in the eye, but you tremble."

She burst into tears and threw herself at his feet, kneeling on a cushion that had been tossed on the floor of the carriage.

"Oh, Monsieur! If only you could help me."

"I'll help you. But do get up."

"It's my brother, Monsieur. He's been taken by Monsieur de Caradeux for having hidden a runaway, and it's killing me."

"What's his name?"

"Joseph Ogé."

"Calm down, dry your tears, my child. I promise I'll help you."

He shouted a quick order to the driver.

"Would you like to get out here?"

"God himself put you on my path. Oh, Monsieur! I swear I'll show you my gratitude some day."

"Go along now, my child."

She got out of the carriage with such elegance and lucidity that she had the feeling she was performing a role – a role that would help her save Joseph. She had barely begun to fight. She would run to the Lamberts' and then she would go to see Céliane de Caradeux. All sorts of ideas took shape in her thoughts suddenly, as if to strengthen her resolve. Yes, she could fight; yes, Joseph would once again be free. The Marquis de Chastenoye admired and respected her. Once again her voice had made a miracle. A noble, rich, powerful white man had said to her: "You charm and you seduce," and he had not asked for anything in exchange for the help she had asked of him.

She barely looked at the passersby and walked quickly to the Lamberts'.

An old black man dressed in rags was walking just ahead of her, limping and holding his hat. One of his arms was wrapped up in a cloth that all of a sudden became soaked with blood. He turned around and Minette saw his terrified face, distraught with suffering. The expression lasted no more than a second. Just as quickly, his thick lips parted in a beatific smile and, holding his filthy straw hat in his free hand, said:

"Anything to spare for me, Miss, anything to spare?"

The old man walked slowly, but from time to time he quickened his step as if hurrying to get off the street before attracting attention. The bandaged arm was still bleeding and the cloth had become red with blood. No one paid him any attention and the bustling crowd passed right by him indifferently. When he looked at the bandage, Minette, who was following close behind him, had the feeling his fear had suddenly become real panic. She removed her shawl and, passing near to the injured man, close enough to touch him, she slipped it to him furtively. She left that first street, then a second, and still he followed her. When she knocked on the Lamberts' door, he came up to her and raised his head.

"My God!" she murmured.

He was so pale that his dark face had become ashen.

The door opened and Zoé appeared.

"Minette!" she exclaimed.

"I'm hurt," breathed the injured man, and he wobbled on his legs as if about to fall.

Zoé looked up and down the street and then seized his wrist.

"Come in," she said to him, closing the door carefully.

As soon as he was inside the house, he dissolved in tears.

"They sawed off my arm, they sawed off my arm…"

"Come."

With Minette's help, she pulled him into Lambert's workshop.

Seeing them come in, Lambert closed the little window that provided all the air in the tiny room.

"Where do you come from?" asked Lambert, bringing his finger to the injured man's chin to force him to look up.

"I come from far away. The workhouse of Monsieur Laplace, on the road to Arcahaie. A slave was condemned to be starved to death; I was caught giving him food. I was condemned to have a limb sawed off every day and then buried alive. Other slaves helped me to escape."

He threw himself to his knees and, indicating his missing arm, said:

"As I was walking, I came across this young lady; my arm was bleeding and she passed me her scarf. I followed her…"

He looked at Minette and, beginning to weep again, said:

"Please don't abandon me, Miss, don't abandon me," he pleaded.

"We must bring him to Louise," said Lambert.

"I'll bring him," answered Zoé.

"Get ready, sister," Lambert answered simply. "And may God bless you for having given yourself so entirely to the work we're trying to do."

Then turning to Minette:

"You've just risked your own freedom."

"Others take greater risks than I."

"That's good. Go with Zoé."

He leaned over the old slave and took his sawed-off limb in his hands, staring at it with his immense eyes with their unendurable gaze:

"We'll bandage you up and then you'll go with my sister to join someone who'll take you into the hills. May you never forget that by protecting you we're risking our own freedom."

"Oh, no, I'll never forget – no, by all the gods of Guinea and by Jesus our Lord and savior, never, never…"

"Hush," said Lambert, "and be strong so as not to scream. I'm going to bandage your wound…"

Minette and Zoé had gone into another room, where they found the old couple seated on their white wooden rockers. They recognized Minette and asked her why she had been gone for so long. The father's eyes, so like those of his children, followed Zoé's gestures as she began to dress.

"Where are you going?" asked the mother, in her Martinican Creole.

"To see Louise, Mama."

"Are you bringing someone?"

"Yes, Mama."

"Be careful, Zoé. I'm old. I need you."

"I know, Mama."

"I paid a high price for our freedom, Zoé…"

The young woman's eyes abruptly changed expression. They were ablaze, as if looking at something white-hot.

"Don't weaken my courage," she protested, as if repressing some horrific suffering.

"Leave her be," intervened the father, raising his eyes to his daughter.

"We're very old – very old, and our children are trying to ruin us."

She lowered her head and kept it down as she spoke, as if ashamed of the words she was speaking.

"Remember the past, Zoé, remember…"

"The past!…"

"Yes, our suffering, your childhood, your brother's…"

She rose from the stool and walked painfully toward her daughter.

"Remember, Zoé – remember the whip, the hunger, the exhaustion, the fear…"

The young woman let out a light cry and threw herself against the table, bent over, her head buried in her arms.

Minette shivered. *What suffering Zoé must be remembering to cause such weakness!* she thought to herself.

"Remember," continued the mother.

"Leave her be," the father cried out a second time.

But she kept talking – and her hesitant steps, her trembling hands, and her anguished face conveyed the despair, the worry, the fear, that terrible, daily fear that had caused the constant trembling in her limbs ever since she was a young girl. She declared to everyone, completely unashamed, raising her deformed hands toward the ceiling:

"I'm afraid, I'm so afraid…"

The words escaped her in a breath that seemed to give them even more weight, to paint them red – the same color as her own blood. She, the former slave who had prostituted herself with the "poor whites" hired by the workhouse and with other slaves, so to buy her own freedom and that of her children. She had sold her favors with the sole purpose of saving money. Every night, upon returning to her hut, her limbs aching, half drunk with exhaustion – she received men whose desires she satisfied on that same hard ground where her husband and children lay asleep.

Minette, at a breaking point, clasped the old woman's hands.

"I'll go with Zoé on this mission – I promise you…"

Zoé raised her head. Minette saw her so calm that she had the impression her every feeling had been buried deep inside of her. Only the wide and still feverish eyes still bore a hint of her despair. Zoé finished dressing, tied her madras scarf over her hair and then, rifling through a drawer, took out a *makandal*, which she looked at steadily for a moment without speaking.

"Come, Minette," she said simply.

"Have you forgotten anything, my child?"

"I haven't forgotten anything, Mama…"

Then the old woman wept with such force that her entire body seemed to shake with spasms. And still, not a single tear ran down her cheeks. The source was dried up, but the fear that called them forth was so fresh that it gripped her entirely.

For a second, Minette felt herself overcome by that uncontrollable fear. She wanted to leave them all there – to run home and never come back. *I'm going to risk my own freedom*, she said to herself, trembling. As if to make her even more nervous, the old woman clutched Zoé's arm:

"Be careful, my child…"

"I'll be careful, Mama."

She went over to her father. For a brief moment their so-similar gazes seemed to become one.

"Be sure not to let anyone look into your eyes," said the old man. "Your eyes give everything away."

Zoé bent over and accidentally kissed him high up on the cheek; the kiss rang hollow, as if it had fallen into a hole. Minette turned to look: one of the man's ears was missing. It had been sliced off at the base.

XXI

Everything had gone well on the trip from Zoé's to Louise Rasteau's house, where they left the slave they wisely had disguised as a market-woman. Minette had suffered no more than a bout of intense emotion, and as soon as she had returned to the Lamberts' she felt herself capable of the most dangerous missions. She left Zoé with her parents and went to find Jean-Pierre in his workshop. She found him sawing a plank and smoking his pipe.

"You want to speak with me, my child," he said once he became aware of her presence.

"I'm going to see Joseph, Lambert," she announced straight off.

"At the Marquis'? That would be madness. The house is guarded by vicious dogs and slaves armed to the teeth."

"Mademoiselle asked me to come see her."

"You?"

"Yes, me. She likes hearing me sing and…"

"If you can do that, if you can manage it…"

He let go of the saw, placed his pipe on the table, and looked at Minette.

"Zoé's right; you're no coward."

"Thank you."

He walked toward Minette and took her shoulders in his powerful hands.

"Can I count on your discretion and your courage?"

"I'm no coward, Lambert," she repeated, looking at him boldly.

"Don't I know it…But I'm not so keen on exposing you…Your talent in the eyes of the white world is useful to us, in a sense. You don't think so, huh? Well, it's true. There are lots of things – both big and small – that can lead to the same goals…If I've never thanked you for singing so beautifully, let me do that here today."

"Thank you, Lambert."

A horse's gallop suddenly broke the silence in the little street. Lambert cocked his ear and Minette saw all the features of his face suddenly tense up with worry.

"Might be a soldier from the constabulary," he said tersely.

The horse stopped with a whinny at the front door of the house, and Minette noticed Lambert shiver and clench his fists. Then the horse galloped away.

"When you leave here," he said, "be very careful, and come back when you have news about Joseph."

"May I leave now?"

"Wait."

He went to the front door, opened it slightly, and looked up and down the street.

"Go ahead."

Obsessed by thoughts of Joseph, she headed toward the Comédie. She found the actors in a state of complete dismay, having just learned of François Saint-Martin's death. Goulard, his eyes reddened, came to greet her. He kissed her hand and wiped his nose. They were all so horribly sad that for a moment Minette wanted to escape back to Arcahaie. Ever since her return, all she heard was bad news. First Joseph, now Saint-Martin. What was Lise going to do? How alone she must feel with this dead man on her hands!

"Poor François," said Macarty. "Dying was the only thing it wasn't like him to do."

"How did he die?" asked Minette, stunned.

"Fever. We got a letter from a notary he told his final wishes to."

"Lise hasn't written?"

"We don't know anything more."

The Acquaires arrived just then. They embraced Minette and fell sobbing into Macarty and Nelanger's arms.

The blonde Dubuisson, slightly less pretentious since being booed, looked at Minette out of the corner of her eye. "What did she have, that girl, that the public found so appealing?" she seemed to be asking herself. Mme Tessyre and Magdeleine Brousse blew their noses with loud sighs. Saint-Martin's death brought back the memory of little Rose, and it was not clear who Mme Tessyre was weeping for. As for Mme Valville, she no longer had her birdlike vivacity and remained locked in an embarrassed silence.

"My God," Magdeleine Brousse let out with difficulty, "death is a horrendous, horrendous thing!"

François Mesplès walked in on these words. He was so overcome with emotion that he did not even notice Minette's presence. He shook all the actors' hands, repeating:

"What terrible news, what terrible news!..."

Minette stood between Goulard and Mlle Dubuisson. He noticed her just as he held out his hand to Goulard, and his unhappy expression was replaced by a sort of grimace, at once irritated and conciliatory. Without extending his hand to her, he said:

"And so here you are. You must be quite happily savoring your little victory. You ditch us. The public demands your return. Someone writes asking you to come back...For heaven's sake!..."

And turning to Mlle Dubuisson:

"And as for you and your famous missed note!..."

"She had a sore throat," said Mme Valville coldly.

"Well then you should have kept her from singing."

"I've been feeling a bit 'off' for some time now," interjected the young Dubuisson, looking slyly in Minette's direction.

"What exactly do you mean by that?" questioned Mesplès.

"Oh, I don't know...That girl left, and the very next day I start going hoarse and am overcome by migraines...In this country, the Whites are at the mercy of these people and their horrible superstitions...."

"Are you crazy?" spat out Minette indignantly.

"Be quiet," interrupted Mesplès. "How dare you call Mademoiselle Dubuisson crazy?"

"She insulted me."

Goulard stepped between them and Mme Acquaire pleaded Minette's case, guaranteeing her innocence.

"Very well," said Mesplès. "I wash my hands of the whole thing. You launched this girl and the public adores her. Up to you to deal with it. As long as I'm paid, I could care less from now on."

Mechanically, he caressed his bulging stomach and held Minette's gaze for a long moment.

"She's the most beautiful little nuisance of a freedwoman I've ever seen in my life," he concluded. "She isn't afraid to look a white man in the eyes…Ah, if she didn't have that voice!…"

He went out, leaving the actors as shocked by Saint-Martin's death as they were upset by the obligations they would have to take on. The Comédie was swimming in debt. The planters had not paid their subscriptions for the past three months. They had signed off on bonds that once again they would have to bring to Mesplès for an advance of the money at a usurious rate of interest. The bohemian Saint-Martin had lived like he was immortal – from strokes of luck to rolls of the dice – and he owed money to the stagehands, the set designers, the porters, and even the guards hired to keep order in the theater. M Acquaire let out an enormous sigh and, his eye twitching grotesquely, said:

"Saint-Martin has left us with an empty till on our hands. Who's going to take responsibility?"

Depoix looked at his bosom-buddy Favart. They smiled at one another and, stepping forward, answered:

"We will."

"Good," said Goulard, "but I warn you: the Comédie owes the actors just as much as it owes the folks backstage."

"If the Government grants us direction of the theater, we'll make good on everything," promised Favart.

"Good luck with that!" said Magdeleine Brousse, inconsolable at the loss of the young director.

"Thanks," Depoix answered coldly.

Everyone went his separate way and Minette went out with Magdeleine Brousse, who had begun railing against life.

"I swear, life is a real bitch; a real nasty bitch. I do my best to forget it by sleeping with everyone I fancy. It's the only way to get old and die without regret."

To prove that her words were more than hot air, Magdeleine left Minette and headed over to a young soldier who was calling her.

"Farewell," she said. "I'm going to go forget about this bitch of a life for a few hours in the arms of this handsome young man."

The soldier looked at Minette. He was tall and slender, with dark hair that fell in unruly curls on his forehead, setting off his splendid blue eyes.

"Bring your friend," he shouted to Magdeleine.

"Do you want to come?" she asked Minette.

"No."

"Bring her," the soldier insisted.

"She refuses."

"She just hasn't had a chance to see me up close…"

He came forward and, his hand on his hip, he lowered his irresistible, smiling young face to Minette.

"So are you coming?"

"No."

"You don't like me?"

"No."

She gave a seductive smile and headed home. Her throat was dry and it suddenly seemed to her that she had lived the last few hours without even knowing whether or not she was suffering. When she arrived at Traversière Street, the vendors had just gone inside, fortunately. She was so tired she would not have been able to speak to them. The painter Perrosier was standing in his doorstep, as filthy and drunk as ever. He called to Minette laughingly:

"Come pose for me, beautiful girl."

She ran away and opened the door to her house, crossing the front room and heading to the bedroom. She threw herself across the bed and remained there, not moving, eyes staring at the ceiling. "Jean, Jean-Baptiste Lapointe!" her heart screamed. "Joseph! Joseph at Caradeux's, Joseph enslaved! No, no, no! My God," she muttered, "take pity, take pity on us." Then she remembered Mlle Dubuisson and Mesplès' recent insults.

Jasmine stuck her head through the partly opened door.

"Are you here? Do you want to eat something?"

"I'd like something to drink, Mama. Please give me something to drink."

Jasmine handed her a big glass of cool water, which she drank down without stopping to breathe. Then she stayed in bed, seated now, not moving, and turning so many things over in her thoughts at once that her head began to hurt. What did she really want? To go back to Boucassin? To save Joseph? To slap every White that had insulted her? She struggled with herself, caught up in the gears of those three impossibilities. She tossed aside those ideas and made an effort to steer her thoughts toward something she could actually accomplish. How much longer was she going to let herself be insulted by the people at the theater? Saint-Martin had died owing her nearly three years of wages; she would go claim what was due her and would demand an apology from Mlle Dubuisson and François Mesplès. She called to her mother.

"Lise is going to come back, Mama," she told her. "Monsieur Saint-Martin has just died in Les Cayes."

"The young director? My God! And Lise is all by herself there!"

"No one's going to eat her, Mama. But I'll never forgive her for not writing to us about any of this."

"She must be on her way – Lord, Lord!…"

Minette stood up and began undressing. She took a bath and went back to bed. That evening, Lise arrived seeming so defeated that, forgetting her anger, Minette took her in her arms and held her there in silence.

"Oh! It was horrible – horrible, Minette!" she immediately confided. "He fought hard; he didn't want to die. He held on to the bed, to my arm, to the doctor's. Oh, I'll never be able to forget it…"

Jasmine quickly made her an infusion of calming leaves and put her to bed.

"Oh, Mama! He was so good, so perfect with me. He was like a brother, like a big brother. I never would have thought that a White could behave that way toward me…"

"Don't talk about all that anymore," advised her mother.

"But I'll never, never be able to forget. He didn't want to die, he didn't want to…"

She kept sobbing as the vendors, who had noticed her arrival, began coming by to ask questions and offer advice. Minette tried to usher them out. They were crowding the tiny little room, all talking at once and shaking their heads wrapped in bright, multicolored scarves. It was at this juncture that Pitchoun showed up and declared that he would be entering the army.

"I'll soon be a uniformed soldier. If you don't find that too unappealing…I…"

He was stammering, as Minette looked at him, amused.

"I'm sure I'll find you very handsome."

He leaned forward suddenly and kissed her cheek.

"Little rascal!" she said to him, mussing his curls with an affectionate caress. "Come say hello to Lise. As for me, I've got some business at the Comédie. You'll have to excuse me…"

As she walked along, she bumped right into a hanged man's feet and was seized with a feeling so strong she felt suddenly unsteady.

A man of color was hanging at the end of a rope. His head had been stuffed into a bag, and a sign hung from his feet. Horrified, Minette read:

CRUSH THEIR DEMANDS

She stayed there for a moment, unable to think and unaware, even, of the passersby who had begun to gather. Then she took off running back home, passing by her mother without looking at her and rushing into the house, where she crashed into Pitchoun, who was just on his way out.

"What's the matter, Minette?"

"Oh, just leave me be."

"But what's the matter?"

"What would you like me to tell you?" she spat out with such rage that he just looked at her, stunned. "That a colored man's just been hanged? Don't you know just as well as I do that these things happen?"

She hid her face in her hands.

"Minette!…"

"I turned right around, you see? I was going to the Comédie to demand the money they've owed me for three years. I was going to demand apologies for their uncalled-for insults. I was going to demand – me, to demand..."

She broke out into a nervous, strident laugh that rang so false Pitchoun seized her hands.

"Listen to me, Minette, listen to me..."

"Oh, leave me alone..."

"I'm not a child anymore. Listen to me..."

"Let me be, I beg you, let me be, let me be!"

He let go of her hands and slammed the door after him. Once she had come to her senses, she ran to call after him. He was already gone.

She sat down for a moment and stayed there looking straight ahead, not moving.

"Minette!" called Lise.

She stood up and opened the bedroom door.

"What's going on with Pitchoun?"

"Nothing," answered Minette.

"You seem terribly upset."

"Yes. But it's nothing."

Lise had a fresh compress on her forehead and her eyes were still red from crying.

"I'm hungry," she stammered, as if ashamed.

"I'll go look for something for you to eat. I don't think there's much at the house. And I don't have a cent. And you, did you make some money in Les Cayes?

"Yes," she admitted, "but I had to buy all my costumes."

Minette went out and came back with a piece of bread and a caramel, which she handed to her sister.

"That's all I could find."

Lise immediately sat down on the bed and began devouring the food.

"I haven't eaten anything since yesterday," she admitted, as if to apologize.

And as she gobbled up mouthful after mouthful, she told Minette about her debut on the stage, her successes, and Saint-Martin's death.

"Oh, if you'd only seen me in the role of Theresa, with my multicolored camisole, my pipe, and my hitched-up skirts! Monsieur Saint-Martin played the role of Papa Simon. What a hit we were!…"

Minette made a mocking little grimace.

"I know you don't much like those local plays. But this one is adorable, trust me. The sets represented Papa Simon's hut and provision grounds, and my partner was a young white man that, unfortunately, we had to do up in blackface. He was handsome, but when he touched me his hands got me all dirty…"

"That's one of the reasons I detest those local plays," said Minette, as if talking to herself.

Lise, lost in her memories, sat on the bed as she held the compress with one hand, covering her forehead.

"Do you think I can keep performing? I'd like to leave for Léogane; that was the advice I got there, in Les Cayes."

"Sure, why not?"

"I'm counting on you to convince Mama."

"Can't you manage that on your own?"

"Of course. But she'll agree quicker if you get involved."

"Okay, then."

Minette stood up and distractedly moved a few objects around on the wood table.

"Mama doesn't have a dime, Lise," she stated dully.

"Oh! But you're going to get a lot of money. Monsieur Saint-Martin dictated his last wishes to the notary, in my presence, and he acknowledged owing you nearly three years' worth of wages."

"Well there's some consolation. But unfortunately the Comédie's till is empty."

"He wrote to Mesplès, telling him to pay you."

"Mesplès! Was Saint-Martin delirious?"

"He also dictated that letter in my presence. He asked him to pay you."

"So I'll never see a cent of that money."

"Why?" asked Lise naively.

Minette gave no answer and left the bedroom. As she headed to join her mother in the street, she saw Mme Acquaire arrive, completely out of breath.

"The Governor has agreed to Depoix and Favart's proposition. They're the new directors. Their enthusiasm is rivaled only by that of poor François Saint-Martin…"

She stopped speaking abruptly, wiped her eyes, then blew her nose.

"Poor François," she exclaimed…"Well, life must go on…The new directors charged me with letting you know that a new show will go up in about two weeks. You'll play the lead role as Iphigenia in the duet with Durand, who has asked for the privilege of acting at your side. Durand's a ward of the King, you know; he's performed in France at the great concert of the Queen. We'll make sure to let the public know in the posters, to drum up the audience…Oh, my dear – the rehearsals are going to be tough! Loads of lines to learn, arias to sing…Bah! It's all child's play for you…All right, goodbye, then. We meet tomorrow morning at the Comédie. Be sure to be on time."

She squeezed Minette's cheek and was about to open the door to leave when the young woman quietly stated:

"I won't perform until I've been paid, Madame."

"You'll tell that to the new directors tomorrow."

"Very well, Madame."

Once Mme Acquaire had left, Minette joined her mother in the street. Jasmine held out her hands to the passersby, presenting her wares to them, and the veins in her neck swelled up as she strained her voice to call out to them. *How tired she seems*, thought Minette. Discouraged, she went to the back of the courtyard and sat down sadly underneath the orange tree. All her projects, all her childish dreams had been torn apart, uprooted. She had worked hard and was still just as poor as before. So many sleepless nights spent learning her long monologues by heart; so many early mornings spent standing next to the piano doing her vocal exercises and learning to sing her more difficult songs! None of that showed: her talent had gone so far as to erase any signs of her diligent training. "Bah! It's all child's play for you," Mme Acquaire had said. But she had worked hard; she knew that. She had overcome horrendous anxiety and felt her heart nearly stop beating from fear. As compensation, she had earned the honor of entering the Whites' ball on the arm of a Prince that one time. A great and enviable honor for a freedwoman. She was happy to have worked for that distinction, that honor, but also would have liked to assure her material well-being. She would have been proud to rent a nice house for her mother, to help her build her business, to buy her a few dresses. It had not been wise, her leaving for Arcahaie. Yet, she felt she should not regret anything about what had happened there, in that little house in Boucassin.

She was no "easy" girl. She truly loved that man, at once complicated, cruel, and so sweet – that young, tortured being who struggled with the duality of his impetuous feelings, as compelled by vengeance and hatred as by forgiveness and love. She suspected somehow that he was only half responsible for some of the things he did, and that he carried them out like a man repressed, out of bravado and a desire to make his mark. There was a revolt in him – a revolt, she thought, that likely would be forever futile – and it transformed his righteous feelings into a burning desire to destroy. She did not yet see clearly how her surroundings were the root of this. But having lived with him for twelve days, she had learned that he did nothing without thinking it through and always with the sole objective of satisfying himself through the most reprehensible acts. He was compelled by hatred. A terrible, mortal hatred that risked enslaving his better instincts. He was torn. He wanted one thing but was forced to do another. He had been so tender with her, yet so harsh and so vicious with his slaves. He hated too much. Hatred is as destructive as poison. It would put a weapon in his hand, freeze his heart, and soon push him, Minette was sure, to take revenge, at the risk of condemning himself. This was the sort of man her heart had chosen to love. How she longed to save him with her love – to make him forget everything and to erase all bitterness from his thoughts. She saw him, his brow furrowed, walking between his two dogs and striking out at his slaves with rage. How she would have loved to leave, to return to him, to forget everything in his arms and to see his wild face become tender with her kisses!

XXII

ONE AFTERNOON, total ruin befell several of the vendors on Traversière Street, in the form of a young white soldier.

They were seated in front of their stands like always. A poor white woman from the neighborhood was selling her soaps to Jasmine as the mixed crowd bustled all around them.

After making some sort of bet, two young officers came bounding through like madmen with their horses at a gallop.

A dog let out a cry of pain. It had been knocked over by one of the horses, which, panic-stricken by the chafing of the bit and the cries of the market-women, whinnied as it pranced about. Left behind by his companion, who was roaring with laughter, the first horseman pulled angrily on his reins. Instead of advancing, the horse began backing up.

"Watch out, watch out…"

Several stands were overturned, including Jasmine's.

A flood of screams and protestations followed, adding to the steed's panic. He stamped in place, held back by his visibly amused rider. The soaps, the bottles of perfume, and the handkerchiefs were soon nothing more than a jumbled-up pile.

Screaming, Jasmine attempted to push the horse away. The officer smacked her hand with his crop.

"Get your paws off of him!"

On their knees, the poor women tried to save whatever they could from the disaster.

The white horseman was about to ride off when he noticed Minette. He immediately had his horse move toward her. She was standing and, fists clenched, looked at him with hate in her eyes.

"Hey, now what do we have here! So this is where you live, 'young person'?"

Without responding, she turned her gaze on Jasmine who, down on all fours, was still gathering up the scattered merchandise.

"Your horse has made quite a mess, Monsieur," she said to him, with rage in her eyes.

"Are these all the wares you possess? They're unworthy of you."

"They allow me to eat, Monsieur."

"Oh! Well you must be so poorly fed that you risk losing your voice. You deserve better. Come with me tonight to the King's Garden and I'll give you ten times the value of this junk."

A black woman touched Minette's arm and whispered:

"Lower your eyes, child, that's the cousin of the King's Bursar."

She became enraged. She felt like throwing herself on the horseman's leg and sinking her teeth into it until she drew blood.

At the same time, a jumble of thoughts stirred within her. If she disrespected a white man, she would be thrown in prison, whipped – who knows? She could lose her place at the Comédie. Jasmine and Lise might also be arrested. Oh! How could she fight? The deck was stacked. Was the only way to get revenge to kill by surprise, to assassinate in the shadows? Lapointe was right.

She clenched her fists even more tightly and closed her eyes for a brief moment.

"So it's settled," repeated the horseman. "Tonight in the King's Garden."

She understood that she had to say something, but she just couldn't contain herself and blurted angrily:

"Thank you, Monsieur, but I'm not part of the merchandise. I'm not for sale."

"Well, well! A proud one, are we? Perhaps you like things a bit rougher?"

She refrained from answering. He turned his horse around.

"I'll still come hear you sing. Good luck..."

He took off at a gallop.

Lise consoled the crying vendors. Jasmine, wracked with tears, wiped her half-smashed soaps and wrinkled, torn madras scarves with her camisole.

"Dear Lord, he did it on purpose. How could he have done that on purpose?" she kept repeating.

"It's unjust!" shouted Minette suddenly, "unjust..."

"Hush!"

She looked around as if she was about to burst.

"Don't you understand we've got to stop being afraid?"

"Hush!" someone said again. "It's the police..."

A few soldiers passed slowly by the anxious vendors. *My God, how I wish I'd just died*, thought Minette.

Her throat was so tight she could barely swallow her saliva. She bent down without a word and helped Jasmine transport what was left of the stand inside the house.

When she woke up the next morning, Minette ran over to Nicolette's house first thing. Only Nicolette could help her get a note to Céliane de Caradeux. Minette had had a horrible night, haunted by thoughts of Joseph and of the soldier who had destroyed Jasmine's stand. She had found herself almost suffocating with rage.

She gave the letter to Nicolette and said:

"Did you see what that white soldier did to the vendors in our neighborhood?"

"Oh! Even if that one gave me a golden chariot to sleep with him I'd say no," spat Nicolette, disgusted.

"He's the cousin of the King's Bursar, my dear," said Minette encouragingly.

Nicolette looked at her with surprise.

"What did you say?"

"Listen, I need you to get this letter to Mademoiselle de Caradeux. Even if you have to give it to my worst enemy…"

"Oh!" said Nicolette.

"Even if that soldier from yesterday were to bring the letter himself," concluded Minette, looking Nicolette straight in the eyes. "And a word of advice, if you really want to help me out – accept a little less than a golden chariot. Otherwise, this might not work."

"Fine, we'll see about that," acquiesced Nicolette, conciliatory.

"Do it," said Minette, "for the cause. And then, avenge us by cuckolding him."

"Okay, fine…"

She made a gesture of farewell to the young courtesan and went to the site of the Comédie. Once there, she found Depoix and Favart suddenly overwhelmed by all of Saint-Martin's debts.

"I'd never have imagined the cashbox could be so empty," confided Favart in a tone of utter distress.

A few notes asking delinquent planters to pay for their subscriptions to the theater immediately appeared in the daily paper. These debtors, some of whom were either cousins of the Governor or the Bursar or friends of the Prosecutor, ignored them and did not pay a single cent.

"We're back at zero," admitted Depoix to the actors gathered around. "Monsieur Saint-Martin is dead, may he rest in peace. May each one of us, out of love for the profession and respect for the memory of our wonderful young director, sacrifice whatever it is the Comédie owes them."

A few furtive glances were exchanged between the actresses from the Saint-Marc Theater, who had not known Saint-Martin well. Minette looked at Goulard and the color drained from her face.

"Here we have a notice that Monsieur Mesplès, executor of Saint-Martin's will, plans to publish very soon," continued Depoix.

He unfolded a piece of paper and read:

Next Wednesday, we'll proceed to an estate sale in Saint-Martin's home of all effects of said estate, including a Negro cook, a driver, a wheelchair, furniture, linens, silver, etcetera, and the creditors of said estate will be welcome to thereby seek compensation for everything that is owed them.

Depoix folded the paper and slipped it in one of his pockets.

"Here's what I propose," he concluded. "After the sale of Saint-Martin's effects, a part of the money will go to the theater's till to take care of likely upcoming expenses and the rest of the actors and workers for the Comédie. We'll sign new contracts once the monies have been distributed and decide whether we'll be fully paid. Do you all accept?"

Goulard was the first to say yes. The actors from Saint-Marc made a face and Mme de Vanancé said frankly that they all might as well stand there with their arms crossed rather than work for a pittance. Mme Tessyre sighed and Mme Valville argued that, when all was said and done, it was better that she and Mlle Dubuisson return to France.

"Our little company," interrupted Depoix, "has both old and new members. I'm counting on those of you who've long known François Saint-Martin – who loved and appreciated him…"

Magdeleine Brousse began to cry, which immediately caused Mme Tessyre to do the same. Goulard cleared his throat and said:

"For my part, I accept Depoix's proposal. I loved Monsieur Saint-Martin too much not to try anything I can think of to take care of all these difficulties."

He cleared his throat again as if he were embarrassed and added:

"Monsieur Saint-Martin died owing more than three years of wages to Minette…"

Favart interrupted him.

"Monsieur Saint-Martin, in his will," began Goulard again, "left me his clothes and his theater costumes, along with five thousand pounds. I accept the clothing and costumes. I refuse the money."

"That's a whole other story," interrupted Depoix. "This is a private affair."

"Why are you refusing the money, Claude?" asked Mme Acquaire.

"I'm leaving it to his kids."

He turned his back and left the Comédie. Minette ran after him. She touched his arm and he turned around. Since her return from Arcahaie, she had avoided speaking to him alone. She hated the idea of breaking things off with him definitively now that, having been in love herself, she understood how painful it would be to be rejected.

"Thank you, Claude," she said simply.

"I loathe you," he said to her so softly that for a moment she thought she had misheard.

She looked at him without responding. Yes, he had to hate her – just as she would have to hate Jean-Baptiste Lapointe if ever he made her suffer by rejecting her. She put her hand on his arm again and said: "Forgive me," in a tone so pleading that he felt things had been broken irreparably and he had to flee. Minette went back to the other actors.

"Monsieur Durand has asked to sing the duet with you as Iphigenia, Minette," said Favart to her.

"I'm flattered, Monsieur."

"He is a graduate of the Royal Academy and..."

"I'm aware, Monsieur."

She took her script and promised to come regularly to the rehearsals.

"We're going to aim," said Depoix, "for a completely full house. The curtain will rise on a Negro dance, executed by Monsieur Acquaire, and then an Indian ballet with Madame Tessyre, Madame Acquaire, Magdeleine Brousse, Favart, Goulard, and me. Then we'll perform a comic opera scene and finish with Iphigenia's duet."

M Acquaire whistled. "That's quite a full night you've got planned."

"I'll collect all the profits and be responsible for everything," said Durand at that moment, with his impeccable accent.

"Great!"

Everyone dispersed and Minette headed back to her house. Goulard, who had been watching her from the street corner, came up beside her.

"It's because I love you that I loathe you," he said to her with such a sorrowful air that she pitied him.

"I understand, Claude."

"Answer me honestly – you owe it to me. Are you in love with someone else?"

She did not lower her eyes and answered:

"Yes."

"That's all I wanted to know."

He began walking alongside her, his eyes dark and his face sorrowful.

"I tried to forget you, to hate you, but I couldn't," he admitted without shame.

"It's not my fault."

"Oh, don't I know it…"

He then asked her if she wanted to accompany him to Zabeth's house.

"She still doesn't know anything, the poor woman. I've got to tell her about François' death before Mesplès seizes all his effects and sells them."

"What did he leave for them – her and the children?"

"Nothing. I couldn't help weeping for the loss of the artist, but my friendship for Saint-Martin was erased when his will was read. He left his home to François Mesplès."

"To Monsieur Mesplès!"

"He died just as he lived: as a total narcissist. I never would have thought him capable of that."

They found Zabeth in the middle of making food for the children. Kneeling next to her, an old slave wearing an apron spoke softly. Noticing Goulard and Minette, she stood and paled horribly. Goulard opened his mouth to speak and she cried out:

"François!"

"He's dead, Zabeth."

She wept and brought her children close to her, still crying out:

"François, François…"

"He thought of you, Zabeth. He sent this for you."

He took the five thousand pounds out of his pocket and gave them to her.

Minette saw that she was trembling and touched her forehead; it was burning.

"She's sick, Claude."

He took the children in his arms and made a gesture to the old slave.

"She doesn't want to take care of herself, Monsieur," the slave immediately confessed. "I know some good herbs. She refuses to take anything."

"Is that so, Zabeth?"

She did not answer. Her beautiful brown face was gaunt and completely drained of color. She wiped her eyes with her flowered calico skirt and left the room without a word, her step faltering and weak.

Goulard handed the infants to the slave.

"Watch over their mother and over them," he asked him.

"Oh! I love them like my own children, Monsieur." He took each in one of his arms and then sat in the rocker to soothe them.

The elder child was named François and the younger was Jean. Goulard especially loved the elder one, as he was more or less his godson.

He caressed the boy's hair and promised to come back the following day.

Early that next day, a messenger on horseback knocked on Jasmine's door and handed her a note addressed to Minette. It was Céliane de Caradeux's response: the requested interview was granted and she would await Minette that very evening at six o'clock. Once the messenger had left, she stuffed the note in her bodice and ran to Nicolette's house.

"Thank you," she said. "I'm grateful for your talents: they're irresistible."

"Oh, my!" said the courtesan coyly. "I didn't have to do much…"

Minette took off with a laugh. Finally, she would be able to fight for Joseph! Until that evening, she remained in a state of feverish agitation that kept her from properly rehearsing her role at the Comédie.

"How nervous you are, my child," said Macarty, making faces in an effort to make her laugh. "Come listen to me play something on the flute. It'll calm you down."

He pulled her into a dark corner and, twisting his lips into a hideous grimace, he asked whether she might consider giving him a kiss. Before she could answer, he had grabbed his flute to play her a gentle, seductive melody.

"Is that better?" he asked her once he had finished.

"Yes, that was kind of you."

"That's how I am with all the pretty ones, all of them…"

He punctuated his remark with a dangerous pirouette. Then righting himself, he took a bow and made the gesture of removing his hat to salute her.

"And now, on to more serious things," he shouted.

Someone told him to quiet down. The rehearsals had begun again and Mme Tessyre and Goulard were singing their duet in the folksy Creole play. Observing them, Minette understood how painful it must have been for them to expend so much effort making others laugh when they were both so unhappy.

Despite Macarty's flute, she was still so anxious that Depoix, discouraged, was forced to send her home.

"But what's going on? What's wrong with you?" asked M Acquaire.

"I just don't feel very well, Sir."

"Well then, go on home and rest," advised Mme Acquaire, mortified to see Minette lose control that way in front of Mmes Valville and Dubuisson, who had never heard her sing.

"Audiences in Saint-Domingue have pretty bad taste, as far as I can tell. Seems to me that's the case throughout the colonies," said the latter mockingly.

"Perhaps," answered Macarty, "but they know what they like."

Durand, who was well aware of Minette's talent, smiled, then ran his fingers through his too-blond hair and shot an amused glance at Mlle Dubuisson. Macarty, who had just slipped behind the curtain to find a shortcut to the wings, jumped back in shock upon discovering Magdeleine Brousse in the arms of Nelanger in a decidedly suggestive position.

"That's a bit much, don't you think?" he said to them as he slipped away.

"What's the matter," asked Favart, "did you just have a run-in with someone?"

"No, it's Nelanger. He's playing the guitar without making a sound," answered Macarty coolly.

"Well that's certainly one way to practice," answered Favart.

"I'm sure."

With that, Macarty headed off, doubled over with laughter.

At exactly a quarter to six, Minette was ready. She had dressed herself simply, with neither jewels nor lace. Minette based her outfit on the modesty she had seen in Céliane de Caradeux on the day she had first met her. She had been as discreetly dressed as those sanctimonious little freedwomen, "as rare as diamonds in the pockets of slaves," as Nicolette always said. Her sister wanted to know where she was going and questioned her about it, but Jasmine stayed quiet.

"Speaking of, how's Joseph?" asked Lise at that very moment. She was no longer ill but had stayed in bed so as to continue to be doted on by her mother. Minette stared at her and said harshly:

"He was hiding runaway slaves. He was arrested and handed over to Monsieur de Caradeux."

Lise let out a cry.

"You'll make her sick," protested Jasmine. "She just had a terrible shock and you're giving her another one."

"It won't kill her, Mama. Come, come, calm down, little sister. I'm going to see what I can do to free him. I'll see you later, Mama. Console yourself and take care of her. She needed to know everything, don't you see?"

She bent down and kissed them both, then went out into the street that led to the sea. The daily flood of vendors, sailors out enjoying themselves, and prostitutes welcomed her with a deafening sound.

She hurried her step and arrived out of breath in Bel-Air. Several homes as rich and luxurious as the Saint-Ars' rose up at the far end of immense courtyards lined with elm trees.

Minette stopped just in front of an enormous gate and knocked. A furious barking of dogs answered her. Trembling, she leaped backward. At the same moment, one of the shutters of the immense doors opened slightly and a Negro's head appeared.

"What do you want?" he said.

"To see Mademoiselle Céliane."

"What's your name?"

"Minette."

"Come in," he said without hesitation, which led Minette to believe she was expected.

"The dogs!"

"Come in," repeated the Negro. "They're chained up."

A long path, guarded by slaves dressed as footmen, led up to the planter's lavish home. Each time he crossed one of the footmen, he made a knowing gesture. As she walked, Minette thought of the expression she would have if she ran into Céliane's uncle. He hated her, that one, as much as Mesplès and all the other horrible, racist Whites. They must hate all people of color just as much as they hated her and Minette was surprised at her inability to figure out why. After all, it was easy to say: "There are too many of us; they're afraid," or "Too many freedmen are rich; that bothers them," or even, "They don't like our color and our blood." But those were nothing but pretexts. The last was an especially weak explanation: the Whites were very fond of pure Negro women. So what then?

As she thought over all of these things, she had arrived with the slave at a gallery that lead to an apartment situated somewhat independently from the rest of the house. The slave ran up to a door, careful to stay hidden, and proceeded to knock. It opened immediately and a woman's voice whispered:

"Who's there?"

"It's me, Mistress," breathed the slave. "The young lady is here."

"Thank you, Tabou. Tell her to come in."

How mysterious, thought Minette to herself. *What's she afraid of?*

She entered into the bedroom, modestly furnished with a bed, a table, and a few ironwood chairs. A large golden crucifix was suspended above the bed and a painting of Saint Cécile hung on the wall. Two young slaves, one a *câpresse* and the other a Negress, were seated in a corner of the room.

"Light the lamp," said Céliane de Caradeux to the *câpresse*.

Then turning, she put her hand on Minette's shoulder.

"You may speak freely. No one here will betray you."

Minette looked at the slaves: they were dressed decently in white gingham, their hair wrapped in white scarves that covered their ears. They wore leather sandals on their feet. On neither of their faces could be seen that trace of brutish stupidity so common among young female slaves. Involuntarily, she compared them to Fleurette and Roseline.

"Someone's coming, Mistress," said the Negress suddenly, leaning toward Mlle de Caradeux.

A footstep fell on the left gallery and someone knocked on the door of the room.

"Who's there?" asked Mlle de Caradeux. "Go and see, Phryné."

The Negress rose and opened the door.

A voice could be heard immediately:

"My master requests Mistress' presence in the salon."

"Very well."

Phryné closed the door. Céliane de Caradeux leaned on the table, trembling.

"I'm going to have to fight again, dear Lord," she muttered. "Give me strength. Quick, Nanouche, pass me my veil."

The *câpresse* handed her a long white veil with which she covered her magnificent blond hair. She was standing near the portrait of Saint Cécile and Minette was struck by the resemblance between the two.

"Wait for me, Minette. This won't take long."

The two slaves opened the door for her and she went out, her hands clasped as if in prayer.

Several long minutes passed in silence. Nanouche took a rosary from her pocket and began to fumble with it, and Phryné began reading a holy book. Observing them with astonishment, Minette saw that their hands were trembling just as those of their mistress had trembled. These were not slaves. Out of two miserable creatures born into a life of brute animals, Mlle de Caradeux had crafted conscious beings who trembled not before the threat of punishment but simply from love and devotion for another being.

"How hard it must be," sighed Phryné, placing next to her the holy book that was none other than the book of Saint Cécile.

"Poor Mistress!"

Abruptly, the sound of voices broke the silence. A man's voice – harsh and sharp – spat out a string of words that sounded like they had been cut with a knife. Heels hammered at the bricks of the left-side gallery and an authoritative hand pushed open the door to the room.

"I've had enough, do you hear me," said the voice. "I've had enough of sending away your suitors. You look ridiculous in that pious little get-up…Your head is filled with all sorts of nonsense and…"

The Marquis de Caradeux entered his daughter's room wearing a velvet doublet. Tall, with a pale face framed by ash-blond hair, he had as much beauty and allure as she did. He was ten years older than his brother, whom he had made his associate and overseer. They were the most feared planters for miles around. Greedy, cruel, ambitious, and criminal, they had turned their home into a political meeting place where, fervent slavers, they battled the slightest signs of relenting on the Government's part in favor of the freedmen and kept their slaves in a state of ignorance and superstition, so better to exploit them. The nobility of their blood made them sacred beings and descendants of Jesus, as far as their slaves believed, scared as they were at the mere sight of them. They had made themselves invulnerable in declaring to the slaves that whoever tried to kill them would be doomed to the eternal flames of hell. Their preferred punishment was most often the penalty by fire, thus rendering this prophecy more concrete. Certain nights, one could see flames from the pyre on which some wretch was dying, gagged, contorted in agony.

The Marquis' wife had died giving birth to Céliane. At the age of twelve, he had sent her to study in Nantes, from which she returned with a calling to the faith. He cared about his daughter, and loved her in his way. The day she told him of her decision, he became blind with rage and, hoping to distract her from what he called "her foolish pietism," he brought her out into society, organized sumptuous parties, and introduced her to the very best members of his entourage. All to no avail...

He closed the door behind him without noticing Minette.

"You will marry, my daughter, whether you want to or not. I have no heir to spare for the convent. I've worked hard to provide you with a dowry. In exchange, you'll give me grandchildren. The Count of Chateaumorond has left disappointed. You looked like a nun wearing that veil of yours. From now on, I forbid you to wear it."

Turning his head to rip it off of her, his eyes met those of Minette.

"Who's this?" he asked, as if trying to figure out where he had seen her face before.

"She's an actress with the Comédie," answered Céliane de Caradeux in a plaintive voice.

Minette rose from her chair. The Marquis walked over to her.

"Yes, I recognize her. It's the 'young person' with the beautiful voice. Well now that's better, young lady," he said more gently to his daughter, placing a long, thin hand on her head. "I wouldn't recommend you associate with someone like her publicly, but for a little distraction, perhaps she's just the thing."

Minette turned pale, as she always did when insulted. Céliane de Caradeux noticed.

"This 'young person,'" she answered sweetly, "ate in my presence at Prince William's table."

"That was the extravagance of a young hothead on holiday. Do you really think, my child, that Prince William would have set such an example in Jamaica?"

Céliane de Caradeux lowered her head.

"That's neither here nor there," the Marquis said sharply. "If this young person is willing to distract us with her talent, I'll happily pay whatever it takes to satisfy her…"

He looked Minette over from head to toe and smiled.

"Farewell, my child. I intend for you to marry very soon," he added, pinching his daughter's cheek.

Once the door closed behind him, Céliane de Caradeux let herself fall onto the bed, where she remained curled up into a ball for several minutes. Then, finally reacting, she turned her sad, sweet face to Minette:

"What did you want to tell me, Minette?"

"Mademoiselle!"

She threw herself down at the foot of the bed and raised her head to the planter's daughter.

"Mademoiselle, will you help me?"

"What can I do for you?"

"A week ago, a young freedman named Joseph Ogé was brought here: he's my brother."

"You've seen the kind of man my father is. There's no way I can help you," she said, as if ashamed.

She seemed to think for a moment and then, suddenly, panic washed over her face and she looked around for her two slaves. Then, lowering her head, she hid her face in her hands and slid to her knees at the foot of the bed, right next to Minette.

"My Lord," she murmured, "have pity on that poor soul."

Minette suddenly had an idea.

"If only the law allowed it, my brother would be a priest," she whispered to the young girl.

"Oh!" whimpered Céliane de Caradeux.

And her gaze lifted, seeking the eyes of the saint in whose footsteps she hoped to follow. She would go find her father and make a deal with him: Joseph Ogé's freedom for her own marriage. Voilà, it was settled. She rose and, without looking at Minette, said:

"Now go. You'll soon see your brother again."

"Oh! Thank you, thank you, Mademoiselle. Bless you."

"Do you know how to pray?"

Faced with such a candid and pure expression, Minette lowered her eyes for the first time in her life.

"Joseph will pray for you, Mademoiselle," she promised.

And clasping her hand, she brought it to her lips. That gesture reminded her of another she had made with Mme Saint-Ar. Was she going to be deceived yet again? No, those blue eyes reminded her of Joseph's, just as her own reminded her of Zoé Lambert's. The eyes, if one knows them well, rarely lie – and Minette had just lowered hers before the celestial glow that dwelled in the depths of the eyes of the planter's daughter.

She left the room, escorted by the two slaves who led her to the gate, where they were met by the furious barking of the dogs.

XXIII

ALTHOUGH EVERYONE remained unsettled by the disaster of the overturned stands, Minette had the feeling that Jasmine's morale was not completely crushed. What was keeping her spirits up? The hope that Joseph would soon be freed? Her daughters' success? Minette could not tell. Too many different feelings were knocking about inside her. It was keeping her from figuring out what was most important. Even her love seemed to have dimmed. She had the impression that her memory of Jean-Baptiste Lapointe was alive in her heart but no longer rose to her brain. She thought about him in flashes of memory quickly overshadowed by the daily battles she was fighting. Her days were spent at the Comédie, at fittings, and in the evening she studied her role late into the night. From the money Durand had given her for her costumes, she had siphoned off a little bit, which was putting food on the table. She was going to find herself back onstage and, in order to show up her white rivals, she was extravagant with her costumes, buying velvet, taffeta, and lace without even thinking about the cost.

Once she had finished her errands, she went back home. Turning the corner, she noticed people gathered around her house. Running, she pushed away the neighbors and tried to open the door, which wouldn't budge. She then began to shout, "It's me, Minette, open the door…" It opened immediately. Lise had propped two chairs against it to keep the vendors from coming in. She was crying. Jasmine was crouched at Joseph's feet and, chin in her hand, was rocking back and forth in a sort of lamentation.

"Joseph!" shouted Minette.

She hurled herself at him, crying with joy. Then, taking his face in her hands:

"Mademoiselle de Caradeux kept her promise. When did they let you go?"

He had changed. His was thin and drawn. He looked at Minette and smiled without answering.

The silence suddenly seemed strange to her.

"Joseph!" she cried. "What's the matter with you? What did they do to you?"

He had a piece of paper and a pencil in his hand. He looked at them nervously. Jasmine grabbed the paper from his hands and handed it to Minette. It was Joseph's handwriting. She read the words she saw there:

They cut off my tongue.

"No, no!" she cried again. "No, no…"

She threw herself to the ground at his feet and began weeping desperately, repeating:

"No, no…"

She was suddenly overcome with a rage that, in the face of her powerlessness, turned back on her. She tore out her hair, ripped her clothing, bit her fist, and felt as if she were going mad. She did not calm down until he took her hand and forced her to look at him. His face was serene and so gentle that she was ashamed of her hateful despair. He looked around for the piece of paper, picked it up, and wrote:

I'm lucky. Thousands of others suffer in the hell of slavery.

In writing, he explained that he had been tortured almost immediately after his arrival. The overseer, M de Caradeux, brother of the Marquis, had caught him talking to the slaves about religion. Then he asked her to be strong and to forget about all of that. Did he not have his books and the voices of his two sisters to console him? Life would carry on as before. He was going to go see Lambert that very night to see how he could be useful again. He then asked for his notebook and pencil, which he slipped into his pocket.

He could not eat yet. Barely healed, the scar was making him suffer horribly and, from time to time, he went out to the courtyard to spit out reddish saliva. He departed at nightfall, leaving the three inconsolable women behind.

The next day, a Sunday, Minette refused to go to mass: she swore, making Jasmine cry and then leave, dragging Lise behind her. They returned accompanied by Joseph.

Minette was seated in the front room, her face hard and tense. Joseph asked her to sing, writing the request in his notebook. She refused, claiming to be tired. She felt as if she would never be able to sing again. She had done too much shouting, too much weeping. All night long she had been screaming inside: *Cursed Whites, cursed white planters.* That smothered rage had inflamed her throat and extinguished her voice. She was seventeen years old but felt as if she had lived a long, long life of suffering and revolt.

She purposely missed rehearsal and remained closed in her bedroom. Durand, already anxious, given that the performance was coming up soon – they were meant to debut in two days – came looking for her himself. Jasmine let him into the room where Minette, still in her nightgown, had hidden herself under the covers.

"Are you ill?" he asked her.

"I'm afraid I won't be able to sing in the show," she answered, looking away.

"Come now, Minette," he pleaded, "don't do this to me. I'm riddled with debt and, as you must have heard, the sale of Saint-Martin's estate isn't going to amount to much. I'm the one meant to take the profits from the show. Are you really going to let me down?"

All her revolt, all her pent-up rage seized the opportunity to explode out of her then. Throwing back the covers, she launched into a tirade against the Whites, calling them brutes and exploiters.

"Oh! So you don't want me to let you down, is that it? You, always you, nothing but you! What's left for any of the other races after the Whites? Have you ever asked yourself whether I might be starving to death? I've worked for more than three years without seeing a penny. That's no big deal, right? Working for free, that suits people like me just fine. It's only natural that I work myself to the bone. I will not perform the day after tomorrow – I'll never perform again, do you hear me? I hate you, I hate the whole world…"

She fell back on the bed, breathless and spent, her eyes shut tight.

Durand, flabbergasted, looked at her without speaking. Jasmine gestured to him to come into the next room and, once he came near her, lowered her eyes and spoke to him softly. Durand left immediately. Then it was Goulard who came, Saint-Martin's children in his arms.

"I'm responsible for these poor souls," he said to Minette. "Zabeth has just died, and Mesplès has begun selling her furniture. Will you help me?"

Saint-Martin's children! How much they resembled him. She remembered the young director's charming, protective smile, his kindness. Alas! He, too, without any ill will, had nevertheless taken advantage of her. She held out her arm and Goulard passed her the youngest of the children.

"What's his name," she asked.

"Jean."

"Jean!"

A wave of memories washed over her, strong enough to knock her over with its force. She reeled with dizziness.

"I'm giving him to you, Minette."

She looked at the child and smiled at Goulard.

"This one is called François. I'll make a great artist of him. Isn't that right, François?"

"Yes, godfather," answered the child in his clear little voice.

"We'll have to work hard, Minette. Little kids don't like to go hungry…A propos, have you gone to see Mesplès about your fees? You're owed a pretty penny. Twenty-four thousand pounds isn't nothing. You should try to get your pay."

Minette shrugged her shoulders.

"With our privately made agreement, what proof do I have?"

"You have justice and what's right."

"You must be kidding, Claude. Or have you forgotten who I am?"

"I haven't forgotten anything. You belong to the class of fighters. So fight, before accepting defeat. Mesplès already made amends by having you come back to perform. He'll relent. As for Mademoiselle Dubuisson, having no idea of your talent, she's preparing to boo you along with the rest of the audience…"

He looked at her and saw that he'd gotten what he wanted. Minette's cheeks had suddenly gotten back their color and her lips parted in a mocking smile.

"We'll see about that…"

She leaned toward the child, who was playing with her earring, and gave him a kiss.

"My word, he's really my responsibility," she concluded.

Goulard went back to see Durand, who awaited him on the street corner, discussing with Jasmine and Lise.

"It seems to be okay," he told them.

"So, has she promised to perform?"

"Don't you know her at all? She'll never concede just because of a promise."

"Well then what did you ask of her?"

"To humiliate Dubuisson and get her revenge on Mesplès."

"Those are pretty Machiavellian tactics."

"Actually, to her credit, I also had to use a third trick."

"What's that."

"An appeal to her maternal instinct: I gave her the kid."

"Well, well!"

Hearing this news, Lise let out a little cry of joy and rushed back into the house...

The next day, Minette went out early to see the seamstress Durand had recommended. Their costumes having been completed, she took them home. She tried them on again for Lise and Jasmine, standing before the little mirror in the bedroom and humming Iphigenia's duet. The costumes were certainly luxurious enough to make Mademoiselle Dubuisson drool with envy.

In the morning, Joseph came by with a play by Racine and handed it to her. She sat down at the table and, without looking at him, began reading certain passages aloud. Then she stood up and went out to the very back of the courtyard, where she blew her nose and wiped away her tears. He who once had read so beautifully! He who once had spoken so beautifully! He who once had recited lines of poetry so beautifully! No, she would never be consoled. She was astonished to discover in herself, ever since Joseph's torture, that same hatred she reproached Jean-Baptiste Lapointe for having inside him. If she had hated Whites before, it was only now that she grasped to what extent that feeling could be violent, bitter, and destructive. At night, she dreamed of sticking large knives into white necks while smiling calmly, as if executing a delightful task. Since then, how close she felt to her lover!

Where was he? What was he doing? Why had he not come? No longer able to live without hearing from him, she wrote him a long letter, which she entrusted to the driver of a carriage who traveled every three days. Every three days, she ran to await the driver's return, hoping for a response. After two weeks of waiting in vain, she wrote a second letter, which she sent to Marie-Rose, asking her to get it to Bou-cassin. She finally got an answer: it was from Marie-Rose herself.

Dear Minette, it said, Jean-Baptiste Lapointe has disappeared. It seems he has killed a planter and is now hiding out in the Spanish part of the island, having made his way through the hills. He has been judged, hanged in effigy, and a bounty has been placed on his head. That's all anyone's talking about in Arcahaie. I'm so sorry to have to give you such sad news…

Minette could not finish reading the letter. Her hand was trembling so violently that she stared at it for a moment, perplexed. He had killed a planter. He had run away. So it was over between the two of them. She would never see him again. She fell into a chair and reread the letter slowly, as if hoping she had misunderstood. *One after the next*, she said to herself. *One tragedy after the next.* Where was that divine mercy – where was that God, so well hidden, who seemed to laugh as he multiplied people's suffering? Who could she call on – pray to? "My God," she murmured, falling into the habit all the same. Oh! It was bound to happen, it was bound to end like that. There was too much unhappiness, too much hatred inside him. That hatred was just looking for the right target and it had landed on some planter. Who was he, anyway – that planter? Some impertinent youth, stiff with haughtiness, or some potbellied fat man, bloodthirsty and ferocious? So he had killed again! Big deal! How could she blame him? He had dared to do what thousands of others dreamed of doing. He had killed a white man –

a planter – after laying his hands on a bunch of drunken sailors. Was he a criminal? "My God, help me," pleaded Minette. She wanted to see more clearly, judge the facts impartially and come to some conclusion – either accuse or forgive Lapointe. He had been forced to do it. Everything had forced him to do it, she concluded. The unhappiness, the humiliations, the injustice, the suffering, and the hatred. Plenty of excuses!

She heard the voice of Saint-Martin's son calling for her. She responded, crying out his name:

"Jean, Jean!"

He ran to her and she held him close to her. Who knows, perhaps tomorrow he would suffer, hate, kill. It could not be expected that all men would have Joseph's sweetness and generosity. Was she, Minette, anything like Céliane de Caradeux? There are some people in whom goodness disappears once they discover the spirit of revolt. That was her type. The Lamberts' type, Jean-Baptiste Lapointe's type, and she had no regrets about it. She had come to admire kindness in others without envying them it. She was keeping her despair to herself, just as she had kept her love story a secret. Without admitting she was ashamed, perhaps, to have feelings for Lapointe, she did not even tell Joseph, for whom her affection had doubled, so great was her desire to love.

Joseph was, for that matter, being well taken care of. As soon as they saw him enter Jasmine's house, everyone in the neighborhood sent over fruit juices and Bavarian creams, which he managed to swallow more easily without too greatly irritating his mutilated tongue. He drank with his eyes closed, and his forehead immediately broke into a heavy sweat, which he quickly wiped away so as not to scare Lise and Minette. Jasmine had agreed to let Lise leave for Léogane. She did not even need to be begged. Their precarious existence and the privations it brought had helped to make up her mind: some days, they had been very hungry, and that was not something that could be easily forgotten.

All the actors from the Comédie, in fact, had lived through similar experiences since Saint-Martin's death. The sale of the Negro chef and the furniture had been just enough to pay half of the theater's debts to the Saint-Marc Company and the French actresses. To buy new sets and pay for the costumes, Depoix and Favart had been obliged to go to François Mesplès, who had agreed to advance them a certain sum, with forty percent interest. Depoix had protested, indignant.

"Take it or leave it, my friend," Mesplès had responded. "I'm helping you out and you're the angry one? Seems the roles have gotten mixed up."

Minette, who had gone with them in the hopes of being paid, found herself being shouted at rudely.

"And what is it you want, girl?"

"My money, Monsieur."

"What money?"

"The twenty-four thousand pounds Monsieur Saint-Martin asked you to pay me in his letter. My sister was there, Monsieur."

"I never got any letter."

"But, Monsieur…"

"Are you questioning my word? Do you want me to have you thrown into prison for grave insult toward a white man? Go on, get the hell out of here."

"You'll make her lose heart, Monsieur," Depoix once again protested. "She might make up her mind not to sing. In that case, we'll go bankrupt, no question."

The usurer grumbled something under his breath, opened a drawer, and took out a bill, which he threw on the desk.

"Here's five thousand pounds, and not another word about it. I never got any letter from Saint-Martin and I will not have my word questioned."

Favart took the bill, folded it, and handed it to Minette.

"Well, we'll have gotten something out of this at least," he said to her, smiling sweetly.

And then, turning toward Mesplès:

"I have fifty-something theater subscriptions here, purchased by high-level people – unpaid subscriptions, of course. At what rate will you take them?"

"Still forty percent."

"Monsieur!…"

"You're wasting your breath and your time. I said forty percent."

Favart took out a wad of subscriptions from a leather suitcase and handed them to the usurer, who counted them after moistening his fingers. Then, looking at the signatures:

"My word, the King's Bursar and Monsieur de Caradeux himself are bad debtees."

"The theater is solid, Monsieur."

"Or the actors are."

He handed them a paper:

"Sign here, will you?"

With this money, the new directors were able to face the numerous expenses demanded by the new piece and to pay the painter Peyret and the stagehand Julian, both very upset at having worked for nothing.

Minette's five thousand pounds bought Jasmine a fully stocked, brand-new stand. But her cashbox remained completely empty.

It remained empty up until the night of the performance. The billboards and the gazette had announced the return of the "young person" – her reappearance in the duet of Iphigenia alongside Durand, ward of the King, as well as a grand ball followed by a masked ball. The theater was full to bursting as of six that evening. Outside, those who had not managed to secure a seat complained loudly. As subscriptions had been suspended by Mesplès as a means of obliging the debtors to pay, several carriages drove away with enraged planters badmouthing the irresponsible new directors.

The evening was a veritable triumph. That night, the soldiers of the regiment, among whom the young horseman who had trampled Jasmine's stand, called to Minette and bestowed her with a new name. The trend was initiated by that blue-eyed officer she had met one day in the company of Magdeleine Brousse. In his enthusiasm, he climbed up on his bench and shouted:

"Long live 'Mademoiselle' Minette!"

Hundreds of delirious voices repeated the words right after him. Minette was no longer the "young person." Her talent had just earned her the enviable title of "demoiselle" – a title to which no woman of color could aspire. Someone threw a crown of flowers at her. Folded notes fell at her feet. High up in the upper mezzanine, Jasmine wept as she clasped Joseph. Her daughter, she could feel it, had been utterly sublime.

Nevertheless, despite the great shows of enthusiasm from the public and the grateful emotion of the new directors, she was refused entry to the ball. That said, she did nothing to try to be admitted. She would have been more than unhappy in that high-society atmosphere. Not that she did not like balls, she enjoyed shining too much not to enjoy them, but her spirit was still convalescing, such that joy could not seduce her but only made her suffer. She was perfectly satisfied. She had enjoyed seeing Mlle Dubuisson's looks of displeasure, astonishment, and fury; she had enjoyed the blissful admiration of the Whites in the audience; she had enjoyed her victory. She left the Comédie triumphantly, on Joseph's arm, amidst the applause of a host of admirers who each promised – with countless compliments – to escort her safely home.

Goulard was among them. He was following her without being noticed, when suddenly two young Whites bet one another that they could give Minette a kiss before she made it to her house.

"What're the stakes?"

"Three thousand pounds."

"Where are the witnesses?"

They chose at random among a group of impudent Whites.

"We'll run up to her together and the first to kiss her is the winner."

"You're on."

The first to arrive, pushing aside Joseph and Lise, who were walking arm in arm with Minette, pulled her to him and shouted:

"Here goes that kiss – and on the lips, at that!"

He pressed his lips to her mouth and ran away. Goulard grabbed him by the collar. Swords were called for and brought. They chose a deserted spot near the church and headed there, followed by the nervous and excited crowd. Joseph dragged away Minette, who was trembling for Goulard. Escorted by the laughing crowd of freedmen, Minette arrived home, where she found little Jean sleeping under the watchful eye of Zulma, an elderly Negress from the neighborhood. She was curled up at the foot of the bed in her filthy rags. Jasmine woke her and, placing some coins in her hand, sent her home saying they would have need of her services again soon.

The child was sleeping on the beds they had joined together to make room for him. His curls spilled across the pillow. Minette and Lise got undressed and lay down, one on each side of the two little beds. Jasmine lay down on hers.

"When are you leaving?" Minette asked her sister.

"As soon as possible. I can't wait to travel."

"Make sure you get paid."

"I have no intention of performing for nothing. I hear the director is a quadroon named Labbé."

"A quadroon – that would surprise me…Will you write to us?"

"Of course."

Lise lay down and looked in Jasmine's direction to see if she had fallen asleep.

"Minette," she whispered, "are you in love with someone?"

"Yes."

"Is it Monsieur Goulard?"

"No."

"Is he the man of your dreams – handsome and good, brave and strong?"

"I don't know, Lise. He suffers far too much. He himself doesn't seem to really know what he is. The only thing I'm certain of is that he's suffering."

"Why is he suffering?"

"He's a freedman."

"Ah!"

She lay down again and, before falling asleep, thought of her sister's last words. That answer, even for Lise, was no mystery.

XXIV

Goulard was only very slightly injured in the duel. The following day, he arrived with his arm in a makeshift sling, an issue of the gazette in his hands.

"Read this," he said to Minette, furious.

She looked at him and said with a slight reproach in her voice:

"Why did you fight over me, Claude?"

He repeated impatiently: "Read this," and threw the paper into her hands.

The anonymous article was devastating. The name of the beautiful Mme Marsan, actress in Cap-Français, was mentioned in the same performance of Iphigenia's duet, comparing Minette's talents unfavorably to those of the white actress. In an effort to denigrate her in the eyes of the public, Minette's social status was recalled in the most unsparing terms, and the article claimed that Port-au-Prince audiences were showing bad taste in their preference for her over the white actress from Cap-Français, whose fame in the Italian theater was surely equal to that of La Dugazon and La Contat.

The article hurt Minette's pride, inasmuch as she had promised herself to garner unanimous praise. Now divided, the spectators fell into two groups: those who remained Minette's fervent admirers and those who agreed with the article. But who had written it? Mozard? She swore to find out.

That same morning, Lise left for Léogane, without any tears this time. She planned to attract an audience by reminding the public that she was "Minette's sister." Whatever her sister's enemies had tried to do, Minette had been launched and was decidedly famous. In every corner of the country, people knew her name and people praised her.

This time, when she signed a new contract, she did so before a notary and proudly signed her name "Mademoiselle" Minette. Aside from a few other scathing, anonymously signed articles, there was an immense crowd for the Christmas performance, for which she took in the profits. She had arranged everything herself, as planned: the choice of the music, the casting, the costumes, the sets, the stage direction. It was a top-notch performance that perhaps even Mme Marsan's admirer's ultimately applauded.

For nearly a year, Minette was praised consistently in every play she brought to the stage. She played the main roles in *Blaise and Babet*, in *The Travels of Rosina*, in *The Village Trial*, and in *The Statue Lover* – in which the part of Célimène had been considered, up until that point, to be the downfall of even the best singers. That evening, two enthusiastic young Whites had come up on the stage and lifted her onto their shoulders in triumph. She reigned supreme on the Saint-Domingue stage, despite Mme Marsan and the anonymous articles. Then, one morning, Macarty ran into the theater, unceremoniously interrupting rehearsal.

"The 'company of Parisian actors' has just landed here," he cried, gesticulating so wildly one would have thought the whole place was on fire.

"What's going on?" screamed Nelanger.

"François Ribié's company – they're here."

There was a moment of blind panic. The backstage was put into some semblance of order, the small reception hall was more or less well arranged, the women powdered their faces, the men adjusted their clothes, and everyone – aside from Mme Tessyre and Magdeleine Brousse, who had been sent to fetch some rum and some glasses – went out to greet the newcomers.

The director, François Ribié, a handsome fellow with a booming voice, greeted the actors with big slaps on the back. He had red cheeks and appeared to be a little tipsy. After pinching Minette's chin and calling her a "Creole beauty," he introduced her to Mlle Thibault, a woman as fair as Minette was dark. Favart called the actors by name and Ribié did the same with his company. As he introduced Claude Gémont, a dashing young man, he pushed him toward Minette and said:

"Now there's something for your mistress to get jealous about, my friend."

He burst out laughing, as Mlle Thibault pursed her lips and looked Minette up and down.

Depoix interrupted the introductions to ask Ribié's company to head over to the Comédie, where they would all raise a glass together.

"That's a lovely idea," said Ribié. "It's hot here in the tropics and the heat makes a man thirsty."

Rhapsodizing about the beauty of the sky, the novelty of the houses, and the women's diverse and fresh-colored garments, the new actors arrived at the theater district.

Crossing a group of slaves carrying planks, Mlle Thibault opened her eyes wide and said:

"Do the Negroes all go around naked in the street like that?"

Her remark made Goulard laugh. He assured her that after a couple of days she would no longer notice.

"I find that quite peculiar," declared Claude Gémont. "Those black, naked bodies remind me of Africa…"

"Are there a lot of them here?" asked Ribié, very intrigued.

"You tell us," answered M Acquaire, his tic in full force. "There are a hundred and sixty thousand of them, fourteen thousand Whites, and twelve thousand people of color – and that's only in the West!"

Ribié let out a quick whistle, and looked around as he wiped his brow.

"Well then! If things start going south one of these days!…"

"Monsieur Ribié," said Favart, with an at once kindly and cutting tone, "we actors try to avoid politics."

Ribié whistled a second time and shook his head.

"A hundred and sixty thousand," he repeated. "And that's only in the West!…"

Mlle Thibault distracted everyone by letting out cries of admiration at the sight of an ivy-covered fountain.

"Oh, have a look, darling," she said, clasping Claude Gémont's arm.

With her finger, she pointed to a young freedwoman wearing a madras scarf and colorful skirt, her breasts half exposed.

"She's lovely," cried Ribié, with his extravagant voice. "What class does that young woman belong to?"

He had turned toward Minette. She was about to respond when Goulard stepped in.

"That's a free Mulatress."

Ponsard, a dancer from Ribié's company, stood on his tiptoes, opened his arms wide as if to embrace the entire country.

"Beautiful skies, delicious nature, beautiful women – why, it's paradise on Earth!"

Mlle Thibault, overexcited by the naked bodies of the slaves, the transparency of the women's bodices, by the sun and the overall scenery, kissed Gémont full on the mouth. He returned her kisses, laughing with slight embarrassment, as his charming and impertinent gaze sought Minette's eyes.

Once arrived at the doors of the Comédie, Ribié let out a few notes of Figaro from *The Barber of Seville*, in his beautiful voice, and grabbed Minette by the waist. They came upon Magdeleine Brousse and Mme Tessyre in the reception hall, in the middle of laying out the glasses. They all drank a first round to the good health of the actors from the Paris Comédie and then a second to the success of the next evening. After that point, Ribié kept the bottle right next to him, to keep from being separated from it again.

Two days later, the billboards announced the arrival of the French company and an upcoming performance of *The Barber of Seville*, a play by Beaumarchais that had spread all over Paris and in which Ribié would play the role of Figaro alongside Mlle Thibault and Mlle Minette.

An even wider public came out to see Ribié's company in a performance for which it had already been decided that the Acquaires would take in the profits. Minette's talent astonished the Parisian company director, who went into the wings to pay her compliments. Then he made some suggestions and critiques to the Acquaires.

"Your stage direction lacked coherence and the actors' performance lacked spirit," he declared. "I'll help you do better. And as for those costumes!…"

If he really intended to help, he had gone about it the wrong way. He was easily carried away and hurt people's feelings at times.

He had brought with him from France a sure eye and a great deal of experience, which he tried to communicate with the local actors. It was a total upending of all the customary ways of that well-meaning, but ultimately very closed little world. Ribié got angry, calling them "little village fairground entertainers." He himself would direct the rehearsals for *The Barber of Seville*. He was severe in every respect and would not tolerate the slightest omission or the slightest change to the original text.

Wearing a white shirt, his sleeves rolled back, he gesticulated, shouted, stormed about, and even went so far as to insult Goulard, who insisted on drawling his words as he sang.

"Beaumarchais didn't write this play in Creole," he screamed, waving around the bottle of rum, which rarely left his side, "Put some effort into it, my friend, put some effort into it…"

Angered, Goulard left the stage and had to be begged by Minette and Mlle Thibault before he would agree to return.

"It's for your own good, my friend," Ribié then said. "Do you think I haven't made the same mistakes myself, for Pete's sake?"

He took several long swallows of rum straight from the bottle then wiped his mouth with the back of his hand while watching Magdeleine Brousse, who was practically swooning and so head over heels this time that she had no problem bringing this new lover home with her while her husband was away. But the latter surprised them in a state of undress that made clear what they were up to. Overcome with rage, the poor wigmaker wept, stormed, threatened.

"This time," he promised the fair Magdeleine, who was unable to come up with any excuses, "for once, this time, I'm going straight to the Governor to ask his permission to stick you in a convent. I've had enough of being ridiculed. And as for you, Monsieur…"

Ribié, like any good actor, threw his clothing on quickly and, bowing deeply to M Brousse, declared loudly:

"I've just learned to appreciate your excellent taste, Monsieur, and I thank you."

He was handsome and strong and, as a mark of his eccentricity, wore a gold ring in his left ear, which made him look like something of a bandit. M Brousse stepped back, fearful, and Magdeleine, seeing her husband all aquiver, was overcome by a fit of the giggles.

Despite it all, rehearsals went along well and, from the very first one, Minette saw in Mlle Thibault a worthy rival. She was very young and very beautiful. Her voice, softened by many years of training, was pure and rich. Hearing the two actresses sing, Ribié declared that Minette's voice was filled with sunlight, whereas Mlle Thibault's was fresh like an April morning. As for their acting skills, their diction and grace, they were equally accomplished and Minette confided to Claude Goulard that, for the first time in her life, she feared being upstaged. Her costume was meant to be sober and modest; she had the ill-advised idea to trim it with chiffon and lace, despite the counsel of Mme Acquaire and Ribié. The fear of being outshined by the new actress made her slightly feverish, and she slept poorly on the night before the performance.

The show's success was unprecedented. The actors were lauded –
especially Ribié, Minette, and Mlle Thibault.

The next day, an article – signed this time by Mozard – directly
criticized Minette for having added too many trimmings to her costumes and accused her, ultimately, of having indulged her desire to
shine at the expense of authenticity.

The critique was legitimate enough to wound Minette's pride
deeply. She went directly to visit Mozard, who welcomed her with the
delighted smile of someone who had already been won over.

"Monsieur," she said to him, looking him straight in the eyes, as
was her way, "are you the one behind this lovely turn of phrase?"

She breathed and, watching her diction, said:

"The papers are lamplights that enlighten the people – and tyrants
do not want people to be enlightened," she stated slowly.

"You're quite young to be so wise," answered the journalist, amused.

"Monsieur, you've been very discouraging."

"How so?"

"Your article…"

"It wasn't that bad, and I love saying what I think."

"The ones before…"

"Those weren't me. As I'm sure you also know, I detest anonym-
ity."

He stared at her for a minute, intrigued.

"Do you know," he said, "that up close you're less beautiful but
more touching?"

She adopted her most seductive pose.

"Is it possible I've touched you, Monsieur?"

"Ha, ha, ha," he immediately protested. "Don't you try putting me on. Let me be touched without you trying to seduce me."

That's not going to work with him, she told herself, changing tactics. So she held his gaze so brazenly that he cried out:

"I prefer that. There's nothing of the coquette about you and I don't appreciate being taken for a ride. I find you very beautiful. Let's go out together this evening, shall we?"

She looked at him. There was certainly nothing of the charming young man about him. He looked like what he was: a hardworking businessman who surely did not make waves in his conjugal life very often. Married to a modest woman, whom he rarely saw due to the demands of his business, his only pleasure consisted of going to the theater, where, as a journalist, he was admitted for free.

Hoping to win him over entirely, Minette accepted his invitation.

To prove to Mozard that his reproaches were undeserved, she had dressed very simply in a dark skirt and a gauze bodice with pleated sleeves that revealed her forearms, and a shawl that discreetly covered her breasts. He came to collect her in a six-horse carriage that Nicolette watched go by with a knowing air. Jasmine and Joseph watched her leave and did not dare ask where she was going. She had become even more respected by friends and neighbors ever since the feat she had managed with the Caradeux – and since she had earned the title "Mademoiselle."

Going out with Mozard, she had prepared for the worst. Jean-Baptiste Lapointe was irretrievably lost to her. And as she had to keep living, even in her despair, she decided to throw herself into the fray – heart and soul. She had to get Mozard to agree not to keep praising

Mme Marsan to the high heavens. She had to blind him with love and get him to stop judging her so severely. If she managed to win over the gazette, she would be saved.

He brought her to the restaurant of a white commoner who received them with flattering low bows. Mozard stared at her as they ate. At the end of the meal, he picked up his glass and, raising it high, said:

"To your success, my dear," he said.

"There won't be any more for me, Monsieur, if you keep bashing me," she answered him without smiling.

She looked right into his eyes. No, she would not be able to seduce him. She could not do it. She who was such a good actress onstage, she could not, despite all her efforts, smile or cry, chit-chat or simper with the sole aim of seducing a man. Her face hardened. She felt like leaving Mozard there and going home. He was a white man, a slave-trader, who excluded freedmen from his paper. What was she doing there with her enemy? Something in her face must have betrayed her, for the journalist exclaimed:

"Whoa, there it is. There's hatred in your eyes."

She did not look away. To her great surprise, he spoke again:

"I like you. There's nothing of the hypocrisy so common with women of your kind, and you look so much better up close."

He drank a glassful of wine.

"But why in heaven's name do you persist in wearing lace when you're playing the part of a peasant?"

"Perhaps because I was afraid of not being charming enough, Monsieur."

Her tone was so sincere that he suddenly understood her fears, her dilemmas, her unending struggles in the face of a capricious and sectarian public, which could turn on her from one moment to the next. Until that very moment he had not truly understood that she was nothing other than a poor little freedwoman, blessed by fortune, striving to climb the rungs of the perilous ladder to fame.

"You don't have to worry anymore," he told her.

He had a kind, jovial, and intelligent face. His behavior toward her had been correct and even courteous. She was on the verge of letting herself go, forgetting her hatred, and crying out to him, "Monsieur Mozard, if a white woman just upstaged me, I'll die. My talent is the only thing I have."

But she kept silent, telling herself that he already knew all of that and that it would be fruitless for him to pity her any further.

"Tell me, why did you agree to go out with me?" he asked roughly.

"I hoped to win you over, Monsieur."

He burst out laughing and rapped her on the hand.

"You've already succeeded," he assured her.

They got back in the carriage, where Mozard maintained the same decorous attitude toward her. They rolled along the coastline, then he asked whether she would enjoy going for a dance at Vaux-Hall. She declined. Then he thought of something that would please her and shouted an address to the driver. He let her out in a sort of boutique where people were coming and going laughingly. It was a museum, she realized on seeing what was on exhibit. He bought two tickets and escorted her into a great room filled with wax statues – those of the royal family surrounded by their guards. Minette was enchanted by

Marie-Antoinette's beauty and pointed out to Mozard that the Queen seemed just as taken with lace and trimmings as she was.

"You don't find it rather bold to compare yourself to a Queen?" he asked her.

"Yes, Monsieur. But, like her Majesty, I'm proud to appreciate costly and beautiful things."

"That's no reason not to heed my advice," he answered her. "And I'll not leave you in peace, for that matter, if you don't obey. Battle your rivals onstage with skillful arms and you'll beat them."

He brought her home and kissed her hand before taking his leave.

"Farewell, young lady. I hope I've not disappointed you," he said with a strange little smile.

"You've been very kind, Monsieur."

And for the first time, she smiled sincerely and so merrily that he almost did not recognize her.

"This evening will have been one of the most delightful of my life. Thank you, Monsieur."

She hurried away and Mozard, left standing alone, shook his head as if mulling over some very private thoughts.

XXV

THE MAROONS continued to terrorize people in the plains and in the towns. They had only been feigning submission. They were now streaming down from the hills in screeching gangs, pillaging the workhouses, which they often would set afire.

Sometimes, during the night, the horns and the drums launched their rallying cries, frightened Whites gathered up their arms, the slaves in the workhouses perked up their ears, and the freedmen – heads lowered, seemingly unmoved – just waited.

One day, news spread that two maroon leaders had just been brought before the Governor. The crowd hurried over and, despite the constabulary's efforts to hold them back, people camped out in front of the Governor's mansion for hours.

When the door opened and the maroon leaders appeared, escorted by a white colonist and two armed guards, a sudden excitement arose among the spectators. What did the rebels want? Why had the Governor received them with honor and respect? A white woman held out her hand to one of the guards, called him by name and shouted:

"Tell me what's going on, Roland?"

"You're far too curious, my dear," he answered.

She ran to him, took his arm familiarly and repeated:

"Come on, tell me what's going on – tell me!"

Annoyed by her persistence, the young soldier finally told her everything.

"Monsieur Desmarrates," he whispered, pointing to the planter, "has just brought these two maroon leaders here. We've signed a treaty with them. We officially recognize their freedom, and in exchange they stop raiding our plantations."

The woman nearly keeled over from shock.

"Oh! Oh!" she exclaimed, bringing her hand to her mouth, "give those wild dogs their freedom – why, it's madness!"

She immediately released the soldier's arm and ran back to the crowd. The news spread like wildfire.

Joseph Ogé was among the freedmen gathered on a corner of the street. As soon as the news reached him, he ran to the Lamberts', where he found Beauvais and Louise Rasteau.

Ever since he had been rendered incapable of speaking, his face had taken on a strained, almost tragic expression. His gentle eyes were open exaggeratedly wide, as if he were making a constant effort to express the intensity of his soul. He looked at Lambert with his expression of a hunted animal, mechanically removed the pad and pencil Minette had given him from his pocket, and wrote:

Santyague has just surrendered and the Governor has recognized officially the freedom of the Bahoruco slaves.

The two men rose and looked at one another, then Beauvais spoke:

"The Whites are more and more afraid."

At that time, a new, subtler kind of marooning had become rampant. After fleeing the plantations, slaves would go into town, where they would blend in, dressed as freedmen. These slaves made a dangerous group of outlaws. Lying in ambush in the woods, they attacked travelers, pillaged and robbed anyone who fell within their grasp. Hunted by the constabulary, they would then return to town, where they would blend in with the crowd, dressed as freedmen to throw off suspicion.

The planters, faced with their impotence to combat these new rebels, organized hunts, during which they often slaughtered perfectly innocent Blacks and mixed-bloods. The tension between the Whites and the latter group was getting worse and worse. The hatred on either side had reached its apogee. The slaves, seen as little more than beasts of burden in the eyes of their masters, had no opportunity to imagine, think about, or prepare any uprisings. Despite the example of the slaves of Bahoruco, the Whites remained skeptical regarding the intelligence and initiative of Africans. So the mixed-bloods were blamed for everything. More than ever, they were humiliated, repressed, and ridiculed. More than ever, the slaves were beaten, tortured, and killed. Slaveholding Blacks and Mulattos, fearing the disappearance of their own slaves, reacted just as brutally toward their black brothers. Proud of the social position their wealth seemed to assure them, they wanted only one thing: to become richer. In this, they so closely resembled the white planters that the latter, always jealous when it came to their exclusivity, had begun to take offense.

One can survive fairly smoothly in the midst of hatred, for habit is a powerful thing. Despite certain suspicious elements, life went on without any great upset. These suspicious elements no longer came from the hills, where a heavy silence reigned now that the *lambi* horns had gone quiet. But it had become visible in thousands of tiny ways – in people's eyes, attitudes, and gestures. The freedmen's silent reproaches turned into a heavy and painful hostility. They gritted their teeth and lowered their eyes beneath the boots and gold-buckled shoes of the important white planters. Cravenly ignoring certain worrisome or unpleasant thoughts, the wealthy planters persuaded themselves that everything was perfectly fine, just to be able to live in peace. And their feasts, their merriment, and their pleasures augmented daily.

For Minette, as for everyone, the years passed with no great shocks. Ever since she had been granted Mozard's protection, she sang, acted, and was paid regularly. She had reached the heights of fame. Young Jean was growing up and Lise continued her successes in Léogane. Everything was going for the best, was it not? In her heart, the memory of Jean-Baptiste Lapointe was little more than a slight shadow that Claude Goulard's affection could not manage to make fade away entirely. At times, she was tempted to fall for him. Yet, her repugnance at the prospect of his kisses and embraces made clear to her that she could be nothing more than a devoted and charming friend to him.

Joseph's suffering, the Whites' haughtiness, the planters' whips – they had all ended up adopting the stunned face of routine and resignation. Strangely, in order to awaken whatever was alive in the depths of people's hearts, the lash of some sort of extraordinary event was needed – something that, with brutal shock, could bring the thousands of dulled consciousnesses out of their torpor.

At the end of that year, Lise returned from Léogane. She brought with her details, news, and a little bag of money, which she proudly showed to her mother and Minette.

"I could buy myself a slave, if I wanted to," she said with a little arrogant tone.

She had grown taller and plumper; her success had brought her confidence and it showed – a bit too much, in Minette's opinion.

The evening of her arrival, she organized a little party, to which she invited Nicolette, Goulard, Joseph, the Acquaires, and a rich young freedwoman named Angevine Roselin, whom she had met in Léogane and about whom she spoke with pride.

"Why Angevine?" protested Minette. "We hardly know her."

"I've got to start frequenting other sorts of people now. Angevine is very rich, you understand?"

No. Minette did not understand at all. But it was not her party and Lise was free to do as she pleased.

"She's a lovely person, you'll see. She came to see me backstage one day, after the performance of *Thérèse and Jeannot*."

So Angevine was invited. She arrived by carriage, escorted by two slave girls. The carriage was driven by a Mulatto in livery who waited for his "mistress" outside the house, which piqued the curiosity of the neighbors on Traversière Street. Angevine wore a magnificent white silk dress, imported from France and ordered by a white boutique owner who worked for her in secret. She was pretty and often showed her perfect teeth in a joyful smile. Nicolette, devouring her with her eyes, noticed her flirting with Goulard. She immediately set out to seduce the young actor herself. Speaking Creole, playing with their fans, they overwhelmed him with batting eyelashes and compliments.

An hour later, Goulard, seduced by Nicolette's expert flirtation, completely abandoned Angevine. Nicolette was right to think herself unbeatable at that particular game.

Minette watched Angevine and her two slave girls, both attentive to her slightest gesture. It reminded her of something she had very nearly managed to forget. The little house in Boucassin, Marie-Rose and the Saint-Ars, Mlle de Caradeux…All those rich slave-owners, served by slaves on their knees, enriched on the backs of slaves. Despite her dark skin, was Angevine not, in a way, in the same position as Mlle de Caradeux? It was money that had performed that miracle. What did it matter that she had to obey certain restrictions if her carriage was just like those of the wealthy white planters, adorned with lace from Utrecht and driven by a coachman in full livery! It was certainly better than nearly being ruined by the hooves of a horse that an impertinent young White laughingly held by the reins as it trampled a poor street vendor's stand. The memory of that scene made her heart beat faster. Yet, it had been some time since they had replaced the stand and refilled it with the best wares in the country. Lise, in her letters, had often slipped in a few crisp bills, and for months they had been eating their fill in the little house on Traversière Street.

During the party, someone asked the two sisters to sing. Lise announced that she would do a whole scene for them. She ran to shut herself up in the bedroom and came back wearing a heavy canvas skirt bunched up at the waist. Barefoot, a pipe in her mouth, and her head wrapped in a red madras scarf, she imitated the gait of workhouse slaves singing a sweet, sad melody.

Suddenly, she fell to her knees, interrupting the song with moans and sobs. Her gestures were perfect and everyone could understand what they meant. She was being hit and trying to dodge the blows. Badly beaten, she lay prostrate and kissed the ground in two places, as if kissing someone's feet. Then, rising, she began to dance a *calenda*, singing and clapping her hands.

Minette looked at her mother: her forehead was covered in sweat. Who knows whether she herself had perhaps twisted like that under someone's blows, moaning and sobbing! Who knew whether, after being beaten, she had had to beg forgiveness and get back in her master's good graces, kissing his feet – her back still bloody – then dancing and singing to amuse him! She put her hands in front of her face and cried:

"Enough!..."

Lise, mute with surprise, looked at her for a moment.

"You don't like that scene? Well, it was a real hit in Léogane..."

Angevine and Nicolette applauded, doubled over with laughter. The two slave girls, crouched in a corner of the room, giggled into their hands as they nibbled on pieces of cake Jasmine had given them. Joseph and Goulard, each with one of Saint-Martin's children on his lap, looked at Lise without flinching, and M Acquaire's tic went wild as he exchanged meaningful glances with his wife.

"And besides, not everyone can sing opera," Lise added, angered.

"Just because you opted for high art doesn't mean you should look down on the local plays."

Unable to respond, Minette busied herself serving refreshments. Handing a glass to Joseph, she noticed his lips trembling.

To lighten the mood, Goulard announced that the Comédie hoped to present very soon an Indian ballet in full costumes, and proceeded to give all the details.

The evening ended without further incident, other than the fact that Goulard quietly slipped away with Nicolette, which made Minette smile.

The next day, they learned that Angevine had been abandoned by her two slaves on the way home and raped by the driver, who had also run away. That morning, Angevine's enraged parents arrived at Jasmine's house, looking for answers.

"What time did she leave here?"

"How were her slaves acting during the party?"

"Were subversive comments made in front of them?"

Angevine's father was a heavyset, light-skinned Mulatto, bearded and potbellied, who spoke a Frenchified Creole and wore boots like those of the wealthy planters. While his wife cried her eyes out, lamenting that her daughter had been a virgin, the black planter screamed and shouted, swearing by all the gods that he would make his other slaves pay for this crime.

"I swear to God, I'll beat and torture them until my anger has been spent!"

They went away, leaving Jasmine stunned.

On hearing the news, Nicolette let out a sarcastic little laugh.

"And so what now? No reason to get all worked up. That Angevine isn't going to die. As for her parents, they should just go ahead and have her bled a bit – that'll calm her down."

Everyone was talking about the incident. Laughing at Angevine, a few young Whites improvised a song about "her virginity, lost in the arms of a handsome slave," and then all was forgotten.

One scandal easily came along to replace another: duels, rapes, hunting down debtors, and the vengeful blows of cuckolded husbands were all the rage. A few days after that, M Brousse swore he would monitor Magdeleine. He followed her, lay in wait for her, and caught her a second time kissing a young officer, who brandished his weapon on seeing him, then burst out laughing at the flabbergasted look on the poor man's face. That time, he would not forgive her and went straight to the public prosecutor to complain about his wife's behavior. Magdeleine Brousse was arrested at the theater in the middle of a rehearsal and, despite her tears and the protests of the other actors, she was brought to prison. The billboards had announced an upcoming opera: *Nina or the Love-Crazed Woman*. Minette was meant to receive the profits from that performance. Magdeleine Brousse's arrest dealt her a harsh blow. The question on everyone's mind: who could replace her? Depoix wrote to Mme de Vanancé, who was vacationing in Cap-Français, asking her to return as soon as possible. Magdeleine Brousse ended up performing the role herself, for she returned two days later, dark circles beneath her eyes and a smile on her lips.

"They took pity on me," she said, wringing her hands with false candidness. "They took pity on me and let me escape. Ah, those officers are decent guys!"

Everyone was so happy to see her that they welcomed her with shouts of joy. The reason behind her liberation was a secret they were perfectly happy to keep. Rehearsals began again with all of the actors in place, and the night of the performance arrived.

It was the month of May. A radiant sky, shining with stars, welcomed a happy, well-dressed, and excited crowd. There were many people gathered outside the Comédie. A half hour before curtain, the actors arrived in their costumes and, as always, caused quite a sensation in the street.

That evening was one of the greatest successes of Minette's entire career. An article signed by Mozard noted as much the following day, while another – signed by François Mesplès – suggested that she would also do well in one of the local plays.

"After all," said Mesplès, "this young person is more capable than anyone else of performing certain Negro sentiments, since she is herself of that race. Mme Marsan," he continued, "performed just as beautifully, just as perfectly in both local plays and the great classics. Why would this young freedwoman have such disdain for something that, at the end of the day, is really her birthright?…"

Those sorts of plays were more popular than ever. M Acquaire himself wrote them in secret, hoping someday to have them performed on the stage. Was Mesplès also writing them? Was he trying to force Minette to change her mind by frightening her? Hundreds of Whites had fashioned themselves as authors and were writing plays that the Comédie often turned down. The youngest writers believed themselves to be poets and the older thought they were dramatic authors. Minette's good taste rebelled at the very reading of such disasters. She stood her ground with Mesplès and refused to accept the role he offered her in *Julien and Zila*, a Creole translation of *Blaise and Babette*.

"I'd be terrible in the role," she repeated stubbornly.

Aside from the fact that it displeased her to play what she knew from experience to be tragic roles in these ephemeral plays, she was ashamed to speak Creole in public, even onstage. Was it not so that the language of black Africans had become a symbol of degradation? She held firm. Mesplès dressed her down in front of the other actors.

"Just who do you think you are to pick your genre?" he shouted.

"An artist, Monsieur."

"An artist of color, accepted in a white company out of pure condescension."

"Yes, Monsieur, but your condescension has been overcome by the public's enthusiasm."

She took out her gloves, announced that she had had enough and that she planned to quit the Comédie for good.

"And I don't want anyone coming after me!" she declared.

Mesplès called her impertinent – and a "descendant of *gens de la côte*."

Despite the pleadings of the Acquaires and Goulard, she went back home, determined never to set foot in the Comédie again unless M Mesplès himself begged her. She felt certain that day would come.

XXVI

FROM THEN ON, she attended the performances with her mother and Joseph, seated in the upper tier in the part of the theater the Whites called "freedmen's heaven." She watched the actors perform, their faces and hands slathered with soot in plays the public seemed to find more and more appealing. She watched them perform new operas in which numerous admirers noted her absence, though Mme Marsan's supporters ultimately won the day. After a few days, an article signed by Mozard called for her return to the theater, demanding – on behalf of the public – a reprisal of *The Statue Lover*. The Acquaires, Goulard, and Magdeleine – sent by Depoix and Favart – arrived one morning at Jasmine's house. Neither Mozard's article nor Goulard's pleadings could change her mind. She refused to return to the theater. As if to call for her return itself, the audience became more and more scarce. They abandoned the Comédie in favor of the Vaux-Halls. After just a few days, the cashbox was empty. Depoix and Favart gambled desperately and lost. Over the course of the next month, debts went unpaid. Depoix insulted Mesplès, who in turn reproached him for not making enough effort. Favart took his partner's side and, enraged, the two friends also quit the Comédie, leaving M Acquaire to take up the role of director. Depoix and Favart left to go on tour in Saint-Marc, and brought Lise with them. A wave of discouragement crashed over the actors. In an attempt to raise morale, M Acquaire announced a special evening, during which they would give an array of performances.

How, though, could they pull off such a project without any resources? As a good Bohemian, he placed his last, meager reserves on the gaming table. Luck was with him, and he won. He left the gambling house gesticulating wildly and ran home. On seeing him arrive, Scipion thought he had gone mad and clasped his hands, chasing after him in the stairwell, where they crossed paths with some other lodgers, who they ended up knocking over.

Once they had reached their rooms, M Acquaire took a wad of bills from his pocket and showed them to his wife, hands trembling.

"Look – look what I've won! Oh, the Comédie is saved!"

His tic was twitching wildly.

His wife looked at him without saying a word, then burst into laughter, all the while giving Scipion mighty slaps on the back. That day, they all got drunk in their rooms and discussed the next play they would put up – which would be a sensation – well into the night.

Good fortune kept smiling on them. Mlle Noël, an actress in Cap-Français, came to Port-au-Prince on a little holiday. Acquaire saw her, was seduced by her youth and beauty, and offered her the lead role. She accepted. Magdeleine Brousse and the other actresses were offended and reproached M Acquaire for favoring an actress from Cap-Français at their expense. During a meeting among the theater stockholders, someone pronounced Minette's name and noted that she was bound by a contract that had not yet expired and so had no right to quit the Comédie before that contract ran out.

"So we're within our rights to sue her," said one of the stock-holders.

M Acquaire alluded to the fact that the rupture had not been entirely unprovoked.

"And what exactly was the provocation?" Mesplès himself had the nerve to ask.

"Your insults, Monsieur," Goulard responded coldly.

The loan-shark pounded his fist on the table and argued that a White could never "insult" a person of color and that he had foreseen that kind of reaction from a freedwoman who had been too well treated and placed on equal footing with white actors.

"Her talent merited that kind of treatment," noted Mme Acquaire, indignant.

"Why did you all let that girl think herself indispensable? We're constantly getting new actors from France and the other towns here in the country...The public will forget her."

M Acquaire introduced Mlle Noël. She was very young and had a pleasant voice.

"Here's the thing that'll make her come out of the shadows," proclaimed Mesplès, smugly. "And this time I'll lend you all some money without interest. Let us spare no expense and make this evening a success like nothing ever seen before. What we need is a director equal to the task. M Acquaire..."

M Acquaire wanted to show himself equal to the task. The sets were overhauled. The painter Jean Peyret and Julian the stage manager worked tirelessly for two weeks. The posters and placards announced "an unparalleled evening, equal in every way to those of the great theaters of the Metropolis." Mlle Noël was touted roundly. Her name was their trump card. Curious, the public came out in force for the performance, and that night the curtains opened onto incomparable sets and staging. François Ribié had left his imprint and his imprint had once again triumphed: it was a total success.

Mlle Noël's youth and beauty won hearts and her talent conquered minds. The audience threw flowers at her feet, she was raised shoulder high in triumph, and people cheered while crying out her name.

Minette, seated between Joseph and Jasmine, had followed the play with little visible emotion. Once the curtain had fallen, she had applauded along with the others, her face impassive and very dignified. She, too, had performed in that play. She, too, had sung those melodies, made those gestures, worn those costumes. That same public had cheered her, raised her up, and called her "Mademoiselle" – and recently, at that. They had forgotten her already – already replaced her, relegated her to the shadows out of which she had emerged only by unhoped-for luck. She finally understood: never again would she climb back up the hill, get back on that pedestal where the most random providence had placed her.

She went home with Jasmine and spent a sleepless night, her eyes filled with memories of the white actress who had eclipsed her. Her pride, her true love for art suffered immensely. To have broken in that way, all of a sudden, with a whole past of successes, unhoped-for honors – to pass by the Comédie as a stranger, never again to sing, never again to sing!…

She knew in her heart that her impulsive move had not been serious and that she had only wanted to prove to M Mesplès that sooner or later he would have to do some real scheming to get her back to the Comédie. She had not wanted anything more. But fortune had just turned abruptly against her. She was nothing, nothing more than a poor freedwoman among so many others – with no real status, with no other reason for being than to resign herself, to lower her head like the others, like all the others. The white man, the only real master, had gotten the better of her. He had beaten her at her own game. M Mesplès, M de Caradeux, M Saint-Ar – all of them, all the masters in the country had gotten the better of her. Why had she been born? Why had her mother not killed herself rather than sleep with that white man? She shuddered at that horrific thought and lay down flat on her stomach, her face hidden in the crook of her elbow. Little Jean slept on Lise's bed. She raised herself onto one elbow and looked over at him. He, too, was a person of color. He was growing up only to resign himself later, just as all the others had resigned themselves. What would he be? Carpenter, tinsmith, manager of a dance hall, cartwright? Even if he turned out to be intelligent and educated, he would spend his life saying yes to the law and accepting like so much charity any crumbs that the Whites might be willing to offer him! She could only hope that he would not become a planter – a big planter who, whip in hand, would count his slaves to be always sure of the exact number. That thought made her shiver. Suddenly, she was back at the little house in Boucassin.

The memory of Lapointe overwhelmed her as it did every time she let those shadows loose from her heart. Breathless, her heart beating wildly, her eyes rolling back, for a moment she relived those delicious hours in which she had first known love…

The next day, to escape her own thoughts, she offered to help Jasmine in the kitchen, which the latter accepted enthusiastically. For a moment, she had the feeling of getting her little girl back, and so, to prove that her authority had remained intact, she babbled senselessly, criticizing her daughters' negligence, pointing out the spider webs and dust as proof:

"You leave me alone here, but I can't take care of everything myself. A young lady should know how to keep house. I'm tired…"

She did, in fact, seem tired. Her wrinkles were apparent. Minette, looking at her with a sidelong glance, realized that for six years she had practically abandoned her mother. Yes, she had been entirely absorbed by her singing – by singing and by her love for Lapointe. Pour Jasmine! How lonely she must have felt!

Minette's eyes fell on the large chest, as if by chance. That was where she kept her treasures.

She waited until her mother had left the bedroom to open it. She then took out a little bag with a few bills in it, which she counted. Everything she had been able to save over the months following Saint-Martin's death. She put them back, alongside the *makandal* good luck charm, Pitchoun's ring, and Lapointe's red roses.

Then, after putting on an Indian-style skirt and matching madras scarf, she went to the market for Jasmine. She found herself immediately caught up in the daily throng. One particularly strident voice dominated the others. A man standing atop a table shouted out his wares at the top of his lungs.

"For sale," cried the voice, "a young Negro violinist, able to read and write. Come forward, ladies and gentlemen. Negro violinist for sale, Negro violinist for sale…"

Suddenly, a violin melody rose up over the tumult and Minette turned around. The violinist was playing a well-known tune. Where had she already heard it played like that? She slipped between the passersby to approach the place where the white man on the table was addressing the crowd, trying to get people's attention. She recognized the Saint-Ars' young slave, Simon. Standing next to the table, he was playing, his eyes lowered. Next to him stood M Saint-Ar, immobile, observing him nervously.

Someone raised his hand and proposed eight hundred pounds.

M Saint-Ar let out an exclamation to protest that derisory sum.

"One thousand pounds," said someone else.

"One thousand five hundred."

M Saint-Ar kept his eyes fixed on Simon's hands, as if he wanted to keep them forcibly attached to the violin. The slave began to turn gray; sweat covered his forehead. He raised pleading eyes to his master. His left hand was cramping, he began missing notes, and then he stopped.

"Why has he stopped playing?" asked the first bidder.

"He seems tired," said the second. "He's a wreck – one thousand five hundred. He isn't worth any more than that."

"One thousand five hundred," shouted the auctioneer, standing on tiptoes. "One thousand five hundred."

"One thousand six hundred," someone stated with a harsh, cutting voice.

Minette turned around. She saw Céliane de Caradeux's uncle.

Upon noticing him, Simon shivered and he begged M Saint-Ar with his eyes.

"One thousand six hundred," shouted the auctioneer once again. "One thousand six for a Negro violinist."

At that moment, Minette jostled her neighbors and ran up to M Saint-Ar to identify herself.

"Bonjour, Monsieur."

"Oh! What's this – you here!"

M de Caradeux, who was inspecting Simon, turned around.

"Ah, there you are. Do you still have white lovers who fight duels over you? Lower those eyes, lower those eyes, you little wench."

Everyone laughed, and the auctioneer himself, forgetting his merchandise, began observing the scene. M Saint-Ar called him back to order with a brief nod of the head.

"A violin-playing Negro," shouted the auctioneer, "one thousand six hundred. Anyone offering more than one thousand six hundred?"

M Saint-Ar looked at Simon without animosity but with cold indifference.

"Play," he muttered to him.

This time, he played a tune from *The Beautiful Arsène*.

For a moment, Minette was transported and forgot everything. Eyes closed, she once again saw the Saint-Ar's home, the masquerade ball, the yellow Harlequin…

"Simon," she whispered to the slave, "how is Marie-Rose?"

"Mademoiselle Marie-Rose! She died two years ago…"

"How did she die, Simon?"

He hesitated a moment then, lowering his head, said:

"She killed herself, Miss."

Saint-Ar had taken M de Caradeux's arm.

"Well then, my friend," said the latter, "we're selling violin-playing Negroes now?"

"I'm not a selfish man, dear Monsieur de Caradeux. I've trained another one and I'm selling this one."

"Might the other one be even better?"

"No, he's merely younger."

"And less tired."

M Saint-Ar turned away abruptly and looked at Simon. The latter was so pale Saint-Ar feared he would faint right there in front of the buyers.

"One thousand six hundred – who'll go higher than one thousand six hundred? A good violin-playing Negro…"

It looked as if M de Caradeux would be Simon's new master. The slave followed him with his head lowered, after Saint-Ar, by way of consolation, clapped him on the shoulder and said:

"Go on now, my boy, you've changed masters."

Simon looked at his hands…

Ah! His hands – those blasted hands were the reason for all of this. The cramps had become more and more frequent. Despite his efforts, after a few minutes of playing his left hand would inevitably cramp up, stiffening his wrist and then the whole length of his arm. And he felt as if his heart, tight in his chest, and somehow also stiff, would simply stop beating. Ah, such suffering! To leave the home where he had been born, where he was called "my boy," where he was clapped on the shoulder! To go with some new and unknown master. Who was this man who sought to buy him? Where would he bring him? What would he do with him? For the first time in his life, Simon was afraid. He turned back, looked at Minette.

"Mademoiselle," he wept, "buy me...buy me in memory of Marie-Rose, buy me..."

Minette raised her eyes and looked all around, panic-stricken. A man smiled at her. It was a young, high-ranking officer who had been following the sale from the beginning, all the while observing Minette from the corner of his eye. As she often did, she made a quick decision and went over to him, hiding her actions from M de Caradeux.

"Buy him, Monsieur," she said to him, looking him straight in the eyes.

"For you?" he asked, with a sly smile. "Is he your lover?"

"Buy him, Monsieur."

Their eyes locked for a moment. The officer smiled again.

"One thousand seven hundred," he shouted.

M de Caradeux, who considered it a done deal, turned around sharply.

"One thousand eight hundred," he shot back.

The officer looked at Minette.

"My word, you're well worth it," he whispered to her.

"One thousand nine hundred."

"One thousand nine hundred," repeated the auctioneer in a booming voice. M de Caradeux went pale.

"Two thousand," he said, furious.

"Two thousand one hundred."

Minette kept her eyes fixed on those of the officer. It seemed to her for a moment as if her gaze was her secret charm and that if she lowered it, she would break the spell.

"Two thousand one hundred," screamed the auctioneer, out of breath, hands raised above his head. "Two thousand one hundred. Anyone ready to go above two thousand one hundred?"

M de Caradeux shrugged his shoulders and, looking the officer up and down, said roguishly:

"I surrender."

Minette trembled. As long as the auction had been going on, she had been able to forget that she, too, would have to pay afterward. Simon rushed toward her, seized her hand, and kissed it. She raised her eyes to the officer. He looked at her smilingly. He was young and handsome and his eyes were not at all brutish.

A woman of color brushed against M de Caradeux as she passed by.

"It's high time," he said disgustedly to M Saint-Ar, "that we designate special areas of the market for those people."

Since that law had not yet been promulgated, the diverse crowd rubbed shoulders shamelessly and shopped at the same stands, bargaining and jostling one another. Minette opened her mouth to speak and the young officer stopped her with a gesture.

"I don't ask anything in exchange," he said. "I love the violin and I needed a slave."

"Thank you, Monsieur."

"My name is Captain Desroches."

She smiled at him.

"Do you know this slave?" he asked her again.

She followed him with Simon, to whom M Saint-Ar had just said:

"Get along, my boy, you've got a new master now."

Minette raised her eyes to the officer and, pointing to Simon, admitted in a gentle voice:

"I was ready to do anything to save him. I heard him play at his master's house. You've made a bad deal, Captain – he suffers from hand cramps."

He turned toward her sharply:

"Well, now, you certainly have some nerve!" he observed flatly.

People looked at them with curiosity. The white women and, especially, the women of color who knew Minette were surprised to see her parading around with a white man at her side.

"Anything's possible," Kiss-Me-Lips shouted at her, laughing. "Look at you, stepping out…and with quite a handsome officer."

And with that she shook her beautiful head, adorned with a bright madras scarf.

A white Creole, wearing a flowing and transparent pink silk *gaule*, brushed so closely against the officer that he turned to stare at her smilingly.

"I'm new in this country," he confessed, with a sidelong glance at Minette.

"That's quite obvious, Captain."

Two young slaves were being sold and wept bitterly. They were likely siblings and were going to be sold separately. They threw themselves in one another's arms, begging to be sold together. Brutally torn apart, the vendor threatened them with thirty lashes unless they kept quiet.

Young Negresses, seated on flat rocks, offered fruits for sale to passersby. Amiably gossiping market-women watched over their stands or their baskets while dangling samples of their wares on their arms. All those black, brown, and yellow heads, decked out in multicolored madras scarves, along with all those long brightly colored skirts gave a touch of originality to the scene, which the officer was observing with great pleasure.

"I think," he said to Minette, "that all these costumes produce a particularly lovely effect against the backdrop of these trees!"

He stopped and leaned abruptly down to her:

"I'd like to see you again."

"If you'd like, Captain."

"I'll let you know."

"Thank you, Captain."

Kiss-Me-Lips arrived at that moment and, under the pretext of wanting to talk to Minette, began mincing about, eyelashes batting and voice lilting.

"Hello, Captain, Monsieur. Minette is a dear friend of mine. Oh, what heat! What terrible heat!"

She fanned herself while eyeing the officer seductively. Annoyed, the latter observed her coldly.

"Are you that hot?" he asked her.

"Yes, Captain," she responded, undulating like a snake.

"Well, then you should go have a bath."

And he turned on his heels after calling for Simon, and glanced once more at Minette.

"You see," said Kiss-Me-Lips, "you made him run away, with your standoffish attitude."

Minette did a bit more shopping then headed back home, where she found Joseph. He had received a letter from his brother Vincent, who hoped soon to be able to return from France. He had asked Joseph to go to Dondon to see their elderly mother and let her know about his imminent return.

"Are you happy to have news from your brother?"

He nodded his head, then took a little book, half torn, from his pocket and perused it with his eyes. It was one of Bossuet's sermons. Minette remembered the sound of his voice when he used to recite certain passages of those sermons and her heart tightened in her chest.

She left the room but ran back when she heard sobs. Joseph, his face hidden in his book, was weeping like a child.

XXVII

MLLE NOËL WAS meant to return to Cap-Français; M Acquaire decided to have her perform in *The Statue Lover* one last time. Unfortunately, she was an unpredictable actress. She did not perform nearly as well, and the public – demanding more from this person who had eclipsed Minette than she was actually capable of giving – was displeased and booed her. The audience drowned out her voice with cries of: "We want Mademoiselle Minette, we want Mademoiselle Minette." It was a real scandal and quite a victory. Unfortunately, though, Minette missed it all. Young Jean was ill and she had stayed home to care for him after having sent for the neighborhood healer, who had prescribed a purge and some herbal infusions.

Beside himself with joy, Goulard came knocking at her door that night to announce the defeat of Mlle Noël.

"The gods are with you, because that actress really is a great talent," he said.

"But what happened?"

"She took a few liberties and our public is demanding, as you well know. Those young people make enough noise to bring down the whole house and they called for you at the top of their lungs."

"My Lord!"

"Will you come back to the Comédie, Minette?"

"Well, I should think so."

In her joy, she threw her arms around Goulard's neck and kissed him. He held her close.

"Has your heart been healed yet?"

"Oh, Claude…Claude…"

"I love you, Minette."

"I know."

"When will you answer, 'I love you, too,' instead of 'I know?'"

"I'd give anything…"

"Oh, hush, just hush."

He pushed her away abruptly and ran off.

The following day, M Acquaire came to see her early in the morning to tell her what had happened at the Comédie the night before.

"Mademoiselle Noël leaves for Cap-Français this morning. The Comédie awaits you, Minette," he told her.

He was counting on bringing her back, triumphantly, to that inconstant public that had once again called for her to perform. He had just finished writing his local play: *Harlequin, Mulatress Protected by Makandal*, in which he hoped to have Lise perform. Minette's last triumph, which he himself had made happen at the Comédie, had made him bold and he had plans to have other actors of color perform. Mme Acquaire wrote a letter to Lise, calling her back to the city. Seduced by the idea of being applauded at the Comédie in Port-au-Prince, she returned immediately, accompanied by a young *griffe* named Julien, who she was more or less in love with, and a few white actors.

Julien was a handsome fellow, had a lovely voice, and played the violin. M Acquaire, encouraged by Minette, hired him immediately to perform in his Creole play alongside Lise. The program for the holidays that week was varied and very promising. Some English horsemen had just come ashore and were beginning to set up camp in an enclosure near the King's Garden. Everyone was talking about their feats of dressage on horses running at full gallop. In addition the municipality had announced an exposition of pyrotechnics in honor of the King, and the Vaux-Halls were organizing their usual balls for Whites and for people of color. There were already more than enough options without the theatrical performance M Acquaire was intent on making "especially sensational."

The billboards announced *Harlequin, Mulatress Protected by Makandal* as an Indian ballet of a new sort; also billed was a musical comedy titled *Renaud from Ast* by Aleyrac, in which Minette would play the lead role. M Acquaire was relying heavily on Lise's youth and talent. Moreover, he meant to prove that henceforth Negro actors would have to be welcomed on the stage to perform in these local comedies, rather than engaging Whites in blackface. Rehearsals for the Creole play got started without M Acquaire letting the theater stakeholders know of his plan, just as they had done for Minette's debut. Mme Marsan was being roundly praised at the time for her performance in *The Beautiful Arsène*. Minette had the program changed at the very last minute, abruptly announcing her own return to stage in the same role in *The Beautiful Arsène*. The public ate up this rivalry, and Minette and Mme Marsan's respective supporters bet wildly on one or the other of the two actresses.

The excitement had reached its peak when it became known that

Mme Marsan had arrived in Port-au-Prince. When the news was announced, it was like a gust of sheer madness at the Comédie. Minette cried from nervousness during a rehearsal, and M Acquaire – with his tic, to boot – tried to manage his nerves by adopting François Ribié's despotic style. During one of the stormier sessions, Durand stepped in, interrupting all the criticisms, tears, and protests:

"I would like to say something," he said with his lovely voice and perfect diction. "If you all do not calm down, Madame Marsan will have a fine time watching you all fail. As for you, Minette, if you do not manage to get a hold of yourself, your rival will return to Cap-Français in triumph…"

These wise words had the effect of a cold shower, and M Acquaire himself, too nervous to reprimand the others, turned to Durand for assistance, which was very effective.

Minette had Jasmine prepare infusions of calming herbs for her, and from then on the rehearsals took place in a calm and orderly fashion. It was time. The date of the performance was nearly upon them and the delinquent subscriptions were being paid by those who did not want to miss this extraordinary evening.

"Madame Marsan has come to watch Minette perform." That latest bit of gossip made the rounds.

Mme Marsan was staying at the "Golden Lion Inn" and had holed herself up there. No one had gotten a glimpse of her. The night of the performance, despite the English horsemen, the fireworks, and the Vaux-Halls with their devilish music, a special garrison had to be arranged to accommodate the great crowds pressing toward the theater entrance.

Five minutes before curtain, the white actress made her appearance in a special box that had been reserved for her near the Governor. Beautiful, calm, smiling, dressed in a sumptuous ensemble adorned with precious stones, she was cheered by the delirious crowd. Minette, hearing the applause, felt a moment of panic – just as she had on the night of her debut. She grabbed Goulard as if he were some sort of life preserver.

"Come, come now, you've got to stay calm. I have every confidence in you," he said, caressing her hair.

M Mesplès himself had come out of his shell that evening. Passing near Minette, radiant in her costume, he looked her over from head to toe.

"Keep in mind that the Comédie's reputation is on the line tonight," he let drop, as if reluctantly.

Minette did not let her chance slip. She looked the loan-shark right in the eyes.

"Am I to believe, Monsieur, that its honor depends on me?"

"It would seem so," answered the white man, defeated.

She smiled. She felt revitalized by the warm, gentle wave of pride that rose in her heart. She took a deep breath.

Macarty went out in front of the closed curtains to speak a few humorous words of welcome to the Governor and to ask for everyone's indulgence and goodwill. He then performed a flute solo, which Nelanger interrupted by breaking in with his guitar. They were cheered enthusiastically. Once they had returned to the wings, Lise and her young *griffe* were ready to go onstage to perform *Harlequin, Mulatress Protected by Makandal*.

If no one booed at the play, M Acquaire owed it all to Lise and her partner's talent. The latter was a smash. It was the first time a dark-skinned person had performed on the stage of the Comédie. Everyone found the idea very original and applauded it as much as they praised the talent of the two young colored actors. M and Mme Acquaire, thrilled, threw themselves into one another's arms and even thumbed their noses at the astonished M Mesplès.

At last, the curtains parted to reveal the set of *The Beautiful Arsène*. When Minette came onstage, the white actress flinched unwittingly and leaned out of her box for a moment.

With the first notes, she raised her head and clasped her hands as if listening intently. She remained this way until the end of the little aria, which she applauded, on her feet along with the rest of the delirious crowd. Then she hastily left her box. Everyone thought she had left and they cheered Minette even more enthusiastically. The curtains were closed. They opened for a fourth time to reveal Minette and Mme Marsan, embracing. The crowd's enthusiasm reached a pinnacle. A few young people attempted to climb onto the stage like acrobats and were intercepted by the bodyguards. Two such hoodlums, standing on their seats, had drawn their swords, while a woman waved her arms and shouted: "Watch out for the spectators – go fight somewhere else." With her gesture, the white actress had just paid sincere and fervent tribute to Minette's talent. Acquaire rushed to the orchestra and they planted a few chords. Silence was reestablished. The violins proposed the first notes of a melody and the voices of the two artists rose in harmony. Then Minette went quiet and Mme Marsan finished the little aria on her own. Her voice was also astonishingly pure and rich.

Neither Mlle Dubuisson, nor Mlle Thibault, nor Mlle Noël had that timber. Minette realized this and, in her joy at finding such a perfect equal in the white songstress, idol of Cap-Français, she threw herself into Mme Marsan's arms and burst into tears. The curtain was lowered on this final tableau.

For a week, the paper wrote incessantly about that evening. Minette and Mme Marsan were unanimously praised to the high heavens and no more foolish comparisons were made to divide the two artists, placed side by side on the same pedestal in the name of artistry, which had triumphed over the law.

At the same time that it lauded the talents of the other colored artists presented for the first time at the Comédie, the paper did not miss the opportunity to provoke the forces of law-and-order with a warning: "Are we prepared to see ourselves overrun by these people?" protested the article's author. "Let us content ourselves with nourishing and favoring a talent like that of Mlle Minette, but do spare us this horde of freedmen with their mediocre talent." The commentary was unfair. Lise – and even Julien – deserved to be encouraged. M Acquaire did not dare object and he urged Lise and Julien to return to touring in less strict towns.

Captain Desroches, sincerely taken by Minette since having seen her perform at the Comédie, began to court her in earnest. He sent her love letters, wreaths of flowers, poems, and love songs.

He was a good poet, and Minette was grateful to him. She agreed to go for walks with him on public holidays and days of celebration. Goulard took offense and made a jealous scene.

"So you prefer white boys who've earned a few stripes, do you?"

"I don't prefer anyone."

"I get the picture, my dear – you're following along with the likes of Nicolette and Kiss-Me-Lips. But what's wrong with me, what's so wrong with me that you can't love me, too?"

"I'll never love again."

He stared at her angrily.

"You're exaggerating."

"It isn't my fault."

"Of course not. To each his own little ways."

That was where they had left off when the door opened and a young soldier entered. Minette looked at him for a moment without recognizing him.

"Pitchoun!" she finally exclaimed.

The soldier took a step backward, brought his hand to his cap and, clacking his heels noisily, said with a smile:

"Officer Alexandre Pétion."

Minette threw herself into his arms.

"Where'd you come up with that name?"

He was of medium height but well proportioned. Black curls brushed his intelligent forehead, half covered by his cap. The blue nankeen cloth of his uniform flattered his bronze skin tone and brought out the elegance of his waist and his limbs.

"My word, what a handsome soldier you make!" exclaimed Minette, slightly amused.

Her frankness showed him that she still looked at him like a little brother.

"So have these years in the barracks been tough, young man?" asked Goulard.

"Yes and no, Monsieur," answered the soldier. "I find heavy artillery fascinating and I love my job."

Nicolette, who had seen him enter Jasmine's home, ran over with Kiss-Me-Lips on her heels. They both began turning around him and, because they were calling him Pitchoun, he once again clacked his heels and for the second time introduced himself by the name he had chosen.

"Alexandre Pétion – what a lovely name!" singsonged Nicolette, eyes batting.

"What a grand name," stated Goulard. "Tell me, young man, did you choose it thinking of the King of Macedonia?"

"No, Monsieur," he answered simply. "Madame Guiole suggested I adopt the name, thinking it would suit me well."

Minette canceled her plans with Captain Desroches in order to go out with Pitchoun. Together they watched the spectacle of the acrobats who had come from France, they laughed over the performance of the show ponies, and they went to dance at the colored balls at the Vaux-Halls.

Everyone in high society was talking about *Beautiful Eloise* and *Margot the Mender*, at that time, so the trend was to master the art of gracefully swooning in the arms of a gentleman.

It was for this reason that, for the last little while, ladies had been going to do their graceful fainting in the home of a charlatan named Rosaldo, an adept of the occult sciences whom ladies consulted, accompanied by a gentleman, to have their future told to them.

One morning, a very excited Nicolette arrived at Minette's and began telling her about the famous fortune-teller's predictions.

"He told me, 'You will die a violent death,'" she confided to her friend, shivering. "He told Kiss-Me-Lips about her past and said that a man had died of love for her. And that's true."

"And how did he say she would die?"

"Violently," said Nicolette, horrified.

"He's a performing fortune-teller," declared Minette laughingly.

Nonetheless, when Nicolette had left she continued to think about him. Her superstitious nature getting the better of her, she decided to go see the fortune-teller and dragged Pitchoun along with her.

They entered into a room where several ladies and their beaus were already waiting. A door opened, leading to an adjoining room, and a man came out, carrying a passed-out woman in his arms. Minette and Pitchoun glanced worriedly at one another. What was the fortune-teller saying to his customers that put them in such a state?

"Let's go," Pitchoun whispered. "You aren't too scared?"

She shook her head no.

A second woman came out in tears. Her partner was passing a vial of smelling salts under her nose to keep her from fainting.

The third woman was stoic. She was inhaling smelling salts on her own and refused to take her partner's arm.

Soon it was Minette and Pitchoun's turn to enter into the mysterious room.

A completely bald, elderly man was seated at a round table. Placed on the table were a compass and an open book, on which he held open his large hands as he looked straight ahead.

Nothing in the room was very unusual aside from the old man himself. He looked up at Minette and Pitchoun with two immense, rheumy eyes that seemed to be looking for a source of light unknown to men.

"Sit down," he said to them.

His voice was deep and quavering, like that of all old men in this world.

"I'm looking at you," he said, "but I do not see you. My eyes are blind to the light of men but they see much further."

He held out two long hands, yellow and veiny.

"Each of you must place a hand in mine," he ordered with his tremulous voice.

Minette and Pitchoun obeyed.

Suddenly, a shiver ran through the old man's body and was transmitted to the two young people.

"I have two large hands in my hands," he stated. "One of these hands is that of a great artist, the other is that of a great man."

Despite his emotion, Pitchoun made a face at Minette, as if to say that the notorious fortune-teller was nothing but a sweet old fool.

"Do not make faces, young man, my eyes are blind but I feel your skepticism. You will someday be a great man and your name will go down in history. You love the military and you will soon prove yourself on the battlefield. That is how your career shall begin."

He suddenly let drop Pitchoun's hand and kept Minette's in his.

"As for you, young lady, you are bound by a terrible love. Artist and lover, this will be your lot on this earth. But terrible events will upend your life and you will die one day of a violent death."

Recalling that he had made the same prediction for both Nicolette and Kiss-Me-Lips, Minette nearly burst into laughter, but she restrained herself and it was she this time who made a face at Pitchoun.

"You, too, are skeptical, young lady. But the future will prove me right."

He let his hands drop and, crossing his arms and closing his strange eyes, concluded:

"Place your offering on the table, please."

When they were back on the street, Minette and Pitchoun burst into laughter, calling the old man a flea-bitten charlatan.

"In your case at least," said Pitchoun, "there's some truth in it – but to tell me I'll be a great man…me! He must have taken me for a white man, that's all, and wanted to flatter me by saying I'd be the future Governor of the country. Oh, that's a good one. And thanks to you I've got no more pocket money. Let's hope Papa Sabès will be feeling generous…"

"Tell me," Minette asked him worriedly, "do you think he's really blind?"

XXVIII

LISE WAS HAVING great success in Saint-Marc. Every so often, Jasmine received letters containing both funny anecdotes and crisp new bills. Her stand had become one of the most well stocked on Traversière Street. Young Jean was old enough that he could be counted on to watch over it on his own and even call out to passersby.

As for Minette, she had one burning desire: to return to Arcahaie. Whatever the cost, she had to see the little house in Boucassin again, to talk to Ninninne, to see what had become of Lapointe's workhouse and his slaves. Every day, pulling her big trunk out from under the bed, she counted her little nest egg, heart pounding. When she finally had enough, she decided to leave immediately.

"Where are you going?"

"To Arcahaie, Mama."

Jasmine did not dare protest. She sighed and went away with the heavy step of the resigned creature she had always been.

When Joseph came that morning, Minette wanted to give him a bit of money so that he might go to Dondon and see Vincent's mother, as he had been asked to do. But he refused to accept her money, shaking his head stubbornly.

"Go on, take the money," she pressed him. "For many years you taught us for free…I'm not giving you a gift. I owe you this money."

And she more or less forced the envelope into his pocket. Then, leaving her luggage half finished, she ran to Mme Acquaire's to let her know of her departure. She found Scipion there, cleaning the bedroom. He looked at her with his air of blissful adoration and told her that "Mistress" had gone out but would soon return.

"Have a seat, Mademoiselle, have a seat."

He offered her some cane sugar, which she refused, and came to crouch dreamily at her feet.

Opening the piano, she played a melody and listened to it distractedly.

"Do you remember, Scipion, how I was afraid of the piano when I saw it for the first time?"

"I do, Miss. You were just a little nightingale back then."

"I've grown up, Scipion, I've grown up so much…"

At that moment, the door opened and Mme Acquaire burst in.

"What's this – is that you, Minette?"

"Yes, Madame."

She seemed worried and her hands fluttered nervously about her scarf as she tried to untie it.

"There's a lot going on out there," she finally admitted. "There's been terrifying news from France. Talk of a revolution."

"A revolution!"

"That's all I know, my dear. But here the big planters are terribly excited and since this morning more than sixty carriages have traversed the driveway at the Governor's palace…What they want, I have no idea."

This business about a revolution in France was of little interest to Minette for the moment. She interrupted Mme Acquaire.

"I've come to say my goodbyes, Madame," she said. "I'm leaving for Arcahaie tomorrow."

"For a long time?"

"I'll be gone for at least a week, Madame."

"Well, then that's all right. Soon we're going to put on an opera that's all the rage in Paris."

"I'll be back in time for that, Madame."

"Well, safe travels."

She kissed Minette and sent her off. The painter Perrosier, standing in his doorway with a bottle of rum in one hand and his paintbrushes in the other, was on the hunt for models. He called out to her as always.

"Come pose for me, my lovely. I'm feeling inspired this morning. It'll be a masterpiece."

"You really have no luck. I'm leaving soon."

"You're leaving, you say?"

"Yes, for Arcahaie."

"Even with all this agitation?"

"What agitation?"

"Hmph, the big planters are all riled up, just like the folks in France…"

She shrugged her shoulders and went home. Jasmine was preparing lunch and young Jean was watching the stand. She finished packing her things, then sat down for a moment and began daydreaming. "Revolution!" Mme Acquaire had said. Her eyes darted around the room and fell on a book by Jean-Jacques Rousseau. She stood up, took the book and began rifling through it feverishly. "The people of France are all riled up," Perrosier had said. She looked at the book again, thoughtfully, then placed it on the bed, stood up, and went out into the street. Two coaches followed by two covered carriages passed at a gallop, causing the pedestrians to scatter. She followed them. Soon they disappeared and she took off along with several others headed toward the Governor's palace. Mme Acquaire had not been exaggerating. More than sixty carriages were lined up around the Governor's palace and a throng of curious passersby had crowded around them. Four planters emerged from their carriages gesticulating furiously, faces red and covered in sweat.

"Apparently the King has convened the Estates General," whispered a young white man to another.

"Is that enough reason for the planters to be panicking?"

"They aren't panicking, they're making demands and being refused."

"What?"

The conversation was interrupted by the parade of carriages leaving the palace. A squad of soldiers came out to the street, armed to the hilt, and Minette recognized Captain Desroches among them. Someone grabbed her by the arm. She turned around to see Joseph. His eyes were gleaming with a strange light and a slight smile played on his parted lips.

"Did you want to tell me something?"

He nodded his head yes and pulled Minette into a quiet corner. Her hand was in his and she could feel him trembling.

"What's the matter, Joseph?"

He looked up and down the street and took out of his pocket a piece of paper on which was written, in round letters, the following words:

The Declaration of the Rights of Man.

Then he folded the paper, put it in his pocket, and wrote in his notebook:

The planters are demanding to be allowed to self-govern the country. I'm not going anywhere. Lambert and Beauvais have asked me to stay.

Minette shook her head abruptly. Oh, no! No one was going to hinder her freedom!

"Well, I for one am leaving."

Joseph shook his head to say no and pointed to something happening in the distance.

A group of poor Whites were shouting as they ran after the carriages. Shaking their fists at the planters, they called them by name and threatened the drivers.

It wouldn't be safe.

The agitation was at its height. The most recent news from France was deeply alarming. A letter from Vincent Ogé to Joseph recounted in great detail all the latest events, among which the storming of the Bastille.

The letter was being re-read at the Lamberts', in the presence of Beauvais, his wife – a young Mulatress named Marguerite – and Louise Rasteau.

"The people of France are demanding their rights," said Beauvais.

"They've seized the Arsenal, armed themselves, and destroyed a fortified prison..." recited Lambert dreamily.

"And they've triumphed, 'class privilege has been abolished,'" continued reading Louise.

"The people of France have revolted!..."

These words, repeated from mouth to mouth, had the effect of a spark in a powder keg. The poor Whites repeated them to the planters' and the freedmen's faces with their heads lifted. "The people of France have revolted." Copies of the Declaration of the Rights of Man were circulated, and as the news heated up people's spirits it also revitalized their sleeping consciousness. The revolt that had been simmering in their hearts sprung up. The cry of disorder was coming from the powerful, the great planters themselves!

Disregarding the King's refusal to recognize Saint-Domingue as a province of the kingdom, they delegated their deputies in the Estates General and formed a General Assembly of the French Sector of Saint-Domingue. Caring nothing for the Governor General, this Assembly interfered in public affairs and prepared to extend its powers by publishing a Constitution that was wholly unacceptable to the Governor.

From then on, hostilities were openly declared. The big planters, more pretentious than ever before, went about whip in hand, smiling with a victorious air. The poor Whites vengefully sided with the Governor, who, as a sign of solidarity, distributed white rosettes among them, which they wore proudly. The colonists, meanwhile, adopted red rosettes in retaliation.

The crowd had begun referring to them as the "White Pompoms" and the "Red Pompoms." Hate had found an outlet and reigned over all. "White Pompoms" and "Red Pompoms" shot murderous glances at one another and sought out the least excuse to fight. Petitions that Beauvais, Lambert, Joseph Ogé, and Labadie had written were proposed to the "Red Pompoms." In these petitions, free men of color and free Negroes demanded to be considered full citizens. In the name of the Black Code and the Declaration of the Rights of Man, they called for political equality. Already infuriated by the articles of the Declaration of the Rights of Man that called for the abolition of slavery, the planters demanded the names of the petitioners. The secret was well kept by their entourage but Labadie was suspected and his home was attacked by a band of enraged Whites. They dragged him into the middle of the street, despite the screams of his slaves, who were kept at bay by the whip, and attached him to the tail of a wild horse, which they then whipped. Followed by a crowd of curious onlookers and by his slaves, who the Whites lashed at any time they made the slightest attempt to save him, Labadie was dragged through the dust, his mouth bloodied, and his ribs half destroyed.

The turmoil had attracted Jasmine, Joseph, and Minette's attention to the street. When they recognized the old man, they rushed outside, screaming. Minette raised her eyes to the planters. She recognized Messieurs Caradeux and Mesplès, red, out of breath, drooling with hatred. A whip lashed the air and struck her face. She threw herself on the old man's body along with Joseph and the slaves.

Despite the blows that rained down on them, they snatched Labadie from certain death and brought him to Jasmine's house. Electrified, the crowd held back the planters. The next day, a young White accused of having encouraged a new petition had his head cut off.

Young Jean was the first to come upon the scene. On hearing his screams, Minette had raced to him and saw the white man's head being paraded around on a pike with the words *Enemy of the Red Pompoms* below it.

Immediately, the freedmen put together a volunteer corps and went as a group to see the Governor, who gave them white pompoms and, flatteringly, promised them the moon. He called them "my dear friends" and "French soldiers," and he showed them every consideration, even welcoming some of them by having them sit down in his presence and putting his hand familiarly on their shoulders.

They would need a leader. Colonel de Mauduit was put in charge.

A White had just attacked a freedman and had killed him. The Colonel, seeing the Governor trembling, cried:

"Good heavens, you're shaking, if I'm not mistaken, Monsieur the Governor."

"My heart is suffering, Colonel," responded the Governor, rubbing the left side of his chest…"What's more, all these receptions seem tedious to me and life on this island would be unbearable without the theater…"

For the rising tensions had not infringed on entertainment, and M de Caradeux never missed an occasion to receive the Governor, despite the fact that his home had become a veritable political club.

At the theater, M Acquaire had decided to soldier on, despite the recent events. He organized a gathering of the artists and called for everyone's complete faith in him, asking them to promise not to get involved in any suspicious goings-on.

"Let's not forget, we're artists. We have nothing to do with politics. And as the late François Saint-Martin would have said to you, let us live for our ideal: Art – our common god…"

They were meant to perform one of Mozard's plays, *The Interrupted Rehearsal*, for which Minette had agreed to take on the lead role.

It was no classic work but, written in French and in the style of the period, it was beautiful in its lively and humorous repartee. At least there were no slaves in the play, Minette could assure herself, and that was for the best.

The evening before the performance, Lise returned from Saint-Marc, eyes red and completely dispirited: her lover had been accused of signing a petition and a colonist had shot him to death right in front of her. She was literally sick over it. The horror of what she had witnessed and her sorrow at having lost the man she loved had rendered her so miserable and weakened that Jasmine could not accompany Minette to the theater. The billboards had announced Charles Mozard's *The Interrupted Rehearsal* on the occasion of the "Meeting of the Three Orders of the State."

A great crowd had come to the theater, after having raised the national rosette. In the course of the military exercises executed by the army of grenadiers, cries of "Long live the King! Long live the nation!" could be heard. The crowd threw rosettes onstage at the actors' feet and asked them to put them on. If the situation was politically tense, it did not seem so during the performance, and the evening ended in a perfectly orderly fashion that everyone made an effort to respect, perhaps so as to make a show of goodwill vis-à-vis the King's orders.

Minette left the theater while the other actors headed to the evening ball, also being held in honor of the "Meeting of the Three Orders of the State," and to which, nonetheless, no persons of color were invited.

At the door of the theater, she ran into Zoé, Lambert, Beauvais, and his pregnant wife. Pétion joined them with a sixteen-year-old, who he promptly introduced.

"This is Charles Pons," he said. "He's a friend."

He was thin and of short stature. Lambert looked like a giant next to him. Seeing that everyone was smiling as they looked at him, he stuttered:

"I may be puny, but I'm brave."

And his voice was so thin that Beauvais laughed heartily. He put his hand on the youth's shoulder and responded reassuringly:

"One can be small and brave. I don't doubt it."

They were joined by a group of men who Lambert introduced to Minette.

"Daguiun, Vissière, Roubiou, and Pierre Pinchinat."

Minette took Joseph's arm and was about to leave her friends when a carriage passed by them and would have run over the Pons boy had

Lambert not grabbed him sharply by the arm. A white man stuck his head out the door:

"Out of the way, monkey, before I have my driver whip you," he screamed at the dumbfounded youth.

Pinchinat exchanged a furtive glance with Beauvais and Lambert. All of their expressions had changed suddenly and Minette, looking at Zoé in that moment, saw that she was biting her lip as her eyes stared hatefully at the carriage.

XXIX

DURING THESE DAYS of turmoil, there were more runaway slaves than ever. The constabulary was dog-tired, for not an hour went by where some slave was not brought back in chains, caught mid-flight. Tipped off to what was going on by the domestic slaves, the slaves in the work-houses listened attentively to those words Liberty and Equality, which a bunch of white people, rising up before the whole world, had written in their own blood. Their revolution, which they knew to be doomed from the start, was trying to declare itself nonetheless. The slaves reignited their old desires for vengeance, poisoning livestock and then killing themselves for fear of punishment. Losses were becoming substantial. M de Caradeux lost ten of his best horses that way. Tortured slaves were brought down from his plantation and paraded through the streets by way of example. Their backs had been sliced up and rubbed with hot peppers. To amplify their suffering, the slave overseers brutally whipped their raw flesh from time to time. Their screams drew the attention of nauseated crowds.

Anarchy reigned during that period, and Saint-Domingue seemed firmly divided. The planters intended to rule the colony in the place of the King's representatives. It was all about humiliation, dishonor, reprisal. They seemed to be everywhere: the tribunal, in the assembly hall, at the Governor's home, at the Bursar's home. From then on, their arrogance was without limit.

The streets were strangely deserted. The people of color, afraid of being provoked, avoided going out, while the poor Whites posted at every crossroads debated in little groups, gesticulating as they conversed.

Despite M Acquaire's best efforts, they were not able to put on a play. Everyone was on high alert and people talked about nothing but politics. In any case, Minette had plenty to worry about between Lise and Labadie, both of whom were still bedridden. She never left the house and spent hours on end by herself, daydreaming. Oddly, she barely thought about the political situation in the country. Memories emerged as if from a thick fog and completely enveloped her; she was more in love than ever with Jean Lapointe. Where was he? What was he doing? She would have given ten years of her life to see him again and to run away with him to the little house in Boucassin.

Desires that had been dormant awakened in her and once again transformed her into a mere love-struck creature for whom nothing mattered but being in love. Whenever she felt afraid, she called his name softly. If a freedman was brutalized for no reason by a White, she thought of him and said to herself, *Ah, if Jean were here, he'd make sure that one got a good old-fashioned knife in the back.* And she loved that he would know so well how to kill – how to exact revenge.

Increasingly impertinent, the poor Whites attacked people of color without provocation, insulting and even killing them. The women, especially, were their scapegoats. They shouted names at them, calling them "freedwoman sluts," and proposed bedding them right in the middle of the street. Without admitting the real reason to herself, Minette also avoided going out in the street and confronting those unwarranted insults.

That evening, Lise had a terrible migraine and needed medication. She asked Minette to go the next street over to buy some. The healer was with Labadie and was rubbing his ribs with bull's fat that Jasmine had been heating. Minette freshened up and went out.

The streets were crowded with poor Whites. Vendors, butchers, bakers, tinsmiths, and shoemakers had gathered and were debating noisily. Groups of sailors out for a drunken night on the town stumbled about, arms linked. A few elderly women out shopping went by them fearfully, while white and Mulatto prostitutes called out to them, their breasts half exposed and their hair undone.

Minette hurried her step. A horse brushed by her at top speed then slowed down. The horseman dismounted and came up to her. It was Captain Desroches.

"Oh, Captain," she said, comforted by his presence. "You're a welcome sight."

"You're afraid, too?"

"Women of color are being insulted, Captain, and the streets are full of drunken sailors."

"Take my arm, and calm down."

She put her trembling hand on the young man's arm and looked timidly at the group of poor Whites.

"It's not right," a fat, apron-clad man who seemed to be a butcher said at just that moment. "Some of those freedmen have land and slaves."

"People like that have land and slaves while we've got nothing. It's time to take away their power," said another.

"They've been given weapons and the white pompom – it's too much!"

"It's time we got to be the big lords – same as the planters."

Minette went into the shop and bought Lise's medication, then ran out to join Captain Desroches, who was waiting for her next to his mount.

"How can I ever thank you, Captain?" she asked him.

"You know very well."

He leaned toward her abruptly and looked her straight in the eyes.

"I've wanted you for a long time now, Minette. I'm so taken with you I can't hold any other woman in my arms without feeling disgusted. Meet me in the King's Garden tonight, won't you?"

"Captain Desroches, I know what I owe you…"

"No, not like that, Minette."

"Would you want to be with me, without love?"

"No."

"Well then I beg of you, Captain, keep being for me the gentleman who purchased a slave out of disinterested admiration for a poor young woman of color."

He looked at her sadly.

"You make a strong case for yourself."

He brought her back to the corner of Traversière Street and left her saying:

"It's a pity."

Minette went in and found Labadie's slaves there preparing to transport him in his carriage. He had spent eight days at Jasmine's and they had been quite cramped for sleeping space. Supported by his slaves, he kissed Jasmine and her daughters.

"Thank you, my children," he said to them. "I hope one day to be able to give back to you all the good you've done for me."

Then, removing a magnificent ring topped with an emerald and holding it out to Minette, he said:

"Keep this as a token of my affection and gratitude."

He had hardly been gone a moment before the market-women rushed into the front room.

"There's fighting outside!" cried one of them.

My God, and with Labadie just leaving.

"There's fighting! Bring in the stands…"

An indescribable din followed and as if to give the words of warning their full weight, the sound of gunfire exploded in the distance. Minette ran out to get young Jean, who was watching the stand. Terrified passersby were trying to figure out was happening and Minette saw the painter Perrosier close his door cautiously. Soldiers from the constabulary went by at a gallop…It was no battle, Minette soon realized. It was a massacre.

Some Whites had just slaughtered a group of freedmen who had reacted to their insults. Several people of color had gathered together and planned to avenge the death of their brothers. The planters chased them away with lashes of the whip and, in the guise of serving justice, went to petition before the court, condemning ten freedmen to be strung up from lampposts.

The planters were going too far. Someone had to rein in their claims and show them that the representatives of the King still had the right to govern the colony. The Colonel, buttressed by the support of the freedmen he had enticed with his promises and signs of friendship, was ready to confront the Committee of the West and disband it. Within the ranks of the "White Pompoms" were the poor Whites from the Assembly of Cap-Haitien who, frightened by the planters of the West's demands, had just broken with them.

Minette was aware of what was going to happen next. It had been spoken about in her presence at Lambert's house and she herself had put the bottles of milk and the crackers in Joseph's bag. In going to fight for Justice against M de Caradeux, he felt full of joy at the prospect of marching in the ranks at his brothers' side and finally battling those ruthless enemies the white planters, one of whom had been his torturer. He forgot all about Christ's magnanimity, he forgot all about religion and its doctrine of conciliation. Everything in him called for revolt, revolt and thirst for vengeance. The sweet and humble young man who recited prayers and sermons had been replaced by a revolutionary, called by the events of the moment to serve as righter of wrongs in the face of his enemies. Once again he had risked his liberty and even his life by continuing to harbor runaway slaves. He had wanted to do more. The events of the moment had constrained him to lower his head and to resign himself. Joseph had been nourished by Rousseau, and the application of those revolutionary ideas in France had torn him and his brothers out of their state of resignation. He would finally act again!

In all of his political gatherings, M de Caradeux drank to the independence of Saint-Domingue. By rising up against the King and his representatives, he had been a dreadful example of insurrection that, according to him, the people he called "those bastards" would never be able to follow. But the example would indeed be followed to the letter, and not only by the freedmen of color.

That day, Nicolette was not exaggerating when she came to announce, with her usual excitement, that there was fighting again on Dauphine Street, in front of the premises of the Committee. Minette made her sit down and served her a little glass of sweetened unrefined rum to calm her down. A volley of musket shots suddenly broke the silence. Worried, the market-women immediately brought in their stands and Lise called to Minette to ask what all the noise was about.

"Sleep, my dear," Minette said to her. "Those are the grenadiers doing their drills. Here, take this pill."

Ever since Julien's murder, she had suffered from migraines and insomnia. Minette tucked her in like a baby and went away gesturing to Nicolette to speak softly...

On Dauphine Street, Colonel de Mauduit had called three times to the Committee of the West, in the name of the Nation, the Law, and the King for them to fall in line with the orders of the Governor. The only response he had gotten was the volley of musket shot that had so frightened all the inhabitants of Traversière Street. He then responded with another volley of musket shot, which sent all the pedestrians running for their homes, caught unawares by the sudden battle. From then on, the tumult exploded. More volleys of musket shot, a few bursts of gunfire, and the thunderous noise of the Rostaing infantry support guns deafened the inhabitants of the whole neighborhood for at least an hour.

The Colonel's troops had left the barrack grounds very early that morning. When they returned victorious, carrying the Committee's flags as trophies, a delirious crowd cheered as it walked alongside them.

The defeated colonists, enraged that people of color had been allowed to fight against them, were clear in showing their rage to the Governor and representatives of the King.

For the moment, the Governor had the upperhand and he knew it. He heightened his despotic authority and was enjoying riling up his enemies. At the slightest provocation, his soldiers raided houses and dragged the "guilty" parties off to prison. People began wearing the white pompom out of fear, as a precautionary measure. The colonists' hatred, though subdued and defeated, was simmering – waiting for the right moment to explode. That same day, in the evening, Joseph received a visit from someone he did not recognize straightaway. It was a market-woman wearing a basket of wares on her head. The market-woman insisted that he buy some handkerchiefs and, as she spoke, it seemed to Joseph that he had heard that voice somewhere before.

"I'll show you my wares in your room. We'll be more comfortable there," she said suddenly, winking at him.

Immediately curious, he went up the stairs, followed by the market-woman, who continued boasting about the quality of her handkerchiefs. All of a sudden, the woman placed her basket on the bed, pulled off her hairpiece and revealed herself. It was his brother Vincent.

Joseph trembled from shock, forgot his injury, opened his mouth to speak and let out a horrific, incomprehensible sound.

"What's happened to you?" cried Vincent, pulling him close.

Joseph opened his mouth to show what was left of his tongue.

Vincent sat down on the bed, his legs shaking.

"My God," he muttered. "Why didn't you tell me about this in your letters?"

He sat there for a moment, utterly dejected. Then, reacting finally, he looked at Joseph.

"Have you seen my mother?"

He shook his head no.

"Have things gotten complicated here?"

He nodded yes.

"We worked hard in France to plead our cause," continued Vincent, "but to no avail. I've come to see if I can be of assistance here, for I've sworn to see our demands triumph. I'll go to Dondon to visit my mother. When I take off this disguise, I'll call myself Poissac – don't forget that, Joseph. And tell the others."

He hugged his brother again and tied the scarf back on his head.

"Farewell, little brother. Things are going to change, you'll see soon enough," he promised.

Though the freedmen had maintained absolute secrecy about Poissac's true identity, the planters were tipped off about the arrival of a Mulatto named Vincent Ogé who had great influence within the "Society of the Friends of the Negroes." They found out that he had left Dondon to visit his friend, Jean-Baptiste Chavannes, in Grande Rivière du Nord.

Two letters signed by these two freedmen were addressed to the Governor and to the Provincial Assembly of the North.

We demand, the letters said, *that the principles promulgated by the National Party be enforced. We demand free access to all jobs, professions, and responsibilities...*

We demand the enforcement of the Decree of March 28, which grants suffrage to all people twenty-five years or older...

They had dared to make fearless demands. Four hundred freedmen had rallied around them to await the decisions of the Governor and the Northern Assembly.

The people of color in Port-au-Prince gathered to wait at Louise Rasteau's home, where Minette, Zoé, and Marguerite Beauvais had gone as well, accompanied by the little Pons fellow and Pétion. Vincent had promised to send a messenger; they would not sleep until he arrived. Louise served punch, which they drank to the success of Ogé and Chavannes' plan. They had barely put down their glasses when a horse galloping at top speed came to a stop in front of the house. They all looked up hopefully. The door opened and a horseman entered the room: it was Jean-Baptiste Lapointe. Minette went pale and leaned on her chair, closing her eyes.

"You!" cried Lambert.

"Yes, me. Bad news. The freedmen were defeated at Cap-Français. Ogé and Chavanne have fled into Spanish territory."

They fell back into their chairs, appalled by the news. Then Louise Rasteau made a sudden gesture of revulsion.

"Oh, no, no!" she wept. "Defeated, always defeated. Does God only exist for the Whites? Are we meant to have no hope at all?"

Marguerite Beauvais put a hand on her shoulder. She was young and expecting a child.

"Let us hope, nonetheless," she said, "for the sake of our children. Perhaps they'll see our cause triumph in the end."

Jean-Baptiste Lapointe moved toward Minette's chair. He stood looking at her for a moment, turning his straw hat in his hands.

"I, I…" he stammered. "I have a message for this young lady. Er, a private message."

Minette rose without saying a word and followed him. He walked out to the courtyard without turning around. He then stopped and, taking her abruptly in his arms:

"Swear to me – swear that you've been waiting for me!" he said, kissing her passionately.

She whimpered with pleasure.

"Do you still love me?"

"I never forgot you."

It was all just as she remembered – his youthful strength, the smell of his body, the feel of his hands and his mouth. Oh! How had she been able to bottle up for so long that wave of desires that now kept her pressed against him, completely weak in his arms?

"I'm afraid for you," she murmured.

"Oh, I have nothing left to fear. Those planters are far too preoccupied with other matters to waste their time chasing me down. I'm returning to Arcahaie tonight and I swear by all the gods that they'll have me to contend with from now on…"

"What are you going to do?" she asked, worried.

"Don't worry. I've got a nice little plan for revenge up my sleeve. If things go the way I expect, I'll carve out an excellent situation for myself that'll set me up definitively, as far as the Whites are concerned."

He pressed her to him forcefully.

"And we'll never be apart again?"

"It's all I hope for."

When they went back into the house, several of the others had already left.

"Where's Joseph?" Minette asked Louise.

"He left with the others."

She headed back home on Lapointe's arm. He had left his horse at Louise's and planned to return for it later on. There were several isolated corners along the way. He pulled her into one of them and took her – half dead with fright and passion. He stayed with her until they had reached her doorstep and after making her promise to see him again as soon as possible.

"You'll come back to Boucassin?"

"Yes."

"When?"

"Soon, I promise…"

They would see one another even sooner than they anticipated. Political events themselves were accelerating and pushed them irresistibly toward one another, thus serving faithfully the ineluctable course of their destiny.

XXX

Frightened by the battle with Ogé and Chavannes, the Assembly of the North sought both to exact revenge and to strike fear in the other freedmen by demanding that the Spanish authorities extradite Ogé, Chavannes, and their collaborators.

"The Spanish authorities will never hand them over," said Lambert to Beauvais with great conviction.

"I certainly hope not," responded Beauvais, decidedly more pessimistic.

The following day, they learned that not only had Ogé and Chavannes been delivered to the Whites in Cap-Français, but that they had been brought before a special tribunal and been condemned to death. Mad with worry, Joseph went to see Minette, who offered on the spot to accompany him to Cap-Français. That evening, Labadie himself brought the money for the trip. Minette entrusted Lise and young Jean to Jasmine's care and left to take her place in the coach alongside Joseph. The journey was exhausting. Knocked about for an entire day, they arrived in Cap-Français completely spent.

The atmosphere there was one of unparalleled agitation.

With its grand houses graced with wide balconies, its picturesque little streets, and its shops decked out in the latest Parisian fashion,

Cap-Français surpassed Port-au-Prince as much by the luxuriousness of its homes as by its bay full of ships. It even seemed to Minette and Joseph that the crowd there was denser, more active, and more diverse.

The news was true. They found out as soon as they entered the hotel. A red-skinned Mulatto came to meet them and take their luggage.

"Would you like one room?"

"No, two rooms."

"Oh!...And I suppose you've come here like all the others to witness the torture of Ogé and Chavannes?"

Minette glanced at Joseph, who had gone horribly ashen. She took his hand.

"And so when's the spectacle?" she asked, feigning indifference.

"Well, it's planned for tomorrow morning. Apparently they've been condemned to breaking on the wheel. The Whites are furious and have sworn not to take mercy on them..."

They went up the stairs and arrived on the first floor, where the big Mulatto pointed out two adjoining rooms.

Once they were alone, Minette took Joseph's face in her hands.

"Listen to me, don't despair. He was probably just exaggerating. We'll get some information soon. Get some rest. I'm going to freshen up and then we'll go out together."

Joseph sat down on the bed with a dejected air and seemed to be conjuring a particularly frightening scene, for his hands trembled. Suddenly, he hid his face in his elbow and threw himself across the bed.

"Come, come," said Minette, caressing his hair.

Then she sighed and went to her own room. She did not bother freshening up. After passing Joseph's room on tiptoes, she raced down the stairs. A couple had just arrived: two middle-aged Negroes that were being led to other rooms by a young slave. Minette scanned the room for the big Mulatto and noticed him behind a counter, in the middle of writing in a notebook. She went up to him and said smilingly, in an effort to hide her anxiousness:

"Are people of color free to attend the punishment of Ogé and Chavannes?" she queried.

"Of course. Yesterday's paper even said we've been invited."

"I'll be there," she promised, still smiling.

"It'll be tough to watch…"

"Do you think so?"

She went back upstairs and knocked at Joseph's door. He opened.

"Listen," she told him, "we won't go out this evening. We'll get some rest. There'll still be time tomorrow to go out to get some news."

He pushed her away with the violence of a madman and headed for the staircase.

"Joseph, where are you going?"

He offered no response and fled the hotel.

She went back into her room and stretched out on the bed. Her head was abuzz and her heart was racing annoyingly. She moaned feebly and turned onto her side. She somehow fell asleep that way. When she awoke, it was already dawn. She jumped up, thinking of Joseph. Opening her door, she went to knock at his room. As there was no answer, she turned the knob and the door opened on its own. The room was empty. She changed her clothes and went downstairs. The big Mulatto, an early riser, was already attending to his business.

"Have you seen my brother, by chance?"

"Your brother? Ah, yes…"

He burst into laughter.

"He must have spent the night in one of those places young people his age like to go to – he still hasn't come back. There are some pretty famous brothels here. In fact, just next door there's apparently a Negress who'll dance naked, one gourde per person…I probably shouldn't be telling such things to a young lady like yourself, but it's just to reassure you. Young people like the fun spots…Well, well, there he is."

He was in quite a state: disheveled, dirty, his hair wild, his eyes beaten, and shaky on his feet!

The big Mulatto burst into laughter once again.

"Oh, they're all the same, those young people!"

Minette dragged Joseph along without asking any questions. He seemed so ashamed to see her that she left him alone and went into her room. Where was he coming from? In what seedy bars had he spent the night? What had he exposed himself to that had so transformed him? His eyes were furtive, his smile constrained, and his movements so awkward that he seemed to be hiding some sort of new character that even he found troubling.

Minette was pondering all of this for more than two hours and then joined Joseph in his room. The door was slightly ajar. She pushed it open: he was sleeping with his fists clenched, laid out on his stomach, with one leg hanging over the side of the bed. She left the room without waking him and went out into the street alone.

An early-morning crowd of people decked out in all their finery jostled one another as they passed by the shops on their way to the central square.

A barricade had been installed around a section of hard-packed earth. As the crowd arrived, people separated into two rows: the Whites went to the right and the people of color went to the left. Minette followed the people of her station and went forward toward the barricades. Two enormous wheels, gleaming in the sunlight, leaned against iron bars that four executioners had just brought in.

"What are those iron bars for?" someone asked.

"I've heard they've been condemned to be broken alive."

"Does that hurt a lot?"

"You can go ask them."

When they brought the two prisoners out, their hands tied behind their backs, Minette tried to figure out which of the two was Vincent Ogé. They both held their heads high and looked directly at the curious onlookers. Slipping adroitly through the crowd, she was able to reach the first row, and stood next to an elderly woman, stout and imposing.

"My Lord," said the woman, making the sign of the cross.

Those who were situated in the first rows were touching the barricade and were no more than a few meters away from the prisoners. Which of them was Vincent? One was a Mulatto with curly hair; the other was darker-skinned and had a complexion more like Joseph's. But it was the Mulatto who looked most like him. His eyes, fixed on the crowd, showed a noble pride. When the executioner approached him, his face took on an expression of terrible revulsion. In that moment, he looked so much like Joseph that Minette no longer had any doubt. That was him, Vincent Ogé. When the executioner untied his hands, he raised them to the heavens and cried:

"Don't forget anything you see here today, my brothers."

It had been so long since Minette had heard Joseph speak that she trembled. It was as if it was him and not his brother who had just spoken. It was the same deep and sonorous tone, the same slow, careful pronunciation.

Jean-Baptiste Chavannes, whose hands had also been untied, held them out to the right side of the barricade.

"I denounce the Whites," he screamed with a ferocious voice. "I denounce the Whites, our torturers, forevermore and I leave to our brothers the task of avenging our martyrdom."

An enormous clamor drowned out his voice. The executioners had just grabbed the prisoners to attach them to the wheels, their arms outstretched and legs spread wide. Minette lowered her head. A feeling of nausea welled up inside her. She put her hand around her neck and raised her head. At the same time, a terrifying scream broke the silence. The executioners, raising high the iron bars, broke the prisoners' limbs. Their screams quickly became horrible bellowings. A freedwoman, weeping as she leaned against a tree, began to vomit. Minette fled, her hands covering her ears. The screams followed her all the way to the hotel, all the way to Joseph's room. He awoke and looked at her with terrified eyes. She threw herself into his arms, put her hands over his ears and sobbed.

"Don't listen, don't listen, Joseph!…"

He threw himself to the ground, sunk his teeth into the sheets and the mattress, with gestures of utter rage, in turn letting out devastating sounds not unlike those of the tortured prisoners. Minette fell to her knees.

"We'll avenge them, we'll avenge them – you'll see," she repeated. "Their suffering and their death won't be for nothing. They spoke out, and that won't have been for nothing…"

She helped him to rise. He collapsed onto the bed, weeping, and covered his head with the pillow so as not to hear the strangely fading but increasingly devastating cries that would keep all the inhabitants of Cap-Français awake through the night.

The next morning, at dawn, it was clear from the silence that had followed their cries and then their whimpers that the tortured men had died. Their remains were brought to their mothers, two old women petrified with horror who had been forcefully kept in the parish and to whom were handed over two coffins, each containing a mutilated cadaver. Joseph stayed in Dondon to be with Vincent's mother, and Minette made the long journey from Cap-Français to Port-au-Prince on her own.

This time, she stopped in Arcahaie. She was demoralized, broken. She needed Jean Lapointe's strength and rugged energy. She went to Boucassin on foot and, carrying her trunk, climbed up the long hill that led to the house. When she saw the little house with its sole gallery, the flood of memories that washed over her was so strong that she collapsed onto her side, her eyes closed and barely breathing. Lucifer and Satan came to lick her hands and ran to alert their master.

She avoided breaking the spell and willingly suppressed the memory of the horrors she had witnessed at Cap-Français. She had not come to talk about such things. Drowning herself in pleasure, she planned to savor the selfish delight of being happy. He asked her all sorts of questions, all of which had only to do with love: "Were you tempted to love someone else? Were you faithful? Was your voice always so beautiful?"

The spell lasted for five days, after which time the manager of the estate came from the workhouse at a full gallop. Six of the best slaves had fled during the night.

Lapointe flew into a terrible rage, saddled his horse, and left for the workhouse, from which there immediately rose terrible screams. The screams reminded Minette of those she had heard from Ogé and Chavannes. She did not want to believe that her beloved was their cause. She waited for him, pale, standing on the gallery and surrounded by trembling slaves. Ninninne came up to her.

"Oh, Lord!" she said to her. "Now he's angry. Too many slaves are escaping."

Her back was bent and she shook her head slowly in her black madras scarf, adding:

"Fleurette and Roseline were the first to leave…"

An indefinable smell coming from the workhouse suddenly flooded her nostrils. The cries immediately turned into screams.

"Fire torture!" said one of the slaves mournfully.

Fearing she would leave like the first time, Lapointe hurried back. He found her packing her things, pale and more shaken even than his servants.

"What are you doing?" he shouted.

"I'm leaving and never coming back."

"Because of a slave I had to punish?"

"You're nothing but a dressed-up white brute," she answered him angrily.

"You'll regret insulting me one day. I'm also fighting for our rights."

"By cutting the throats of the Blacks?"

"They're slaves."

"I see! Just be quiet, then."

He tried to win her over by changing the subject.

"Between lovers, there should only ever be reproaches that have to do with love."

"Love gets mixed up in everything these days. Times have changed."

He saw that she was intent on carrying out her threat and tried to take her in his arms.

"You don't want to leave, do you?"

"Let me go. Don't touch me. I loathe you."

She pushed him away with such a look of revulsion that he stared at her, astonished.

"Twice now you will have left me over these slaves. Perhaps one day you'll come back to me because of them."

He was suddenly enraged.

"But understand that without them I would be nothing, nothing…I've got to do everything in my power to keep them."

As she offered no response, he shrugged his shoulders and helped her mount a horse. Then, handing the reins to a slave, said with a smile both mysterious and cynical:

"Bring Mademoiselle back."

XXXI

Minette's arrival in Port-au-Prince coincided with the expedition
of French reinforcements that had been announced several days earlier.
The spineless Governor had left and been replaced by someone equally
incompetent, who let loose hundreds of undisciplined, pro-revolution-
ary soldiers on the shores of Saint-Domingue. They came from regiments in Artois and Normandy and were known for their spirit of
insubordination. They immediately sided with the "Red Pompoms"
and riled the local troops and the people into a frightening state of agitation.

People went to the docks en masse to see them disembark. Minette
left Lise and young Jean with Jasmine and hurried to the harbor with
Joseph, Nicolette, and Pétion. M de Caradeux, at the head of the "Red
Pompoms," greeted several soldiers with cheers and had his slaves serve
them tall glasses of rum. A few moments after their arrival, they were
roaming the streets singing revolutionary couplets that joyful groups
of children picked up and sung along with them.

That same day, the Colonel, who had received an order from
the Governor to leave for the South at the head of enough troops to
suppress an insurrection of freedmen, returned to Port-au-Prince
victorious, with a large number of prisoners. The crowd of people of

color, silent and enigmatic, watched them pass. Among the prisoners was André Rigaud, a young Mulatto with a proud, military bearing who walked with his head held high as he looked attentively all around him.

Pétion pointed him out to Pons:

"That's André Rigaud, the head of the freedmen who fought at Les Cayes against the white troops."

"What's going to happen to him and the other prisoners?" asked Pons worriedly.

"They'll probably be thrown in prison."

"To be tortured?"

"No. Even if he hasn't kept his promises to us, Colonel de Mauduit still wants to handle us carefully. He'll pardon the prisoners."

A dozen or so freedmen between the ages of seventeen and twenty surrounded Pétion at that very moment.

"You saw that, right, Pétion," whispered one of them. "The Colonel is fighting our people and arresting them."

Pétion slowly brought his hand to his white pompom and tore it off.

"I'm not with them anymore," he said coldly.

"Me neither," said Pons, also tearing off his pompom.

The twelve other young freedmen immediately followed suit.

"We can only count on ourselves," spoke Pétion again, and his gaze, gleaming and harsh, followed the path of the Colonel's troops.

The Colonel had lost the support of the freedmen. The perfect moment for the planters to avenge themselves had come.

The situation was tragic, for the soldiers from Artois and Normandy, encouraged by the planters, had converted the Colonel's own grenadiers to their side. Stubbornly refusing to believe the betrayal, he and Captain Desroches, who had warned him, went to the barracks to interrogate the men.

"Don't go, Colonel," Captain Desroches advised him. "Your grenadiers have betrayed you, I'm sure of it…"

"I refuse to believe that."

His arrival provoked a sudden tumult among the soldiers. Rising from their stations and without even standing at attention, they ran into the interior of the barracks.

"Colonel," insisted Captain Desroches, pulling on the reins of his horse, "don't go."

"Forward march, Captain. That's an order…"

They entered a room crammed with soldiers and as soon as the Colonel opened his mouth to speak:

"Let's place Colonel de Mauduit under arrest," shouted one of his grenadiers.

"Bunch of fools," replied the Colonel, trembling. "You've all let yourselves be bamboozled by the planters."

"Let's place Colonel de Mauduit under arrest," repeated the grenadier, seeming far less sure of himself.

Captain Desroches, unsheathing his sword, protected the Colonel with his body.

He was seized and disarmed.

As soon as the news made its way throughout the crowd, Pétion and Charles Pons ran to the Lamberts'.

"Colonel de Mauduit has been arrested," announced Pétion, his voice choked with emotion.

"Let him figure it out," responded Roubiou, a young freedman with harsh, accusing features.

"No," said Lambert, "we'll help him – if only to prove we're better than he is."

"Okay," agreed Pétion. "Do you want to take charge of this, Pons?"

"Very well," the young man accepted, conciliatory. "What do I have to do?"

That evening, young Pons, disguised as a woman, fled into a thick hedge separating the Governor's palace from the barracks' courtyard. The streets were under military guard by the newly arrived soldiers. At every crossroads, armed planters came out of their carriages to hold lengthy discussions with them. The Vaux-Halls – the theater as well as the pleasure houses – were completely deserted.

Outfoxing the guards, who were in something of a rum-soaked stupor, young Pons managed to get to the door of the room where the Colonel had been imprisoned. In the neighboring room, people were noisily debating his fate. Someone shouted:

"Down with Mauduit!"

Another responded:

"Hang him from the lamppost!"

Pons inserted tweezers into the lock and was about to force open the door and help the Colonel escape when the planters and the half-drunk soldiers burst into the room. Pons headed back into the hedges and stayed hidden there for a long while, listening to the group threaten the Colonel and condemn him for the sacrilege of having joined forces with the freedmen.

"You defeated us with a band of wretches," shouted one of them.

"You'll make serious amends for that," said someone else. "Tomorrow, you yourself will bring back the flags that were removed from the Committee's great hall."

Pons quickly escaped the hedges and ran to Lambert's. Powerless, they watched the execution of the Colonel the next day.

Surrounded by a half-drunk crowd of Whites, he walked with his head held high, carrying the flag. A disheveled woman passed in front of him and shouted, her fists raised:

"Let's hang him from that lamppost!"

A drunken sailor, jostling the grenadiers, moved toward him and slapped him. Another woman threw herself on him and spit in his face.

Two tears ran down the Colonel's cheeks. Tearing off his insignia, he threw them to his feet, thus signaling that he was no longer fit to wear them.

An arm raised a sword and dealt the Colonel a blow to the face. A vast wound opened on his cheek, revealing the bone.

Young Pons and Pétion, followed by a few Whites and some freedmen, threw themselves into the scuffle in an attempt to free the Colonel from the hands of his enemies. They were about to carry him off when a soldier thrust a sword into his back. He fell to the ground, blood streaming from his nose and mouth. His bloody corpse was then dragged through the street as people shouted, "Down with Mauduit, friend to sons of bitches…"

In the jail cells, the curious prisoners listened to the sounds of the mob, which intensified with every passing minute.

"They're fighting!" exclaimed Rigaud, surprised.

"And we're trapped in here," whimpered one of his companions, a strapping, dark-skinned young man named Boury. "How awful..."

The guard approached.

"Shh!" said Rigaud. "Everyone pretend to be asleep, as well as you can. And you, Boury, get to work...it's our last chance..."

They threw themselves to the ground and stayed there unmoving. The guard opened the door of the cell, carrying bread, which he threw on the ground.

"Your meal, Messieurs," he said mockingly.

Two strong hands suddenly grabbed his neck.

"Squeeze him tight, Boury," whispered Rigaud, breathless with worry.

The keys fell out of the guard's hand. Rigaud grabbed them.

Boury continued squeezing the man's neck although he was long dead. After opening the door to the cell, Rigaud signaled to his companions to stay quiet. He stole a glance into the courtyard; everything was deserted. They were then able to slink along the walls and reach the exit without encountering a living soul.

Once outside, they were immediately engulfed by a vociferous crowd of Whites, brandishing cut-up parts of a human body.

"Down with Mauduit!"

"Where's his head?"

It appeared at that very moment, at the end of a pike, and was greeted with shouts and insults.

Rigaud and his companions made their way to an out-of-the-way path without being noticed. They walked through the night and arrived exhausted in Mirebalais, where they met up with Beauvais and Pierre Pinchinat who, suspected by the planters, were waiting in the sidelines for the opportunity to react and rejoin the struggle.

XXXII

THE NEW GOVERNOR fled to Cap-Français and the palace remained unoccupied. For days, the Colonel's mutilated corpse haunted the inhabitants of Port-au-Prince. Cap-Français had barely recovered from the horrific death of Ogé and Chavannes when news of Colonel de Mauduit's assassination by his own soldiers became known. Moreover, despite the planters' triumphant smiles, the princely teams of horses, and the costly receptions thrown to receive the regiments from Artois and Normandy, a terrifying sadness remained in the people's hearts.

Was it some sort of forewarning? It seemed to everyone that they would never again recover their carefree ways and love of life. Although the planters were celebrating, they were still unsettled. Their victory did not keep them from being overcome by worry from time to time. Where could the danger come from? They still did not know. But this fraught and mysterious atmosphere they at times felt all around them became more and more intense with each passing day. Their worry made them a hundred times more arrogant and cruel. For some time, their insulting dominance spread throughout the entire colony and brought it to its knees, defeated. Defeated, but not at all resigned, for the freedmen had been completely disillusioned as far as the Governor and the King's functionaries' promises were concerned. Realizing that they had simply been used without there ever having been an intention of giving them real rights, they gathered around their own leaders, Beauvais and Lambert, to organize in secret.

Rather than lessening their resolve, Ogé and Chavannes' defeat, torture, and death had unleashed the spirit of revolt that had long remained dormant in them. They threw themselves desperately and headlong into the fight and swore an oath to emerge victorious. The Colonel's assassination had just shown them that the Whites were capable of ruthlessness, even toward their own brothers.

Their attitude changed completely. If the Whites would assassinate their brothers, why should they show the Whites any respect?

That was their attitude when Joseph returned from Dondon. He was so thin that Lise cried when she saw him. She pulled herself together and began to forget about the bloody spectacle she had witnessed in Saint-Marc. Because of her, they spoke only in low tones about Ogé and Chavannes' torture and the Colonel's murder. Bizarrely, even Nicolette seemed interested in the latest turn of events. She arrived at Jasmine's house, her eyes gleaming, overexcited, and gently asking for details about the torture and death of the two freedmen.

Even more astonishing was the fact that she had raced to Jasmine's to announce that the King of France had just been dethroned. It was important and overwhelming news – and had spread nearly everywhere within the blink of an eye. Who had informed Nicolette? they worried. A white soldier. Was the information reliable? No one could say. When the news became official, the white planters celebrated their victory loudly. They began imagining their autonomy. They were already in charge of the colony; they held a half-terrorized population under their heel.

From then on, hiding their true thoughts beneath indifferent smiles, the people of Saint-Domingue returned to their old ways. The theater reopened its doors and the Vaux-Halls brought back its salons and gambling rooms. M Acquaire, having been in dire straits for several weeks, was intent on refilling the empty coffers immediately. All the events had dealt the actors a real shock. Mme Tessyre had had to sell a wet nurse she had purchased during better days. Magdeleine Brousse was living off of prostitution, and the others by their wits. They came back to the Comédie with gaunt, defeated faces that betrayed their recent privations. To eat and to pay the rent, Mme Acquaire had gone to Mesplès. Unfortunately, M Acquaire continued playing dice and promptly lost whatever they earned from giving their dance and elocution lessons. This deeply worried Scipion, who feared being sold in a moment of desperation, so he did his best to make himself useful while hoping the Comédie would return to its former activity. It did so, but without Minette, who refused to perform in the play that had been announced on the weekly billboards. Despite Acquaire and Goulard's pleading, she refused to sign a new contract and would not give any reason. M Mesplès, though on the side of the white planters, also wanted to see her return to the theater. When he learned of her refusal, he went to her house himself to try and convince her.

"You, Monsieur!" she exclaimed, surprised. She pointed to a chair he seemed not to see.

"Yes, me. It would seem you've abandoned the theater. I've come to find out your reasons."

"I have none, Monsieur."

"Well then why do you persist in refusing to perform?"

"The Comédie has done me great honor for a long time, Monsieur. I now refuse that honor."

"Ah! So you want us to beg you?"

"As I've gotten older, I couldn't care less about being begged to do anything."

"Too bad. We'll go on without you."

"The Comédie means a great deal to me, Monsieur. I wish the actors all the success they deserve."

Devastated in her love for Lapointe, saddened by the spectacle of the victorious white planters, troubled by the changes she had seen in Joseph since the deaths of Vincent and Chavannes, she lived among the group of freedmen and, like them, had thrown herself headlong into the struggle. She felt less alone at their side, and sought in their revolt a means of combating her despair. This revolt, no matter what the Whites believed, was not powerless. It was just being cleverly hidden by the dispersal of their leadership. They knew they were being watched, monitored; they became stealthy. Their whole lives, they had hidden their discontent. So it was easy for them to present serene countenances as they developed their plan of attack. They would soon demand their rights, weapons in hand.

One evening, with Beauvais and Lambert in charge, they all left together for Louise Rasteau's plantation. Beauvais decided on the rankings and placed Pétion, whose calm bravery he admired, at the head of the artillery. Then, unfurling a flag with the national colors, he brandished it and demanded that everyone swear with him to obtain the rights so long denied them, even if it should cost them their lives.

"Let Justice always be our guide," he added with a determined and animated voice.

Everyone swore the oath.

The young people were called upon: Pétion, Roubiou, Pons, Joseph, and some others were charged with rallying to their cause the slaves hidden in the neighboring area. They returned triumphant, with three hundred committed slaves who they immediately enrolled in their army.

During the night, they decided to move farther away from Port-au-Prince and headed toward Caïman Hole. Lambert and Beauvais led the way and were explaining their battle plan to the young people when a group of white soldiers suddenly attacked them from the rear.

"Watch out!" someone screamed.

Hidden in the cane fields, the Whites shot at them from point-blank.

Lambert and Beauvais dismounted their horses and began opening fire, when the slaves shouted and began lighting torches, which they threw into the cane fields. The fields immediately caught fire, sowing panic in the ranks of the Whites, soon surrounded by the crackling flames.

When the flames diminished, the Whites had fled, abandoning the dead and wounded among the calcified crops.

That had been, on the spot, an initial victory, which the freedmen celebrated with great song. The future seemed full of promise and their courage invincible. The first real sign of victory came with the peace offering made by the frightened Whites of Port-au-Prince. They accepted the proposal without condition and delegates from the two parties met in Damiens. The Whites signed an accord recognizing the freedmen's political rights. M de Caradeux, conciliatory, held out his hand to Beauvais and Lambert, saying to them:

"And now that's settled, freedmen."

When the freedmen's army, composed of fifteen hundred men, among whom the slaves who had been responsible for their success in battle, entered Port-au-Prince, it was welcomed by a crowd of people of color screaming: "Long live the Confederates!" Flags unfurled and drums beating, Lambert and Beauvais' army traversed the city and gathered at Bursar's Square.

A mass was meant to be performed to celebrate and sanctify this unexpected reconciliation. Everyone put down his weapons and M de Caradeux, who led the National Guard, took Beauvais and Lambert by the arm, while a soldier in charge of the artillery put his hand familiarly on Pétion's shoulder.

"My name is Praloto," he said. "I'm in charge of the national artillery."

"And I am Pétion. I'm leader of the Confederate artillery."

Praloto had a sly smile and a hypocritical look in his eye that Pétion did not like.

That one, he said to himself, *must hate us more than any other White.*

After the meal offered in the Confederate barracks, M de Caradeux was named Commander General of the National Guard of the West, and Beauvais his second in command, to great joy and enthusiasm.

To prove to everyone that peace had been reestablished and that they had generously accepted coming to terms with the freedmen, M de Caradeux appeared in public again, linking arms with Beauvais, who had just established his troops at the Government palace and in Bel-Air.

The victors and the defeated showed unprecedented joy. They were tired of fighting, of hating one another, and of living in fear. These were days of mad celebration during which the Comédie, the Vaux-Halls, and all public places had enormous success.

Minette and Lise saw a lot of Zoé Lambert during this time. The triumph of their cause had finally uprooted the implacable hatred she felt for the Whites, and she had begun to smile. All the freedmen held up their heads again, embracing the future with a smile. The Whites were no longer their enemies. With great joy, they rid themselves of bitterness, refusing to acknowledge even the insults hurled at them by the poor Whites, jealous of their victory.

Goulard and Acquaire had come to congratulate Minette and kissed her affectionately.

"Will you come back to the theater now?" Mme Acquaire asked, giving her a sidelong glance as if to say she was well aware of her political activities.

"I promise I will, Madame."

"Will you perform in our next play?"

"I will, Madame."

M Mesplès, M de Caradeux – they had been defeated. And so? A deep sense of joy took her breath away for a moment. She and those like her had become the equal of Whites. Ah! How Ogé and Chavannes must be feeling proud and happy in their graves! Joseph himself had a peaceful look in his eye that she had not seen for a long time. Lise was better; she had begun curling her hair in front of the mirror again and went dancing with Pétion and the others at the Vaux-Halls.

Young Jean had grown up and looked more and more like his father.

"You're not even ten years old and you've already seen our cause prevail," Minette said to him one day as she caressed his hair.

"What cause?" he asked, astonished.

"Well, let me explain it all to you. Thanks to your older brothers, when you're a young man you'll be able to choose the profession you want, you'll give your opinion in public meetings, and you'll be a full-fledged citizen in a country that is truly yours."

"It wasn't always like that?"

"No. Brave and courageous men suffered so we could have these rights. They died under the worst torture. Others fought so that tomorrow you and all other freedmen could be seen as men in this world..."

"I'll fight, too..."

"Of course. I'll talk to the leaders about it," she answered him with a laugh. "But I'm afraid that battle has been won already."

XXXIII

THUS PEACE HAD returned. At least, people tried to make themselves believe that, working twice as hard to make up for lost time. The cabarets, the Vaux-Halls, and the restaurants all were going non-stop, adding a touch of madness to an already too sensual atmosphere. Couples kissed full on the mouth, whores invaded the waterfront, where the sailors welcomed them with triumphant cheers. They dangled bags of money to tempt them and led them off, whispering obscenities in their ears. The irresistible stench of a warm, perverse wind reached all the way to the freedmen soldiers confined to the Governor's palace. Despite their leaders' refusal to let them venture out, they abandoned their posts and went to rejoin their families.

"It's just normal," stammered young Pons to Lambert, won over. "We're young, and we've got to, to, to…"

"Fine," Lambert interrupted, "but don't forget that the Whites still have their eyes on you."

For the moment, they were completely unconcerned. One only ever saw them entangled in the arms of some woman, in the gambling dens, the cabarets, and the Vaux-Halls for people of color. They, too, wanted to make up for all they had been missing out on.

Though he hosted lavish parties every evening, on seeing the dispersal of the freedmen's forces M de Caradeux immediately decided to break the Damiens Accord. Without their well-established battalions, they seemed so unimpressive to him that he had come to regret ever ceding to them.

"We were stupid to have accorded them those rights," he said to Praloto. "Now they're taking advantage of them, parading around with white whores on their arms. They think they've won, with those arrogant airs of theirs..."

The feeling got the better of him – the freedmen seemed to be everywhere he turned. As he confessed to a group of planters in formal dress who had come to his reception from a neighboring area, he had a hard time seeing himself on the same level as those mixed-bloods, so many of whom were sons of former slaves. He had played his role well enough to appease them and to force them back into the shadows. Now it was time to act as quickly as possible. Giving one's word to the freedmen and then taking it back was child's play. Who possibly could have believed that that whole production had been serious?

"The freedmen themselves," pointed out a powdered Marquis, fanning himself nonchalantly.

"Well that's their problem," said Praloto coldly.

An hour later, as the women were off together talking about clothes, the men deliberated, surrounded by slaves who were hanging on their every word.

"We'll break the accord," they decided, "and as soon as possible..."

The sight of the slaves who had fought alongside the freedmen troubled them, for they feared that other slaves might follow their example. So they demanded that the slaves be sent away from Port-au-Prince, promising to free them afterward.

"They'll be free – they just have to leave," M de Caradeux had insisted.

Beauvais and Lambert asked for a few days to consider this. They were accorded them.

Would M de Caradeux and the other planters keep their promise? Would the slaves be freed? Who knows whether they would be abandoned in some godforsaken place?…

After numerous discussions, in which the women also participated, it was decided: concerned that the Whites would otherwise rip up the accord, they agreed to meet their terms.

"No," pleaded Minette. "Don't do it. Don't abandon the slaves to the Whites…"

"You may come to regret this," added Zoé.

The men dismissed this feminine sensitivity, unwarranted in a struggle such as this one, they said. Any of the men who agreed with the women they called weak.

"But those slaves helped us win that battle…"

"Yes," answered Beauvais. "But if their deportation can keep the Whites from breaking the accord, we've got to cede…We aren't sending them to their death, for heaven's sake!…"

All the same, watching them leave with the Whites, they couldn't help feel – like Minette and Zoé – terribly worried.

For Minette, it was a rift in what she had thought was deep solidarity. So then Lapointe was right! The freedmen exploited the slaves to plead their own cause and obtain rights for themselves!

When they learned several days later that, instead of being freed, the slaves had been beheaded on the pontoons of Môle Saint-Nicolas, confusion, remorse, and dissension spread through the ranks of the freedmen.

Minette realized once again that the battle being waged before her eyes was a pitiless one. The three hundred decapitated slaves often haunted her thoughts, as they did those of the freedmen. The lovely harmony of the recent past seemed broken. An unease that everyone recognized all too well turned those who once had been brothers, firmly united in bloodshed and in battle, into enemies. The Whites had cut deeply into the very heart of the peace. Unsettled and anxious, they began to divide up. The Whites had been waiting for this moment to launch their attack, this time publicly threatening to break the accord.

As soon as they became aware of this, the freedmen united and rallied around their leaders, banishing any past grievances from their thoughts and focusing only on the moment at hand.

They had to fight and they had to fight together. Otherwise the Whites were sure to be victorious. They had to forget about anything other than their abiding will to fight; they had to forget about the three hundred murdered slaves; they had to forget about the past and live only with the present desperate passion to triumph at whatever cost.

Minette understood this immediately.

She had been made aware of the situation by the Lamberts themselves. Their disappointment, their bitterness, and their rebellion had been terrifying. And when Beauvais had cried out, "We would rather die and take them with us!" she had understood that they were all prepared for the very worst.

She had returned from her visit utterly depressed and so overwhelmed that she did not think she would be able to sing that evening at the theater.

So the Whites were once again going back on their word! So those three hundred slaves had been sacrificed for nothing! No, it wasn't possible, they couldn't; they had no right…But then suddenly remembering their strength and their power, Minette felt her hatred for them swell. *I hate them, I hate them*, she said to herself. And for the first time in her life she had the courage to look her hatred in the face. Ah, yes! Truly, her hatred extended not just to all the planters, but to all the Whites in the world. She had had enough of suppressing her feelings and holding back her reactions. "I hate them, I hate them…" she repeated. And her throat contracted so violently in response to this harsh burning sensation that it was as if the roof of her mouth were being stabbed with a lancet.

When she returned home, Jasmine gave her the same news she had just heard from the Lamberts.

"They say the Whites have ripped up the Damiens Accord. It's like we were born only to keep being defeated."

"We'll beat them someday, Mama."

"I'll already be dead."

Minette said nothing and got dressed to head to the theater with Lise and her mother.

There were too many carriages and too many stagecoaches for anyone to notice the absence of a few cars. The atmosphere was the same everywhere: in the crowd, in the wings, and on the stage. Nothing had changed on the outside. Everyone knew that the Whites had promised to give the freedmen their rights and that a new Colonial Assembly was to be formed. Everyone also knew that the Whites were thinking of going back on their promise and breaking the accord. Everyone was talking about it in the theater. It was the most recent news on everyone's mind – some being for and others against the planters' decision. The fact that several seats were empty first became apparent from the stage, though this was not necessarily that odd. Yet, everyone had been so happy to go back to the old amusements after so much conflict, that these absences seemed bizarre. The play, which had been advertised with Minette in the lead role, should have been an irresistible temptation. Why had these seats remained empty?

During the intermission, a few people pointed out the empty seats.

"I'll bet," said a young man in a frilled shirt, "that the Committee of the West is going back on its word. I'll bet a hundred pounds."

"I'll take that bet. They're afraid of the freedmen. They'll cow to them completely."

"Monsieur de Caradeux has been talking about annulling the Treaty of Damiens."

"That's impossible – it'll start up the fighting again."

"You taking the bet?"

"Okay."

As the curtains were about to rise, the conversations stopped, and Minette made her appearance in a dazzling costume.

She looked toward the empty seats. Where were the planters? Deliberating on the freedmen's fate? Tearing up the accord? A surge of revolt rumbled so deeply inside her that she feared she would be incapable of singing. It was too late to do anything about it – the orchestra had already launched into the first bars. That day, she sang like she had never sung before. But when the triumphant applause began she made a few vain attempts to smile before fleeing the stage, making clear she would not return.

As soon as the curtains had been lowered, the political discussions began again unabated. The police had difficulty containing the various tussles that had broken out. At the exit, a police officer jostled a black Confederate, who then grabbed him by the collar. Such a tumult broke out that Minette ended up separated from Jasmine and Lise. The black Confederate had just seized the white man and was about to disarm him when the horsemen of the constabulary invaded the square and arrested the black man. At that point, the din had become so deafening that the police had to fire into the crowd to get them to disperse. All the people of color shook their fists at the policemen, threatening to have their heads. One White, standing near Minette, protested openly against the unjust treatment the black Confederate had received. When the police withdrew with their prisoner, more than a thousand people of color followed behind them.

Jasmine had been searching for Minette and finally found her.

"Come," she said, "let's join the crowd of demonstrators. As for you, Lise, be strong, no matter what happens…"

Minette looked at her, astonished. Her resigned expression had disappeared. She had raised her head high, like someone who had just become conscious of her own value.

A poor White passed by them and Minette recognized the painter Perrosier. He was filthier than ever and stumbled as he walked. He raised his arms to the sky and cried:

"It's unjust…"

He reached the crowd of people of color, repeating the same words:
"It's unjust, it's unjust, it's unjust…"

A thousand voices repeated after him.

"It's unjust!" screamed Minette.

At that moment, Joseph rushed up to her.

Unable to speak, his eyes were bulging out of his head. Minette took his hand in hers. To think that he had once roused crowds with his words! The time had come – the moment he had been waiting for his whole life. The first serious revolts were beginning and he could not speak to his people. The miracles he had dreamed of in spreading the good word, he could no longer conjure into being with his words – and his brothers risked straying from the righteous path, taking hatred alone for their guide. Where was it about to lead them? Blinded with anger, spurred on by this word "Justice" they were repeating publicly for the first time in their lives, they would end up being slaughtered by the National Guard.

Minette looked at Joseph. His forehead was drenched in sweat and his features were so tense that she immediately understood she needed to help him. What did he want? To hold back a crowd headed toward certain death…

She then remembered a passage from Bossuet's sermons that Joseph used to recite with such eloquence. And with her most beautiful voice, she began to sing it to the melody of a well-known tune:

Christians, let us reflect on those whose
power seems stronger than everything else.

Think of the final hour,
which will enshroud all their greatness...

Becalmed by these great words, the crowd began to sing as one. Joseph was so moved, he began to weep. In their calmer state, the demonstrators accompanied the prisoner to the Municipality, where the Guard awaited them, muskets drawn.

But what were they supposed to do with this crowd of people singing?

Not a single shot was fired, not one body was left dead on the cobblestones. Their numbers remained intact for the final battle.

XXXIV

THE NEXT DAY was Saint Cécile's Day. The bells had been ringing out joyful melodies all morning in the hopes of attracting some of the faithful to the church where the saint, covered in bouquets of flowers, graced all who entered with a smile that greatly resembled that of Mlle de Caradeux.

Young flower merchants set up on the street corners proposed bouquets to the passersby. A limpid sky, speckled with just a few light clouds, brightened the horizon.

Groups of freedmen in multicolored costumes spoke in low tones about the demonstration of the day before and about the fate that awaited the prisoner, who, they had learned, had been hanged on the parade grounds. At that moment, the freedmen's indignation had reached its peak. No longer would they be controlled. They gathered in groups and protested openly. The time of fear had long passed for them. No longer would they tolerate being humiliated. Indifferent to whatever consequences might follow, they would return blow for blow. As one of Praloto's gunners passed by, a freedman who had been immersed in a passionate discussion noticed him and, losing his head, killed him with a gunshot before anyone could stop him.

The Whites immediately commanded the drummers to beat the assembly.

The footsoldiers and officers ran back to the barracks and, while the crowd of ardent congregants leaving the church began to spill out onto the street, the joyful ringing of the bells became a death knell.

Already at the command of his post, Pétion saw M de Caradeux and his men emerge from the street.

"Destroy that fort!" he cried to Praloto's men, pointing to the Governor's palace, where Pétion was stationed.

Pétion caressed his artillery.

"There you go, Gluttonous One," he said. "There's a nice meal for you."

And he immediately launched a violent response to Praloto's bullets.

The battle was so intense that the room had become stiflingly overheated.

Pétion looked for water. The buckets were empty and the fountain across the way directly faced Praloto.

"A brave man," he shouted, "I need a brave man."

Pons grabbed the buckets and headed toward the fountain as fast as he could run. Bullets whizzed by him so close that several times he feared he had been hit. Once he had filled the buckets, he had to cross the street again. How could he run with these weights on his arms?

He had come so close to death that, reaching Pétion, he fell into a seat on the cannon, the full buckets in his hands.

"They missed you – they're bad shots," said Pétion, hugging him.

Realizing that he was being attacked both by the regiments from Artois and from Normandy, he cried:

"We need help – we need help! Let Beauvais' camp know!"

Help fell from the sky at that very moment, in the form of Jean-Baptiste Lapointe. Leading his men, he arrived at the parade grounds, causing Praloto's shocked soldiers to cease firing.

Surrounded by his men, Lapointe sowed panic among the Whites stationed in the square. Bullets whistling right by his ears, he invaded the Municipality, seized the ledgers where the names of condemned freedmen were inscribed and burned them in the street. Eyes blazing and a cruel smile playing at the corners of his lips, he began violently stabbing the Whites.

Soon the battle between his men and the French soldiers turned into a tremendous hand-to-hand combat.

After two hours of battle, Pétion was beginning to run out of munitions.

"My Lord!" he said, "the 'Gluttonous One' has already eaten up everything we've got. Someone bring me some rocks – bring me some rocks!"

Noticing the diminished firepower, Beauvais and Lambert gave the order to retreat toward Croix des Bouquets. They brought the wounded along with them. Twenty dead freedmen remained on the cobblestones. The Whites had lost more than a hundred of their soldiers, including Captain Desroches.

Suddenly, a fire broke out in Bel-Air. Lit by mercenaries who had been paid by the planters to increase dissent and disorder, it spread rapidly. Rather than try to put it out, the Whites chased after the freed-men and tried to kill them. All those who had not had the time to join up with Beauvais' troops were murdered: men, women, and children. Homes were broken into and looted, their inhabitants killed. Cries and screams rang out. Fearing the appearance of armed Whites, people of color abandoned their homes and fled. Women fell to their knees, pleading with Saint Cécile to rescue them.

Panic had reached the inhabitants of Traversière Street. Jasmine sobbed as she held the terrified Lise and little Jean against her shoulder.

"We've got to leave," screamed Nicolette, bursting in. "The Whites are killing people in their homes."

Minette and Jasmine quickly packed some bedding.

A screaming horde arrived at the Comédie, brandishing swords and rifles.

"My God," murmured Jasmine, feeling her old fears overwhelm her again, "have pity on the young, at least."

"Quiet, Mama," pleaded Minette softly, "or we'll all lose our heads."

All of a sudden, a big black body emerged from the shadows. It was Scipion.

"You've got to go, ladies," he said. "The Whites are coming."

They did not have time to leave. Six Whites armed with rifles invaded the front room. Scipion immediately cut two of their throats. Then, grabbing their weapons, he threw one to Minette while at the same time smashing in the skull of a White who was about to fire on Lise.

"Use your weapon, young lady," he shouted to Minette.

She shouldered the rifle and aimed at one of the murderers. He fell to the ground. Young Jean screamed. Jasmine hid him in the back room and came back with an iron bar with which she threatened one of the invaders. Abandoning Lise to her tears, Nicolette threw herself into the battle. She had surprised one of the invaders by jumping on his back and was now digging her fingers into his eyes like some kind of she-devil. A shot was fired but hit no one. With a solid kick, Scipion had disarmed Jasmine's attacker. He picked up the rifle and broke it over one of the Whites' head. Minette tried to fire a second time, but her rifle was out of bullets. She went to the second room and returned with a knife. Her eyes blazing and her lips taut, she struck one of the Whites with all her strength. The knife stayed planted in the man's body as he fell, curled into a ball, without making a sound. Nicolette was biting and scratching, dodging bullets. Scipion seized her adversary and crushed his head against a wall. Minette looked at her feet: they were swimming in a sea of blood. The entire room was filled with corpses. Jasmine ran to get young Jean and together they went out to the street where panicked escapees turned in place, unable to move forward.

"Saint Cécile, come to our aid," murmured Jasmine, making the sign of the cross.

"Let us put our souls in the hands of our Lord Jesus. May he consider our suffering and welcome us in our last hours."

"Stop praying, Mama, please. I'm scared – I'm too scared to die…"

Lise clutched her mother, whimpering.

They took a few steps forward and were immediately blocked by the crowd.

"Move forward, clear the street; do you want to die where you're standing?" someone shouted.

"We can't. The Whites are waiting for us on the other side of the street."

"So then we're surrounded."

Minette turned her head and saw flames rising. The surrounding houses were on fire. A suffocating heat engulfed the escapees, and terrifying flashes of light blazed, filling the atmosphere. Women and children passed out; people trampled their bodies. They could barely breathe.

"Please, please, go forward. Have pity..."

The blaze had reached indescribable proportions. Four pumps had been brought from the ships; they burned up immediately.

All of a sudden, someone began firing on the crowd at point-blank range. Twenty or so people fell to the ground. Trampled cadavers, their insides hanging out, lay on the ground. Those who had only been wounded tried with cries of pain to keep away the feet that were crushing them and more than one died in this final misery.

Jasmine held Lise and young Jean close to her as Minette, protected by Scipion, walked ahead of them. The crowd moved step by step, with frustrating slowness, as the houses blazed like torches. The fire was coming from the north and the south. It quickly reached the area of the Comédie and the Great Clock. The city had become an immense inferno. Her throat dry, her eyes burning, Minette looked out for Jasmine. She saw her holding Lise and young Jean close to her. Behind them, Nicolette wept as she tried to cut through the crowd. All of a sudden, a horde of demons with bloodied clothes threw themselves on the inhabitants of Traversière Street. A thick-necked white man seized Nicolette and sunk his weapon into her back. She fell at Jasmine's feet, as she clasped Lise and young Jean closer to her.

"You're all almost there, Mama, Mama," called Minette.

She let out a scream of horror and tried to run to them:

"Mama, Mama…Lise…"

Jasmine had faltered on her feet. A white man pulled a knife from her heart and then plunged it into Lise's back. Young Jean fell from Jasmine's lifeless arms. Minette tore herself from Scipion's arms and, fighting desperately, tried to reach the child. But she couldn't move. Holding out her hand, she called him to her. A white man turned around, and with one hand grabbed the boy's neck and strangled him; with the other he threw a knife, which hit Minette in the chest.

Scipion grabbed her and pulled her toward him:

"Stay here, miss. Don't move."

She tried to speak, and a stream of blood flowed from her mouth. She turned her eyes toward Jasmine and Lise's entangled corpses. A sob left her throat along with a second trickle of blood.

"Don't be afraid, Miss. You'll go to pray on their graves one day."

Lifting her up, Scipion held her above the crowd in his powerful arms. She did not move at all; she had fainted.

As soon as he had seen the blaze, Lapointe had stopped fighting. Fleeing the square, he had run with his rifle in one hand and a knife in the other. A white man, blinded in one eye and covered in rags, threatened him and tried to block his way. He felled him with a single rifle shot. Near the Comédie, right at the corner of Traversière Street, fifty or so white men were chasing the freedmen, gathered in the narrow street.

He called out:

"Minette!"

His voice was lost in the tumult of sobs, screams, and cries of rage.

He ran through a mob of poor Whites.

"There's one – kill him!"

He ducked down, and the bullets just missed him, whizzing past him as he ran. He reached the last row of freedmen, who were headed to the docks.

Two solid black arms were carrying a woman through the suffocating crowd. He recognized Minette. An expression of relief came over his face.

He called out again:

"Minette!"

But despite his efforts, he could not move forward. He stood next to a pile of corpses, among which were Lise, Jasmine, and young Jean. He turned back in the other direction and, as the Whites were headed toward him, hid in the debris of a smoking house and shot down more than a dozen.

At last free from the narrow street, the escapees began approaching the harbor in wild disarray. Women pushed terrified children ahead of them, others headed off on the road to the barracks where the soldiers from Artois and Normandy welcomed them to protect them and tend to their wounds…Scipion followed them, still carrying Minette passed out in his arms.

The next day, five hundred homes and shops were in ruins. The streets, strewn with the dead and the wounded, were covered in blood and body parts. Hundreds of women and children had perished in the harbor, bogged down by the mangroves; their bodies now floated on the surface of the water.

Joseph, Pétion, and the other freedmen, who had gathered in the Cul-de-Sac plains and taken on the name the "Confederates of Croix des Bouquets," were about to send for news when the soldiers from Artois and Normandy arrived accompanied by the escapees. Minette, Zoé, and Louise Rasteau were with them.

Zoé, who had also lost her parents, told Lambert what had happened as she held him in her arms. Joseph, Pétion, and all the men from Beauvais' troop were appalled by the horrific news, and their resentment grew even more intense. Swearing to get vengeance, the Confederates of Croix des Bouquets called on the southern troops, commanded by André Rigaud, and cut off the water supply. Dying of hunger and thirst, surrounded on one side by Rigaud's troops and by Beauvais' on the other, the population wandered the streets for days like starving animals.

XXXV

FOUR DAYS LATER, the silence in the hills broke. The *lambi* horn sounded lugubriously as it transmitted messages to the four corners of the island. Thousands of slaves, armed with pikes, sticks, and machetes descended from the hills to join those in the workhouses, sowing terror and death in their wake. Massacring, pillaging, and burning, they arrived at the doors of Cap-Français. The white population took up arms to defend itself against the revolting slaves. In the West and in the South, the slaves had risen up and were waging war under other leaders. Just as in the North, they were massacring, pillaging, and burning. After killing their masters, they raped their wives and daughters before slitting their throats. Not even the convents were respected and one could see terrified nuns fleeing as they implored the heavens for rescue. Although drunk with vengeance and hatred, the slaves remained lucid enough to choose the cruelest masters for their first targets. Thus was the Marquis de Caradeux's home raided and burned to the ground. Hidden in a trunk where no one had thought to look for him, he heard his daughter's screams of horror as the slaves raped her and his brother and son-in-law's cries of agony. When the house was set afire, he left his hiding place and crawled to his daughter's bedroom. She lay there, passed out. He took her in his arms, fled into the night, and reached a boat heading to the United States. More than a thousand white families were murdered that night and buried under the rubble of their homes, reduced to ashes.

The volcano, which for long years the planters did not believe existed, was erupting. Like lava and ashes, the slaves poured from the hills, left the workhouses and the forests as if vomited up from a crater. Armed, they took their turn bringing their weapons down over and over, without mercy…

Blaming the people of color for this terrible insurrection, the Whites killed them in droves. Free Blacks and Mulattos, hunted and persecuted, fled into the hills. These were indescribably terrifying times for everyone. Fossette Square, in Cap-Français, was filled with gallows from which hung Negroes and Mulattos, slave and free, often wrongly accused.

The hospitals were overflowing with the wounded. The dead, piled up and poorly buried, gave off a nauseating smell. As if to add to the horror, yellow fever began to ravage hundreds of families, many of whom perished for lack of medical care…

Praloto and M de Caradeux schemed with the planters of Arcahaie to seize that parish by surprise and thereby cut off all communication between the freedmen of Saint-Marc and those of the West. Jean-Baptiste Lapointe, warned by his spies, chose among his most intelligent slaves and sent them to rally slaves from the neighboring workhouses. Then, arming all of them, he sent them to attack the Whites in their homes and slaughter them.

After the uprising, he gathered the revolting slaves with his own and led them into town, where the Whites, despite their suspicions, welcomed him as a savior. He had indeed entered as a peacemaker and publicly asked the slaves to return to their workhouses. How could anyone stand up to such a dangerous mixed-blood?

For some time, the little house in Boucassin had become an important political salon, just like M de Caradeux's luxurious home. Ever since Lapointe had returned from the Spanish side of the island, the most vindictive and hate-filled freedmen had been gathering there. He shrewdly kept their hatred alive by showing them the proof of the Whites' bad faith toward them. Soon, he reigned over them like a dictator, naming himself head of the National Guard, then head of the police force and, finally, Mayor of Arcahaie. All the slaves of the region obeyed him blindly. His power was accepted and his will was law. It was the Whites' turn to lower their heads in fear. He had them in the palm of his hand and he would not release them. He had sworn to make the Whites pay back bit by bit all the humiliation, all the dishonor, and all the disdain he and the other freedmen had felt for so long.

In the meantime, he wanted to see Minette again and make her his wife. Her hold over him was as strong as the one he held over the Whites. All other women paled in comparison to her. Her reproaches made him admire and love her even more. Where was she? Had the black slave that was carrying her been able to save her? Mad with worry, he left Arcahaie and went to Croix des Bouquets, to the Confederates. The first person he encountered was Pétion:

"There's Jean Lapointe," he cried.

Minette, still recovering, was seated with Zoé on a flat rock surrounded by greenery. All around them, wildflowers trembling in the breeze shook their delicate petals. He came slowly toward them, restraining his fiery horse. They looked at one another in silence for a moment.

"I was looking for you…"

She said nothing and squeezed Zoé's hand in hers.

He dismounted his horse and took two steps toward her.

"Did you see what happened?"

Her voice was choked with emotion and full of tears as she spoke these words. Then, rising, she stood up and remained immobile, her hands clasped to her heart.

"They killed my mother and sister."

"I know."

She raised her head, looked at him for a moment, and threw herself into his open arms. Then she cried. After a minute, her badly healed wound hurt so much that she had to close her eyes.

"Humanity is made in the image of vultures. We have to fight, Minette, not with tears or prayers. Pity's no longer in fashion. How many times will I have to tell you that?"

She calmed down and wiped her tears.

Beauvais, Lambert, Joseph, Pétion, and a few others came over to them.

"Lapointe," said Beauvais, "your latest maneuver in Arcahaie was an unparalleled feat of arms. Without your intervention, communication would have been cut between the freedmen of Saint-Marc and those of the West; we would have had to surrender unconditionally. Allow me to thank you…"

He shook his hand and, once a glass of rum had been served to everyone, drank to the success of the Confederate cause. That evening,

Lapointe was alone with Minette and asked her to return to Boucassin with him.

"I've proven to you that I, too, have been fighting for our cause. What do you hold against me? That I own slaves? That I beat them? Do you think that Ogé and Chavannes and all the people here would fight for their freedom? Everyone thinks only of himself, fights only for himself, and that's already beautiful enough."

It had been some time since she had come to think the same way. Despair and all the fighting had aged her. Her idealism had been destroyed and she could see the truth of things more clearly.

"I'll join you very soon, Jean," she promised him.

"And this time, if you leave me, I'll kill you."

He tried to take her in his arms again, so she had to admit to him that she had been wounded and was still suffering.

"Wounded!" he cried out. "Oh, but you'll get better. You'll see a doctor tomorrow. I'll bring him here myself."

She smiled weakly and caressed his face.

"What strength you have in you!"

He departed that night, leaving Minette, if not consoled, at least somewhat reassured. His vitality and energy had left some small mark on her wounded soul.

The next day, he returned with a white doctor and had Minette show him her wound. It was deep, badly cared for, and half gangrened. The doctor made a bandage and advised her to rest. He said nothing to Lapointe, but in passing by Zoé, said:

"It's a nasty wound; this young girl needs the kind of regular care she can't get here."

Zoé tried to get her to leave for Arcahaie. She refused. What was she afraid of? She herself did not know. She felt calm around her friends and, though she was in pain because of her wound, she had no desire to leave Croix des Bouquets. Weakened and distraught, perhaps she feared that some new conflict might separate her once again from Lapointe. It was better for her, she thought, to remain there and have him arrive at a gallop, impatient and lovelorn. She was also closer to the battle, more intimately involved in making decisions and getting news, which came daily and was more and more shocking. Thus it was that two days after the doctor's visit, they learned that a boat arriving from France had left three civil commissioners on the shores of Cap-Français and that, astounded by the state of the colony, they had tried to restore order by entering into negotiations with the leaders of the revolting slaves.

Beauvais asked for two volunteers: Joseph and Pétion were then sent to Port-au-Prince, from which they returned that afternoon with all sorts of information. Yes, the commissioners had indeed begun negotiations with the slave leaders. But the latter had demanded fifty autonomies in exchange for their surrender and the planters had refused to cede.

"Haven't they had enough of all this killing?" cried Lambert. "For heaven's sake what kind of men are these?"

And Minette, remembering the pile of corpses cluttering Traversière Street, hid her face in her hands.

But all of this had to end; everyone had had enough. They made their final arrangements and decided to march on the Assembly of the West. Their numbers were small. Many had died in battle on the day of the massacre. The morning of their departure was a heartbreaking moment for the women. Marguerite Beauvais, who had lost the child she was carrying due to all she had lived through, Louise Rasteau, Zoé, and Minette all cried openly: these men were all they had left in the world. With their relatives dead, the freedmen's army was their only consolation. Minette grabbed on to Jean Lapointe, Zoé clutched her brother, Marguerite Beauvais held on to her husband. They went from one to the other, telling them to be cautious, going to their satchels and adding a few last treats. Minette hugged Joseph and Pétion to her, kissed her lover one last time, and fled into the house. An indefinable taste rose in her throat. She took her handkerchief and spat. It was blood. She looked ahead with a strange expression and raised her hand to the spot on her chest where she had been wounded. Hearing the galloping of a horse, she raced outside. A messenger had arrived, out of breath. The news was staggering: three more commissioners had arrived from France with an expeditionary army of six thousand men and with an order to execute a decree favorable to the people of color. Everyone was overjoyed. The Confederates of Croix des Bouquets, learning that a mixed commission made up of six Whites and six freedmen had been formed, rallied to the side of the commissioners and the Governor and headed for Port-au-Prince. A brutal combat ensued for two days, after which the planters were defeated. Finally, it was the great and definitive victory they had sought for so many long years. Many of them had died, but many had stayed alive to bless this day and see their cause triumph. Welcomed by the jubilant population, the freedmen's army entered the town, accompanied by the commissioners and the Governor. This time they marched along the main street, heads held high and cheered by the Whites themselves, as they headed toward the

Municipality, where they proceeded to sign the decree recognizing their civil and political rights.

Despite all of this satisfaction, hearts remained heavy: the city was in ruins. Port-au-Prince was no longer recognizable. Fire, death, and desolation had left violent traces everywhere. The actors of the Comédie had left for France and the site was nothing more than burned-out rubble. On Traversière Street, the market-women – half of whom had been killed – had become traveling vendors. The magnificent homes of Bel-Air, the boutiques, the Vaux-Halls – there was nothing left but a pile of ashes. The doors of the houses having been torn off, the looted homes stood wide open and completely emptied. The gaunt and ragged populace wandered through the streets, utterly distraught. Children – orphans – held out their hands to beg, and wept as they followed passersby, while starving dogs sniffed at them.

The freedwomen in Croix des Bouquets could not look at the town without weeping. There was no one there to greet them – no homes, no relatives. Some few acquaintances came up to them, spoke to them about those who had died of hunger and thirst, those who had been murdered, those who had died on the battlefield. The dead, the dead, nothing but the dead. *Such horror!* Minette thought to herself. When she saw Scipion in the crowd, she let out a cry of relief. He would help her find out what had happened to her loved ones.

"I've been waiting for you, Miss," he said simply.

He brought her to a grave, recognizable by the immense cross comprised of two branches nailed together. A slight taste of blood rose in her throat, as it did every time she exerted herself at all.

"Why, God, why?" she murmured, her eyes fixed on the cross.

XXXVI

TRYING TO FORGET the dead and regain their taste for living, the townspeople built dreams for the future on the still-smoking ruins of the town.

Zoé's house had been spared and Minette took shelter there. The army had dispersed. The men courageously rebuilt the homes that had been destroyed, and those who still had theirs opened their doors to those without shelter. After having searched in vain for a doctor to treat Minette, Lapointe had returned to his land in the hopes of finding someone there. The trip from Croix des Bouquets to Port-au-Prince had unleashed a frightening hemorrhage and Lapointe, desperately worried, had nearly lost his mind when Minette fainted. A local healer and Zoé had done their best to care for her, but Lapointe insisted on finding a doctor.

The day after his departure for Arcahaie, Minette revealed to Zoé that she had decided to get married in just a few days.

"That makes me very happy," responded Zoé. "You two need one another…He'll help you get well, and you'll help him to change."

Minette had lowered her head without answering. Him – change? She had a hard time imagining him forgiving his tormentors, holding his hand out to the Whites, and forgetting the past. He had fought at his brothers' sides to win this fight. Now that the battle had been won, he stayed firm in his judgments, and looked at the present situation with a clear eye.

The situation was not ideal, and Minette, kept informed by Lapointe, anxiously observed what was happening all around her. It wasn't over, and she sensed that Lapointe was right again. The planters' hatred had not abated. Praloto was dead, M de Caradeux had left, but there were others to take their place. And those others, miraculous survivors of the slaves' massacre, were still numerous. But more than ever, the colony needed everyone's help: an enemy was knocking at its borders, hoping to exploit the dissension and disorder that reigned there. Rather than accept the decree favorable to the freedmen, the planters had allied themselves with a coalition of English and Spanish forces, enemies of Saint-Domingue.

Sonthonax, the High Commissioner, was a hotheaded young revolutionary. Of medium height, he had the round, rosy cheeks of a young girl, which was decidedly misleading, given his pugnacious temperament. Three days after his arrival, he had installed a young Negress in his home to help, as he put it, cool the ardor of his blood. Treating her like a princess, he went around with her on his arm and, in this imitating the late François Saint-Martin, went about saying that white women paled in comparison to a goddess like his. He had made himself unlikeable to the planters with his revolutionary ideas, and he became even more hated once he began publicly declaring his preference for women of color. He understood immediately that if he wanted to get into the planters' good graces he would have to work within the rules and do what he wanted in secret. Even love. But he refused.

For the time being, the battle he was waging against hundreds of reactionary colonists was at its paroxysm. He had already had to capitulate to several of his aggressors, despite the aid of the freedmen. The enemy was exploiting the situation; the Spanish were already invading the neighboring market towns.

"I'll bring them to heel," cried the young Commissioner, slamming his fist on the deliberation table, surrounded by some of his supporters.

"The Spanish already occupy Vallière, Fort Dauphin, Grande Rivière du Nord…"

"Enough," interrupted Sonthonax, a bundle of nerves. "I want to be left alone."

He was backed into a corner, he realized. It was only a matter of a few hours before the Spanish troops invaded the northern province…

He put his head between his hands, elbows on the table.

All of a sudden, he sat up with an expression of strange satisfaction.

He slammed his fist down on the table for a second time, but this time with a burst of laughter.

"I'll bring them to heel," he screamed.

Then taking a sheet of paper, he feverishly wrote the following words:

The lands of Saint-Domingue should be the property of the Blacks; they have earned them by the sweat of their brow.

A freedman entered at that very moment. Breathless and drenched in sweat, he had clearly traveled a long way on horseback.

"Monsieur the Commissioner," he began, out of breath, "the enemy has just invaded Limbé and Borgne…"

"Very well, but they'll retreat soon enough," responded Sonthonax with such certainty in his voice that the freedman stared at him in astonishment. "Yes, they'll retreat even if I have to make the forces of liberty shoot out of the very ground in Saint-Domingue…"

Seeing that the freedman was staring at him wide-eyed, he continued:

"The slaves, the slaves…Only they can help us win this fight! Now do you understand? Go on, get me the other freedmen. I need messengers to reach the bands of rebels hiding in the area…What am I promising them in return? Huh? What am I promising them? Why, their freedom, of course, their freedom – do you hear me?" he sang in a terrible voice. "So what are you waiting for? Run along!"

And thus it was that three completely distinct classes, divided for hundreds of years, were integrated for the first time. The enemy defeated, Commissioner Sonthonax proclaimed the freedom of the slaves in the North.

Surrounded and cheered by the crowd, the young Commissioner declared all Negroes and mixed-bloods of the northern provinces to be Frenchmen.

This time, Scipion was the one to give Minette the news. She was sitting on her bed, softly humming an opera melody. She stopped from time to time, astonished by her breathlessness and by the sharp little pains that kept her from forgetting her wound.

"Zoé," she called, "do you think I'll ever get better? Do you think I'll ever be able to sing again?"

"The healer says not for another three months…"

"She doesn't know what she's talking about, that healer. I feel like I've lost my voice…"

"Come now, don't go exaggerating. Your wound was poorly treated. You need rest, lots of rest, and good care. Lapointe promised to move heaven and earth to find a doctor for you – a good one…"

Scipion entered at that moment.

"Mistress," he cried, "there are no more slaves. The commissioners freed us all!"

"What are you saying?"

"Commissioner Sonthonax just arrived from Cap-Français. He's at the parade grounds with the crowd…There are no more slaves…"

Minette and Zoé ran outside.

The populace had gathered at the parade grounds, where an altar to the Fatherland was being erected. Women carrying garlands and flags helped to decorate it. The main street, covered with palm fronds and flowers, awaited the procession. A delightful sensation suffused Minette's heart. She saw herself in the bed she had slept in as a little girl, arms wrapped around Lise, telling her:

"I'd like to buy all the slaves in Saint-Domingue and then free them…"

At last her dream had become a reality. She had lived long enough to see the cause of the freedmen and the slaves emerge victorious…

All around her, the ruins and the cadavers seemed revived. Her eyes fixed on a pile of ashes, she once again saw the Comédie. Everything was in its place again – everything and everyone: Jasmine, Lise, young Jean, Goulard, the Acquaires, the missing – all the missing – communed with the crowd on that day with the same enthusiastic energy.

It was Polvérel who spoke. He called the former slaves "French citizens" and explained to them what Liberty was.

Labadie was among them. After having signed, he embraced some of his people. They cheered him. The crowd, overcome with emotion, following the Commissioner, began to intone a sublime song of love and peace.

"I'm going to sing," Minette said to Zoé, grasping her hand.

"Have you forgotten your wound?"

"No, but I've got to sing."

"Don't be foolish…"

But Zoé had the impression that Minette was not listening to her. Minette seemed to be alone in the midst of the crowd, alone or with someone with whom she was pleading. Her hands joined and her tense attitude betrayed a determination that had nothing to with a simple desire to sing. It was something else – an escape to the beyond, perhaps just the simple idea that she could help with the miracle – a little girl's dream, drawn from a well of superstition, to which she could not help but cede.

The crowd had just stopped singing. Minette looked up at the sky. It was so blue that her heart swelled with a feeling of gentle gratitude. In the end, it deserved to be lived, this life. Yes, despite all those who had departed, despite the bitter struggles, the evils, and the injustices… Such a day deserved to be celebrated spectacularly. Her whole life, Minette had dreamed of living just that. She thought of Lapointe at that moment and her expression became almost pained.

It was for him that she would sing – only for him. She knew it. To sing so that the miracle would reach him. Because, My God, she had just learned that nothing was sure in this world. No matter how long it took, the struggle was never in vain. She had just had the proof that the world could be transformed and rebuilt. Had Saint-Domingue not been reborn from its fraught past, erasing three centuries' worth of disgrace in a single day?…

With her two hands, Minette pressed against her heart and launched her magnificent voice into a final effort, taking up the song of peace all alone.

The commissioners looked around for the citizen they heard singing. Her voice, mixed with the sound of the bells, was an unparalleled message of gratitude directed toward the heavens.

A message that reached Lapointe, perhaps, on the road leading to Port-au-Prince, for he was only a few minutes from the center of town.

He had finally found a doctor for Minette. The man was an old Jesuit priest, dressed in a filthy cassock, whom he had managed to load onto a lazy, shriveled mule. Lapointe was giving him an aggressive sidelong glance. At that pace, they risked arriving in Port-au-Prince at nightfall. Clutching the mule's saddle, his skinny legs almost touching the ground, the old priest made for a sad picture on his mount.

"Tell me, Father, is there no way to make you go any faster?"

"My son, I didn't hide the fact that this is the first time I've ever been in a saddle. And if it weren't for this gentle old mule, I would have refused to follow you categorically…"

Ahead of them, the road stretched out, sunny in places, shady in others, reflecting their distorted silhouette.

Lapointe boiled with impatience. At several points he had to fight the urge to dump the old Jesuit and race back to Port-au-Prince.

"I'm told that Sonthonax has proclaimed the liberty of all the slaves in the North," said the priest.

"It would seem…"

"The way things are going, soon there'll be no more slaves left in the country."

"If they move as slowly as our horses, this may very well last for some time."

Surprised by Lapointe's angry gaze, the priest tried to spur on his mule by giving him several awkward kicks in the stomach. Having slipped from the saddle, he did his best to prop himself up and lowered his head timidly.

Since learning of what had happened in the North, Lapointe had been struggling with a serious personal conflict. He had read the Abbé Raynal, the Abbé Grégoire, and Jean-Jacques Rousseau…He was aware that there were Whites who fought on behalf of the slaves, who called for the end of class divisions, and who denounced slavery as the most shameful of institutions. And here was this young Girondist, fresh from France, who had set himself up as righter of wrongs – taking on the planters and declaring the emancipation of the slaves.

And so what about that? Sonthonax had no need of slaves to help him establish his social position. Whites could make and even unmake the laws. It was only natural that some of them were slaveholders for the love of profit while others were abolitionists out of dilettantism. He could not help thinking that he had collected enough enviable titles to do without slaves. Had he not just recently been named Mayor of Arcahaie? Henceforth, he had an established social position. To hell with everyone else…After a restless night of strange dreams, he had awoken with the painful feeling that he had dreamed of his mother, the little slave girl with the soulful and fearful gaze…

Lapointe lifted his straw hat and mopped at the sweat on his forehead. Memories came into his thoughts with a tenacity that seemed almost obsessive. He saw himself as a little boy, playing in front of his father's hut. His father had been a despotic, unintelligent Mulatto who made his slaves tremble merely by looking at them. How old was he then? Six, seven years – he could not recall anymore, but he relived that scene as if it had been just yesterday: the big hunting dog that had attacked him, and his mother, so small and thin, fighting desperately to tear him from the jaws of the beast, rolling on the ground with it and strangling it. After the struggle, she had been left so weak and trembling that someone had carried her back to the hut, where the master had shouted at her for killing his animal…

"There it is – Port-au-Prince!" cried the priest triumphantly. "My mule truly will have made a fine journey."

Lapointe shivered as if he had just awoken from a dream. On the other side of the road, Bel-Air seemed to be cluttered with the burned-up debris of the former homes. An odor of wet smoke, slaked lime, and death emanated from the ruins.

"It's all of this, all of this that keeps me from forgiving them," said Lapointe angrily as he looked around.

"Civilization comes from great men, but just as with small men, 'they know not what they do.' It's their only excuse, my son."

On the parade grounds, they came upon a meditative crowd. A woman's voice was singing a divine melody and the priest found the voice so singular that he stopped for a moment to listen.

"I was in Italy once, a long time ago. Who in this country can sing that melody if not La Dugazon herself?"

He had turned to Lapointe, but the latter had abandoned him right there and dismounted his horse to run into the crowd.

Minette was singing, surrounded by her friends: Joseph, Pétion, Labadie, Zoé, Beauvais, Lambert, and the others...

She was foolish to sing with her wound so badly healed. How had they allowed her to do that? He looked around for Zoé and then gestured toward Minette with his chin and frowned. She answered him with a gesture of helplessness.

The old priest had managed to catch up to him. Adjusting his glasses on his nose, he looked at Minette curiously.

"So, young man, shall we go see about that sick friend of yours?"

"There she is, Father."

Minette had just noticed him in the crowd. A slight smile played across her lips then disappeared, replaced by a worried expression as she noted the shock in his eyes. He took two steps forward, as if to interrupt her singing. She stopped him with a gesture, without breaking his gaze. He looked anxiously at the crowd, for once all together without hatred or prejudice – at these men who yesterday had been planters now coming to the altar and accepting the transformation of their slaves into free men. Was he going to side with them or with those who would rather see the colony destroyed than accept the idea of Equality for all?

The memory of his mother once again passed through his thoughts. He smiled to himself as if to recognize that he had fallen prey to a certain romanticism. But how nice it was not to feel ashamed of that. So he had gotten the better of himself – he, Lapointe, was going to cede, to abdicate, to renounce all those things to which he had clutched his whole life, like some sort of lifeline. Another smile danced across his face. Removing his straw hat, he turned it around in his fingers, as if intimidated. Then shrugging his shoulders, he walked up to the altar. He was about to sign, when Minette's voice faltered on the final note. He turned around, anguished. Supported by Zoé, she was vomiting blood. He reached her in a flash and took her in his arms.

The crowd gathered around them, curious.

"She's fainted! Is there a doctor here?" whimpered Zoé.

With difficulty, the old priest made his way through the crowd. With an authoritative gesture, he stopped Lapointe who, trembling, had been unbuttoning Minette's bodice.

"Wait…"

He bent down, placed his ear to Minette's left breast and then to her face. He finally raised his head with a strangely dazed expression and, without looking at Lapointe, muttered as if talking to himself.

"Truly, truly…with a voice like that…"

Lapointe glanced at him with an expressionless look in which the priest could nonetheless see a despair so dismal that he could not speak to him.

He advanced slowly, looking straight ahead of himself with that faraway gaze, so blank it was almost terrifying. His face drenched with sweat, his breathing ragged, he carried her to Zoé's house. When Joseph tried to help him, he shook his head stubbornly and placed her on the bed without looking at her. Her eyes were open. Joseph leaned over her, made the sign of the cross and, with the gesture of a priest officiating for the very first time, closed her eyes.

For a moment, Lapointe seemed to be struggling desperately with himself. He was holding back his tears with a stoic attitude that was fooling no one. Then suddenly throwing himself on the bed, he hid his head in his hands and wept.

When he stood up, Zoé could see an unspeakable expression of bitterness and hatred in his eyes.

"They killed her – they killed her, Zoé," he muttered, as if lost…

She placed her hand on his shoulder.

"Calm yourself."

"It's their fault – it's their fault and they will pay dearly."

"Be quiet," said Pétion, a lump in his throat.

Joseph was praying next to the bed.

Lapointe took his watch, looked at it and then, throwing it aside in a gesture of terrifying rage, broke it on the floorboards.

Zoé jumped. Had he gone mad? His eyes were haggard, his mouth trembling, and the veins in his face seemed ready to burst.

"Calm yourself," she repeated gently.

He fell to his knees and stretched out his hand toward the bed:

"I swear to avenge your death," he said. "The Whites will pay dearly for this crime. I swear it…"

At that moment, Jean-Baptiste Lapointe's eyes met Joseph's, and he lowered them.

He spent the night at her bedside without saying another word and without even seeming to notice Pétion and Joseph, who were also sitting up with her.

The burial took place the next day. He followed along with the others, head lowered, arms folded across his chest, without speaking a word. Only in hearing someone weep near him did he notice and recognize Scipion.

That very day, he returned to Arcahaie. Learning that a plot had been hatched against him, he seized the occasion and arrested the conspirators. With his own hands, he cut the throats of thirty Whites without even a semblance of a trial. He then boarded a ship along with his men and, without the slightest hesitation, cut off another twenty heads on a hastily assembled scaffold. His shirt, his arms, his breeches – they were all stained with blood and bits of flesh. He had been transformed into a horrific butcher.

His sorry task completed, he looked at his hands and burst into a laugh that the men in his company knew was truly diabolical.

Two days later, following the example of the white colonists and the mulatto slaveholders, he turned Arcahaie over to the English.

AUTHOR'S NOTE

This book is based on historical documents. The two heroines and all the principal characters are real figures, and all have kept their real names.* The major events of their lives, as well as all historical events recounted here, are completely authentic.

* Theater in Saint-Domingue, by Jean Fouchard. (note in original)

archipelago books
is a not-for-profit literary press devoted to
promoting cross-cultural exchange through innovative
classic and contemporary international literature
www.archipelagobooks.org